**Praise for *New York Times* bestselling author
Diana Palmer**

"Diana Palmer is a mesmerizing storyteller who captures the essence of what a romance should be."
—*Affaire de Coeur*

"You just can't do better than a Diana Palmer story to make your heart lighter and smile brighter."
—*Fresh Fiction* on *Wyoming Rugged*

"Diana Palmer is an amazing storyteller, and her long-time fans will enjoy *Wyoming Winter* with satisfaction!"
—*RT Book Reviews*

**Praise for *New York Times* bestselling author
Maisey Yates**

"Her characters excel at defying the norms and providing readers with…an emotional investment."
—*RT Book Reviews* on *Claim Me, Cowboy* (Top Pick)

"Yates's thrilling…contemporary proves that friendship can evolve into scintillating romance…. This is a surefire winner not to be missed."
—*Publishers Weekly* on *Slow Burn Cowboy* (starred review)

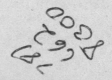

A prolific author of more than one hundred books, **Diana Palmer** got her start as a newspaper reporter. A *New York Times* bestselling author and voted one of the top ten romance writers in America, she has a gift for telling the most sensual tales with charm and humor. Diana lives with her family in Cornelia, Georgia. Visit her website at dianapalmer.com.

New York Times bestselling author **Maisey Yates** lives in rural Oregon with her three children and her husband, whose chiseled jaw and arresting features continue to make her swoon. She feels the epic trek she takes several times a day from her office to her coffee maker is a true example of her pioneer spirit.

New York Times Bestselling Author

DIANA PALMER

SUTTON'S WAY

HARLEQUIN
BESTSELLING
AUTHOR
COLLECTION

**HARLEQUIN®
BESTSELLING
AUTHOR
COLLECTION**

Recycling programs
for this product may
not exist in your area.

ISBN-13: 978-1-335-44857-6

Sutton's Way
First published in 1989. This edition published in 2020.
Copyright © 1989 by Diana Palmer

The Rancher's Baby
First published in 2017. This edition published in 2020.
Copyright © 2017 by Harlequin Books S.A.

This edition published by arrangement with Harlequin Books S.A.

For questions and comments about the quality of this book, please contact us at CustomerService@Harlequin.com.

Harlequin Enterprises ULC
22 Adelaide St. West, 40th Floor
Toronto, Ontario M5H 4E3, Canada
www.Harlequin.com

Printed in U.S.A.

SUTTON'S WAY

Diana Palmer

To Barry Call
of Charbons in Gainesville, GA
Many thanks

CONTENTS

Books by Diana Palmer

Long, Tall Texans

Fearless
Heartless
Dangerous
Merciless
Courageous
Protector
Invincible
Untamed
Defender
Undaunted

The Wyoming Men

Wyoming Tough
Wyoming Fierce
Wyoming Bold
Wyoming Strong
Wyoming Rugged
Wyoming Brave

Visit her Author Profile page
on Harlequin.com, or dianapalmer.com,
for more titles!

CHAPTER ONE

THE NOISE OUTSIDE the cabin was there again, and Amanda shifted restlessly with the novel in her lap, curled up in a big armchair by the open fireplace in a rug. Until now, the cabin had been paradise. There was three feet of new snow outside, she had all the supplies she needed to get her through the next few wintery weeks of Wyoming weather, and there wasn't a telephone in the place. Best of all, there wasn't a neighbor.

Well, there was, actually. But nobody in their right mind would refer to that man on the mountain as a neighbor. Amanda had only seen him once and once was enough.

She'd met him, if their head-on encounter could be referred to as a meeting, on a snowy Saturday last week. Quinn Sutton's majestic ranch house overlooked this cabin nestled against the mountainside. He'd been out in the snow on a horse-drawn sled that contained huge square bales of hay, and he was heaving them like feather pillows to a small herd of red-and-white cattle. The sight had touched Amanda, because it indicated concern. The tall, wiry rancher out in a blizzard feeding his starving cattle. She'd even smiled at the tender picture it made.

And then she'd stopped her four-wheel-drive vehicle

and stuck her blond head out the window to ask directions to the Blalock Durning place, which was the cabin one of her aunt's friends was loaning her. And the tender picture dissolved into stark hostility.

The tall rancher turned toward her with the coldest black eyes and the hardest face she'd ever seen in her life. He had a day's growth of stubble, but the stubble didn't begin to cover up the frank homeliness of his lean face. He had amazingly high cheekbones, a broad forehead and a jutting chin, and he looked as if someone had taken a straight razor to one side of his face, which had a wide scratch. None of that bothered Amanda because Hank Shoeman and the other three men who made music with her group were even uglier than Quinn Sutton. But at least Hank and the boys could smile. This man looked as if he invented the black scowl.

"I said," she'd repeated with growing nervousness, "can you tell me how to get to Blalock Durning's cabin?"

Above the sheepskin coat, under the battered gray ranch hat, Quinn Sutton's tanned face didn't move a muscle. "Follow the road, turn left at the lodgepoles," he'd said tersely, his voice as deep as a rumble of thunder.

"Lodgepoles?" she'd faltered. "You mean Indian lodgepoles? What do they look like?"

"Lady," he said with exaggerated patience, "a lodgepole is a pine tree. It's tall and piney, and there are a stand of them at the next fork in the road."

"You don't need to be rude, Mr...?"

"Sutton," he said tersely. "Quinn Sutton."

"Nice to meet you," she murmured politely. "I'm

Amanda." She wondered if anyone might accidentally recognize her here in the back of beyond, and on the off chance, she gave her mother's maiden name instead of her own last name. "Amanda Corrie," she added untruthfully. "I'm going to stay in the cabin for a few weeks."

"This isn't the tourist season," he'd said without the slightest pretense at friendliness. His black eyes cut her like swords.

"Good, because I'm not a tourist," she said.

"Don't look to me for help if you run out of wood or start hearing things in the dark," he added coldly. "Somebody will tell you eventually that I have no use whatsoever for women."

While she was thinking up a reply to that, a young boy of about twelve had come running up behind the sled.

"Dad!" he called, amazingly enough to Quinn Sutton. "There's a cow in calf down in the next pasture. I think it's a breech!"

"Okay, son, hop on," he told the boy, and his voice had become fleetingly soft, almost tender. He looked back at Amanda, though, and the softness left him. "Keep your door locked at night," he'd said. "Unless you're expecting Durning to join you," he added with a mocking smile.

She'd stared at him from eyes as black as his own and started to tell him that she didn't even know Mr. Durning, who was her aunt's friend, not hers. But she bit her tongue. It wouldn't do to give this man an opening. "I'll do that little thing," she agreed. She glanced at the boy, who was eyeing her curiously from his perch on the sled. "And it seems that you do have at least one use for women," she added with a vacant smile. "My condolences to your wife, Mr. Sutton."

She'd rolled up the window before he could speak and she'd whipped the four-wheel-drive down the road with little regard for safety, sliding all over the place on the slick and rutted country road.

She glared into the flames, consigning Quinn Sutton to them with all her angry heart. She hoped and prayed that there wouldn't ever be an accident or a reason she'd have to seek out his company. She'd rather have asked help from a passing timber wolf. His son hadn't seemed at all like him, she recalled. Sutton was as dangerous looking as a timber wolf, with a face like the side of a bombed mountain and eyes that were coal-black and cruel. In the sheepskin coat he'd been wearing with that raunchy Stetson that day, he'd looked like one of the old mountain men might have back in Wyoming's early days. He'd given Amanda some bad moments and she'd hated him after that uncomfortable confrontation. But the boy had been kind. He was redheaded and blue-eyed, nothing like his father, not a bit of resemblance.

She knew the rancher's name only because her aunt had mentioned him, and cautioned Amanda about going near the Sutton ranch. The ranch was called Ricochet, and Amanda had immediately thought of a bullet going awry. Probably one of Sutton's ancestors had thrown some lead now and again. Mr. Sutton looked a lot more like a bandit than he did a rancher, with his face unshaven, that wide, awful scrape on his cheek and his crooked nose. It was an unforgettable face all around, especially those eyes....

She pulled the rug closer and gave the book in her slender hand a careless glance. She wasn't really in the mood to read. Memories kept tearing her heart. She leaned her blond head back against the chair and her dark eyes studied the flames with idle appreciation of their beauty.

The nightmare of the past few weeks had finally caught up with her. She'd stood onstage, with the lights beating down on her long blond hair and outlining the beige leather dress that was her trademark, and her voice had simply refused to cooperate. The shock of being unable to produce a single note had caused her to faint, to the shock and horror of the audience.

She came to in a hospital, where she'd been given what seemed to be every test known to medical science. But nothing would produce her singing voice, even though she could talk. It was, the doctor told her, purely a psychological problem, caused by the trauma of what had happened. She needed rest.

So Hank, who was the leader of the group, had called her Aunt Bess and convinced her to arrange for Amanda to get away from it all. Her aunt's rich boyfriend had this holiday cabin in Wyoming's Grand Teton Mountains and was more than willing to let Amanda recuperate there. Amanda had protested, but Hank and the boys and her aunt had insisted. So here she was, in the middle of winter, in several feet of snow, with no television, no telephone and facilities that barely worked. Roughing it, the big, bearded bandleader had told her, would do her good.

She smiled when she remembered how caring and kind the guys had been. Her group was called Desperado, and her leather costume was its trademark. The four men who made up the rest of it were fine musicians, but they looked like the Hell's Angels on stage in denim and leather with thick black beards and mustaches and untrimmed hair. They were really pussycats under that rough exterior, but nobody had ever been game enough to try to find out if they were.

Hank and Deke and Jack and Johnson had been trying to get work at a Virginia night spot when they'd run into Amanda Corrie Callaway, who was also trying to get work there. The club needed a singer and a band, so it was a match made in heaven, although Amanda with her sheltered upbringing had been a little afraid of her new backup band. They, on the other hand, had been nervous around her because she was such a far cry from the usual singers they'd worked with. The shy, introverted young blonde made them self-conscious about their appearance. But their first performance together had been a phenomenal hit, and they'd been together four years now.

They were famous, now. Desperado had been on the music videos for two years, they'd done television shows and magazine interviews, and they were recognized everywhere they went. Especially Amanda, who went by the stage name of Mandy Callaway. It wasn't a bad life, and it was making them rich. But there wasn't much rest or time for a personal life. None of the group was married except Hank, and he was already getting a divorce. It was hard for a homebound spouse to accept the frequent absences that road tours required.

She still shivered from the look Quinn Sutton had given her, and now she was worried about her Aunt Bess, though the woman was more liberal minded and should know the score. But Sutton had convinced Amanda that she wasn't the first woman to be at Blalock's cabin. She should have told that arrogant rancher what her real relationship with Blalock Durning was, but he probably wouldn't have believed her.

Of course, she could have put him in touch with Jerry and proved it. Jerry Allen, their road manager, was one of the best in the business. He'd kept them from starving during the beginning, and they had an expert crew of electricians and carpenters who made up the rest of the retinue. It took a huge bus to carry the people and equipment, appropriately called the "Outlaw Express."

Amanda had pleaded with Jerry to give them a few weeks rest after the tragedy that had cost her her nerve, but he'd refused. Get back on the horse, he'd advised. And she'd tried. But the memories were just too horrible.

So finally he'd agreed to Hank's suggestion and she was officially on hiatus, as were the other members of the group, for a month. Maybe in that length of time she could come to grips with it, face it.

It had been a week and she felt better already. Or she would, if those strange noises outside the cabin would just stop! She had horrible visions of wolves breaking in and eating her.

"Hello?"

The small voice startled her. It sounded like a boy's. She got up, clutching the fire poker in her hand and went to the front door. "Who's there?" she called out tersely.

"It's just me. Elliot," he said. "Elliot Sutton."

She let out a breath between her teeth. Oh, no, she thought miserably, what was he doing here? His father would come looking for him, and she couldn't bear to have that…that savage anywhere around!

"What do you want?" she groaned.

"I brought you something."

It would be discourteous to refuse the gift, she guessed, especially since he'd apparently come through several feet of snow to bring it. Which brought to mind a really interesting question: where was his father?

She opened the door. He grinned at her from under a thick cap that covered his red hair.

"Hi," he said. "I thought you might like to have some roasted peanuts. I did them myself. They're nice on a cold night."

Her eyes went past him to a sled hitched to a sturdy draft horse. "Did you come in that?" she asked, recognizing the sled he and his father had been riding the day she'd met them.

"Sure," he said. "That's how we get around in winter, what with the snow and all. We take hay out to the livestock on it. You remember, you saw us. Well, we usually take hay out on it, that is. When Dad's not laid up," he added pointedly, and his blue eyes said more than his voice did.

She knew she was going to regret asking the question before she opened her mouth. She didn't want to ask. But no young boy came to a stranger's house in the middle of a snowy night just to deliver a bag of roasted peanuts.

"What's wrong?" she asked with resigned perception.

He blinked. "What?"

"I said, what's wrong?" She made her tone gentler. He couldn't help it that his father was a savage, and he was worried under that false grin. "Come on, you might as well tell me."

He bit his lower lip and looked down at his snow-covered boots. "It's my dad," he said. "He's bad sick and he won't let me get the doctor."

So there it was. She knew she shouldn't have asked.

"Can't your mother do something?" she asked hopefully.

"My mom ran off with Mr. Jackson from the livestock association when I was just a little feller," he replied, registering Amanda's shocked expression. "She and Dad got divorced and she died some years ago, but Dad doesn't talk about her. Will you come, miss?"

"I'm not a doctor," she said, hesitating.

"Oh, sure, I know that," he agreed eagerly, "but you're a girl. And girls know how to take care of sick folks, don't they?" The confidence slid away and he looked like what he was—a terrified little boy with nobody to turn to. "Please, lady," he added. "I'm scared. He's hot and shaking all over and—!"

"I'll get my boots on," she said. She gathered them from beside the fireplace and tugged them on, and then she went for a coat and stuffed her long blond hair under a stocking cap. "Do you have cough syrup, aspirins, throat lozenges—that sort of thing?"

"Yes, ma'am," he said eagerly, then sighed. "Dad won't take them, but we have them."

"Is he suicidal?" Amanda asked angrily as she went out the door behind him and locked the cabin before she climbed on the sled with the boy.

"Well sometimes things get to him," he ventured. "But he doesn't ever get sick, and he won't admit that he is. But he's out of his head and I'm scared. He's all I got."

"We'll take care of him," she promised, and hoped she could deliver on the promise. "Let's go."

"Do you know Mr. Durning well?" he asked as he called to the draft horse and started him back down the road and up the mountain toward the Sutton house.

"He's sort of a friend of a relative of mine," she said evasively. The sled ride was fun, and she was enjoying the cold wind and snow in her face, the delicious mountain air. "I'm only staying at the cabin for a few weeks. Just time to...get over something."

"Have you been sick, too?" he asked curiously.

"In a way," she said noncommittally.

The sled went jerkily up the road, around the steep hill. She held on tight and hoped the big draft horse had steady feet. It was a harrowing ride at the last, and then they were up, and the huge redwood ranch house came into sight, blazing with light from its long, wide front porch to the gabled roof.

"It's a beautiful house," Amanda said.

"My dad added on to it for my mom, before they married," he told her. He shrugged. "I don't remember much about her, except she was redheaded. Dad sure hates women." He glanced at her apologetically. "He's not going to like me bringing you...."

"I can take care of myself," she returned, and smiled reassuringly. "Let's go see how bad it is."

"I'll get Harry to put up the horse and sled," he said, yelling toward the lighted barn until a grizzled old man appeared. After a brief introduction to Amanda, Harry left and took the horse away.

"Harry's been here since Dad was a boy," Elliot told her as he led her down a bare-wood hall and up a steep staircase to the second storey of the house. "He does most everything, even cooks for the men." He paused outside a closed door, and gave Amanda a worried look. "He'll yell for sure."

"Let's get it over with, then."

She let Elliot open the door and look in first, to make sure his father had something on.

"He's still in his jeans," he told her, smiling as she blushed. "It's okay."

She cleared her throat. So much for pretended so-phistication, ~~she thought, and here she was twenty-four~~ years old. She avoided Elliot's grin and walked into the room.

Quinn Sutton was sprawled on his stomach, his bare muscular arms stretched toward the headboard. His back gleamed with sweat, and his thick, black hair was damp with moisture. Since it wasn't hot in the room, Amanda decided that he must have a high fever. He was moaning and talking unintelligibly.

"Elliot, can you get me a basin and some hot water?" she asked. She took off her coat and rolled up the sleeves of her cotton blouse.

"Sure thing," Elliot told her, and rushed out of the room.

"Mr. Sutton, can you hear me?" Amanda asked softly. She sat down beside him on the bed, and lightly touched his bare shoulder. He was hot, all right—burning up. "Mr. Sutton," she called again.

"No," he moaned. "No, you can't do it…!"

"Mr. Sutton…"

He rolled over and his black eyes opened, glazed with fever, but Amanda barely noticed. Her eyes were on the rest of him, male perfection from shoulder to narrow hips. He was darkly tanned, too, and thick, black hair wedged from his chest down his flat stomach to the wide belt at his hips. Amanda, who was remarkably innocent not only for her age, but for her profession as well, stared like a star-struck girl. He was beautiful, she thought, amazed at the elegant lines of his body, at the ripple of muscle and the smooth, glistening skin.

"What the hell do you want?" he rasped.

So much for hero worship, she thought dryly. She lifted her eyes back to his. "Elliot was worried," she said quietly. "He came and got me. Please don't fuss at him. You're raging with fever."

"Damn the fever, get out," he said in a tone that might have stopped a charging wolf.

"I can't do that," she said. She turned her head toward the door where Elliot appeared with a basin full of hot water and a towel and washcloth over one arm.

"Here you are, lady," he said. "Hi, Dad," he added with a wan smile at his furious father. "You can beat me when you're able again."

"Don't think I won't," Quinn growled.

"There, there, you're just feverish and sick, Mr. Sutton," Amanda soothed.

"Get Harry and have him throw her off my land," Quinn told Elliot in a furious voice.

"How about some aspirin, Elliot, and something for him to drink? A small whiskey and something hot—"

"I don't drink whiskey," Quinn said harshly.

"He has a glass of wine now and then," Elliot ventured.

"Wine, then." She soaked the cloth in the basin. "And you might turn up the heat. We don't want him to catch a chill when I sponge him down."

"You damned well aren't sponging me down!" Quinn raged.

She ignored him. "Go and get those things, please, Elliot, and the cough syrup, too."

"You bet, lady!" he said, grinning.

"My name is Amanda," she said absently.

"Amanda," the boy repeated, and went back downstairs.

"God help you when I get back on my feet," Quinn said with fury. He laid back on the pillow, shivering when she touched him with the cloth. "Don't...!"

"I could fry an egg on you. I have to get the fever down. Elliot said you were delirious."

"Elliot's delirious to let you in here," he shuddered. Her fingers accidentally brushed his flat stomach and he arched, shivering. "For God's sake, don't," he groaned.

"Does your stomach hurt?" she asked, concerned. "I'm sorry." She soaked the cloth again and rubbed it against his shoulders, his arms, his face.

His black eyes opened. He was breathing roughly, and his face was taut. The fever, she imagined. She brushed back her long hair, and wished she'd tied it up. It kept flowing down onto his damp chest.

"Damn you," he growled.

"Damn you, too, Mr. Sutton." She smiled sweetly. She finished bathing his face and put the cloth and basin aside. "Do you have a long-sleeved shirt?"

"Get out!"

Elliot came back with the medicine and a small glass of wine. "Harry's making hot chocolate," he said with a smile. "He'll bring it up. Here's the other stuff."

"Good," she said. "Does your father have a pajama jacket or something long-sleeved?"

"Sure!"

"Traitor," Quinn groaned at his son.

"Here you go." Elliot handed her a flannel top, which she proceeded to put on the protesting and very angry Mr. Sutton.

"I hate you," Quinn snapped at her with his last ounce of venom.

"I hate you, too," she agreed. She had to reach around him to get the jacket on, and it brought her into much too close proximity to him. She could feel the hair on his chest rubbing against her soft cheek, she could feel her own hair smoothing over his bare shoulder and chest. Odd, that shivery feeling she got from contact with him. She ignored it forcibly and got his other arm into the pajama jacket. She fastened it, trying to keep her fingers from touching his chest any more than necessary because the feel of that pelt of hair disturbed her. He shivered violently at the touch of her hands and her long, silky hair, and she assumed it was because of his fever.

"Are you finished?" Quinn asked harshly.

"Almost." She pulled the covers over him, found the electric-blanket control and turned it on. Then she ladled cough syrup into him, gave him aspirin and had him take a sip of wine, hoping that she wasn't overdosing him in the process. But the caffeine in the hot chocolate would probably counteract the wine and keep it from doing any damage in combination with the medicine. A sip of wine wasn't likely to be that dangerous anyway, and it might help the sore throat she was sure he had.

"Here's the cocoa," Harry said, joining them with a tray of mugs filled with hot chocolate and topped with whipped cream.

"That looks delicious. Thank you so much," Amanda said, and smiled shyly at the old man.

He grinned back. "Nice to be appreciated." He glared

at Quinn. "Nobody else ever says so much as a thank-you!"

"It's hard to thank a man for food poisoning," Quinn rejoined weakly.

"He ain't going to die," Harry said as he left. "He's too damned mean."

"That's a fact," Quinn said and closed his eyes.

He was asleep almost instantly. Amanda drew up a chair and sat down beside him. He'd still need looking after, and presumably the boy went to school. It was past the Christmas holidays.

"You go to school, don't you?" she asked Elliot.

He nodded. "I ride the horse out to catch the bus and then turn him loose. He comes to the barn by himself. You're staying?"

"I'd better, I guess," she said. "I'll sit with him. He may get worse in the night. He's got to see a doctor tomorrow. Is there one around here?"

"There's Dr. James in town, in Holman that is," he said. "He'll come out if Dad's bad enough. He has a cancer patient down the road and he comes to check on her every few days. He could stop by then."

"We'll see how your father is feeling. You'd better get to bed," she said and smiled at him.

"Thank you for coming, Miss... Amanda," Elliot said. He sighed. "I don't think I've ever been so scared."

"It's okay," she said. "I didn't mind. Good night, Elliot."

He smiled at her. "Good night."

He went out and closed the door. Amanda sat back in her chair and looked at the sleeping face of the wild man. He seemed vulnerable like this, with his black eyes closed. He had the thickest lashes she'd ever seen, and his eyebrows were thick and well shaped above his deep-set eyes. His mouth was rather thin, but it was perfectly shaped, and the full lower lip was sensuous. She liked that jutting chin, with its hint of stubbornness. His nose was formidable and straight, and he wasn't that bad looking…asleep. Perhaps it was the coldness of his eyes that made him seem so much rougher when he was awake. Not that he looked that unintimidating even now. He had so many coarse edges….

She waited a few minutes and touched his forehead. It was a little cooler, thank God, so maybe he was going to be better by morning. She went into the bathroom and washed her face and went back to sit by him. Somewhere in the night, she fell asleep with her blond head pillowed on the big arm of the chair. Voices woke her.

"Has she been there all night, Harry?" Quinn was asking.

"Looks like. Poor little critter, she's worn out."

"I'll shoot Elliot!"

"Now, boss, that's no way to treat the kid. He got scared, and I didn't know what to do. Women know things about illness. Why, my mama could doctor people and she never had no medical training. She used herbs and things."

Amanda blinked, feeling eyes on her. She found Quinn Sutton gazing steadily at her from a sitting position on the bed.

"How do you feel?" she asked without lifting her sleepy head.

"Like hell," he replied. "But I'm a bit better."

"Would you like some breakfast, ma'am?" Harry asked with a smile. "And some coffee?"

"Coffee. Heavenly. But no breakfast, thanks, I won't

impose," she said drowsily, yawning and stretching un-
inhibitedly as she sat up, her full breasts beautifully outlined against the cotton blouse in the process.

Quinn felt his body tautening again, as it had the
night before so unexpectedly and painfully when her
hands had touched him. He could still feel them, and
the brush of her long, silky soft hair against his skin.
She smelled of gardenias and the whole outdoors, and
he hated her more than ever because he'd been briefly
vulnerable.

"Why did you come with Elliot?" Quinn asked her
when Harry had gone.

She pushed back her disheveled hair and tried not
to think how bad she must look without makeup and
with her hair uncombed. She usually kept it in a tight
braid on top of her head when she wasn't performing.
It made her feel vulnerable to have its unusual length
on display for a man like Quinn Sutton.

"Your son is only twelve," she answered him belatedly. "That's too much responsibility for a kid," she
added. "I know. I had my dad to look after at that age,
and no mother. My dad drank," she added with a bitter
smile. "Excessively. When he drank he got into trouble. I can remember knowing how to call a bail bonds-
man at the age of thirteen. I never dated, I never took
friends home with me. When I was eighteen, I ran away
from home. I don't even know if he's still alive, and I
don't care."

"That's one problem Elliot won't ever have," he replied quietly. "Tough girl, aren't you?" he added, and
his black eyes were frankly curious.

She hadn't meant to tell him so much. It embarrassed
her, so she gave him her most belligerent glare. "Tough

enough, thanks," she said. She got out of the chair. "If you're well enough to argue, you ought to be able to take care of yourself. But if that fever goes up again, you'll need to see the doctor."

"I'll decide that," he said tersely. "Go home."

"Thanks, I'll do that little thing." She got her coat and put it on without taking time to button it. She pushed her hair up under the stocking cap, aware of his eyes on her the whole time.

"You don't fit the image of a typical hanger-on," he said unexpectedly.

She glanced at him, blinking with surprise. "I beg your pardon?"

"A hanger-on," he repeated. He lifted his chin and studied her with mocking thoroughness. "You're Durning's latest lover, I gather. Well, if it's money you're after, he's the perfect choice. A pretty little tramp could go far with him... Damn!"

She stood over him with the remains of his cup of hot chocolate all over his chest, shivering with rage.

"I'm sorry," she said curtly. "That was a despicable thing to do to a sick man, but what you said to me was inexcusable."

She turned and went to the door, ignoring his muffled curses as he threw off the cover and sat up.

"I'd cuss, too," she said agreeably as she glanced back at him one last time, her eyes running helplessly over the broad expanse of hair-roughened skin. "All that sticky hot chocolate in that thicket on your chest," she mused. "It will probably take steam cleaning to remove it. Too bad you can't attract a 'hanger-on' to help you bathe it out. But, then, you aren't as rich as Mr. Durning, are you?" And she walked out, her nose in the air. As she went toward the stairs, she imagined that she heard laughter. But of course, that couldn't have been possible.

CHAPTER TWO

AMANDA REGRETTED THE hot-chocolate incident once she was back in the cabin, even though Quinn Sutton had deserved every drop of it. How dare he call her such a name!

Amanda was old-fashioned in her ideas. A real country girl from Mississippi who'd had no example to follow except a liberated aunt and an alcoholic parent, and she was like neither of them. She hardly even dated these days. Her working gear wasn't the kind of clothing that told men how conventional her ideals were. They saw the glitter and sexy outfit and figured that Amanda, or just "Mandy" as she was known onstage, lived like her alter ego looked. There were times when she rued the day she'd ever signed on with Desperado, but she was too famous and making too much money to quit now.

She put her hair in its usual braid and kept it there for the rest of the week, wondering from time to time about Quinn Sutton and whether or not he'd survived his illness. Not that she cared, she kept telling herself. It didn't matter to her if he turned up his toes.

There was no phone in the cabin, and no piano. She couldn't play solitaire, she didn't have a television. There was only the radio and the cassette player for company, and Mr. Durning's taste in music was really extreme.

He liked opera and nothing else. She'd have died for some soft rock, or just an instrument to practice on. She could play drums as well as the synthesizer and piano, and she wound up in the kitchen banging on the counter with two stainless-steel knives out of sheer boredom.

When the electricity went haywire in the wake of two inches of freezing rain on Sunday night, it was almost a relief. She sat in the darkness laughing. She was trapped in a house without heat, without light, and the only thing she knew about fireplaces was that they required wood. The logs that were cut outside were frozen solid under the sleet and there were none in the house. There wasn't even a pack of matches.

She wrapped up in her coat and shivered, hating the solitude and the weather and feeling the nightmares coming back in the icy night. She didn't want to think about the reason her voice had quit on her, but if she spent enough time alone, she was surely going to go crazy reliving that night onstage.

Lost in thought, in nightmarish memories of screams and her own loss of consciousness, she didn't hear the first knock on the door until it came again.

"Miss Corrie!" a familiar angry voice shouted above the wind.

She got up, feeling her way to the door. "Keep your shirt on," she muttered as she threw it open.

Quinn Sutton glared down at her. "Get whatever you'll need for a couple of days and come on. The power's out. If you stay here you'll freeze to death. It's going below zero tonight. My ranch has an extra generator, so we've still got the power going."

She glared back. "I'd rather freeze to death than go anywhere with you, thanks just the same."

He took a slow breath. "Look, your morals are your own business. I just thought—"

She slammed the door in his face and turned, just in time to have him kick in the door and come after her.

"I said you're coming with me, lady," he said shortly. He bent and picked her up bodily and started out the door. "And to hell with what you'll need for a couple of days."

"Mr....Sutton!" she gasped, stunned by the unexpected contact with his hard, fit body as he carried her easily out the door and closed it behind them.

"Hold on," he said tautly and without looking at her. "The snow's pretty heavy right through this drift."

In fact, it was almost waist deep. She hadn't been outside in two days, so she hadn't noticed how high it had gotten. Her hands clung to the old sheepskin coat he was wearing. It smelled of leather and tobacco and whatever soap he used, and the furry collar was warm against her cold cheek. He made her feel small and helpless, and she wasn't sure she liked it.

"I don't like your tactics," she said through her teeth as the wind howled around them and sleet bit into her face like tiny nails.

"They get results. Hop on." He put her up on the sled, climbed beside her, grasped the reins and turned the horse back toward the mountain.

She wanted to protest, to tell him to take his offer and go to hell. But it was bitterly cold and she was shivering too badly to argue. He was right, and that was the hell of it. She could freeze to death in that cabin easily enough, and nobody would have found her until spring came or until her aunt persuaded Mr. Durning to come and see about her.

"I don't want to impose," she said curtly.

"We're past that now," he replied. "It's either this or bury you."

"I'm sure I know which you'd prefer," she muttered, huddling in her heavy coat.

"Do you?" he asked, turning his head. In the daylight glare of snow and sleet, she saw an odd twinkle in his black eyes. "Try digging a hole out there."

She gave him a speaking glance and resigned herself to going with him.

He drove the sled right into the barn and left her to wander through the aisle, looking at the horses and the two new calves in the various stalls while he dealt with unhitching and stalling the horse.

"What's wrong with these little things?" she asked, her hands in her pockets and her ears freezing as she nodded toward the two calves.

"Their mamas starved out in the pasture," he said quietly. "I couldn't get to them in time."

He sounded as if that mattered to him. She looked up at his dark face, seeing new character in it. "I didn't think a cow or two would matter," she said absently.

"I lost everything I had a few months back," he said matter-of-factly. "I'm trying to pull out of bankruptcy, and right now it's a toss-up as to whether I'll even come close. Every cow counts." He looked down at her. "But it isn't just the money. It disturbs me to see anything die from lack of attention. Even a cow."

"Or a mere woman?" she said with a faint smile. "Don't worry, I know you don't want me here. I'm… grateful to you for coming to my rescue. Most of the firewood was frozen and Mr. Durning apparently doesn't smoke, because there weren't a lot of matches around."

He scowled faintly. "No, Durning doesn't smoke. Didn't you know?"

She shrugged. "I never had reason to ask," she said, without telling him that it was her aunt, not herself, who would know about Mr. Durning's habits. Let him enjoy his disgusting opinion of her.

"Elliot said you'd been sick."

She lifted a face carefully kept blank. "Sort of," she replied.

"Didn't Durning care enough to come with you?"

"Mr. Sutton, my personal life is none of your business," she said firmly. "You can think whatever you want to about me. I don't care. But for what it's worth, I hate men probably as much as you hate women, so you won't have to hold me off with a stick."

His face went hard at the remark, but he didn't say anything. He searched her eyes for one long moment and then turned toward the house, gesturing her to follow.

Elliot was overjoyed with their new house guest. Quinn Sutton had a television and all sorts of tapes, and there was, surprisingly enough, a brand-new keyboard on a living-room table.

She touched it lovingly, and Elliot grinned at her. "Like it?" he asked proudly. "Dad gave it to me for Christmas. It's not an expensive one, you know, but it's nice to practice on. Listen."

He turned it on and flipped switches, and gave a pretty decent rendition of a tune by Genesis.

Amanda, who was formally taught in piano, smiled at his efforts. "Very good," she praised. "But try a

B-flat instead of a B at the end of that last measure and see if it doesn't give you a better sound."

Elliot cocked his head. "I play by ear," he faltered.

"Sorry." She reached over and touched the key she wanted. "That one." She fingered the whole chord. "You have a very good ear."

"But I can't read music," he sighed. His blue eyes searched her face. "You can, can't you?"

She nodded, smiling wistfully. "I used to long for piano lessons. I took them in spurts and then begged a... friend to let me use her piano to practice on. It took me a long time to learn just the basics, but I do all right."

"All right" meant that she and the boys had won a Grammy award for their last album and it had been one of her own songs that had headlined it. But she couldn't tell Elliot that. She was convinced that Quinn Sutton would have thrown her out the front door if he'd known what she did for a living. He didn't seem like a rock fan, and once he got a look at her stage costume and her group, he'd probably accuse her of a lot worse than being his neighbor's live-in lover. She shivered. Well, at least she didn't like Quinn Sutton, and that was a good thing. She might get out of here without having him find out who she really was, but just in case, it wouldn't do to let herself become interested in him.

"I don't suppose you'd consider teaching me how to read music?" Elliot asked. "For something to do, you know, since we're going to be snowed in for a while, the way it looks."

"Sure, I'll teach you," she murmured, smiling at him. "If you dad doesn't mind," she added with a quick glance at the doorway.

Quinn Sutton was standing there, in jeans and red-checked flannel shirt with a cup of black coffee in one hand, watching them.

"None of that rock stuff," he said shortly. "That's a bad influence on kids."

"Bad influence?" Amanda was almost shocked, despite the fact that she'd gauged his tastes very well.

"Those raucous lyrics and suggestive costumes, and satanism," he muttered. "I confiscated his tapes and put them away. It's indecent."

"Some of it is, yes," she agreed quietly. "But you can't lump it all into one category, Mr. Sutton. And these days, a lot of the groups are even encouraging chastity and going to war on drug use..."

"You don't really believe that bull, do you?" he asked coldly.

"It's true, Dad," Elliot piped up.

"You can shut up," he told his son. He turned. "I've got a lot of paperwork to get through. Don't turn that thing on high, will you? Harry will show you to your room when you're ready to bed down, Miss Corrie," he added, and looked as if he'd like to have shown her to a room underwater. "Or Elliot can."

"Thanks again," she said, but she didn't look up. He made her feel totally inadequate and guilty. In a small way, it was like going back to that night...

"Don't stay up past nine, Elliot," Quinn told his son.

"Okay, Dad."

Amanda looked after the tall man with her jaw hanging loose. "What did he say?" she asked.

"He said not to stay up past nine," Elliot replied. "We all go to bed at nine," he added with a grin at her expression. "There, there, you'll get used to it. Ranch life, you know. Here, now, what was that about a B-flat? What's a B-flat?"

She was obviously expected to go to bed with the chickens and probably get up with them, too. Absently she picked up the keyboard and began to explain the basics of music to Elliot.

"Did he really hide all your tapes?" she asked curiously.

"Yes, he did," Elliot chuckled, glancing toward the stairs. "But I know where he hid them." He studied her with pursed lips. "You know, you look awfully familiar somehow."

Amanda managed to keep a calm expression on her face, despite her twinge of fear. Her picture, along with that of the men in the group, was on all their albums and tapes. God forbid that Elliot should be a fan and have one of them, but they were popular with young people his age. "They say we all have a counterpart, don't they?" she asked and smiled. "Maybe you saw somebody who looked like me. Here, this is how you run a C scale...."

She successfully changed the subject and Elliot didn't bring it up again. They went upstairs a half hour later, and she breathed a sigh of relief. Since the autocratic Mr. Sutton hadn't given her time to pack, she wound up sleeping in her clothes under the spotless white sheets. She only hoped that she wasn't going to have the nightmares here. She couldn't bear the thought of having Quinn Sutton ask her about them. He'd probably say that she'd gotten just what she deserved.

But the nightmares didn't come. She slept with delicious abandon and didn't dream at all. She woke up the next morning oddly refreshed just as the sun was com-

ing up, even before Elliot knocked on her door to tell
her that Harry had breakfast ready downstairs.

She combed out her hair and rebraided it, wrapping
it around the crown of her head and pinning it there
as she'd had it last night. She tidied herself after she'd
washed up, and went downstairs with a lively step.

Quinn Sutton and Elliot were already making great
inroads into huge, fluffy pancakes smothered in syrup
when she joined them.

Harry brought in a fresh pot of coffee and grinned at
her. "How about some hotcakes and sausage?" he asked.

"Just a hotcake and a sausage, please," she said and
grinned back. "I'm not much of a breakfast person."

"You'll learn if you stay in these mountains long,"
Quinn said, sparing her a speaking glance. "You need
more meat on those bones. Fix her three, Harry."

"Now, listen…" she began.

"No, you listen," Quinn said imperturbably, sipping
black coffee. "My house, my rules."

She sighed. It was just like old times at the orphanage, during one of her father's binges when she'd had to
live with Mrs. Brim's rules. "Yes, sir," she said absently.

He glared at her. "I'm thirty-four, and you aren't
young enough to call me 'sir.'"

She lifted startled dark eyes to his. "I'm twenty-
four," she said. "Are you really just thirty-four?" She
flushed even as she said it. He did look so much older,
but she hadn't meant to say anything. "I'm sorry. That
sounded terrible."

"I look older than I am," he said easily. "I've got a
friend down in Texas who thought I was in my late thir-
ties, and he's known me for years. No need to apologize." He didn't add that he had a lot of mileage on him,

thanks to his ex-wife. "You look younger than twenty-four," he did add.

He pushed away his empty plate and sipped coffee, staring at her through the steam rising from it. He was wearing a blue-checked flannel shirt this morning, buttoned up to his throat, with jeans that were well fitting but not overly tight. He didn't dress like the men in Amanda's world, but then, the men she knew weren't the same breed as this Teton man.

"Amanda taught me all about scales last night," Elliot said excitedly. "She really knows music."

"How did you manage to learn?" Quinn asked her, and she saw in his eyes that he was remembering what she'd told him about her alcoholic father.

She lifted her eyes from her plate. "During my dad's binges, I stayed at the local orphanage. There was a lady there who played for her church. She taught me."

"No sisters or brothers?" he asked quietly.

She shook her head. "Nobody in the world, except an aunt." She lifted her coffee cup. "She's an artist, and she's been living with her latest lover—"

"You'd better get to school, son," Quinn interrupted tersely, nodding at Elliot.

"I sure had, or I'll be late. See you!"

He grabbed his books and his coat and was gone in a flash, and Harry gathered the plates with a smile and vanished into the kitchen.

"Don't talk about things like that around Elliot," Quinn said shortly. "He understands more than you think. I don't want him corrupted."

"Don't you realize that most twelve-year-old boys know more about life than grown-ups these days?" she asked with a faint smile.

"In your world, maybe. Not in mine."

She could have told him that she was discussing the way things were, not the way she preferred them, but she knew it would be useless. He was so certain that she was wildly liberated. She sighed. "Maybe so," she murmured.

"I'm old-fashioned," he added. His dark eyes narrowed on her face. "I don't want Elliot exposed to the liberated outlook of the so-called modern world until he's old enough to understand that he has a choice. I don't like a society that ridicules honor and fidelity and innocence. So I fight back in the only way I can. I go to church on Sunday, Miss Corrie," he mused, smiling at her curious expression. "Elliot goes, too. You might not know it from watching television or going to movies, but there are still a few people in America who also go to church on Sunday, who work hard all week and find their relaxation in ways that don't involve drugs, booze or casual sex. How's that for a shocking revelation?"

"Nobody ever accused Hollywood of portraying real life," she replied with a smile. "But if you want my honest opinion, I'm pretty sick of gratuitous sex, filthy language and graphic violence in the newer movies. In fact, I'm so sick of it that I've gone back to watching the old-time movies from the 1940s." She laughed at his expression. "Let me tell you, these old movies had real handicaps—the actors all had to keep their clothes on and they couldn't swear. The writers were equally limited, so they created some of the most gripping dramas ever produced. I love them. And best of all, you can even watch them with kids."

He pursed his lips, his dark eyes holding hers. "I like George Brent, George Sanders, Humphrey Bogart,

Bette Davis and Cary Grant best," he confessed. "Yes, I watch them, too."

"I'm not really all that modern myself," she confessed, toying with the tablecloth. "I live in the city, but not in the fast lane." She put down her coffee cup. "I can understand why you feel the way you do, about taking Elliot to church and all. Elliot told me a little about his mother…"

He closed up like a plant. "I don't talk to outsiders about my personal life," he said without apology and got up, towering over her. "If you'd like to watch television or listen to music, you're welcome. I've got work to do."

"Can I help?" she asked.

His heavy eyebrows lifted. "This isn't the city."

"I know how to cut open a bale of hay," she said. "The orphanage was on a big farm. I grew up doing chores. I can even milk a cow."

"You won't milk the kind of cows I keep," he returned. His dark eyes narrowed. "You can feed those calves in the barn, if you like. Harry can show you where the bottle is."

Which meant that he wasn't going to waste his time on her. She nodded, trying not to feel like an unwanted guest. Just for a few minutes she'd managed to get under that hard reserve. Maybe that was good enough for a start. "Okay."

His black eyes glanced over her hair. "You haven't worn it down since the night Elliot brought you here," he said absently.

"I don't ever wear it down at home, as a rule," she said quietly. "It…gets in my way." It got recognized, too, she thought, which was why she didn't dare let it loose around Elliot too often.

His eyes narrowed for an instant before he turned and shouldered into his jacket.

"Don't leave the perimeter of the yard," he said as he stuck his weather-beaten Stetson on his dark, thick hair. "This is wild country. We have bears and wolves, and a neighbor who still sets traps."

"I know my limitations, thanks," she said. "Do you have help, besides yourself?"

He turned, thrusting his big, lean hands into work gloves. "Yes, I have four cowboys who work around the place. They're all married."

She blushed. "Thank you for your sterling assessment of my character."

"You may like old movies," he said with a penetrating stare. "But no woman with your kind of looks is a virgin at twenty-four," he said quietly, mindful of Harry's sharp ears. "And I'm a backcountry man, but I've been married and I'm not stupid about women. You won't play me for a fool."

She wondered what he'd say if he knew the whole truth about her. But it didn't make her smile to reflect on that. She lowered her eyes to the thick white mug. "Think what you like, Mr. Sutton. You will anyway."

"Damned straight."

He walked out without looking back, and Amanda felt a vicious chill even before he opened the door and went out into the cold white yard.

She waited for Harry to finish his chores and then went with him to the barn, where the little calves were curled up in their stalls of hay.

"They're only days old," Harry said, smiling as he brought the enormous bottles they were fed from. In fact, the nipples were stretched across the top of buckets and filled with warm mash and milk. "But they'll grow. Sit down, now. You may get a bit dirty…"

"Clothes wash," Amanda said easily, smiling. But this outfit was all she had. She was going to have to get the elusive Mr. Sutton to take her back to the cabin to get more clothes, or she'd be washing out her things in the sink tonight.

She knelt down in a clean patch of hay and coaxed the calf to take the nipple into its mouth. Once it got a taste of the warm liquid, it wasn't difficult to get it to drink. Amanda loved the feel of its silky red-and-white coat under her fingers as she stroked it. The animal was a Hereford, and its big eyes were pink rimmed and soulful. The calf watched her while it nursed.

"Poor little thing," she murmured softly, rubbing between its eyes. "Poor little orphan."

"They're tough critters, for all that," Harry said as he fed the other calf. "Like the boss."

"How did he lose everything, if you don't mind me asking?"

He glanced at her and read the sincerity in her expression. "I don't guess he'd mind if I told you. He was accused of selling contaminated beef."

"Contaminated…how?"

"It's a long story. The herd came to us from down in the Southwest. They had measles. Not," he added when he saw her puzzled expression, "the kind humans get. Cattle don't break out in spots, but they do develop cysts in the muscle tissue and if it's bad enough, it means that the carcasses have to be destroyed." He shrugged. "You can't spot it, because there are no definite symptoms, and you can't treat it because there isn't a drug that cures it. These cattle had it and contaminated the rest of our herd. It was like the end of the world. Quinn had sold the beef cattle to the packing-plant operator. When the meat was ordered destroyed, he came back on Quinn to recover his money, but Quinn had already spent it to buy new cattle. We went to court... Anyway, to make a long story short, they cleared Quinn of any criminal charges and gave him the opportunity to make restitution. In turn, he sued the people who sold him the contaminated herd in the first place." He smiled ruefully. "We just about broke even, but it meant starting over from scratch. That was last year. Things are still rough, but Quinn's a tough customer and he's got a good business head. He'll get through it. I'd bet on him."

Amanda pondered that, thinking that Quinn's recent life had been as difficult as her own. At least he had Elliot. That must have been a comfort to him. She said as much to Harry.

He gave her a strange look. "Well, yes, Elliot's special to him," he said, as if there were things she didn't know. Probably there were.

"Will these little guys make it?" she asked when the calf had finished his bottle.

"I think so," Harry said. "Here, give me that bottle and I'll take care of it for you."

She sighed, petting the calf gently. She liked farms and ranches. They were so real, compared to the artificial life she'd known since she was old enough to leave home. She loved her work and she'd always enjoyed performing, but it seemed sometimes as if she lived in another world. Values were nebulous, if they even existed, in the world where she worked. Old-fashioned ideas like morality, honor, chastity were laughed at or ignored. Amanda kept hers to herself, just as she kept her privacy intact. She didn't discuss her inner feelings with anyone. Probably her friends and associates would have died laughing if they'd known just how many hang-ups she had, and how distant her outlook on life was from theirs.

"Here's another one," Quinn said from the front of the barn.

Amanda turned her head, surprised to see him because he'd ridden out minutes ago. He was carrying another small calf, but this one looked worse than the younger ones did.

"He's very thin," she commented.

"He's got scours." He laid the calf down next to her. "Harry, fix another bottle."

"Coming up, boss."

Amanda touched the wiry little head with its rough hide. "He's not in good shape," she murmured quietly.

Quinn saw the concern on her face and was surprised by it. He shouldn't have been, he reasoned. Why would she have come with Elliot in the middle of the night to nurse a man she didn't even like, if she wasn't a kind woman?

"He probably won't make it," he agreed, his dark eyes searching hers. "He'd been out there by himself for a long time. It's a big property, and he's a very small calf," he defended when she gave him a meaningful look. "It wouldn't be the first time we missed one, I'm sorry to say."

"I know." She looked up as Harry produced a third bottle, and her hand reached for it just as Quinn's did. She released it, feeling odd little tingles at the brief contact with his lean, sure hand.

"Here goes," he murmured curtly. He reached under

the calf's chin and pulled its mouth up to slide the nipple in. The calf could barely nurse, but after a minute it seemed to rally and then it fed hungrily.

"Thank goodness," Amanda murmured. She smiled at Quinn, and his eyes flashed as they met hers, searching, dark, full of secrets. They narrowed and then abruptly fell to her soft mouth, where they lingered with a kind of questioning irritation, as if he wanted very much to kiss her and hated himself for it. Her heart leaped at the knowledge. She seemed to have a new, built-in insight about this standoffish man, and she didn't understand either it or her attitude toward him. He was domineering and hardheaded and unpredictable and she should have disliked him. But she sensed a sensitivity in him that touched her heart. She wanted to get to know him.

"I can do this," he said curtly. "Why don't you go inside?"

She was getting to him, she thought with fascination. He was interested in her, but he didn't want to be. She watched the way he avoided looking directly at her again, the angry glance of his eyes.

Well, it certainly wouldn't do any good to make him furious at her, especially when she was going to be his unwanted houseguest for several more days, from the look of the weather.

"Okay," she said, giving in. She got to her feet slowly. "I'll see if I can find something to do."

"Harry might like some company while he works in the kitchen. Wouldn't you, Harry?" he added, giving the older man a look that said he'd damned sure better like some company.

"Of course I would, boss," Harry agreed instantly.

Amanda pushed her hands into her pockets with a last glance at the calves. She smiled down at them. "Can I help feed them while I'm here?" she asked gently.

"If you want to," Quinn said readily, but without looking up.

"Thanks." She hesitated, but he made her feel shy and tongue-tied. She turned away nervously and walked back to the house.

Since Harry had the kitchen well in hand, she volunteered to iron some of Quinn's cotton shirts. Harry had the ironing board set up, but not the iron, so she went into the closet and produced one. It looked old, but maybe it would do, except that it seemed to have a lot of something caked on it.

She'd just started to plug it in when Harry came into the room and gasped.

"Not that one!" he exclaimed, gently taking it away from her. "That's Quinn's!"

She opened her mouth to make a remark, when Harry started chuckling.

"It's for his skis," he explained patiently.

She nodded. "Right. He irons his skis. I can see that."

"He does. Don't you know anything about skiing?"

"Well, you get behind a speedboat with them on..."

"Not waterskiing. *Snow* skiing," he emphasized.

She shrugged. "I come from southern Mississippi." She grinned at him. "We don't do much business in snow, you see."

"Sorry. Well, Quinn was an Olympic contender in giant slalom when he was in his late teens and early twenties. He would have made the team, but he got married and Elliot was on the way, so he gave it up. He still gets in plenty of practice," he added, shuddering. "On old Ironside peak, too. Nobody, but nobody, skis it except Quinn and a couple of other experts from Larry's Lodge over in Jackson Hole."

"I haven't seen that one on a map…" she began, because she'd done plenty of map reading before she came here.

"Oh, that isn't its official name, it's what Quinn calls it." He grinned. "Anyway, Quinn uses this iron to put wax on the bottom of his skis. Don't feel bad, I didn't know any better, either, at first, and I waxed a couple of shirts. Here's the right iron."

He handed it to her, and she plugged it in and got started. The elusive Mr. Sutton had hidden qualities, it seemed. She'd watched the winter Olympics every four years on television, and downhill skiing fascinated her. But it seemed to Amanda that giant slalom called for a kind of reckless skill and speed that would require ruthlessness and single-minded determination. Considering that, it wasn't at all surprising to her that Quinn Sutton had been good at it.

CHAPTER THREE

AMANDA HELPED HARRY do dishes and start a load of clothes in the washer. But when she took them out of the dryer, she discovered that several of Quinn's shirts were missing buttons and had loose seams.

Harry produced a needle and some thread, and Amanda set to work mending them. It gave her something to do while she watched a years-old police drama on television.

Quinn came in with Elliot a few hours later.

"Boy, the snow's bad," Elliot remarked as he rubbed his hands in front of the fire Harry had lit in the big stone fireplace. "Dad had to bring the sled out to get me, because the bus couldn't get off the main highway."

"Speaking of the sled," Amanda said, glancing at Quinn, "I've got to have a few things from the cabin. I'm really sorry, but I'm limited to what I'm wearing...."

"I'll run you down right now, before I go out again."

She put the mending aside. "I'll get my coat."

"Elliot, you can come, too. Put your coat back on," Quinn said unexpectedly, ignoring his son's surprised glance.

Amanda didn't look at him, but she understood why he wanted Elliot along. She made Quinn nervous. He was attracted to her and he was going to fight it to the bitter end. She wondered why he considered her such a threat.

He paused to pick up the shirt she'd been working on, and his expression got even harder as he glared at her. "You don't need to do that kind of thing," he said curtly.

"I've got to earn my keep somehow." She sighed. "I can feed the calves and help with the housework, at least. I'm not used to sitting around doing nothing," she added. "It makes me nervous."

He hesitated. An odd look rippled over his face as he studied the neat stitches in his shirtsleeve where the rip had been. He held it for a minute before he laid it gently back on the sofa. He didn't look at Amanda as he led the way out the door.

It didn't take her long to get her things together. Elliot wandered around the cabin. "There are knives all over the counter," he remarked. "Want me to put them in the sink?"

"Go ahead. I was using them for drumsticks," she called as she closed her suitcase.

"They don't look like they'd taste very good." Elliot chuckled.

She came out of the bedroom and gave him an amused glance. "Not that kind of drumsticks, you turkey. Here." She put down the suitcase and took the blunt stainless-steel knives from him. She glanced around to make sure Quinn hadn't come into the house and then she broke into an impromptu drum routine that made Elliot grin even more.

"Say, you're pretty good," he said.

She bowed. "Just one of my minor talents," she said. "But I'm better with a keyboard. Ready to go?"

"Whenever you are."

She started to pick up her suitcase, but Elliot reached down and got it before she could, a big grin on his freckled face. She wondered again why he looked so little like his father. She knew that his mother had been a redhead, too, but it was odd that he didn't resemble Quinn in any way at all.

Quinn was waiting on the sled, his expression unreadable, impatiently smoking his cigarette. He let them get on and turned the draft horse back toward his own house. It was snowing lightly and the wind was blowing, not fiercely but with a nip in it. Amanda sighed, lifting her face to the snow, not caring that her hood had fallen back to reveal the coiled softness of her blond hair. She felt alive out here as she never had in the city, or even back East. There was something about the wilderness that made her feel at peace with herself for the first time since the tragedy that had sent her retreating here.

"Enjoying yourself?" Quinn asked unexpectedly.

"More than I can tell you," she replied. "It's like no other place on earth."

He nodded. His dark eyes slid over her face, her cheeks flushed with cold and excitement, and they lingered there for one long moment before he forced his gaze back to the trail. Amanda saw that look and it brought a sense of foreboding. He seemed almost angry.

In fact, he was. Before the day was out, it was pretty apparent that he'd withdrawn somewhere inside himself and had no intention of coming out again. He barely said two words to Amanda before bedtime.

"He's gone broody," Elliot mused before he and Amanda called it a night. "He doesn't do it often, and not for a long time, but when he's got something on his mind, it's best not to get on his nerves."

"Oh, I'll do my best," Amanda promised, and crossed her heart.

But that apparently didn't do much good, in her case, because he glared at her over breakfast the next morning and over lunch, and by the time she finished mending a window curtain in the kitchen and helped Harry bake a cake for dessert, she was feeling like a very unwelcome guest.

She went out to feed the calves, the nicest of her daily chores, just before Quinn was due home for supper. Elliot had lessons and he was holed up in his room trying to get them done in time for a science-fiction movie he wanted to watch after supper. Quinn insisted that homework came first.

She fed two of the three calves and Harry volunteered to feed the third, the little one that Quinn had brought home with scours, while she cut the cake and laid the table. She was just finishing the place settings when she heard the sled draw up outside the door.

Her heart quickened at the sound of Quinn's firm, measured stride on the porch. The door opened and he came in, along with a few snowflakes.

He stopped short at the sight of her in an old white apron with wisps of blond hair hanging around her flushed face, a bowl of whipped potatoes in her hands.

"Don't you look domestic?" he asked with sudden, bitter sarcasm.

The attack was unexpected, although it shouldn't have been. He'd been irritable ever since the day before, when he'd noticed her mending his shirt.

"I'm just helping Harry," she said. "He's feeding the calves while I do this."

"So I noticed."

She put down the potatoes, watching him hang up his hat and coat with eyes that approved his tall, fit physique, the way the red-checked flannel shirt clung to his muscular torso and long back. He was such a lonely man, she thought, watching him. So alone, even with Elliot and Harry here. He turned unexpectedly, catching her staring and his dark eyes glittered.

He went to the sink to wash his hands, almost vibrating with pent-up anger. She sensed it, but it only piqued her curiosity. He was reacting to her. She felt it, knew it, as she picked up a dish towel and went close to him to wrap it gently over his wet hands. Her big black eyes searched his, and she let her fingers linger on his while time seemed to end in the warm kitchen.

His dark eyes narrowed, and he seemed to have stopped breathing. He was aware of so many sensations. Hunger. Anger. Loneliness. Lust. His head spun with them, and the scent of her was pure, soft woman, drifting up into his nostrils, cocooning him in the smell of cologne and shampoo. His gaze fell helplessly to her soft bow of a mouth and he wondered how it would feel to bend those few inches and take it roughly under his own. It had been so long since he'd kissed a woman, held a woman. Amanda was particularly feminine, and she appealed to everything that was masculine in him. He almost vibrated with the need to reach out to her.

But that way lay disaster, he told himself firmly. She was just another treacherous woman, probably bored with confinement, just keeping her hand in with attracting men. He probably seemed like a pushover, and she was going to use her charms to make a fool of him. He took a deep, slow breath and the glitter in his eyes became even more pronounced as he jerked the towel out of her hands and moved away.

"Sorry," she mumbled. She felt her cheeks go hot, because there had been a cold kind of violence in the action that warned her his emotions weren't quite under control. She moved away from him. Violence was the one thing she did expect from men. She'd lived with it for most of her life until she'd run away from home.

She went back to the stove, stirring the sauce she'd made to go with the boiled dumpling.

"Don't get too comfortable in the kitchen," he warned her. "This is Harry's private domain and he doesn't like trespassers. You're just passing through."

"I haven't forgotten that, Mr. Sutton," she replied, and her eyes kindled with dark fire as she looked at him. There was no reason to make her feel so unwelcome. "Just as soon as the thaw comes, I'll be out of your way for good."

"I can hardly wait," he said, biting off the words.

Amanda sighed wearily. It wasn't her idea of the perfect rest spot. She'd come away from the concert stage needing healing, and all she'd found was another battle to fight.

"You make me feel so at home, Mr. Sutton," she said wistfully. "Like part of the family. Thanks so much for your gracious hospitality, and do you happen to have a jar of rat poison...?"

Quinn had to bite hard to keep from laughing. He turned and went out of the kitchen as if he were being chased.

After supper, Amanda volunteered to wash dishes, but Harry shooed her off. Quinn apparently did book work every night, because he went into his study and closed the door, leaving Elliot with Amanda for company. They'd watched the science-fiction movie Elliot had been so eager to see and now they were working on the keyboard.

"I think I've got the hang of C major," Elliot announced, and ran the scale, complete with turned under thumb on the key of F.

"Very good," she enthused. "Okay, let's go on to G major."

She taught him the scale and watched him play it, her mind on Quinn Sutton's antagonism.

"Something bothering you?" Elliot asked suspiciously.

She shrugged. "Your dad doesn't want me here."

"He hates women," he said. "You knew that, didn't you?"

"Yes. But why?"

He shook his head. "It's because of my mother. She did something really terrible to him, and he never talks about her. He never has. I've got one picture of her, in my room."

"I guess you look like her," she said speculatively.

He handed her the keyboard. "I've got red hair and freckles like she had," he confessed. "I'm just sorry that I...well, that I don't look anything like Dad. I'm glad he cares about me, though, in spite of everything. Isn't it great that he likes me?"

What an odd way to talk about his father, Amanda thought as she studied him. She wanted to say something else, to ask about that wording, but it was too soon. She hid her curiosity in humor.

"'There are more things in heaven and earth, Horatio, than are dreamt of in your philosophy,'" she intoned deeply.

He chuckled. "Hamlet," he said. "Shakespeare. We did that in English class last month."

"Culture in the high country." She applauded. "Very good, Elliot."

"I like rock culture best," he said in a stage whisper. "Play something."

She glanced toward Quinn's closed study door with a grimace. "Something soft."

"No!" he protested, and grinned. "Come on, give him hell."

"Elliot!" she chided.

"He needs shaking up, I tell you, he's going to die an old maid. He gets all funny and red when unmarried ladies talk to him at church, and just look at how grumpy he's been since you've been around. We've got to save him, Amanda," he said solemnly.

She sighed. "Okay. It's your funeral." She flicked switches, turning on the auto rhythm, the auto chords, and moved the volume to maximum. With a mischievous glance at Elliot, she swung into one of the newest rock songs, by a rival group, instantly recognizable by the reggae rhythm and sweet harmony.

"Good God!" came a muffled roar from the study.

Amanda cut off the keyboard and handed it to Elliot.

"No!" Elliot gasped.

But it was too late. His father came out of the study and saw Elliot holding the keyboard and started smoldering.

"It was her!" Elliot accused, pointing his finger at her.

She peered at Quinn over her drawn-up knees.

"Would I play a keyboard that loud in your house, after you warned me not to?" she asked in her best meek voice.

Quinn's eyes narrowed. They went back to Elliot.

"She's lying," Elliot said. "Just like the guy in those truck commercials on TV...!"

"Keep it down," Quinn said without cracking a smile. "Or I'll give that thing the decent burial it really needs. And no more damned rock music in my house! That thing has earphones. Use them!"

"Yes, sir," Elliot groaned.

Amanda saluted him. "We hear and obey, excellency!" she said with a deplorable Spanish accent. "Your wish is our command. We live only to serve...!"

The slamming of the study door cut her off. She burst into laughter while Elliot hit her with a sofa cushion.

"You animal," he accused mirthfully. "Lying to Dad, accusing me of doing something I never did! How could you?"

"Temporary insanity," she gasped for breath. "I couldn't help myself."

"We're both going to die," he assured her. "He'll lie awake all night thinking of ways to get even and when we least expect it, pow!"

"He's welcome. Here. Run that G major scale again."

He let her turn the keyboard back on, but he was careful to move the volume switch down as far as it would go.

It was almost nine when Quinn came out of the study and turned out the light.

"Time for bed," he said.

Amanda had wanted to watch a movie that was coming on, but she knew better than to ask. Presumably they did occasionally watch television at night. She'd have to ask one of these days.

"Good night, Dad. Amanda," Elliot said, grinning as he went upstairs with a bound.

"Did you do your homework?" Quinn called up after him.

"Almost."

"What the hell does that mean?" he demanded.

"It means I'll do it first thing in the morning! 'Night, Dad!"

A door closed.

Quinn glared at Amanda. "That won't do," he said tersely. "His homework comes first. Music is a nice hobby, but it's not going to make a living for him."

Why not, she almost retorted, it makes a six-figure annual income for me, but she kept her mouth shut.

"I'll make sure he's done his homework before I offer to show him anything else on the keyboard. Okay?"

He sighed angrily. "All right. Come on. Let's go to bed."

She put her hands over her chest and gasped, her eyes wide and astonished. "Together? Mr. Sutton, really!"

His dark eyes narrowed in a veiled threat. "Hell will freeze over before I wind up in bed with you," he said icily. "I told you, I don't want used goods."

"Your loss," she sighed, ignoring the impulse to lay a lamp across his thick skull. "Experience is a valuable commodity in my world." She deliberately smoothed her hands down her waist and over her hips, her eyes faintly coquettish as she watched him watching her movements. "And I'm very experienced," she drawled. In music, she was.

His jaw tautened. "Yes, it does show," he said.

"Kindly keep your attitudes to yourself. I don't want my son corrupted."

"If you really meant that, you'd let him watch movies and listen to rock music and trust him to make up his own mind about things."

"He's only twelve."

"You aren't preparing him to live in the real world," she protested.

"This," he said, "is the real world for him. Not some fancy apartment in a city where women like you lounge around in bars picking up men."

"Now you wait just a minute," she said. "I don't lounge around in bars to pick up men." She shifted her stance. "I hang out in zoos and flash elderly men in my trench coat."

He threw up his hands. "I give up."

"Good! Your room or mine?"

He whirled, his dark eyes flashing. Her smile was purely provocative and she was deliberately baiting him, he could sense it. His jaw tautened and he wanted to pick her up and shake her for the effect her teasing was having on him.

"Okay, I quit," Amanda said, because she could see that he'd reached the limits of his control and she wasn't quite brave enough to test the other side of it. "Good night. Sweet dreams."

He didn't answer her. He followed her up the stairs and watched her go into her room and close the door. After a minute, he went into his own room and locked the door. He laughed mirthlessly at his own rash action, but he hoped she could hear the bolt being thrown.

She could. It shocked her, until she realized that he'd done it deliberately, probably trying to hurt her. She laid

back on her bed with a long sigh. She didn't know what
to do about Mr. Sutton. He was beginning to get to her
in a very real way. She had to keep her perspective. This
was only temporary. It would help to keep it in mind.

Quinn was thinking the same thing. But when he
turned out the light and closed his eyes, he kept feeling Amanda's loosened hair brushing down his chest,
over his flat stomach, his loins. He shuddered and woke
up sweating in the middle of the night. It was the worst
and longest night of his life.

The next morning, Quinn glared at Amanda across
the breakfast table after Elliot had left for school.

"Leave my shirts alone," he said curtly. "If you find
any more tears, Harry can mend them."

Her eyebrows lifted. "I don't have germs," she
pointed out. "I couldn't contaminate them just by stitch-
ing them up."

"Leave them alone," he said harshly.

"Okay. Suit yourself." She sighed. "I'll just busy myself making lacy pillows for your bed."

He said something expressive and obscene; her lips
fell open and she gaped at him. She'd never heard him
use language like that.

It seemed to bother him that he had. He put down
his fork, left his eggs and went out the door as if leop-
ards were stalking him.

Amanda stirred her eggs around on the plate, feeling
vaguely guilty that she'd given him such a hard time
that he'd gone without half his breakfast. She didn't
know why she needled him. It seemed to be a new habit,
maybe to keep him at bay, to keep him from noticing
how attracted she was to him.

"I'm going out to feed the calves, Harry," she said after a minute.

"Dress warm. It's snowing again," he called from upstairs.

"Okay."

She put on her coat and hat and wandered out to the barn through the path Quinn had made in the deep snow. She'd never again grumble at little two-and three-foot drifts in the city, she promised herself. Now that she knew what real snow was, she felt guilty for all her past complaints.

The barn was warmer than the great outdoors. She pushed snowflakes out of her eyes and face and went to fix the bottles as Harry had shown her, but Quinn was already there and had it done.

"No need to follow me around trying to get my attention," Amanda murmured with a wicked smile. "I've already noticed how sexy and handsome you are."

He drew in a furious breath, but just as he was about to speak she moved closer and put her fingers against his cold mouth.

"You'll break my heart if you use ungentlemanly language, Mr. Sutton," she told him firmly. "I'll just feed the calves and admire you from afar, if you don't mind. It seems safer than trying to throw myself at you."

He looked torn between shaking her and kissing her. She stood very still where he towered above her, even bigger than usual in that thick shepherd's coat and his tall, gray Stetson. He looked down at her quietly, his narrowed eyes lingering on her flushed cheeks and her soft, parted mouth.

Her hands were resting against the coat, and his were on her arms, pulling. She could hardly breathe as she realized that he'd actually touched her voluntarily. He jerked her face up under his, and she could see anger and something like bitterness in the dark eyes that held hers until she blushed.

"Just what are you after, city girl?" he asked coldly.

"A smile, a kind word and, dare I say it, a round of hearty laughter?" she essayed with wide eyes, trying not to let him see how powerfully he affected her.

His dark eyes fell to her mouth. "Is that right? And nothing more?"

Her breath came jerkily through her lips. "I…have to feed the calves."

His eyes narrowed. "Yes, you do." His fingers on her arms contracted, so that she could feel them even through the sleeves of her coat. "Be careful what you offer me," he said in a voice as light and cold as the snow outside the barn. "I've been without a woman for one hell of a long time, and I'm alone up here. If you're not what you're making yourself out to be, you could be letting yourself in for some trouble."

She stared up at him only half comprehending what he was saying. As his meaning began to filter into her consciousness, her cheeks heated and her breath caught in her throat.

"You…make it sound like a threat," she breathed.

"It is a threat, Amanda," he replied, using her name for the first time. "You could start something you might not want to finish with me, even with Elliot and Harry around."

She bit her lower lip nervously. She hadn't considered that. He looked more mature and formidable than he ever had before, and she could feel the banked-down fires in him kindling even as he held her.

"Okay," she said after a minute.

He let her go and moved away from her to get the bottles. He handed them to her with a long, speculative look.

"It's all right," she muttered, embarrassed. "I won't attack you while your back is turned. I almost never rape men."

He lifted an eyebrow, but he didn't smile. "You crazed female sex maniac," he murmured.

"Goody Two Shoes," she shot back.

A corner of his mouth actually turned up. "You've got that one right," he agreed. "Stay close to the house while it's snowing like this. We wouldn't want to lose you."

"I'll just bet we wouldn't," she muttered and stuck her tongue out at his retreating back.

She knelt down to feed the calves, still shaken by her confrontation with Quinn. He was an enigma. She was almost certain that he'd been joking with her at the end of the exchange, but it was hard to tell from his poker face. He didn't look like a man who'd laughed often or enough.

The littlest calf wasn't responding as well as he had earlier. She cuddled him and coaxed him to drink, but he did it without any spirit. She laid him back down with a sigh. He didn't look good at all. She worried about him for the rest of the evening, and she didn't argue when the television was cut off at nine o'clock. She went straight to bed, with Quinn and Elliot giving her odd looks.

CHAPTER FOUR

AMANDA WAS SUBDUED at the breakfast table, more so when Quinn started watching her with dark, accusing eyes. She knew she'd deliberately needled him for the past two days, and now she was sorry. He'd hinted that her behavior was about to start something, and she was anxious not to make things any worse than they already were.

The problem was that she was attracted to him. The more she saw of him, the more she liked him. He was different from the superficial, materialistic men in her own world. He was hardheaded and stubborn. He had values, and he spoke out for them. He lived by a rigid code of ethics, and *honor* was a word that had great meaning for him. Under all that, he was sensitive and caring. Amanda couldn't help the way she was beginning to feel about him. She only wished that she hadn't started off on the wrong foot with him.

She set out to win him over, acting more like her real self. She was polite and courteous and caring, but without the rough edges she'd had in the beginning. She still did the mending, despite his grumbling, and she made cushions for the sofa out of some cloth Harry had put away. But all her domestic actions only made things worse. Quinn glared at her openly now, and his lack of politeness raised even Harry's eyebrows.

Amanda had a sneaking hunch that it was attraction to her that was making him so ill-humored. He didn't act at all like an experienced man, despite his marriage, and the way he looked at her was intense. If she could bring him out into the open, she thought, it might ease the tension a little.

She did her chores, including feeding the calves, worrying even more about the littlest one because he wasn't responding as well today as he had the day before. When Elliot came home, she refused to help him with the keyboard until he did his homework. With a rueful smile and a knowing glance at his dad, he went up to his room to get it over with.

Meanwhile, Harry went out to get more firewood and Amanda was left in the living room with Quinn watching an early newscast.

The news was, as usual, all bad. Quinn put out his cigarette half angrily, his dark eyes lingering on Amanda's soft face.

"Don't you miss the city?" he asked.

She smiled. "Sure. I miss the excitement and my friends. But it's nice here, too." She moved toward the big armchair he was sitting in, nervously contemplating her next move. "You don't mind all that much, do you? Having me around, I mean?"

He glared up at her. He was wearing a blue-checked flannel shirt, buttoned up to the throat, and the hard muscles of his chest strained against it. He looked twice as big as usual, his dark hair unruly on his broad forehead as he stared up into her eyes.

"I'm getting used to you, I guess," he said stiffly. "Just don't get too comfortable."

"You really don't want me here, do you?" she asked quietly.

He sighed angrily. "I don't like women," he muttered.

"I know." She sat down on the arm of his chair, facing him. "Why not?" she asked gently.

His body went taut at the proximity. She was too close. Too female. The scent of her got into his nostrils and made him shift restlessly in the chair. "It's none of your damned business why not," he said evasively. "Will you get up from there?"

She warmed at the tone of his voice. So she did disturb him! Amanda smiled gently as she leaned forward. "Are you sure you want me to?" she asked and suddenly threw caution to the wind and slid down into his lap, putting her soft mouth hungrily on his.

He stiffened. He jerked. His big hands bit into her arms so hard they bruised. But for just one long, sweet moment, his hard mouth gave in to hers and he gave her back the kiss, his lips rough and warm, the pressure bruising, and he groaned as if all his dreams had come true at once.

He tasted of smoke for the brief second that he allowed the kiss. Then he was all bristling indignation and cold fury. He slammed to his feet, taking her with him, and literally threw her away, so hard that she fell against and onto the sofa.

"Damn you," he ground out. His fists clenched at his sides. His big body vibrated with outrage. "You cheap little tart!"

She lay trembling, frightened of the violence in his now white face and blazing dark eyes. "I'm not," she defended feebly.

"Can't you live without it for a few days, or are you

desperate enough to try to seduce me?" he hissed. His eyes slid over her with icy contempt. "It won't work. I've told you already, I don't want something that any man can have! I don't want any part of you, least of all your overused body!"

She got to her feet on legs that threatened to give way under her, backing away from his anger. She couldn't even speak. Her father had been like that when he drank too much, white-faced, icy hot, totally out of control. And when he got that way, he hit. She cringed away from Quinn as he moved toward her and suddenly, she whirled and ran out of the room.

He checked his instinctive move to go after her. So she was scared, was she? He frowned, trying to understand why. He'd only spoken the truth; did she not like hearing what she was? The possibility that he'd been wrong, that she wasn't a cheap little tart, he wouldn't admit even to himself.

He sat back down and concentrated on the television without any real interest. When Elliot came downstairs, Quinn barely looked up.

"Where's Amanda going?" he asked his father.

Quinn raised an eyebrow. "What?"

"Where's Amanda going in such a rush?" Elliot asked again. "I saw her out the window, tramping through waist-deep snow. Doesn't she remember what you told her about old McNaber's traps? She's headed straight for them if she keeps on the way she's headed... Where are you going?"

Quinn was already on his feet and headed for the back door. He got into his shepherd's coat and hat without speaking, his face pale, his eyes blazing with mingled fear and anger.

"She was crying," Harry muttered, sparing him a glance. "I don't know what you said to her, but—"

"Shut up," Quinn said coldly. He stared the older man down and went out the back door and around the house, following in the wake Amanda's body had made. She was already out of sight, and those traps would be buried under several feet of snow. Bear traps, and she wouldn't see them until she felt them. The thought of that merciless metal biting her soft flesh didn't bear thinking about, and it would be his fault because he'd hurt her.

Several meters ahead, into the woods now, Amanda was cursing silently as she plowed through the snowdrifts, her black eyes fierce even through the tears. Damn Quinn Sutton, she panted. She hoped he got eaten by moths during the winter, she hoped his horse stood on his foot, she hoped the sled ran over him and packed him into the snow and nobody found him until spring. It was only a kiss, after all, and he'd kissed her back just for a few seconds.

She felt the tears burning coldly down her cheeks as they started again. Damn him. He hadn't had to make her feel like such an animal, just because she'd kissed him. She cared about him. She'd only wanted to get on a friendlier footing with him. But now she'd done it. He hated her for sure, she'd seen it in his eyes, in his face, when he'd called her those names. Cheap little tart, indeed! Well, Goody Two Shoes Sutton could just hold his breath until she kissed him again, so there!

She stopped to catch her breath and then plowed on. The cabin was somewhere down here. She'd stay in it even if she did freeze to death. She'd shack up with a grizzly bear before she'd spend one more night under

Quinn Sutton's roof. She frowned. Were there grizzly bears in this part of the country?

"Amanda, stop!"

She paused, wondering if she'd heard someone call her name, or if it had just been the wind. She was in a break of lodgepole pines now, and a cabin was just below in the valley. But it wasn't Mr. Durning's cabin. Could that be McNaber's...?

"Amanda!"

That was definitely her name. She glanced over her shoulder and saw the familiar shepherd's coat and dark worn Stetson atop that arrogant head.

"Eat snow, Goody Two Shoes!" she yelled back. "I'm going home!"

She started ahead, pushing hard now. But he had the edge, because he was walking in the path she'd made. He was bigger and faster, and he had twice her stamina. Before she got five more feet, he had her by the waist.

She fought him, kicking and hitting, but he simply wrapped both arms around her and held on until she finally ran out of strength.

"I hate you," she panted, shivering as the cold and the exertion got to her. "I hate you!"

"You'd hate me more if I hadn't stopped you," he said, breathing hard. "McNaber lives down there. He's got bear traps all over the place. Just a few more steps, and you'd have been up to your knees in them, you little fool! You can't even see them in snow this deep!"

"What would you care?" she groaned. "You don't want me around. I don't want to stay with you anymore. I'll take my chances at the cabin!"

"No, you won't, Amanda," he said. His embrace didn't even loosen. He whipped her around, his big hands rough on her sleeves as he shook her. "You're coming back with me, if I have to carry you!"

She flinched, the violence in him frightening her. She swallowed, her lower lip trembling and pulled feebly against his hands.

"Let go of me," she whispered. Her voice shook, and she hated her own cowardice.

He scowled. She was paper white. Belatedly he realized what was wrong and his hands released her. She backed away as far as the snow would allow and stood like a young doe at bay, her eyes dark and frightened.

"Did he hit you?" he asked quietly.

She didn't have to ask who. She shivered. "Only when he drank," she said, her voice faltering. "But he always drank." She laughed bitterly. "Just…don't come any closer until you cool down, if you please."

He took a slow, steadying breath. "I'm sorry," he said, shocking her. "No, I mean it. I'm really sorry. I wouldn't have hit you, if that's what you're thinking. Only a coward would raise his hand to a woman," he said with cold conviction.

She wrapped her arms around herself and stood, just breathing, shivering in the cold.

"We'd better get back before you freeze," he said tautly. Her very defensiveness disarmed him. He felt guilty and protective all at once. He wanted to take her to his heart and comfort her, but even as he stepped toward her, she backed away. He hadn't imagined how much that would hurt until it happened. He stopped and stood where he was, raising his hands in an odd gesture of helplessness. "I won't touch you," he promised. "Come on, honey. You can go first."

Tears filmed her dark eyes. It was the first endear-

ment she'd ever heard from him and it touched her
deeply. But she knew it was only casual. Her behavior
had shocked him and he didn't know what to do. She
let out a long breath.

Without a quip or comeback, she eased past him
warily and started back the way they'd come. He followed her, giving thanks that he'd been in time, that she
hadn't run afoul of old McNaber's traps. But now he'd
really done it. He'd managed to make her afraid of him.

She went ahead of him into the house. Elliot and
Harry took one look at her face and Quinn's and didn't
ask a single question.

She sat at the supper table like a statue. She didn't
speak, even when Elliot tried to bring her into the conversation. And afterward, she curled up in a chair in the
living room and sat like a mouse watching television.

Quinn couldn't know the memories he'd brought
back, the searing fear of her childhood. Her father had
been a big man, and he was always violent when he
drank. He was sorry afterward, sometimes he even
cried when he saw the bruises he'd put on her. But
it never stopped him. She'd run away because it was
more than she could bear, and fortunately there'd been
a place for runaways that took her in. She'd learned vol-
umes about human kindness from those people. But the
memories were bitter and Quinn's bridled violence had
brought them sweeping in like storm clouds.

Elliot didn't ask her about music lessons. He excused
himself a half hour early and went up to bed. Harry had
long since gone to his own room.

Quinn sat in his big chair, smoking his cigarette, but
he started when Amanda put her feet on the floor and
glanced warily at him.

"Don't go yet," he said quietly. "I want to talk to you."

"We don't have anything to say to each other," she said quietly. "I'm very sorry for what I did this afternoon. It was impulsive and stupid, and I promise I'll never do it again. If you can just put up with me until it thaws a little, you'll never have to see me again."

He sighed wearily. "Is that what you think I want?" he asked, searching her face.

"Of course it is," she replied simply. "You've hated having me here ever since I came."

"Maybe I have. I've got more reason to hate and distrust women than you'll ever know. But that isn't what I want to talk about," he said, averting his gaze from her wan face. He didn't like thinking about that kiss and how disturbing it had been. "I want to know why you thought I might hit you."

She dropped her eyes to her lap. "You're big, like my father," she said. "When he lost his temper, he always hit."

"I'm not your father," Quinn pointed out, his dark eyes narrowing. "And I've never hit anyone in a temper, except maybe another man from time to time when it was called for. I never raised my hand to Elliot's mother, although I felt like it a time or two, in all honesty. I never lifted a hand to her even when she told me she was pregnant with Elliot."

"Why should you have?" she asked absently. "He's your son."

He laughed coldly. "No, he isn't."

She stared at him openly. "Elliot isn't yours?" she asked softly.

He shook his head. "His mother was having an affair with a married man and she got caught out." He shrugged. "I was twenty-two and grass green and she mounted a campaign to marry me. I guess I was pretty much a sitting duck. She was beautiful and stacked and she had me eating out of her hand in no time. We got married and right after the ceremony, she told me what she'd done. She laughed at how clumsy I'd been during the courtship, how she'd had to steel herself not to be sick when I'd kissed her. She told me about Elliot's father and how much she loved him, then she dared me to tell people the truth about how easy it had been to make me marry her." He blew out a cloud of smoke, his eyes cold with memory. "She had me over a barrel. I was twice as proud back then as I am now. I couldn't bear to have the whole community laughing at me. So I stuck it out. Until Elliot was born, and she and his father took off for parts unknown for a weekend of love. Unfortunately for them, he wrecked the car in his haste to get to a motel and killed both of them outright."

"Does Elliot know?" she asked, her voice quiet as she glanced toward the staircase.

"Sure," he said. "I couldn't lie to him about it. But I took care of him from the time he was a baby, and I raised him. That makes me his father just as surely as if I'd put the seed he grew from into his mother's body. He's my son, and I'm his father. I love him."

She studied his hard face, seeing behind it to the pain he must have suffered. "You loved her, didn't you?"

"Calf love," he said. "She came up on my blind side and I needed somebody to love. I'd always been shy and clumsy around girls. I couldn't even get a date when I was in school because I was so rough-edged. She paid me a lot of attention. I was lonely." His big shoulders shrugged. "Like I said, a sitting duck. She taught me some hard lessons about your sex," he added, his narrowed eyes on her face. "I've never forgotten them. And nobody's had a second chance at me."

Her breath came out as a sigh. "That's what you thought this afternoon, when I kissed you," she murmured, reddening at her own forwardness. "I'm sorry. I didn't realize you might think I was playing you for a sucker."

He frowned. "Why did you kiss me, Amanda?"

"Would you believe, because I wanted to?" she asked with a quiet smile. "You're a very attractive man, and something about you makes me weak in the knees. But you don't have to worry about me coming on to you again," she added, getting to her feet. "You teach a pretty tough lesson yourself. Good night, Mr. Sutton. I appreciate your telling me about Elliot. You needn't worry that I'll say anything to him or to anybody else. I don't carry tales, and I don't gossip."

She turned toward the staircase, and Quinn's dark eyes followed her. She had an elegance of carriage that touched him, full of pride and grace. He was sorry now that he'd slapped her down so hard with cruel words. He really hadn't meant to. He'd been afraid that she was going to let him down, that she was playing. It hadn't occurred to him that she found him attractive or that she'd kissed him because she'd really wanted to.

He'd made a bad mistake with Amanda. He'd hurt her and sent her running, and now he wished he could take back the things he'd said. She wasn't like any woman he'd ever been exposed to. She actually seemed unaware of her beauty, as if she didn't think much of it. Maybe he'd gotten it all wrong and she wasn't much more experienced than he was. He wished he could ask her. She disturbed him very much, and now he wondered if it wasn't mutual.

Amanda was lying in bed, crying. The day had been horrible, and she hated Quinn for the way he'd treated her. It wasn't until she remembered what he'd told her that she stopped crying and started thinking. He'd said that he'd never slept with Elliot's mother, and that he hadn't been able to get dates in high school. Presumably that meant that his only experience with women had been after Elliot's mother died. She frowned. There hadn't been many women, she was willing to bet. He seemed to know relatively nothing about her sex. She frowned. If he still hated women, how had he gotten any experience? Finally her mind grew tired of trying to work it out and she went to sleep.

AMANDA WAS UP helping Harry in the kitchen the next morning when Quinn came downstairs after a wild, erotic dream that left him sweating and swearing when he woke up. Amanda had figured largely in it, with her blond hair loose and down to her lower spine, his hands twined in it while he made love to her in the stillness of his own bedroom. The dream had been so vivid that he could almost see the pink perfection of her breasts through the bulky, white-knit sweater she was wearing, and he almost groaned as his eyes fell to the rise and fall of her chest under it.

She glanced at Quinn and actually flushed before she dragged her eyes back down to the pan of biscuits she was putting into the oven.

"I didn't know you could make biscuits," Quinn murmured.

"Harry taught me," she said evasively. Her eyes went back to him again and flitted away.

He frowned at that shy look until he realized why he was getting it. He usually kept his shirts buttoned up to his throat, but this morning he'd left it open halfway down his chest because he was still sweating from that dream. He pursed his lips and gave her a speculative stare. He wondered if it were possible that he disturbed her as much as she disturbed him. He was going to make it his business to find out before she left here. If for no other reason than to salve his bruised ego.

He went out behind Elliot, pausing in the doorway. "How's the calf?" he asked Amanda.

"He wasn't doing very well yesterday," she said with a sigh. "Maybe he's better this morning."

"I'll have a look at him before I go out." He glanced out at the snow. "Don't try to get back to the cabin again, will you? You can't get through McNaber's traps without knowing where they are."

He actually sounded worried. She studied his hard face quietly. That was nice. Unless, of course, he was only worried that she might get laid up and he'd have to put up with her for even longer.

"Is the snow ever going to stop?" she asked.

"Hard to say," he told her. "I've seen it worse than this even earlier in the year. But we'll manage, I suppose."

"I suppose." She glared at him.

He pulled on his coat and buttoned it, propping his hat over one eye. "In a temper this morning, are we?" he mused.

His eyes were actually twinkling. She shifted back against the counter, grateful that Harry had gone off to clean the bedrooms. "I'm not in a temper. Cheap little tarts don't have tempers."

One eyebrow went up. "I called you that, didn't I?" He let his eyes run slowly down her body. "You shouldn't have kissed me like that. I'm not used to aggressive women."

"Rest assured that I'll never attack you again, Goody Two Shoes."

He chuckled softly. "Won't you? Well, disappointment is a man's lot, I suppose."

Her eyes widened. She wasn't sure she'd even heard him. "You were horrible to me!"

"I guess I was." His dark eyes held hers, making little chills up and down her spine at the intensity of the gaze. "I thought you were playing games. You know, a little harmless fun at the hick's expense."

"I don't know how to play games with men," she said stiffly, "and nobody, anywhere, could call you a hick with a straight face. You're a very masculine man with a keen mind and an overworked sense of responsibility. I wouldn't make fun of you even if I could."

His dark eyes smiled into hers. "In that case, we might call a truce for the time being."

"Do you think you could stand being nice to me?" she asked sourly. "I mean, it would be a strain, I'm sure."

"I'm not a bad man," he pointed out. "I just don't know much about women, or hadn't that thought occurred?"

She searched his eyes. "No."

"We'll have to have a long talk about it one of these days." He pulled the hat down over his eyes. "I'll check on the calves for you."

"Thanks." She watched him go, her heart racing at the look in his eyes just before he closed the door. She was more nervous of him now than ever, but she didn't know what to do about it. She was hoping that the chinook would come before she had to start worrying too much. She was too confused to know what to do anymore.

CHAPTER FIVE

AMANDA FINISHED THE breakfast dishes before she went out to the barn. Quinn was still there, his dark eyes quiet on the smallest of the three calves. It didn't take a fortune teller to see that something was badly wrong. The small animal lay on its side, its dull, lackluster red-and-white coat showing its ribs, its eyes glazed and unseeing while it fought to breathe.

She knelt beside Quinn and he glanced at her with concern.

"You'd better go back in the house, honey," he said.

Her eyes slid over the small calf. She'd seen pets die over the years, and now she knew the signs. The calf was dying. Quinn knew it, too, and was trying to shield her.

That touched her, oddly, more than anything he'd said or done since she'd been on Ricochet. She looked up at him. "You're a nice man, Quinn Sutton," she said softly.

He drew in a slow breath. "When I'm not taking bites out of you, you mean?" he replied. "It hurts like hell when you back away from me. You'll never know how sorry I am for what happened yesterday."

One shock after another. At least it took her mind off the poor, laboring creature beside them. "I'm sorry, too," she said. "I shouldn't have been so..." She stopped, averting her eyes. "I don't know much about men,

Quinn," she said finally. "I've spent my whole adult life
backing away from involvement, emotional or physical.
I know how to flirt, but not much more." She risked a
glance at him, and relaxed when she saw his face. "My
aunt is Mr. Durning's lover, you know. She's an artist. A little flighty, but nice. I've...never had a lover."

He nodded quietly. "I've been getting that idea since
we wound up near McNaber's cabin yesterday. You reacted pretty violently for an experienced woman." He
looked away from her. That vulnerability in her pretty
face was working on him again. "Go inside now. I can
deal with this."

"I'm not afraid of death," she returned. "I saw my
mother die. It wasn't scary at all. She just closed her
eyes."

His dark eyes met hers and locked. "My father went
the same way." He looked back down at the calf. "It
won't be long now."

She sat down in the hay beside him and slid her small
hand into his big one. He held it for a long moment. Finally his voice broke the silence. "It's over. Go have a
cup of coffee. I'll take care of him."

She hadn't meant to cry, but the calf had been so
little and helpless. Quinn pulled her close, holding her
with quiet comfort, while she cried. Then he wiped the
tears away with his thumbs and smiled gently. "You'll
do," he murmured, thinking that sensitivity and courage was a nice combination in a woman.

She was thinking the exact same thing about him.
She managed a watery smile and with one last, pitying
look at the calf, she went into the house.

Elliot would miss it, as she would, she thought. Even
Quinn had seemed to care about it, because she saw

him occasionally sitting by it, petting it, talking to it. He loved little things. It was evident in all the kittens and puppies around the place, and in the tender care he took of all his cattle and calves. And although Quinn cursed old man McNaber's traps, Elliot had told her that he stopped by every week to check on the dour old man and make sure he had enough chopped wood and supplies. For a taciturn iceman, he had a surprisingly warm center.

She told Harry what had happened and sniffed a little while she drank black coffee. "Is there anything I can do?" she asked.

He smiled. "You do enough," he murmured. "Nice to have some help around the place."

"Quinn hasn't exactly thought so," she said dryly.

"Oh, yes he has," he said firmly as he cleared away the dishes they'd eaten his homemade soup and corn bread in. "Quinn could have taken you to Mrs. Pearson down the mountain if he'd had a mind to. He doesn't have to let you stay here. Mrs. Pearson would be glad of the company." He glanced at her and grinned at her perplexed expression. "He's been watching you lately. Sees the way you sew up his shirts and make curtains and patch pillows. It's new to him, having a woman about. He has a hard time with change."

"Don't we all?" Amanda said softly, remembering how clear her own life had been until that tragic night. But it was nice to know that Quinn had been watching her. Certainly she'd been watching him. And this morning, everything seemed to have changed between them. "When will it thaw?" she asked, and now she was dreading it, not anticipating it. She didn't want to leave Ricochet. Or Quinn.

Harry shrugged. "Hard to tell. Days. Weeks. This is raw mountain country. Can't predict a chinook. Plenty think they can, though," he added, and proceeded to tell her about a Blackfoot who predicted the weather with jars of bear grease.

She was much calmer, but still sad when Quinn finally came back inside.

He spared her a glance before he shucked his coat, washed his hands and brawny forearms and dried them on a towel.

He didn't say anything to her, and Harry, sensing the atmosphere, made himself scarce after he'd poured two cups of coffee for them.

"Are you all right?" he asked her after a minute, staring down at her bent head.

"Sure." She forced a smile. "He was so little, Quinn." She stopped when her voice broke and lowered her eyes to the table. "I guess you think I'm a wimp."

"Not really." Without taking time to think about the consequences, his lean hands pulled her up by the arms, holding her in front of him so that her eyes were on a level with his deep blue, plaid flannel shirt. The sleeves were rolled up, and it was open at the throat, where thick, dark hair curled out of it. He looked and smelled fiercely masculine and Amanda's knees weakened at the unexpected proximity. His big hands bit into her soft flesh, and she wondered absently if he realized just how strong he was.

The feel of him so close was new and terribly exciting, especially since he'd reached for her for the first time. She didn't know what to expect, and her heart was going wild. She lowered her eyes to his throat. His pulse was jumping and she stared at it curiously, only half aware of his hold and the sudden increase of his breathing.

He was having hell just getting a breath. The scent of her was in his nostrils, drowning him. Woman smell. Sweet and warm. His teeth clenched. It was bad enough having to look at her, but this close, she made his blood run hot and wild as it hadn't since he was a young man. He didn't know what he was doing, but the need for her had haunted him for days. He wanted so badly to kiss her, the way she'd kissed him the day before, but in a different way. He wasn't quite sure how to go about it.

"You smell of flowers," he said roughly.

That was an interesting comment from a nonpoetic man. She smiled a little to herself. "It's my shampoo," she murmured.

He drew in a steadying breath. "You don't wear your hair down at all, do you?"

"Just at night," she replied, aware that his face was closer than it had been, because she could feel his breath on her forehead. He was so tall and overwhelming this close. He made her feel tiny and very feminine.

"I'm sorry about the calf, Amanda," he said. "We lose a few every winter. It's part of ranching."

The shock of her name on his lips made her lift her head. She stared up at him curiously, searching his dark, quiet eyes. "I suppose so. I shouldn't have gotten so upset, though. I guess men don't react to things the way women do."

"You don't know what kind of man I am," he replied. His hands felt vaguely tremulous. He wondered if she knew the effect she had on him. "As it happens, I get attached to the damned things, too." He sighed heavily.

"Little things don't have much choice in this world. They're at the mercy of everything and everybody."

Her eyes softened as they searched his. He sounded different when he spoke that way. Vulnerable. Almost tender. And so alone.

"You aren't really afraid of me, are you?" he asked, as if the thought was actually painful.

She grimaced. "No. Of course not. I was ashamed of what I'd done, and a little nervous of the way you reacted to it, that's all. I know you wouldn't hurt me." She drew in a soft breath. "I know you resent having me here," she confessed. "I resented having to depend on you for shelter. But the snow will melt soon, and I'll leave."

"I thought you'd had lovers," he confessed quietly. "The way you acted…well, it just made all those suspicions worse. I took you at face value."

Amanda smiled. "It was all put-on. I don't even know why I did it. I guess I was trying to live down to your image of me."

He loved the sensation her sultry black eyes aroused in him. Unconsciously his hands tightened on her arms. "You haven't had a man, ever?" he asked huskily.

The odd shadow of dusky color along his cheekbones fascinated her. She wondered about the embarrassment asking the question had caused. "No. Not ever," she stammered.

"The way you look?" he asked, his eyes eloquent.

"What do you mean, the way I look?" she said, bristling.

"You know you're beautiful," he returned. His eyes darkened. "A woman who looks like you do could have her pick of men."

"Maybe," she agreed without conceit. "But I've never wanted a man in my life, to be dominated by a man. I've made my own way in the world. I'm a musician," she told him, because that didn't give away very much. "I support myself by playing a keyboard."

"Yes, Elliot told me. I've heard you play for him. You're good." He felt his heartbeat increasing as he looked at her. She smelled so good. He looked down at her mouth and remembered how it had felt for those few seconds when he'd given in to her playful kiss. Would she let him do it? He knew so little about those subtle messages women were supposed to send out when they wanted a man's lovemaking. He couldn't read Amanda's eyes. But her lips were parted and her breath was coming rather fast from between them. Her face was flushed, but that could have been from the cold.

She gazed up into his eyes and couldn't look away. He wasn't handsome. His face really seemed as if it had been chipped away from the side of the Rockies, all craggy angles and hard lines. His mouth was thin and faintly cruel looking. She wondered if it would feel as hard as it looked if he was in control, dominating her lips. It had been different when she'd kissed him....

"What are you thinking?" he asked huskily, because her eyes were quite frankly on his mouth.

"I...was wondering," she whispered hesitantly, "how hard your mouth would be if you kissed me."

His heart stopped and then began to slam against his chest. "Don't you know already?" he asked, his voice deeper, harsher. "You kissed me."

"Not...properly."

He wondered what she meant by properly. His wife had only kissed him when she had to, and only in the very beginning of their courtship. She always pushed him away and murmured something about mussing her makeup. He couldn't remember one time when he'd kissed anyone with passion, or when he'd ever been kissed by anyone else like that.

His warm, rough hands let go of her arms and came up to frame her soft oval face. His breath shuddered out of his chest when she didn't protest as he bent his dark head.

"Show me what you mean…by properly," he whispered.

He had to know, she thought dizzily. But his lips touched hers and she tasted the wind and the sun on them. Her hands clenched the thick flannel shirt and she resisted searching for buttons, because she wanted very much to touch that thicket of black, curling hair that covered his broad chest. She went on her tiptoes and pushed her mouth against his, the force of the action parting his lips as well as her own, and she felt him stiffen and heard him groan as their open mouths met.

She dropped back onto her feet, her wide, curious eyes meeting his stormy ones.

"Like that?" he whispered gruffly, bending to repeat the action with his own mouth. "I've never done it…with my mouth open," he said, biting off the words against her open lips.

She couldn't believe he'd said that. She couldn't believe, either, the sensations rippling down to her toes when she gave in to the force of his ardor and let him kiss her that way, his mouth rough and demanding as one big hand slid to the back of her head to press her even closer.

A soft sound passed her lips, a faint moan, because

she couldn't get close enough to him. Her breasts were flattened against his hard chest, and she felt his heartbeat against them. But she wanted to be closer than that, enveloped, crushed to him.

"Did I hurt you?" he asked in a shaky whisper that touched her lips.

"What?" she whispered back dizzily.

"You made a sound."

Her eyes searched his, her own misty and half closed and rapt. "I moaned," she whispered. Her nails stroked him through the shirt and she liked the faint tautness of his body as he reacted to it. "I like being kissed like that." She rubbed her forehead against him, smelling soap and detergent and pure man. "Could we take your shirt off?" she whispered.

Her hands were driving him nuts, and he was wondering the same thing himself. But somewhere in the back of his mind he remembered that Harry was around, and that it might look compromising if he let her touch him that way. In fact, it might get compromising, because he felt his body harden in a way it hadn't since his marriage. And because it made him vulnerable and he didn't want her to feel it, he took her gently by the arms and moved her away from him with a muffled curse.

"Harry," he said, his breath coming deep and rough.

She colored. "Oh, yes." She moved back, her eyes a little wild.

"You don't have to look so threatened. I won't do it again," he said, misunderstanding her retreat. Had he frightened her again?

"Oh, it's not that. You didn't frighten me." She lowered her eyes to the floor. "I'm just wondering if you'll think I'm easy...."

He scowled. "Easy?"

"I don't usually come on to men," she said softly.
"And I've never asked anybody to take his shirt off before." She glanced up at him, fascinated by the expression on his face. "Well, I haven't," she said belligerently.
"And you don't have to worry; I won't throw myself at
you anymore, either. I just got carried away in the heat
of the moment...."

His eyebrows arched. None of what she was saying
made sense. "Like you did yesterday?" he mused, liking
the color that came and went in her face. "I did accuse
you of throwing yourself at me," he said on a long sigh.

"Yes. You seem to think I'm some sort of liberated
sex maniac."

His lips curled involuntarily. "Are you?" he asked,
and sounded interested.

She stamped her foot. "Stop that. I don't want to stay
here anymore!"

"I'm not sure it's a good idea myself," he mused,
watching her eyes glitter with rage. God, she was pretty!
"I mean, if you tried to seduce me, things could get
sticky."

The red in her cheeks got darker. "I don't have any
plans to seduce you."

"Well, if you get any, you'd better tell me in ad-
vance," he said, pulling a cigarette from his shirt pocket.
"Just so I can be prepared to fight you off."

That dry drawl confused her. Suddenly he was a
different man, full of male arrogance and amusement.
Things had shifted between them during that long, hard
kiss. The distance had shortened, and he was looking at
her with an expression she couldn't quite understand.

"How did you get to the age you are without winding up in someone's bed?" Quinn asked then. He'd wondered at her shyness with him and then at the way she blushed all the time. He didn't know much about women, but he wanted to know everything about her.

Amanda wrapped her arms around herself and shrugged. When he lit his cigarette and still stood there waiting for an answer, she gave in and replied. "I couldn't give up control," she said simply. "All my life I'd been dominated and pushed around by my father. Giving in to a man seemed like throwing away my rights as a person. Especially giving in to a man in bed," she stammered, averting her gaze. "I don't think there's anyplace in the world where a man is more the master than in a bedroom, despite all the liberation and freedom of modern life."

"And you think that women should dominate there."

She looked up. "Well, not dominate." She hesitated. "But a woman shouldn't be used just because she's a woman."

His thin mouth curled slightly. "Neither should a man."

"I wasn't using you," she shot back.

"Did I accuse you?" he returned innocently.

She swallowed. "No, I guess not." She folded her arms over her breasts, wincing because the tips were hard and unexpectedly tender.

"That hardness means you feel desire," he said, grinning when she gaped and then glared at him. She made him feel about ten feet tall. "I read this book about sex," he continued. "It didn't make much sense to me at the time, but it's beginning to."

"I am not available as a living model for sex education!"

He shrugged. "Suit yourself. But it's a hell of a loss to my education."

"You don't need educating," she muttered. "You were married."

He nodded. "Sure I was." He pursed his lips and let his eyes run lazily over her body. "Except that she never wanted me, before or after I married her."

Amanda's lips parted. "Oh, Quinn," she said softly. "I'm sorry."

"So was I, at the time." He shook his head. "I used to wonder at first why she pulled back every time I kissed her. I guess she was suffering it until she could get me to put the ring on her finger. Up until then, I thought it was her scruples that kept me at arm's length. But she never had many morals." He stared at Amanda curiously, surprised at how easy it was to tell her things he'd never shared with another human being. "After I found out what she really was, I couldn't have cared less about sharing her bed."

"No, I don't suppose so," she agreed.

He lifted the cigarette to his lips and his eyes narrowed as he studied her. "Elliot's almost thirteen," he said. "He's been my whole life. I've taken care of him and done for him. He knows there's no blood tie between us, but I love him and he loves me. In all the important ways, I'm his father and he's my son."

"He loves you very much," she said with a smile. "He talks about you all the time."

"He's a good boy." He moved a little closer, noticing how she tensed when he came close. He liked that reaction a lot. It told him that she was aware of him, but shy and reticent. "You don't have men," he said softly. "Well, I don't have women."

"Not for…a few months?" she stammered, because she couldn't imagine that he was telling the truth.

He shrugged his powerful shoulders. "Well, not for a bit longer than that. Not much opportunity up here. And I can't go off and leave Elliot while I tomcat around town. It's been a bit longer than thirteen years."

"A bit?"

He looked down at her with a curious, mocking smile. "When I was a boy, I didn't know how to get girls. I was big and clumsy and shy, so it was the other boys who scored." He took another draw, a slightly jerky one, from his cigarette. "I still have the same problem around most women. It's not so much hatred as a lack of ability, and shyness. I don't know how to come on to a woman," he confessed with a faint smile.

Amanda felt as if the sun had just come out. She smiled back. "Don't you, really?" she asked softly. "I thought it was just that you found me lacking, or that I wasn't woman enough to interest you."

He could have laughed out loud at that assumption. "Is that why you called me Goody Two Shoes?" he asked pleasantly.

She laughed softly. "Well, that was sort of sour grapes." She lowered her eyes to his chest. "It hurt my feelings that you thought I didn't have any morals, when I'd never made one single move toward any other man in my whole life."

He felt warm all over from that shy confession. It took down the final brick in his wall of reserve. She wasn't like any woman he'd ever known. "I'm glad to know that. But you and I have more in common than a lack of technique," he said, hesitating.

"We do?" she asked. Her soft eyes held his. "What do you mean?"

He turned and deliberately put out his cigarette in the ashtray on the table beside them. He straightened and looked down at her speculatively for a few seconds before he went for broke. "Well, what I mean, Amanda," he replied finally, "is that you aren't the only virgin on the place."

CHAPTER SIX

"I DIDN'T HEAR THAT," Amanda said, because she knew she hadn't. Quinn Sutton couldn't have told her that he was a virgin.

"Yes, you did," he replied. "And it's not all that far-fetched. Old McNaber down the hill's never had a woman, and he's in his seventies. There are all sorts of reasons why men don't get experience. Morals, scruples, isolation, or even plain shyness. Just like women," he added with a meaningful look at Amanda. "I couldn't go to bed with somebody just to say I'd had sex. I'd have to care about her, want her, and I'd want her to care about me. There are idealistic people all over the world who never find that particular combination, so they stay celibate. And really, I think that people who sleep around indiscriminately are in the minority even in these liberated times. Only a fool takes that sort of risk with the health dangers what they are."

"Yes, I know." She watched him with fascinated eyes. "Haven't you ever…wanted to?" she asked.

"Well, that's the problem, you see," he replied, his dark eyes steady on her face.

"What is?"

"I have…wanted to. With you."

She leaned back against the counter, just to make sure she didn't fall down. "With me?"

"That first night you came here, when I was so sick, and your hair drifted down over my naked chest. I shivered, and you thought it was with fever," he mused. "It was a fever, all right, but it didn't have anything to do with the virus."

Her fingers clenched the counter. She'd wondered about his violent reaction at the time, but it seemed so unlikely that a cold man like Quinn Sutton would feel that way about a woman. He was human, she thought absently, watching him.

"That's why I've given you such a hard time," he confessed with narrowed, quiet eyes. "I don't know how to handle desire. I can't throw you over my shoulder and carry you upstairs, not with Elliot and Harry around, even if you were the kind of woman I thought at first you were. The fact that you're as innocent as I am only makes it more complicated."

She looked at him with new understanding, as fascinated by him as he seemed to be by her. He wasn't that bad looking, she mused. And he was terribly strong, and sexy in an earthy kind of way. She especially liked his eyes. They were much more expressive than that poker face.

"Fortunately for you, I'm kind of shy, too," she murmured.

"Except when you're asking men to take their clothes off," Quinn said, nodding.

Harry froze in the doorway with one foot lifted while Amanda gaped at him and turned red.

"Put your foot down and get busy," Quinn muttered irritably. "Why were you standing there?"

"I was getting educated." Harry chuckled. "I didn't know Amanda asked people to take their clothes off!"

"Only me," Quinn said, defending her. "And just my shirt. She's not a bad girl."

"Will you stop!" Amanda buried her face in her hands. "Go away!"

"I can't. I live here," Quinn pointed out. "Did I smell brandy on your breath?" he asked suddenly.

Harry grimaced even as Amanda's eyes widened. "Well, yes you do," he confessed. "She was upset and crying and all…"

"How much did you give her?" Quinn persisted.

"Only a few drops," Harry promised. "In her coffee, to calm her."

"Harry, how could you!" Amanda laughed. The coffee had tasted funny, but she'd been too upset to wonder why.

"Sorry," Harry murmured dryly. "But it seemed the thing to do."

"It backfired," Quinn murmured and actually smiled.

"You stop that!" Amanda told him. She sat down at the table. "I'm not tipsy. Harry, I'll peel those apples for the pie if I can have a knife."

"Let me get out of the room first, if you please," Quinn said, glancing at her dryly. "I saw her measuring my back for a place to put it."

"I almost never stab men with knives," she promised impishly.

He chuckled. He reached for his hat and slanted it over his brow, buttoning his old shepherd's coat because it was snowing outside again.

Amanda looked past him, the reason for all the upset coming back now as she calmed down. Her expression became sad.

"If you stay busy, you won't think about it so much," Quinn said quietly. "It's part of life, you know."

"I know." She managed a smile. "I'm fine. Despite Harry," she added with a chuckle, watching Harry squirm before he grinned back.

Quinn's dark eyes met hers warmly for longer than he meant, so that she blushed. He tore his eyes away finally, and went outside.

Harry didn't say anything, but his smile was speculative.

Elliot came home from school and persuaded Amanda to get out the keyboard and give him some more pointers. He admitted that he'd been bragging about her to his classmates and that she was a professional musician.

"Where do you play, Amanda?" Elliot asked curiously, and he stared at her with open puzzlement. "You look so familiar somehow."

She sat very still on the sofa and tried to stay calm. Elliot had already told her that he liked rock music and she knew Quinn had hidden his tapes. If there was a tape in his collection by Desperado, it would have her picture on the cover along with that of her group.

"Do I really look familiar?" she asked with a smile. "Maybe I just have that kind of face."

"Have you played with orchestras?" he persisted.

"No. Just by myself, sort of. In nightclubs," she improvised. Well, she had once sang in a nightclub, to fill in for a friend. "Mostly I do backup. You know, I play with groups for people who make tapes and records."

"Wow!" he exclaimed. "I guess you know a lot of famous singers and musicians?"

"A few," she agreed.

"Where do you work?"

"In New York City, in Nashville," she told him. "All over. Wherever I can find work."

He ran his fingers up and down the keyboard. "How did you ever wind up here?"

"I needed a rest," she said. "My aunt is...a friend of Mr. Durning. She asked him if I could borrow the cabin, and he said it was all right. I had to get away from work for a while."

"This doesn't bother you, does it? Teaching me to play, I mean?" he asked and looked concerned.

"No, Elliot, it doesn't bother me. I'm enjoying it." She ran a scale and taught it to him, then showed him the cadences of the chords that went with it.

"It's so complicated," he moaned.

"Of course it is. Music is an art form, and it's complex. But once you learn these basics, you can do anything with a chord. For instance..."

She played a tonic chord, then made an impromptu song from its subdominant and seventh chords and the second inversion of them. Elliot watched, fascinated.

"I guess you've studied for years," he said with a sigh.

"Yes, I have, and I'm still learning," she said. "But I love it more than anything. Music has been my whole life."

"No wonder you're so good at it."

She smiled. "Thanks, Elliot."

"Well, I'd better get my chores done before supper," he said, sighing. He handed Amanda the keyboard. "See you later."

She nodded. He went out. Harry was feeding the two calves that were still alive, so presumably he'd tell

Elliot about the one that had died. Amanda hadn't had the heart to talk about it.

Her fingers ran over the keyboard lovingly and she began to play a song that her group had recorded two years back, a sad, dreamy ballad about hopeless love that had won them a Grammy. She sang it softly, her pure, sweet voice haunting in the silence of the room as she tried to sing for the first time in weeks.

"Elliot, for Pete's sake, turn that radio down, I'm on the telephone!" came a pleading voice from the back of the house.

She stopped immediately, flushing. She hadn't realized that Harry had come back inside. Thank God he hadn't seen her, or he might have asked some pertinent questions. She put the keyboard down and went to the kitchen, relieved that her singing voice was back to normal again.

Elliot was morose at the supper table. He'd heard about the calf and he'd been as depressed as Amanda had. Quinn didn't look all that happy himself. They all picked at the delicious chili Harry had whipped up; nobody had much of an appetite.

After they finished, Elliot did his homework while Amanda put the last stitches into a chair cover she was making for the living room. Quinn had gone off to do his paperwork and Harry was making bread for the next day.

It was a long, lazy night. Elliot went to bed at eight-thirty and not much later Harry went to his room.

Amanda wanted to wait for Quinn to come back, but something in her was afraid of the new way he looked at her. He was much more a threat now than he had been before, because she was looking at him with new and interested eyes. She was drawn to him more than ever. But he didn't know who she really was, and she couldn't tell him. If she were persuaded into any kind of close relationship with him, it could lead to disaster.

So when Elliot went to bed, so did Amanda. She sat at the dresser and let down her long hair, brushing it with slow, lazy strokes, when there was a knock at the door.

She was afraid that it might be Quinn, and she hesitated. But surely he wouldn't make any advances toward her unless she showed that she wanted them. Of course he wouldn't.

She opened the door, but it wasn't Quinn. It was Elliot. And as he stared at her, wheels moved and gears clicked in his young mind. She was wearing a long granny gown in a deep beige, a shade that was too much like the color of the leather dress she wore onstage. With her hair loose and the color of the gown, Elliot made the connection he hadn't made the first time he saw her hair down.

"Yes?" she prompted, puzzled by the way he was looking at her. "Is something wrong, Elliot?"

"Uh, no," he stammered. "Uh, I forgot to say goodnight. Good night!" He grinned.

He turned, red faced, and beat a hasty retreat, but not to his own room. He went to his father's and searched quickly through the hidden tapes until he found the one he wanted. He held it up, staring blankly at the cover. There were four men who looked like vicious bikers surrounding a beautiful woman in buckskin with long, elegant, blond hair. The group was one of his favorites—Desperado. And the woman was Mandy. Amanda. His Amanda. He caught his breath. Boy, would she be in for it if his dad found out who she was! He put the tape into his pocket, feeling guilty for taking it when Quinn had told him not to. But these were desperate circumstances. He had to protect Amanda until he could figure out how to tell her that he knew the truth. Meanwhile, having her in the same house with him was sheer undiluted heaven! Imagine, a singing star that famous in his house. If only he could tell the guys! But that was too risky, because it might get back to Dad. He sighed. Just his luck, to find a rare jewel and have to hide it to keep someone from stealing it. He closed the door to Quinn's bedroom and went quickly back to his own.

Amanda slept soundly, almost missing breakfast. Outside, the sky looked blue for the first time in days, and she noticed that the snow had stopped.

"Chinook's coming," Harry said with a grin. "I knew it would."

Quinn's dark eyes studied Amanda's face. "Well, it will be a few days before they get the power lines back up again," he muttered. "So don't get in an uproar about it."

"I'm not in an uproar," Harry returned with a frown. "I just thought it was nice that we'll be able to get off the mountain and lay in some more supplies. I'm getting tired of beef. I want a chicken."

"So do I!" Elliot said fervently. "Or bear, or beaver or moose, anything but beef!"

Quinn glared at both of them. "Beef pays the bills around here," he reminded them.

They looked so guilty that Amanda almost laughed out loud.

"I'm sorry, Dad," Elliot sighed. "I'll tell my stomach to shut up about it."

Quinn's hard face relaxed. "It's all right. I wouldn't mind a chicken stew, myself."

"That's the spirit," Elliot said. "What are we going to do today? It's Saturday," he pointed out. "No school."

"You could go out with me and help me feed cattle," Quinn said.

"I'll stay here and help Harry," Amanda said, too quickly.

Quinn's dark eyes searched hers. "Harry can manage by himself. You can come with me and Elliot."

"You'll enjoy it," Elliot assured her. "It's a lot of fun. The cattle see us and come running. Well, as well as they can run in several feet of snow," he amended.

It was fun, too. Amanda sat on the back of the sled with Elliot and helped push the bales of hay off. Quinn cut the strings so the cattle could get to the hay. They did come running, reminding Amanda so vividly of women at a sale that she laughed helplessly until the others had to be told why she was laughing.

They came back from the outing in a new kind of harmony, and for the first time, Amanda understood what it felt like to be part of a family. She looked at Quinn and wondered how it would be if she never had to leave here, if she could stay with him and Elliot and Harry forever.

But she couldn't, she told herself firmly. She had to remember that this was a vacation, with the real world just outside the door.

Elliot was allowed to stay up later on Saturday night, so they watched a science-fiction movie together while Quinn grumbled over paperwork. The next morning they went to church on the sled, Amanda in the one skirt and blouse she'd packed, trying not to look too

conspicuous as Quinn's few neighbors carefully scru-
tinized her.

When they got back home, she was all but shaking.
She felt uncomfortable living with him, as if she really was a fallen woman now. He cornered her in the
kitchen while she was washing dishes to find out why
she was so quiet.

"I didn't think about the way people would react
if you went with us this morning," he said quietly. "I
wouldn't have subjected you to that if I'd just thought."

"It's okay," she said, touched by his concern. "Really. It was just a little uncomfortable."

He sighed, searching her face with narrowed eyes.
"Most people around here know how I feel about
women," he said bluntly. "That was why you attracted
so much attention. People get funny ideas about woman
haters who take in beautiful blondes."

"I'm not beautiful," she stammered shyly.

He stepped toward her, towering over her in his dress
slacks and good white shirt and sedate gray tie. He
looked handsome and strong and very masculine. She
liked the spicy cologne he wore. "You're beautiful, all
right," he murmured. His big hand touched her cheek,
sliding down it slowly, his thumb brushing with soft
abrasion over her full mouth.

Her breath caught as she looked up into his dark, soft
eyes. "Quinn?" she whispered.

He drew her hands out of the warm, soapy water,
still holding her gaze, and dried them on a dishcloth.
Then he guided them, first one, then the other, up to
his shoulders.

"Hold me," he whispered as his hands smoothed

over her waist and brought her gently to him. "I want
to kiss you."

She shivered from the sensuality in that soft whisper, lifting her face willingly.

He bent, brushing his mouth lazily over hers. "Isn't
this how we did it before?" he breathed, parting his lips
as they touched hers. "I like the way it feels to kiss you
like this. My spine tingles."

"So...does mine." She slid her hands hesitantly into
the thick, cool strands of hair at his nape and she went
on tiptoe to give him better access to her mouth.

He accepted the invitation with quiet satisfaction, his
mouth growing slowly rougher and hungrier as it fed
on hers. He made a sound under his breath and all at
once he bent, lifting her clear off the floor in a bearish
embrace. His mouth bit hers, parting her lips, and she
clung to him, moaning as the fever burned in her, too.

He let her go at once when Elliot called, "What?"
from the living room. "Amanda, did you say something?"

"No... No, Elliot," she managed in a tone pitched a
little higher than normal. Her answer appeared to satisfy him, because he didn't ask again. Harry was outside, but he probably wouldn't stay there long.

She looked up at Quinn, surprised by the intent stare
he was giving her. He liked the way she looked, her face
flushed, her mouth swollen from his kisses, her eyes
wide and soft and faintly misty with emotion.

"I'd better get out of here," he said hesitantly.

"Yes." She touched her lips with her fingers and he
watched the movement closely.

"Did I hurt your mouth?" he asked quietly.

She shook her head. "No. Oh, no, not at all," she said huskily.

Quinn nodded and sighed heavily. He smiled faintly and then turned and went back into the living room without another word.

It was a long afternoon, made longer by the strain Amanda felt being close to him. She found her eyes meeting his across the room and every time she flushed from the intensity of the look. Her body was hungry for him, and she imagined the reverse was equally true. He watched her openly now, with smoldering hunger in his eyes. They had a light supper and watched a little more television. But when Harry went to his room and Elliot called good-night and went up to bed, Amanda weakly stayed behind.

Quinn finished his cigarette with the air of a man who had all night, and then got up and reached for Amanda, lifting her into his arms.

"There's nothing to be afraid of," he said quietly, searching her wide, apprehensive eyes as he turned and carried her into his study and closed the door behind them.

It was a fiercely masculine room. The furniture was dark wood with leather seats, the remnants of more prosperous times. He sat down in a big leather armchair with Amanda in his lap.

"It's private here," he explained. His hand moved one of hers to his shirt and pressed it there, over the tie. "Even Elliot doesn't come in when the door's shut. Do you still want to take my shirt off?" he asked with a warm smile.

Amanda sighed. "Well, yes," she stammered. "I haven't done this sort of thing before...."

"Neither have I, honey," he murmured dryly. "I guess we'll learn it together, won't we?"

She smiled into his dark eyes. "That sounds nice." She lowered her eyes to the tie and frowned when she saw how it was knotted.

"Here, I'll do it." He whipped it off with the ease of long practice and unlooped the collar button. "Now. You do the rest," he said deeply, and looked like a man anticipating heaven.

Her fingers, so adept on a keyboard, fumbled like two left feet while she worried buttons out of button-holes. He was heavily muscled, tanned skin under a mass of thick, curling black hair. She remembered how it had looked that first night she'd been here, and how her hands had longed to touch it. Odd, because she'd never cared what was under a man's shirt before.

She pressed her hands flat against him, fascinated by the quick thunder of his heartbeat under them. She looked up into dark, quiet eyes.

"Shy?" he murmured dryly.

"A little. I always used to run a mile when men got this close."

The smile faded. His big hand covered hers, press-ing them closer against him. "Wasn't there ever any-one you wanted?"

She shook her head. "The men I'm used to aren't like you. They're mostly rounders with a line a mile long. Everything is just casual to them, like eating mints." She flushed a little. "Intimacy isn't a casual thing to me."

"Or to me." His chest rose and fell heavily. He touched her bright head. "Now will you take your hair down, Amanda?" he asked gently. "I've dreamed about it for days."

Amanda smiled softly. "Have you, really? It's something of a nuisance to wash and dry, but I've gotten sort of used to it." She unbraided it and let it down, enchanted by Quinn's rapt fascination with it. His big hands tangled in it, as if he loved the feel of it. He brought his face down and kissed her neck through it, drawing her against his bare chest.

"It smells like flowers," he whispered.

"I washed it before church this morning," she replied. "Elliot loaned me his blow-dryer but it still took all of thirty minutes to get the dampness out." She relaxed with a sigh, nuzzling against his shoulder while her fingers tugged at the thick hair on his chest. "You feel furry. Like a bear," she murmured.

"You feel silky," he said against her hair. With his hand, Quinn tilted her face up to his and slid his mouth onto hers in the silent room. He groaned softly as her lips parted under his. His arms lifted and turned her, wrapped her up, so that her breasts were lying on his chest and her cheek was pressed against his shoulder by the force of the kiss.

He tasted of smoke and coffee, and if his mouth wasn't expert, it was certainly ardent. She loved kissing him. She curled her arms around his neck and turned a little more, hesitating when she felt the sudden stark arousal of his body.

Her eyes opened, looking straight into his, and she colored.

"I'm sorry," he murmured, starting to shift her, as if his physical reaction to her embarrassed him.

"No, Quinn," she said, resisting gently, holding his

gaze as she relaxed into him, shivering a little. "There's nothing to apologize for. I…like knowing you want me," she whispered, lowering her eyes to his mouth. "It just takes a little getting used to. I've never let anyone hold me like this."

His chest swelled with that confession. His cheek rested on her hair as he settled into the chair and relaxed himself, taking her weight easily. "I'm glad about that," he said. "But it isn't just physical with me. I wanted you to know."

She smiled against his shoulder. "It isn't just physical with me, either." She touched his hard face, her fingers moving over his mouth, loving the feel of it, the smell of his body, the warmth and strength of it. "Isn't it incredible?" She laughed softly. "I mean, at our ages, to be so green…"

He laughed, too. It would have stung to have heard that from any other woman, but Amanda was different. "I've never minded less being inexperienced," he murmured.

"Oh, neither have I." She sighed contentedly.

His big hand smoothed over her shoulder and down her back to her waist and onto her rib cage. He wanted very much to run it over her soft breast, but that might be too much too soon, so he hesitated.

Amanda smiled to herself. She caught his fingers and, lifting her face to his eyes, deliberately pulled them onto her breast, her lips parting at the sensation that steely warmth imparted. The nipple hardened and she caught her breath as Quinn's thumb rubbed against it.

"Have you ever seen a woman…without her top on?" she whispered, her long hair gloriously tangled around her face and shoulders.

"No," he replied softly. "Only in pictures." His dark eyes watched the softness his fingers were tracing. "I want to see you that way. I want to touch your skin… like this."

She drew his hand to the buttons of her blouse and lay quietly against him, watching his hard face as he loosened the buttons and pulled the fabric aside. The bra seemed to fascinate him. He frowned, trying to decide how it opened.

"It's a front catch," she whispered. She shifted a little, and found the catch. Her fingers trembled as she loosened it. Then, watching him, she carefully peeled it away from the high, taut throb of her breasts and watched him catch his breath.

"My God," he breathed reverently. He touched her with trembling fingers, his eyes on the deep mauve of her nipples against the soft pink thrust of flesh, his body taut with sudden aching longing. "My God, I've never seen anything so beautiful."

He made her feel incredibly feminine. She closed her eyes and arched back against his encircling arm, moaning softly.

"Kiss me…there," she whispered huskily, aching for his mouth.

"Amanda…" He bent, delighting in her femininity, the obvious rapt fascination of the first time in her actions so that even if he hadn't suspected her innocence he would have now. His lips brushed over the silky flesh, and his hands lifted her to him, arched her even more. She tasted of flower petals, softly trembling under his warm, ardent mouth, her breath jerking past her parted lips as she lay with her eyes closed, lost in him.

"It's so sweet, Quinn," she whispered brokenly.

His lips brushed up her body to her throat, her chin, and then they locked against her mouth. He turned her slowly, so that her soft breasts lay against the muted thunder of his hair-roughened chest. He felt her shiver before her arms slid around his neck and she deliberately pressed closer, drawing herself against him and moaning.

"Am I hurting you?" he asked huskily, his mouth poised just above hers, a faint tremor in his arms. "Amanda, am I hurting you?"

"No." She opened her eyes and they were like black pools, soft and deep and quiet. With her blond hair waving at her temples, her cheeks, her shoulders, she was so beautiful that Quinn's breath caught.

He sat just looking at her, indulging his hunger for the sight of her soft breasts, her lovely face. She lay quietly in his arms without a protest, barely breathing as the spell worked on them.

"I'll live on this the rest of my life," he said roughly, his voice deep and soft in the room, with only an occasional crackle from the burning fire in the potbellied stove to break the silence.

"So will I," she whispered. She reached up to his face, touching it in silence, adoring its strength. "We shouldn't have done this," she said miserably. "It will make it...so much more difficult, when I have to leave. The thaw...!"

His fingers pressed against her lips. "One day at a time," he said. "Even if you leave, you aren't getting away from me completely. I won't let go. Not ever."

Tears stung her eyes. The surplus of emotion sent them streaming down her cheeks and Quinn caught his breath, brushing them away with his long fingers.

"Why?" he whispered.

"Nobody ever wanted to keep me before," she explained with a watery smile. "I've always felt like an extra person in the world."

He found that hard to imagine, as beautiful as she was. Perhaps her reticence made her of less value to sophisticated men, but not to him. He found her a pearl beyond price.

"You're not an extra person in my world," he replied. "You fit."

She sighed and nuzzled against him, closing her eyes as she drank in the exquisite pleasure of skin against skin, feeling his heart beat against her breasts. She shivered.

"Are you cold?" he asked.

"No. It's...so wonderful, feeling you like this," she whispered. "Quinn?"

He eased her back in his arm and watched her, understanding as she didn't seem to understand what was wrong.

His big, warm hand covered her breast, gently caressing it. "It's desire," he whispered softly. "You want me."

"Yes," she whispered.

"You can't have me. Not like this. Not in any honorable way." He sighed heavily and lifted her against him to hold her, very hard. "Now hold on, real tight. It will pass."

She shivered helplessly, drowning in the warmth of his body, in its heat against her breasts. But he was right. Slowly the ache began to ease away and her body stilled with a huge sigh.

"How do you know so much when you've...when you've never...?"

"I told you, I read a book. Several books." He chuckled, the laughter rippling over her sensitive breasts. "But, my God, reading was never like this!"

She laughed, too, and impishly bit his shoulder right through the cloth.

Then he shivered. "Don't," he said huskily.

She lifted her head, fascinated by the expression on his face. "Do you like it?" she asked hesitantly.

"Yes, I like it," he said with a rueful smile. "All too much." He gazed down at her bareness and his eyes darkened. "I like looking at your breasts, too, but I think we'd better stop this while we can."

He tugged the bra back around her with a grimace and hooked the complicated catch. He deftly buttoned her blouse up to her throat, his eyes twinkling as they met hers.

"Disappointed?" he murmured. "So am I. I have these dreams every night of pillowing you on your delicious hair while we make love until you cry out."

She could picture that, too, and her breath lodged in her throat as she searched his dark eyes. His body, bare and moving softly over hers on white sheets, his face above her...

She moaned.

"Oh, I want it, too," he whispered, touching his mouth with exquisite tenderness to hers. "You in my bed, your arms around me, the mattress moving under us." He lifted his head, breathing unsteadily. "I might have to hurt you a little at first," he said gruffly. "You understand?"

"Yes." She smoothed his shirt, absently drawing it back together and fastening the buttons with a sense of possession. "But only a little, and I could bear it for what would come afterward," she said, looking up. "Because you'd pleasure me then."

"My God, would I," he whispered. "Pleasure you until you were exhausted." He framed her face in his hands and kissed her gently. "Please go to bed, Amanda, before I double over and start screaming."

She smiled against his mouth and let him put her on her feet. She laughed when she swayed and he had to catch her.

"See what you do to me?" she mused. "Make me dizzy."

"Not half as dizzy as you make me." He smoothed down her long hair, his eyes adoring it. "Pretty little thing," he murmured.

"I'm glad you like me," she replied. "I'll do my best to stay this way for the next fifty years or so, with a few minor wrinkles."

"You'll be beautiful to me when you're an old lady. Good night."

She moved away from him with flattering reluctance, her dark eyes teasing his. "Are you sure you haven't done this before?" she asked with a narrow gaze. "You're awfully good at it for a beginner."

"That makes two of us," he returned dryly.

She liked the way he looked, with his hair mussed and his thin mouth swollen from her kisses, and his shirt disheveled. It made her feel a new kind of pride that she could disarrange him so nicely. After one long glance, she opened the door and went out.

"Lock your door," he whispered.

She laughed delightedly. "No, you lock yours the way you did the other night."

He shifted uncomfortably. "That was a low blow. I'm sorry."

"Oh, I was flattered," she corrected. "I've never felt so dangerous in all my life. I wish I had one of those long, black silk negligees…"

"Will you get out of here?" he asked pleasantly. "I think I did mention the urge to throw you on the floor and ravish you?"

"With Elliot right upstairs? Fie, sir, think of my reputation."

"I'm trying to, if you'll just go to bed!"

"Very well, if I must." She started up the staircase, her black eyes dancing as they met his. She tossed her hair back and smiled at him. "Good night, Quinn."

"Good night, Amanda. Sweet dreams."

"They'll be sweet from now on," she agreed. She turned reluctantly and went up the staircase. He watched her until she went into her room and closed the door.

It wasn't until she was in her own room that she realized just what she'd done.

She wasn't some nice domestic little thing who could fit into Quinn's world without any effort. She was Amanda Corrie Callaway, who belonged to a rock group with a worldwide reputation. On most streets in most cities, her face was instantly recognizable. How was Quinn going to take the knowledge of who she really was—and the fact that she'd deceived him by leading him to think she was just a vacationing keyboard player? She groaned as she put on her gown. It didn't bear thinking about. From sweet heaven to nightmare in one hour was too much.

CHAPTER SEVEN

AMANDA HARDLY SLEPT from the combined shock of Quinn's ardor and her own guilt. How could she tell him the truth now? What could she say that would take away the sting of her deceit?

She dressed in jeans and the same button-up pink blouse she'd worn the night before and went down to breakfast.

Quinn looked up as she entered the room, his eyes warm and quiet.

"Good morning," she said brightly.

"Good morning yourself," Quinn murmured with a smile. "Sleep well?"

"Barely a wink," she said, sighing, her own eyes holding his.

He chuckled, averting his gaze before Elliot became suspicious. "Harry's out feeding your calves," he said, "and I'm on my way over to Eagle Pass to help one of my neighbors feed some stranded cattle. You'll have to stay with Elliot—it's teacher workday."

"I forgot," Elliot wailed, head in hands. "Can you imagine that I actually forgot? I could have slept until noon!"

"There, there," Amanda said, patting his shoulder. "Don't you want to learn some more chords?"

"Is that what you do?" Quinn asked curiously, because now every scrap of information he learned about her was precious. "You said you played a keyboard for a living. Do you teach music?"

"Not really," she said gently. "I play backup for various groups," she explained. "That rock music you hate…" she began uneasily.

"That's all right," Quinn replied, his face open and kind. "I was just trying to get a rise out of you. I don't mind it all that much, I guess. And playing backup isn't the same thing as putting on those god-awful costumes and singing suggestive lyrics. Well, I'm gone. Stay out of trouble, you two," he said as he got to his feet in the middle of Amanda's instinctive move to speak, to correct his assumption that all she did was play backup. She wanted to tell him the truth, but he winked at her and Elliot and got into his outdoor clothes before she could find a way to break the news. By the time her mind was working again, he was gone.

She sat back down, sighing. "Oh, Elliot, what a mess," she murmured, her chin in her hands.

"Is that what you call it?" he asked with a wicked smile. "Dad's actually grinning, and when he looked at you, you blushed. I'm not blind, you know. Do you like him, even if he isn't Mr. America?"

"Yes, I like him," she said with a shy smile, lowering her eyes. "He's a pretty special guy."

"I think so, myself. Eat your breakfast. I want to ask you about some new chords."

"Okay."

They were working on the keyboard when the sound of an approaching vehicle caught Amanda's attention. Quinn hadn't driven anything motorized since the snow had gotten so high.

"That's odd," Elliot said, peering out the window curtain. "It's a four-wheel drive... Oh, boy." He glanced at Amanda. "You aren't gonna like this."

She lifted her eyebrows. "I'm not?" she asked, puzzled.

The knock at the back door had Harry moving toward it before Amanda and Elliot could. Harry opened it and looked up and up and up. He stood there staring while Elliot gaped at the grizzly-looking man who loomed over him in a black Western costume, complete with hat.

"I'm looking for Mandy Callaway," he boomed.

"Hank!"

Amanda ran to the big man without thinking, to be lifted high in the air while he chuckled and kissed her warmly on one cheek, his whiskers scratching.

"Hello, peanut!" he grinned. "What are you doing up here? The old trapper down the hill said you hadn't been in Durning's cabin since the heavy snow came."

"Mr. Sutton took me in and gave me a roof over my head. Put me down," she fussed, wiggling.

He put her back on her feet while Harry and Elliot still gaped.

"This is Hank," she said, holding his enormous hand as she turned to face the others. "He's a good friend, and a terrific musician, and I'd really appreciate it if you wouldn't tell Quinn he was here just yet. I'll tell him myself. Okay?"

"Sure," Harry murmured. He shook his head. "You for real, or do you have stilts in them boots?"

"I used to be a linebacker for the Dallas Cowboys." Hank grinned.

"That would explain it," Harry chuckled. "Your secret's safe with me, Amanda." He excused himself and went to do the washing.

"Me, too," Elliot said, grinning, "as long as I get Mr. Shoeman's autograph before he leaves."

Amanda let out a long breath, her eyes frightened as they met Elliot's.

"That's right," Elliot said. "I already knew you were Mandy Callaway. I've got a Desperado tape. I took it out of Dad's drawer and hid it as soon as I recognized you. You'll tell him when the time's right. Won't you?"

"Yes, I will, Elliot," she agreed. "I'd have done it already except that…well, things have gotten a little complicated."

"You can say that again." Elliot led the way into the living room, watching Hank sit gingerly on a sofa that he dwarfed. "I'll just go make sure that tape's hidden," he said, leaving them alone.

"Complicated, huh?" Hank said. "I hear this Sutton man's a real woman hater."

"He was until just recently." She folded her hands in her lap. "And he doesn't approve of rock music." She sighed and changed the subject. "What's up, Hank?"

"We've got a gig at Larry's Lodge," he said. "I know, you don't want to. Listen for a minute. It's to benefit cystic fibrosis, and a lot of other stars are going to be in town for it, including a few pretty well-known singers." He named some of them and Amanda whistled. "See what I mean? It's strictly charity, or I wouldn't have come up here bothering you. The boys and I want to do it." His dark eyes narrowed. "Are you up to it?"

"I don't know. I tried to sing here a couple of times, and my voice seems to be good enough. No more lapses.

But in front of a crowd…" She spread her hands. "I don't know, Hank."

"Here." He handed her three tickets to the benefit. "You think about it. If you can, come on up. Sutton might like the singers even if he doesn't care for our kind of music." He studied her. "You haven't told him, have you?"

She shook her head, smiling wistfully. "Haven't found the right way yet. If I leave it much longer, it may be too late."

"The girl's family sent you a letter," he said. "Thanking you for what you tried to do. They said you were her heroine…aw, now, Mandy, stop it!"

She collapsed in tears. He held her, rocking her, his face red with mingled embarrassment and guilt.

"Mandy, come on, stop that," he muttered. "It's all over and done with. You've got to get yourself together. You can't hide out here in the Tetons for the rest of your life."

"Can't I?" she wailed.

"No, you can't. Hiding isn't your style. You have to face the stage again, or you'll never get over it." He tilted her wet face. "Look, would you want somebody eating her guts out over you if you'd been Wendy that night? It wasn't your fault, damn it! It wasn't anybody's fault; it was an accident, pure and simple."

"If she hadn't been at the concert…"

"If, if, if," he said curtly. "You can't go back and change things to suit you. It was her time. At the concert, on a plane, in a car, however, it would still have been her time. Are you listening to me, Mandy?"

She dabbed her eyes with the hem of her blouse. "Yes, I'm listening."

"Come on, girl. Buck up. You can get over this if you set your mind to it. Me and the guys miss you, Mandy. It's not the same with just the four of us. People are scared of us when you aren't around."

That made her smile. "I guess they are. You do look scruffy, Hank," she murmured.

"You ought to see Johnson." He sighed. "He's let his beard go and he looks like a scrub brush. And Deke says he won't change clothes until you come back."

"Oh, my God," Amanda said, shuddering, "tell him I'll think hard about this concert, okay? You poor guys. Stay upwind of him."

"We're trying." He got up, smiling down at her. "Everything's okay. You can see the letter when you come to the lodge. It's real nice. Now stop beating yourself. Nobody else blames you. After all, babe, you risked your life trying to save her. Nobody's forgotten that, either."

She leaned against him for a minute, drawing on his strength. "Thanks, Hank."

"Anytime. Hey, kid, you still want that autograph?" he asked.

Elliot came back into the room with a pad and pen. "Do I!" he said, chuckling.

Hank scribbled his name and Desperado's curly-Q logo underneath. "There you go."

"He's a budding musician," Amanda said, putting an arm around Elliot. "I'm teaching him the keyboard. One of these days, if we can get around Quinn, we'll have him playing backup for me."

"You bet." Hank chuckled, and ruffled Elliot's red hair. "Keep at it. Mandy's the very best. If she teaches you, you're taught."

"Thanks, Mr. Shoeman."

"Just Hank. See you at the concert. So long, Mandy."

"So long, pal."

"What concert?" Elliot asked excitedly when Hank had driven away.

Amanda handed him the three tickets. "To a benefit in Jackson Hole. The group's going to play there. Maybe. If I can get up enough nerve to get back onstage again."

"What happened, Amanda?" he asked gently.

She searched his face, seeing compassion along with the curiosity, so she told him, fighting tears all the way.

"Gosh, no wonder you came up here to get away," Elliot said with more than his twelve years worth of wisdom. He shrugged. "But like he said, you have to go back someday. The longer you wait, the harder it's going to be."

"I know that," she groaned. "But Elliot, I..." She took a deep breath and looked down at the floor. "I love your father," she said, admitting it at last. "I love him very much, and the minute he finds out who I am, my life is over."

"Maybe not," he said. "You've got another week until the concert. Surely in all that time you can manage to tell him the truth. Can't you?"

"I hope so," she said with a sad smile. "You don't mind who I am, do you?" she asked worriedly.

"Don't be silly." He hugged her warmly. "I think you're super, keyboard or not."

She laughed and hugged him back. "Well, that's half the battle."

"Just out of curiosity," Harry asked from the doorway, "who was the bearded giant?"

"That was Hank Shoeman," Elliot told him. "He's the drummer for Desperado. It's a rock group. And Amanda—"

"—plays backup for him," she volunteered, afraid to give too much away to Harry.

"Well, I'll be. He's a musician?" Harry shook his head. "Would have took him for a bank robber," he mumbled.

"Most people do, and you should see the rest of the group." She grinned. "Don't give me away, Harry, okay? I promise I'll tell Quinn, but I've got to do it the right way."

"I can see that," he agreed easily. "Be something of a shock to him to meet your friend after dark, I imagine."

"I imagine so," she said, chuckling. "Thanks, Harry."

"My pleasure. Desperado, huh? Suits it, if the rest of the group looks like he does."

"Worse," she said, and shuddered.

"Strains the mind, don't it?" Harry went off into the kitchen and Amanda got up after a minute to help him get lunch.

Quinn wasn't back until late that afternoon. Nobody mentioned Hank's visit, but Amanda was nervous and her manner was strained as she tried not to show her fears.

"What's wrong with you?" he asked gently during a lull in the evening while Elliot did homework and Harry washed up. "You don't seem like yourself tonight."

She moved close to him, her fingers idly touching the sleeve of his red flannel shirt. "It's thawing outside," she said, watching her fingers move on the fabric. "It won't be long before I'll be gone."

He sighed heavily. His fingers captured hers and

held them. "I've been thinking about that. Do you really have to get back?"

She felt her heart jump. Whatever he was offering, she wanted to say yes and let the future take care of itself. But she couldn't. She grimaced. "Yes, I have to get back," she said miserably. "I have commitments to people. Things I promised to do." Her fingers clenched his. "Quinn, I have to meet some people at Larry's Lodge in Jackson Hole next Friday night." She looked up. "It's at a concert and I have tickets. I know you don't like rock, but there's going to be all kinds of music." Her eyes searched his. "Would you go with me? Elliot can come, too. I...want you to see what I do for a living."

"You and your keyboard?" he mused gently.

"Sort of," she agreed, hoping she could find the nerve to tell him everything before next Friday night.

"Okay," he replied. "A friend of mine works there—I used to be with the Ski Patrol there, too. Sure, I'll go with you." The smile vanished, and his eyes glittered down at her. "I'll go damned near anywhere with you."

Amanda slid her arms around him and pressed close, shutting her eyes as she held on for dear life. "That goes double for me, mountain man," she said half under her breath.

He bent his head, searching for her soft mouth. She gave it to him without a protest, without a thought for the future, gave it to him with interest, with devotion, with ardor. Her lips opened invitingly, and she felt his hands on her hips with a sense of sweet inevitability, lifting her into intimate contact with the aroused contours of his body.

"Frightened?" he whispered unsteadily just over her mouth when he felt her stiffen involuntarily.

"Of you?" she whispered back. "Don't be absurd. Hold me any way you want. I adore you...!"

He actually groaned as his mouth pressed down hard on hers. His arms contracted hungrily and he gave in to the pleasure of possession for one long moment.

Her eyes opened and she watched him, feeding on the slight contortion of his features, his heavy brows drawn over his crooked nose, his long, thick lashes on his cheek as he kissed her. She did adore him, she thought dizzily. Adored him, loved him, worshiped him. If only she could stay with him forever like this.

Quinn lifted his head and paused as he saw her watching him. He frowned slightly, then bent again. This time his eyes stayed open, too, and she went under as he deepened the kiss. Her eyes closed in self-defense and she moaned, letting him see the same vulnerability she'd seen in him. It was breathlessly sweet.

"This is an education," he said, laughing huskily, when he drew slightly away from her.

"Isn't it, though?" she murmured, moving his hands from her hips up to her waist and moving back a step from the blatant urgency of his body. "Elliot and Harry might come in," she whispered.

"I wouldn't mind," he said unexpectedly, searching her flushed face. "I'm not ashamed of what I feel for you, or embarrassed by it."

"This from a confirmed woman hater?" she asked with twinkling eyes.

"Well, not exactly confirmed anymore," he confessed. He lifted her by the waist and searched her eyes at point-blank range until she trembled from the intensity of the look. "I couldn't hate you if I tried, Amanda," he said quietly.

"Oh, I hope not," she said fervently, thinking ahead to when she would have to tell him the truth about herself.

He brushed a lazy kiss across her lips. "I think I'm getting the hang of this," he murmured.

"I think you are, too," she whispered. She slid her arms around his neck and put her warm mouth hungrily against his, sighing when he caught fire and answered the kiss with feverish abandon.

A slight, deliberate cough brought them apart, both staring blankly at the small redheaded intruder.

"Not that I mind," Elliot said, grinning, "but you're blocking the pan of brownies Harry made."

"You can think of brownies at a time like this?" Amanda groaned. "Elliot!"

"Listen, he can think of brownies with a fever of a hundred and two," Quinn told her, still holding her on a level with his eyes. "I've seen him get out of a sickbed to pinch a brownie from the kitchen."

"I like brownies, too," Amanda confessed with a warm smile, delighted that Quinn didn't seem to mind at all that Elliot had seen them in a compromising position. That made her feel lighter than air.

"Do you?" Quinn smiled and brushed his mouth gently against hers, mindless of Elliot's blatant interest, before he put her back on her feet. "Harry makes his from scratch, with real baker's chocolate. They're something special."

"I'll bet they are. Here. I'll get the saucers," she volunteered, still catching her breath.

Elliot looked like the cat with the canary as she dished up brownies. It very obviously didn't bother him that Amanda and his dad were beginning to notice each other.

"Isn't this cozy?" he remarked as they went back into the living room and Amanda curled up on the sofa beside his dad, who never sat there.

"Cozy, indeed," Quinn murmured with a warm smile for Amanda.

She smiled back and laid her cheek against Quinn's broad chest while they watched television and ate brownies. She didn't move even when Harry joined them. And she knew she'd never been closer to heaven.

That night they were left discreetly alone, and she lay in Quinn's strong arms on the long leather couch in his office while wood burned with occasional hisses and sparks in the potbellied stove.

"I've had a raw deal with this place," he said eventually between kisses. "But it's good land, and I'm building a respectable herd of cattle. I can't offer you wealth or position, and we've got a ready-made family. But I can take care of you," he said solemnly, looking down into her soft eyes. "And you won't want for any of the essentials."

Her fingers touched his lean cheek hesitantly. "You don't know anything about me," she said. "When you know my background, you may not want me as much as you think you do." She put her fingers against his mouth. "You have to be sure."

"Damn it, I'm already sure," he muttered.

But was he? She was the first woman he'd ever been intimate with. Couldn't that blind him to her real suitability? What if it was just infatuation or desire? She was afraid to take a chance on his feelings, when she didn't really know what they were.

"Let's wait just a little while longer before we make any plans, Quinn. Okay?" she asked softly, turning in his hard arms so that her body was lying against his. "Make love to me," she whispered, moving her mouth up to his. "Please…"

He gave in with a rough groan, gathering her to him, crushing her against his aroused body. He wanted her beyond rational thought. Maybe she had cold feet, but he didn't. He knew what he wanted, and Amanda was it.

His hands smoothed the blouse and bra away with growing expertise and he fought out of his shirt so that he could feel her soft skin against his. But it wasn't enough. He felt her tremble and knew that it was reflected in his own arms and legs. He moved against her with a new kind of sensuousness, lifting his head to hold her eyes while he levered her onto her back and eased over her, his legs between both of hers in their first real intimacy.

She caught her breath, but she didn't push him to try to get away.

"It's just that new for you, isn't it?" he whispered huskily as his hips moved lazily over hers and he groaned. "God, it burns me to…feel you like this."

"I know." She arched her back, loving his weight, loving the fierce maleness of his body. Her arms slid closer around him and she felt his mouth open on hers, his tongue softly searching as it slid inside, into an intimacy that made her moan. She began to tremble.

His lean hand slid under her, getting a firm grip, and he brought her suddenly into a shocking, shattering position that made her mindless with sudden need. She clutched him desperately, shuddering, her nails digging into him as the contact racked her like a jolt of raw electricity.

He pulled away from her without a word, shuddering as he lay on his back, trying to get hold of himself.

"I'm sorry," he whispered. "I didn't mean to let it go so far with us."

She was trembling, too, trying to breathe while great hot tears rolled down her cheeks. "Gosh, I wanted you," she whispered tearfully. "Wanted you so badly, Quinn!"

"As badly as I wanted you, honey," he said heavily. "We can't let things get that hot again. It was a close call. Closer than you realize."

"Oh, Quinn, couldn't we make love?" she asked softly, rolling over to look down into his tormented face. "Just once…?"

He framed his face in his hands and brought her closed eyes to his lips. "No. I won't compromise you."

She hit his big, hair-roughened chest. "Goody Two Shoes…!"

"Thank your lucky stars that I am," he chuckled. His eyes dropped to her bare breasts and lingered there before he caught the edges of her blouse and tugged them together. "You sex-crazed female, haven't you ever heard about pregnancy?"

"That condition where I get to have little Quinns?"

"Stop it, you're making it impossible for me," he said huskily. "Here, get up before I lose my mind."

She sat up with a grimace. "Spoilsport."

"Listen to you," he muttered, putting her back into her clothes with a wry grin. "I'll give you ten to one that you'd be yelling your head off if I started taking off your jeans."

She went red. "My jeans…!"

His eyebrows arched. "Amanda, would you like me to explain that book I read to you? The part about how men and women…"

She cleared her throat. "No, thanks, I think I've got the hang of it now," she murmured evasively.

"We might as well add a word about birth control," he added with a chuckle when he was buttoning up his own shirt. "You don't take the pill, I assume?"

She shook her head. The whole thing was getting to be really embarrassing!

"Well, that leaves prevention up to me," he explained. "And that would mean a trip into town to the drugstore, since I never indulged, I never needed to worry about prevention. *Now* do you get the picture?"

"Boy, do I get the picture." She grimaced, avoiding his knowing gaze.

"Good girl. That's why we aren't lying down anymore."

She sighed loudly. "I guess you don't want children."

"Sure I do. Elliot would love brothers and sisters, and I'm crazy about kids." He took her slender hands in his and smoothed them over with his thumbs. "But kids should be born inside marriage, not outside it. Don't you think so?"

She took a deep breath, and her dark eyes met his. "Yes."

"Then we'll spend a lot of time together until you have to meet your friends at this concert," he said softly. "And afterward, you and I will come in here again and I'll ask you a question."

"Oh, Quinn," she whispered with aching softness.

"Oh, Amanda," he murmured, smiling as his lips

softly touched hers. "But right now, we go to bed. Separately. Quick!"

"Yes, sir, Mr. Sutton." She got up and let him lead her to the staircase.

"I'll get the lights," he said. "You go on up. In the morning after we get Elliot off to school you can come out with me, if you want to."

"I want to," she said simply. She could hardly bear to be parted from him even overnight. It was like an addiction, she thought as she went up the staircase. Now if only she could make it last until she had the nerve to tell Quinn the truth....

The next few days went by in a haze. The snow began to melt and the skies cleared as the long-awaited chinook blew in. In no time at all it was Friday night and Amanda was getting into what Elliot would recognize as her stage costume. She'd brought it, with her other things, from the Durning cabin. She put it on, staring at herself in the mirror. Her hair hung long and loose, in soft waves below her waist, in the beige leather dress with the buckskin boots that matched, she was the very picture of a sensuous woman. She left off the headband. There would be time for that if she could summon enough courage to get onstage. She still hadn't told Quinn. She hadn't had the heart to destroy the dream she'd been living. But tonight he'd know. And she'd know if they had a future. She took a deep breath and went downstairs.

CHAPTER EIGHT

AMANDA SAT IN the audience with Quinn and Elliot at a far table while the crowded hall rang with excited whispers. Elliot was tense, like Amanda, his eyes darting around nervously. Quinn was frowning. He hadn't been quite himself since Amanda came down the staircase in her leather dress and boots, looking expensive and faintly alien. He hadn't asked any questions, but he seemed as uptight as she felt.

Her eyes slid over him lovingly, taking in his dark suit. He looked out of place in fancy clothes. She missed the sight of him in denim and his old shepherd's coat, and wondered fleetingly if she'd ever get to see him that way again after tonight—if she'd ever lie in his arms on the big sofa and warm to his kisses while the fire burned in the stove. She almost groaned. Oh, Quinn, she thought, I love you.

Elliot looked uncomfortable in his blue suit. He was watching for the rest of Desperado while a well-known Las Vegas entertainer warmed up the crowd and sang his own famous theme song.

"What are you looking for, son?" Quinn asked.

Elliot shifted. "Nothing. I'm just seeing who I know."

Quinn's eyebrows arched. "How would you know anybody in this crowd?" he muttered, glancing around.

"My God, these are show people. Entertainers. Not people from our world."

That was a fact. But hearing it made Amanda heartsick. She reached out and put her hand over Quinn's.

"Your fingers are like ice," he said softly. He searched her worried eyes. "Are you okay, honey?"

The endearment made her warm all over. She smiled sadly and slid her fingers into his, looking down at the contrast between his callused, work-hardened hand and her soft, pale one. His was a strong hand, hers was artistic. But despite the differences, they fit together perfectly. She squeezed her fingers. "I'm fine," she said. "Quinn…"

"And now I want to introduce a familiar face," the Las Vegas performer's voice boomed. "Most of you know the genius of Desperado. The group has won countless awards for its topical, hard-hitting songs. Last year, Desperado was given a Grammy for 'Changes in the Wind,' and Hank Shoeman's song 'Outlaw Love' won him a country music award and a gold record. But their fame isn't the reason we're honoring them tonight."

To Amanda's surprise, he produced a gold plaque. "As some of you may remember, a little over a month ago, a teenage girl died at a Desperado concert. The group's lead singer leaped into the crowd, disregarding her own safety, and was very nearly trampled trying to protect the fan. Because of that tragedy, Desperado went into seclusion. We're proud to tell you tonight that they're back and they're in better form than ever. This plaque is a token of respect from the rest of us in the performing arts to a very special young woman whose compassion and selflessness have won the respect of all."

He looked out toward the audience where Amanda sat frozen. "This is for you—Amanda Corrie Callaway. Will you come up and join the group, please? Come on, Mandy!"

She bit her lower lip. The plaque was a shock. The boys seemed to know about it, too, because they went to their instruments grinning and began to play the downbeat that Desperado was known for, the deep throbbing counter rhythm that was their trademark.

"Come on, babe!" Hank called out in his booming voice, he and Johnson and Deke and Jack looking much more like backwoods robbers than musicians with their huge bulk and outlaw gear.

Amanda glanced at Elliot's rapt, adoring face, and then looked at Quinn. He was frowning, his dark eyes searching the crowd. She said a silent goodbye as she got to her feet. She reached into her pocket for her headband and put it on her head. She couldn't look at him, but she felt his shocked stare as she walked down the room toward the stage, her steps bouncing as the rhythm got into her feet and her blood.

"Thank you," she said huskily, kissing the entertainer's cheek as she accepted the plaque. She moved in between Johnson and Deke, taking the microphone. She looked past Elliot's proud, adoring face to Quinn's. He seemed to be in a state of dark shock. "Thank you all. I've had a hard few weeks. But I'm okay now, and I'm looking forward to better times. God bless, people. This one is for a special man and a special boy, with all my love." She turned to Hank, nodded, and he began the throbbing drumbeat of "Love Singer."

It was a song that touched the heart, for all its mad beat. The words, in her soft, sultry, clear voice caught every ear in the room. She sang from the heart, with the heart, the words fierce with meaning as she sang them to Quinn. "Love you, never loved anybody but you, never leave me lonely, love…singer."

But Quinn didn't seem to be listening to the words. He got to his feet and jerked Elliot to his. He walked out in the middle of the song and never looked back once.

Amanda managed to finish, with every ounce of willpower she had keeping her onstage. She let the last few notes hang in the air and then she bowed to a standing ovation. By the time she and the band did an encore and she got out of the hall, the truck they'd come in was long gone. There was no note, no message. Quinn had said it all with his eloquent back when he walked out of the hall. He knew who she was now, and he wanted no part of her. He couldn't have said it more clearly if he'd written it in blood.

She kept hoping that he might reconsider. Even after she went backstage with the boys, she kept hoping for a phone call or a glimpse of Quinn. But nothing happened.

"I guess I'm going to need a place to stay," Amanda said with a rueful smile, her expression telling her group all they needed to know.

"He couldn't handle it, huh?" Hank asked quietly. "I'm sorry, babe. We've got a suite, there's plenty of room for one more. I'll go up and get your gear tomorrow."

"Thanks, Hank." She took a deep breath and clutched the plaque to her chest. "Where's the next gig?"

"That's my girl," he said gently, sliding a protective arm around her. "San Francisco's our next stop. The boys and I are taking a late bus tomorrow." He grimaced at her knowing smile. "Well, you know how I feel about airplanes."

"Chicken Little," she accused. "Well, I'm not going to sit on a bus all day. I'll take the first charter out and meet you guys at the hotel."

"Whatever turns you on," Hank chuckled. "Come on. Let's get out of here and get some rest."

"You did good, Amanda," Johnson said from behind her. "We were proud."

"You bet," Deke and Jack seconded.

She smiled at them all. "Thanks, group. I shocked myself, but at least I didn't go dry the way I did last time." Her heart was breaking in two, but she managed to hide it. Quinn, she moaned inwardly. Oh, Quinn, was I just an interlude, an infatuation?

She didn't sleep very much. The next morning Amanda watched Hank start out for Ricochet then went down to a breakfast that she didn't even eat while she waited for him to return.

He came back three hours later, looking ruffled.

"Did you get my things?" she asked when he came into the suite.

"I got them." He put her suitcase down on the floor. "Part at Sutton's place, part at the Durning cabin. Elliot sent you a note." He produced it.

"And...Quinn?"

"I never saw him," he replied tersely. "The boy and the old man were there. They didn't mention Sutton and I didn't ask. I wasn't feeling too keen on him at the time."

"Thanks, Hank."

He shrugged. "That's the breaks, kid. It would have

been a rough combination at best. You're a bright-lights girl."

"Am I?" she asked, thinking how easily she'd fit into Quinn's world. But she didn't push it. She sat down on the couch and opened Elliot's scribbled note.

Amanda,
I thought you were great. Dad didn't say anything all the way home and last night he went into his study and didn't come out until this morning. He went hunting, he said, but he didn't take any bullets. I hope you are okay. Write me when you can.
I love you.
Your friend, Elliot.

She bit her lip to keep from crying. Dear Elliot. At least he still cared about her. But her fall from grace in Quinn's eyes had been final, she thought bitterly. He'd never forgive her for deceiving him. Or maybe it was just that he'd gotten over his brief infatuation with her when he found out who she really was. She didn't know what to do. She couldn't remember ever feeling so miserable. To have discovered something that precious, only to lose it forever. She folded Elliot's letter and put it into her purse. At least it would be something to remember from her brief taste of heaven.

For the rest of the day, the band and Jerry, the road manager, got the arrangements made for the San Francisco concert, and final travel plans were laid. The boys were to board the San Francisco bus the next morning. Amanda was to fly out on a special air charter that specialized in flights for business executives.

They'd managed to fit her in at the last minute when a computer-company executive had canceled his flight.

"I wish you'd come with us," Hank said hesitantly. "I guess I'm overreacting and all, but I hate airplanes."

"I'll be fine," she told him firmly. "You and the boys have a nice trip and stop worrying about me. I'll be fine."

"If you say so," Hank mumbled.

"I do say so." She patted him on the shoulder. "Trust me."

He shrugged and left, but he didn't look any less worried. Amanda, who'd gotten used to his morose predictions, didn't pay them any mind.

She went to the suite and into her bedroom early that night. Her fingers dialed the number at Ricochet. She had to try one last time, she told herself. There was at least the hope that Quinn might care enough to listen to her explanation. She had to try.

The phone rang once, twice, and she held her breath, but on the third ring the receiver was lifted.

"Sutton," came a deep weary-sounding voice.

Her heart lifted. "Oh, Quinn," she burst out. "Quinn, please let me try to explain—"

"You don't have to explain anything to me, Amanda," he said stiffly. "I saw it all on the stage."

"I know it looks bad," she began.

"You lied to me," he said. "You let me think you were just a shy little innocent who played a keyboard, when you were some fancy big-time entertainer with a countrywide following."

"I knew you wouldn't want me if you knew who I was," she said miserably.

"You knew I'd see right through you if I knew," he

corrected, his voice growing angrier. "You played me for a fool."

"I didn't!"

"All of it was a lie. Nothing but a lie! Well, you can go back to your public, Miss Callaway, and your outlaw buddies, and make some more records or tapes or whatever the hell they are. I never wanted you in the first place except in bed, so it's no great loss to me." He was grimacing, and she couldn't see the agony in his eyes as he forced the words out. Now that he knew who and what she was, he didn't dare let himself weaken. He had to make her go back to her own life, and stay out of his. He had nothing to give her, nothing that could take the place of fame and fortune and the world at her feet. He'd never been more aware of his own inadequacies as he had been when he'd seen Amanda on that stage and heard the applause of the audience. It ranked as the worst waking nightmare of his life, putting her forever out of his reach.

"Quinn!" she moaned. "Quinn, you don't mean that!"

"I mean it," he said through his teeth. He closed his eyes. "Every word. Don't call here again, don't come by, don't write. You're a bad influence on Elliot now that he knows who you are. I don't want you. You've worn out your welcome at Ricochet." He hung up without another word.

Amanda stared at the telephone receiver as if it had sprouted wings. Slowly she put it back in the cradle just as the room splintered into wet crystal around her.

She put on her gown mechanically and got into bed, turning out the bedside light. She lay in the dark and Quinn's words echoed in her head with merciless coolness. *Bad influence. Don't want you. Worn out your welcome. Never wanted you anyway except in bed.*

She moaned and buried her face in her pillow. She didn't know how she was going to go on, with Quinn's cold contempt dogging her footsteps. He hated her now. He thought she'd been playing a game, enjoying herself while she made a fool out of him. The tears burned her eyes. How quickly it had all ended, how finally. She'd hoped to keep in touch with Elliot, but that wouldn't be possible anymore. She was a bad influence on Elliot, so he wouldn't be allowed to contact her. She sobbed her hurt into the cool linen. Somehow, being denied contact with Elliot was the last straw. She'd grown so fond of the boy during those days she'd spent at Ricochet, and he cared about her, too. Quinn was being unnecessarily harsh. But perhaps he was right, and it was for the best. Maybe she could learn to think that way eventually. Right now she had a concert to get to, a sold-out one from what the boys and Jerry had said. She couldn't let the fans down.

Amanda got up the next morning, looking and feeling as if it were the end of the world. The boys took her suitcase downstairs, not looking too closely at her face without makeup, her long hair arranged in a thick, haphazard bun. She was wearing a dark pantsuit with a cream-colored blouse, and she looked miserable.

"We'll see you in San Francisco," Jerry told her with a smile. "I have to go nursemaid these big, tough guys, so you make sure the pilot of your plane has all his marbles, okay?"

"I'll check him out myself," she promised. "Take care of yourselves, guys. I'll see you in California."

"Okay. Be good, babe," Hank called. He and the

others filed into the bus Jerry had chartered and Jerry hugged her impulsively and went in behind them.

She watched the bus pull away, feeling lost and alone, not for the first time. It was cold and snowy, but she hadn't wanted her coat. It was packed in her suitcase, and had already been put on the light aircraft. With a long sigh, she went back to the cab and sat disinterestedly in it as it wound over the snowy roads to the airport.

Fortunately the chinook had thawed the runways so that the planes were coming and going easily. She got out at the air charter service hangar and shook hands with the pilot.

"Don't worry, we're in great shape," he promised Amanda with a grin. "In fact, the mechanics just gave us another once-over to be sure. Nothing to worry about."

"Oh, I wasn't worried," she said absently and allowed herself to be shepherded inside. She slid into an empty aisle seat on the right side and buckled up. Usually she preferred to sit by the window, but today she wasn't in the mood for sight-seeing. One snow-covered mountain looked pretty much like another to her, and her heart wasn't in this flight or the gig that would follow it. She leaned back and closed her eyes.

It seemed to take forever for all the businessmen to get aboard. Fortunately there had been one more cancellation, so she had her seat and the window seat as well. She didn't feel like talking to anyone, and was hoping she wouldn't have to sit by some chatterbox all the way to California.

She listened to the engines rev up and made sure that her seat belt was properly fastened. They would be off as soon as the tower cleared them, the pilot announced. Amanda sighed. She called a silent goodbye to Quinn Sutton, and Elliot and Harry, knowing that once this plane lifted off, she'd never see any of them again. She winced at the thought. Oh, Quinn, she moaned inwardly, why wouldn't you *listen?*

The plane got clearance and a minute later, it shot down the runway and lifted off. But it seemed oddly sluggish. Amanda was used to air travel, even to charter flights, and she opened her eyes and peered forward worriedly as she listened to the whine become a roar.

She was strapped in, but a groan from behind took her mind off the engine. The elderly man behind her was clutching his chest and groaning.

"What's wrong?" she asked the worried businessman in the seat beside the older man.

"Heart attack, I think." He grimaced. "What can we do?"

"I know a little CPR," she said. She unfastened her seat belt; so did the groaning man's seat companion. But just as they started to lay him on the floor, someone shouted something. Smoke began to pour out of the cockpit, and the pilot called for everyone to assume crash positions. Amanda turned, almost in slow motion. She could feel the force of gravity increase as the plane started down. The floor went out from under her and her last conscious thought was that she'd never see Quinn again....

Elliot was watching television without much interest, wishing that his father had listened when Amanda had phoned the night before. He couldn't believe that he was going to be forbidden to even speak to her again, but Quinn had insisted, his cold voice giving nothing away as he'd made Elliot promise to make no attempt to contact her.

It seemed so unfair, he thought. Amanda was no wild party girl, surely his father knew that? He sighed heavily and munched on another potato chip.

The movie he was watching was suddenly interrupted as the local station broke in with a news bulletin. Elliot listened for a minute, gasped and jumped up to get his father.

Quinn was in the office, not really concentrating on what he was doing, when Elliot burst in. The boy looked odd, his freckles standing out in an unnaturally pale face.

"Dad, you'd better come here," he said uneasily. "Quick!"

Quinn's first thought was that something had happened to Harry, but Elliot stopped in front of the television. Quinn frowned as his dark eyes watched the screen. They were showing the airport.

"What's this all—" he began, then stopped to listen.

"...plane went down about ten minutes ago, according to our best information," the man, probably the airport manager, was saying. "We've got helicopters flying in to look for the wreckage, but the wind is up, and the area the plane went down in is almost inaccessible by road."

"What plane?" Quinn asked absently.

"To repeat our earlier bulletin," the man on television seemed to oblige, "a private charter plane has been reported lost somewhere in the Grand Teton Mountains just out of Jackson Hole. One eyewitness interviewed by KWJC-TV newsman Bill Donovan stated that he saw flames shooting out of the cockpit of the twin-engine aircraft and that he watched it plummet into the mountains and vanish. Aboard the craft were prominent San Francisco businessmen Bob Doyle and Harry Brown, and the lead singer of the rock group Desperado, Mandy Callaway."

Quinn sat down in his chair hard enough to shake it. He knew his face was as white as Elliot's. In his mind, he could hear his own voice telling Mandy he didn't want her anymore, daring her to ever contact him again. Now she was dead, and he felt her loss as surely as if one of his arms had been severed from his body.

That was when he realized how desperately he loved her. When it was too late to take back the harsh words, to go after her and bring her home where she belonged. He thought of her soft body lying in the cold snow, and a sound broke from his throat. He'd sent her away because he loved her, not because he'd wanted to hurt her, but she wouldn't have known that. Her last memory of him would have been a painful, hateful one. She'd have died thinking he didn't care.

"I don't believe it," Elliot said huskily. He was shaking his head. "I just don't believe it. She was onstage Friday night, singing again—" His voice broke and he put his face in his hands.

Quinn couldn't bear it. He got up and went past a startled Harry and out the back door in his shirtsleeves, so upset that he didn't even feel the cold. His eyes went to the barn, where he'd watched Amanda feed the calves, and around the back where she'd run from him that snowy afternoon and he'd had to save her from McNaber's bear traps. His big fists clenched by his sides and he shuddered with the force of the grief he felt, his face contorting.

"Amanda!" He bit off the name.

A long time later, he was aware of someone standing nearby. He didn't turn because his face would have said too much.

"Elliot told me," Harry said hesitantly. He stuck his hands into his pockets. "They say where she is, they may not be able to get her out."

Quinn's teeth clenched. "I'll get her out," he said huskily. "I won't leave her out there in the cold." He swallowed. "Get my skis and my boots out of the storeroom, and my insulated ski suit out of the closet. I'm going to call the lodge and talk to Terry Meade."

"He manages Larry's Lodge, doesn't he?" Harry recalled.

"Yes. He can get a chopper to take me up."

"Good thing you've kept up your practice," Harry muttered. "Never thought you'd need the skis for something this awful, though."

"Neither did I." He turned and went back inside. He might have to give up Amanda forever, but he wasn't giving her up to that damned mountain. He'd get her out somehow.

He grabbed the phone, ignoring Elliot's questions, and called the lodge, asking for Terry Meade in a tone that got instant action.

"Quinn!" Terry exclaimed. "Just the man I need. Look, we've got a crash—"

"I know," Quinn said tightly. "I know the singer. Can you get me a topo map of the area and a chopper? I'll need a first-aid kit, too, and some flares—"

"No sooner said than done," Terry replied tersely. "Although I don't think that first-aid kit will be needed, Quinn, I'm sorry."

"Well, pack it anyway, will you?" He fought down nausea. "I'll be up there in less than thirty minutes."

"We'll be waiting."

Quinn got into the ski suit under Elliot's fascinated gaze.

"You don't usually wear that suit when we ski together," he told his father.

"We don't stay out that long," Quinn explained. "This suit is a relatively new innovation. It's such a tight weave that it keeps out moisture, but it's made in such a way that it allows sweat to get out. It's like having your own heater along."

"I like the boots, too," Elliot remarked. They were blue, and they had a knob on the heel that allowed them to be tightened to fit the skier's foot exactly. Boots had to fit tight to work properly. And the skis themselves were equally fascinating. They had special brakes that unlocked when the skier fell, which stopped the ski from sliding down the hill.

"Those sure are long skis," Elliot remarked as his father took precious time to apply hot wax to them.

"Longer than yours, for sure. They fit my height," Quinn said tersely. "And they're short compared to jumping skis."

"Did you ever jump, Dad, or did you just do downhill?"

"Giant slalom," he replied. "Strictly Alpine skiing. That's going to come in handy today."

Elliot sighed. "I don't guess you'll let me come along?"

"No chance. This is no place for you." His eyes darkened. "God knows what I'll find when I get to the plane."

Elliot bit his lower lip. "She's dead, isn't she, Dad?" he asked in a choked tone.

Quinn's expression closed. "You stay here with Harry, and don't tie up the telephone. I'll call home as soon as I know anything."

"Take care of yourself up there, okay?" Elliot murmured as Quinn picked up the skis and the rest of his equipment, including gloves and ski cap. "I don't say it a lot, but I love you, Dad."

"I love you, too, son." Quinn pulled him close and gave him a quick, rough hug. "I know what I'm doing. I'll be okay."

"Good luck," Harry said as Quinn went out the back door to get into his pickup truck.

"I'll need it," Quinn muttered. He waved, started the truck, and pulled out into the driveway.

Terry Meade was waiting with the Ski Patrol, the helicopter pilot, assorted law enforcement officials and the civil defense director and trying to field the news media gathered at Larry's Lodge.

"This is the area where we think they are," Terry said grimly, showing Quinn the map. "What you call Ironside peak, right? It's not in our patrol area, so we don't have anything to do with it officially. The helicopter tried and failed to get into the valley below it because of the wind. The trees are dense down there and visibility is limited by blowing snow. Our teams are going to start here," he pointed at various places on the map. "But this hill is a killer." He grinned at Quinn. "You cut your teeth on it when you were practicing for the Olympics all those years ago, and you've kept up your practice there. If anyone can ski it, you can."

"I'll get in. What then?"

"Send up a flare. I'm packing a cellular phone in with the other stuff you asked for. It's got a better range than our walkie-talkies. Everybody know what to do? Right. Let's go."

He led them out of the lodge. Quinn put on his goggles, tugged his ski cap over his head and thrust his hands into his gloves. He didn't even want to think about what he might have to look at if he was lucky enough to find the downed plane. He was having enough trouble living with what he'd said to Amanda the last time he'd talked to her.

He could still hear her voice, hear the hurt in it when he'd told her he didn't want her. Remembering that was like cutting open his heart. For her sake, he'd sent her away. He was a poor man. He had so little to offer such a famous, beautiful woman. At first, at the lodge, his pride had been cut to ribbons when he discovered who she was, and how she'd fooled him, how she'd deceived him. But her adoration had been real, and when his mind was functioning again, he realized that. He'd almost phoned her back, he'd even dialed the number. But her world was so different from his. He couldn't let her give up everything she'd worked all her life for, just to live in the middle of nowhere. She deserved so much more. He sighed wearily. If she died, the last conversation would haunt him until the day he died. He didn't think he could live with it. He didn't want to have to try. She had to be alive. Oh, dear God, she had to be!

CHAPTER NINE

THE SUN WAS bright, and Quinn felt its warmth on his face as the helicopter set him down at the top of the mountain peak where the plane had last been sighted.

He was alone in the world when the chopper lifted off again. He checked his bindings one last time, adjusted the lightweight backpack and stared down the long mountainside with his ski poles restless in his hands. This particular slope wasn't skied as a rule. It wasn't even connected with the resort, which meant that the Ski Patrol didn't come here, and that the usual rescue toboggan posted on most slopes wouldn't be in evidence. He was totally on his own until he could find the downed plane. And he knew that while he was searching this untamed area, the Ski Patrol would be out in force on the regular slopes looking for the aircraft.

He sighed heavily as he stared down at the rugged, untouched terrain, which would be a beginning skier's nightmare. Well, it was now or never. Amanda was down there somewhere. He had to find her. He couldn't leave her there in the cold snow for all eternity.

He pulled down his goggles, suppressed his feelings and shoved the ski poles deep as he propelled himself down the slope. The first couple of minutes were tricky as he had to allow for the slight added weight of the backpack. But it took scant time to adjust, to balance his weight on the skis to compensate.

The wind bit his face, the snow flew over his dark ski suit as he wound down the slopes, his skis throwing up powdered snow in his wake. It brought back memories of the days when he'd maneuvered through the giant slalom in Alpine skiing competition. He'd been in the top one percent of his class, a daredevil skier with cold nerve and expert control on the slopes. This mountain was a killer, but it was one he knew like the back of his hand. He'd trained on this peak back in his early days of competition, loving the danger of skiing a slope where no one else came. Even for the past ten years or so, he'd honed his skill here every chance he got.

Quinn smiled to himself, his body leaning into the turns, not too far, the cutting edge of his skis breaking his speed as he maneuvered over boulders, down the fall line, around trees and broken branches or over them, whichever seemed more expedient.

His dark eyes narrowed as he defeated the obstacles. At least, thank God, he was able to do something instead of going through hell sitting at home waiting for word. That in itself was a blessing, even if it ended in the tragedy everyone seemed to think it would. He couldn't bear to imagine Amanda dead. He had to think positively. There were people who walked away from airplane crashes. He had to believe that she could be one of them. He had to keep thinking that or go mad.

He'd hoped against hope that when he got near the bottom of the hill, under those tall pines and the deadly updrafts and downdrafts that had defeated the helicopter's reconnoitering, that he'd find the airplane. But it wasn't there. He turned his skis sideways and skidded to a stop, looking around him. Maybe the observer had gotten his sighting wrong. Maybe it was another peak, maybe it was miles away. He bit his lower lip raw, tasting the lip balm he'd applied before he came onto the slope. If anyone on that plane was alive, time was going to make the difference. He had to find it quickly, or Amanda wouldn't have a prayer if she'd managed to survive the initial impact.

He started downhill again, his heartbeat increasing as the worry began to eat at him. On an impulse, he shot across the fall line, parallel to it for a little while before he maneuvered back and went down again in lazy *S* patterns. Something caught his attention. A sound. Voices!

He stopped to listen, turning his head. There was wind, and the sound of pines touching. But beyond it was a voice, carrying in the silence of nature. Snow blanketed most sound, making graveyard peace out of the mountain's spring noises.

Quinn adjusted his weight on the skis and lifted his hands to his mouth, the ski poles dangling from his wrists. "Hello! Where are you?" he shouted, taking a chance that the vibration of his voice wouldn't dislodge snow above him and bring a sheet of it down on him.

"Help!" voices called back. "We're here! We're here!"

He followed the sound, praying that he wasn't following an echo. But no, there, below the trees, he saw a glint of metal in the lowering sun. The plane! Thank God, there were survivors! Now if only Amanda was one of them...

He went the rest of the way down. As he drew closer, he saw men standing near the almost intact wreckage of the aircraft. One had a bandage around his head, another was nursing what looked like a broken arm. He saw one woman, but she wasn't blond. On the ground were two still forms, covered with coats. Covered up.

Please, God, no, he thought blindly. He drew to a stop.

"I'm Sutton. How many dead?" he asked the man who'd called to him, a burly man in a gray suit and white shirt and tie.

"Two," the man replied. "I'm Jeff Coleman, and I sure am glad to see you." He shook hands with Quinn. "I'm the pilot. We had a fire in the cockpit and it was all I could do to set her down at all. God, I feel bad! For some reason, three of the passengers had their seat belts off when we hit." He shook his head. "No hope for two of them. The third's concussed and looks comatose."

Quinn felt himself shaking inside as he asked the question he had to ask. "There was a singer aboard," he said. "Amanda Callaway."

"Yeah." The pilot shook his head and Quinn wanted to die, he wanted to stop breathing right there... "She's the concussion."

Quinn knew his hand shook as he pushed his goggles up over the black ski cap. "Where is she?" he asked huskily.

The pilot didn't ask questions or argue. He led Quinn past the two bodies and the dazed businessmen who were standing or sitting on fabric they'd taken from the plane, trying to keep warm.

"She's here," the pilot told him, indicating a makeshift stretcher constructed of branches and pillows from the cabin, and coats that covered the still body.

"Amanda," Quinn managed unsteadily. He knelt beside her. Her hair was in a coiled bun on her head. Her face was alabaster white, her eyes closed, long black lashes lying still on her cheekbones. Her mouth was as pale as the rest of her face, and there was a bruise high on her forehead at the right temple. He stripped off his glove and felt the artery at her neck. Her heart was still beating, but slowly and not very firmly. Unconscious. Dying, perhaps. "Oh, God," he breathed.

He got to his feet and unloaded the backpack as the pilot and two of the other men gathered around him.

"I've got a modular phone," Quinn said, "which I hope to God will work." He punched buttons and waited, his dark eyes narrowed, holding his breath.

It seemed to take forever. Then a voice, a recognizable voice, came over the wire. "Hello."

"Terry!" Quinn called. "It's Sutton. I've found them."

"Thank God!" Terry replied. "Okay, give me your position."

Quinn did, spreading out his laminated map to verify it, and then gave the report on casualties.

"Only one unconscious?" Terry asked again.

"Only one," Quinn replied heavily.

"We'll have to airlift you out, but we can't do it until the wind dies down. You understand, Quinn, the same downdrafts and updrafts that kept the chopper out this morning are going to keep it out now."

"Yes, I know, damn it," Quinn yelled. "But I've got to get her to a hospital. She's failing already."

Terry sighed. "And there you are without a rescue toboggan. Listen, what if I get Larry Hale down there?" he asked excitedly. "You know Larry; he was national champ in downhill a few years back, and he's a senior member of the Ski Patrol now. We could airdrop you the toboggan and some supplies for the rest of the survivors by plane. The two of you could tow her to a point accessible by chopper. Do you want to risk it, Quinn?"

"I don't know if she'll be alive in the morning, Terry," Quinn said somberly. "I'm more afraid to risk doing nothing than I am of towing her out. It's fairly level, if I remember right, all the way to the pass that leads from Caraway Ridge into Jackson Hole. The chopper might be able to fly down Jackson Hole and come in that way, without having to navigate the peaks. What do you think?"

"I think it's a good idea," Terry said. "If I remember right, they cleared that pass from the Ridge into Jackson Hole in the fall. It should still be accessible."

"No problem," Quinn said, his jaw grim. "If it isn't cleared, I'll clear it, by hand if necessary."

Terry chuckled softly. "Hale says he's already on the way. We'll get the plane up—hell of a pity he can't land where you are, but it's just too tricky. How about the other survivors?"

Quinn told him their conditions, along with the two bodies that would have to be airlifted out.

"Too bad," he replied. He paused for a minute to talk to somebody. "Listen, Quinn, if you can get the woman to Caraway Ridge, the chopper pilot thinks he can safely put down there. About the others, can they manage until morning if we drop the supplies?"

Quinn looked at the pilot. "Can you?"

"I ate snakes in Nam and Bill over there served in Antarctica." He grinned. "Between us, we can keep these pilgrims warm and even feed them. Sure, we'll be okay. Get that little lady out if you can."

"Amen," the man named Bill added, glancing at Amanda's still form. "I've heard her sing. It would be a crime against art to let her die."

Quinn lifted the cellular phone to his ear. "They say they can manage, Terry. Are you sure you can get them out in the morning?"

"If we have to send the snowplow in through the valley or send in a squad of snowmobiles and a horse-drawn sled, you'd better believe we'll get them out. The Ski Patrol is already working out the details."

"Okay."

Quinn unloaded his backpack. He had flares and matches, packets of high-protein dehydrated food, the first-aid kit and some cans of sterno.

"Paradise," the pilot said, looking at the stores. "With that, I can prepare a seven-course meal, build a bonfire and make a house. But those supplies they're going to drop will come in handy, just the same."

Quinn smiled in spite of himself. "Okay."

"We can sure use this first-aid kit, but I've already set a broken arm and patched a few cuts. Before I became a pilot, I worked in the medical corps."

"I had rescue training when I was in the Ski Patrol," Quinn replied. He grinned at the pilot. "But if I ever come down in a plane, I hope you're on it."

"Thanks. I hope none of us ever come down again." He glanced at the two bodies. "God, I'm sorry about them." He glanced at Amanda. "I hope she makes it."

Quinn's jaw hardened. "She's a fighter," he said. "Let's hope she cares enough to try." He alone knew

how defeated she'd probably felt when she left the lodge.
He'd inflicted some terrible damage with his coldness.
Pride had forced him to send her away, to deny his own
happiness. Once he knew how famous and wealthy she
was in her own right, he hadn't felt that he had the right
to ask her to give it all up to live with him and Elliot in
the wilds of Wyoming. He'd been doing what he thought
was best for her. Now he only wanted her to live.

He took a deep breath. "Watch for the plane and
Hale, will you? I'm going to sit with her."

"Sure." The pilot gave him a long look that he didn't
see before he went back to talk to the other survivors.

Quinn sat down beside Amanda, reaching for one
cold little hand under the coats that covered her. It was
going to be a rough ride for her, and she didn't need any
more jarring. But if they waited until morning, without medical help, she could die. It was much riskier to
do nothing than it was to risk moving her. And down
here in the valley, the snow was deep and fairly level. It
would be like Nordic skiing; cross-country skiing. With
luck, it would feel like a nice lazy sleigh ride to her.

"Listen to me, honey," he said softly. "We've got
a long way to go before we get you out of here and to
a hospital. You're going to have to hold on for a long
time." His hand tightened around hers, warming it. "I'll
be right with you every step of the way. I won't leave
you for a second. But you have to do your part, Amanda.
You have to fight to stay alive. I hope that you still want
to live. If you don't, there's something I need to tell you.
I sent you away not because I hated you, Amanda, but
because I loved you so much. I loved you enough to let
you go back to the life you needed. You've got to stay

alive so that I can tell you that," he added, stopping because his voice broke.

He looked away, getting control back breath by breath. He thought he felt her fingers move, but he couldn't be sure. "I'm going to get you out of here, honey, one way or the other, even if I have to walk out with you in my arms. Try to hold on, for me." He brought her hand to his mouth and kissed the palm hungrily. "Try to hold on, because if you die, so do I. I can't keep going unless you're somewhere in the world, even if I never see you again. Even if you hate me forever."

He swallowed hard and put down her hand. The sound of an airplane in the distance indicated that supplies were on the way. Quinn put Amanda's hand back under the cover and bent to brush his mouth against her cold, still one.

"I love you," he whispered roughly. "You've got to hold on until I can get you out of here."

He stood, his face like the stony crags above them, his eyes glittering as he joined the others.

The plane circled and seconds later, a white parachute appeared. Quinn held his breath as it descended, hoping against hope that the chute wouldn't hang up in the tall trees and that the toboggan would soft-land so that it was usable. A drop in this kind of wind was risky at best.

But luck was with them. The supplies and the sled made it in one piece. Quinn and the pilot and a couple of the sturdier survivors unfastened the chute and brought the contents back to the wreckage of the commuter plane. The sled was even equipped with blankets and a pillow and straps to keep Amanda secured.

Minutes later, the drone of a helicopter whispered on the wind, and not long after that, Hale started down the mountainside.

It took several minutes. Quinn saw the flash of rust that denoted the distinctive jacket and white waist pack of the Ski Patrol above, and when Hale came closer, he could see the gold cross on the right pocket of the jacket—a duplicate of the big one stenciled on the jacket's back. He smiled, remembering when he'd worn that same type of jacket during a brief stint as a ski patrolman. It was a special kind of occupation, and countless skiers owed their lives to those brave men and women. The National Ski Patrol had only existed since 1938. It was created by Charles Dole of Connecticut, after a skiing accident that took the life of one of his friends. Today, the Ski Patrol had over 10,000 members nationally, of whom ninety-eight percent were volunteers. They were the first on the slopes and the last off, patroling for dangerous areas and rescuing injured people. Quinn had once been part of that elite group and he still had the greatest respect for them.

Hale was the only color against the whiteness of the snow. The sun was out, and thank God it hadn't snowed all day. It had done enough of that last night.

Quinn's nerves were stretched. He hadn't had a cigarette since he'd arrived at the lodge, and he didn't dare have one now. Nicotine and caffeine tended to constrict blood vessels, and the cold was dangerous enough without giving it any help. Experienced skiers knew better than to stack the odds against themselves.

"Well, I made it." Hale grinned, getting his breath. "How are you, Quinn?" He extended a hand and Quinn shook it.

The man in the Ski Patrol jacket nodded to the others, accepted their thanks for the supplies he'd brought with him, which included a makeshift shelter and plenty of food and water and even a bottle of cognac. But he didn't waste time. "We'd better get moving if we hope to get Miss Callaway out of here by dark."

"She's over here," Quinn said. "God, I hate doing this," he added heavily when he and Hale were standing over the unconscious woman. "If there was any hope, any at all, that the chopper could get in here…"

"You can feel the wind for yourself," Hale replied, his eyes solemn. "We're the only chance she has. We'll get her to the chopper. Piece of cake," he added with a reassuring smile.

"I hope so," Quinn said somberly. He bent and nodded to Hale. They lifted her very gently onto the long sled containing the litter. It had handles on both ends, because it was designed to be towed. They attached the towlines, covered Amanda carefully and set out, with reassurances from the stranded survivors.

There was no time to talk. The track was fairly straightforward, but it worried Quinn, all the same, because there were crusts that jarred the woman on the litter. He towed, Hale guided, their rhythms matching perfectly as they made their way down the snow-covered valley. Around them, the wind sang through the tall firs and lodgepole pines, and Quinn thought about the old trappers and mountain men who must have come through this valley a hundred, two hundred years before. In those days of poor sanitation and even poorer medicine, Amanda wouldn't have stood a chance.

He forced himself not to look back. He had to concentrate on getting her to the Ridge. All that was important now, was that she get medical help while it could still do her some good. He hadn't come all this way to find her alive, only to lose her.

It seemed to take forever. Once Quinn was certain that they'd lost their way as they navigated through the narrow pass that led to the fifty-mile valley between the Grand Tetons and the Wind River Range, an area known as Jackson Hole. But he recognized landmarks as they went along, and eventually they wound their way around the trees and along the sparkling river until they reached the flats below Caraway Ridge.

Quinn and Hale were both breathing hard by now. They'd changed places several times, so that neither got too tired of towing the toboggan, and they were both in peak condition. But it was still a difficult thing to do.

They rested, and Quinn reached down to check Amanda's pulse. It was still there, and even seemed to be, incredibly, a little stronger than it had been. But she was pale and still and Quinn felt his spirits sink as he looked down at her.

"There it is," Hale called, sweeping his arm over the ridge. "The chopper."

"Now if only it can land," Quinn said quietly, and he began to pray.

The chopper came lower and lower, then it seemed to shoot up again and Quinn bit off a hard word. But the pilot corrected for the wind, which was dying down, and eased the helicopter toward the ground. It seemed to settle inch by inch until it landed safe. The pilot was out of it before the blades stopped.

"Let's get out of here," he called to the men. "If that

wind catches up again, I wouldn't give us a chance in hell of getting out. It was a miracle that I even got in!"

Quinn released his bindings in a flash, leaving his skis and poles for Hale to carry, along with his own. He got one side of the stretcher while the pilot, fortunately no lightweight himself, got the other. They put the stretcher in the back of the broad helicopter, on the floor, and Quinn and Hale piled in —Hale in the passenger seat up front, Quinn behind with Amanda, carefully laying ski equipment beside her.

"Let's go!" the pilot called as he revved up the engine.

It was touch and go. The wind decided to play tag with them, and they almost went into a lodgepole pine on the way up. But the pilot was a tenacious man with good nerves. He eased down and then up, down and up until he caught the wind off guard and shot up out of the valley and over the mountain.

Quinn reached down and clasped Amanda's cold hand in his. Only a little longer, honey, he thought, watching her with his heart in his eyes. Only a little longer, for God's sake, hold on!

It was the longest ride of his entire life. He spared one thought for the people who'd stayed behind to give Amanda her chance and he prayed that they'd be rescued without any further injuries. Then his eyes settled on her pale face and stayed there until the helicopter landed on the hospital lawn.

The reporters, local, state and national, had gotten word of the rescue mission. They were waiting. Police kept them back just long enough for Amanda to be carried into the hospital, but Quinn and Hale were caught. Quinn volunteered Hale to give an account of the rescue and then he ducked out, leaving the other man to field the enthusiastic audience while he trailed quickly behind the men who'd taken Amanda into the emergency room.

He drank coffee and smoked cigarettes and glared at walls for over an hour until someone came out to talk to him. Hale had to go back to the lodge, to help plan the rescue of the rest of the survivors, but he promised to keep in touch. After he'd gone, Quinn felt even more alone. But at last a doctor came into the waiting room, and approached him.

"Are you related to Miss Callaway?" the doctor asked with narrowed eyes.

Quinn knew that if he said no, he'd have to wait for news of her condition until he could find somebody who was related to her, and he had no idea how to find her aunt.

"I'm her fiancé," he said without moving a muscle in his face. "How is she?"

"Not good," the doctor, a small wiry man, said bluntly. "But I believe in miracles. We have her in intensive care, where she'll stay until she regains consciousness. She's badly concussed. I gather she hasn't regained consciousness since the crash?" Quinn shook his head. "That sleigh ride and helicopter lift didn't do any good, either," he added firmly, adding when he saw the expression on Quinn's tormented face, "but I can understand the necessity for it. Go get some sleep. Come back in the morning. We won't know anything until then. Maybe not until much later. Concussion is tricky. We can't predict the outcome, as much as we'd like to."

"I can't rest," Quinn said quietly. "I'll sit out here and drink coffee, if you don't mind. If this is as close to her as I can get, it'll have to do."

The doctor took a slow breath. "We keep spare beds in cases like this," he said. "I'll have one made up for you when you can't stay awake any longer." He smiled faintly. "Try to think positively. It isn't medical, exactly, but sometimes it works wonders. Prayer doesn't hurt, either."

"Thank you," Quinn said.

The doctor shrugged. "Wait until she wakes up. Good night."

Quinn watched him go and sighed. He didn't know what to do next. He phoned Terry at the lodge to see if Amanda's band had called. Someone named Jerry and a man called Hank had been phoning every few minutes, he was told. Quinn asked for a phone number and Terry gave it to him.

He dialed the area code. California, he figured as he waited for it to ring.

"Hello?"

"This is Quinn Sutton," he began.

"Yes, I recognize your voice. It's Hank here. How is she?"

"Concussion. Coma, I guess. She's in intensive care and she's still alive. That's about all I know."

There was a long pause. "I'd hoped for a little more than that."

"So had I," Quinn replied. He hesitated. "I'll phone you in the morning. The minute I know anything. Is there anybody we should notify...her aunt?"

"Her aunt is a scatterbrain and no help at all. Anyway, she's off with Blalock Durning in the Bahamas on one of those incommunicado islands. We couldn't reach her if we tried."

"Is there anybody else?" Quinn asked.

"Not that I know of." There was a brief pause. "I feel bad about the way things happened. I hate planes, you know. That's why the rest of us went by bus. We stopped here in some hick town to make sure Amanda got her plane, and Terry told us what happened. We got a motel room and we're waiting for a bus back to Jackson. It will probably be late tomorrow before we get there. We've already canceled the gig. We can't do it without Amanda."

"I'll book a room for you," Quinn said.

"Make it a suite," Hank replied, "and if you need anything, you know, anything, you just tell us."

"I've got plenty of cigarettes and the coffee machine's working. I'm fine."

"We'll see you when we get there. And Sutton— thanks. She really cares about you, you know?"

"I care about her," he said stiffly. "That's why I sent her away. My God, how could she give all that up to live on a mountain in Wyoming?"

"Amanda's not a city girl, though," Hank said slowly. "And she changed after those days she spent with you. Her heart wasn't with us anymore. She cried all last night…"

"Oh, God, don't," Quinn said.

"Sorry, man," Hank said quietly. "I'm really sorry, that's the last thing I should have said. Look, go smoke a cigarette. I think I'll tie one on royally and have the boys put me to bed. Tomorrow we'll talk. Take care."

"You, too."

Quinn hung up. He couldn't bear to think of Amanda crying because of what he'd done to her. He might lose her even yet, and he didn't know how he was going to go on living. He felt so alone.

He was out of change after he called the lodge and booked the suite for Hank and the others, but he still had to talk to Elliot and Harry. He dialed the operator and called collect. Elliot answered the phone immediately.

"How is she?" he asked quickly.

Quinn went over it again, feeling numb. "I wish I knew more," he concluded. "But that's all there is."

"She can't die," Elliot said miserably. "Dad, she just can't!"

"Say a prayer, son," he replied. "And don't let Harry teach you any bad habits while I'm gone."

"No, sir, I won't," Elliot said with a feeble attempt at humor. "You're going to stay, I guess?"

"I have to," Quinn said huskily. He hesitated. "I love her."

"So do I," Elliot said softly. "Bring her back when you come."

"If I can. If she'll even speak to me when she wakes up," Quinn said with a total lack of confidence.

"She will," Elliot told him. "You should have listened to some of those songs you thought were so horrible. One of hers won a Grammy. It was all about having to give up things we love to keep from hurting them. She always seemed to feel it when somebody was sad or hurt, you know. And she risked her own life trying to save that girl at the concert. She's not someone who thinks about getting even with people. She's got too much heart."

Quinn drew deeply from his cigarette. "I hope so, son," he said. "You get to bed. I'll call you tomorrow."

"Okay. Take care of yourself. Love you, Dad."

"Me, too, son," Quinn replied. He hung up. The waiting area was deserted now, and the hospital seemed to have gone to sleep. He sat down with his Styrofoam cup of black coffee and finished his cigarette. The room looked like he felt—empty.

CHAPTER TEN

I_T WAS LATE_ morning when the nurse came to shake Quinn gently awake. Apparently around dawn he'd gone to sleep sitting up, with an empty coffee cup in his hand. He thought he'd never sleep at all.

He sat up, drowsy and disheveled. "How is Amanda?" he asked immediately.

The nurse, a young blonde, smiled at him. "She's awake and asking for you."

"Oh, thank God," he said heavily. He got quickly to his feet, still a little groggy, and followed her down to the intensive-care unit, where patients in tiny rooms were monitored from a central nurses' station and the hum and click and whir of life-supporting machinery filled the air. If she was asking for him, she must not hate him too much. That thought sustained him as he followed the nurse into one of the small cubicles where Amanda lay.

Amanda looked thinner than ever in the light, her face pinched, her eyes hollow, her lips chapped. They'd taken her hair down somewhere along the way and tied it back with a pink ribbon. She was propped up in bed, still with the IV in position, but she'd been taken off all the other machines.

She looked up and saw Quinn and all the weariness and pain went out of her face. She brightened, became beautiful despite her injuries, her eyes sparkling. Her last thought when she'd realized in the plane what was going to happen had been of Quinn. Her first thought when she'd regained consciousness had been of him. The pain, the grief of having him turn away from her was forgotten. He was here, now, and that meant he had to care about her.

"Oh, Quinn!" she whispered tearfully, and held out her arms.

He went to her without hesitation, ignoring the nurses, the aides, the whole world. His arms folded gently around her, careful of the tubes attached to her hand, and his head bent over hers, his cheek on her soft hair, his eyes closed as he shivered with reaction. She was alive. She was going to live. He felt as if he were going to choke to death on his own rush of feeling.

"My God," he whispered shakily. "I thought I'd lost you."

That was worth it all, she thought, dazed from the emotion in his voice, at the tremor in his powerful body as he held her. She clung to him, her slender arms around his neck, drowning in pleasure. She'd wondered if he hadn't sent her away in a misguided belief that it was for her own good. Now she was sure of it. He couldn't have looked that haggard, that terrible, unless she mattered very much to him. Her aching heart soared. "They said you brought me out."

"Hale and I did," he said huskily. He lifted his head, searching her bright eyes slowly. "It's been the longest night of my life. They said you might die."

"Oh, we Callaways are tough birds," she said, wiping away a tear. She was still weak and sore and her headache hadn't completely gone away. "You look terrible, my darling," she whispered on a choked laugh.

The endearment fired his blood. He had to take a deep breath before he could even speak. His fingers linked with hers. "I felt pretty terrible when we listened to the news report, especially when I remembered the things I said to you." He took a deep breath. "I didn't know if you'd hate me for the rest of your life, but even if you did, I couldn't just sit on my mountain and let other people look for you." His thumb gently stroked the back of her pale hand. "How do you feel, honey?"

"Pretty bad. But considering it all, I'll do. I'm sorry about the men who died. One of them was having a heart attack," she explained. "The other gentleman who was sitting with him alerted me. We both unfastened our seat belts to try and give CPR. Just after I got up, the plane started down," she said. "Quinn, do you believe in predestination?"

"You mean, that things happen the way they're meant to in spite of us?" He smiled. "I guess I do." His dark eyes slid over her face hungrily. "I'm so glad it wasn't your time, Amanda."

"So am I." She reached up and touched his thin mouth with just the tips of her fingers. "Where is it?" she asked with an impish smile as a sudden delicious thought occurred to her.

He frowned. "Where's what?"

"My engagement ring," she said. "And don't try to back out of it," she added firmly when he stood there looking shocked. "You told the doctor and the whole medical staff that I was your fiancée, and you're not ducking out of it now. You're going to marry me."

His eyebrows shot up. "I'm what?" he said blankly.

"You're going to marry me. Where's Hank? Has any-body phoned him?"

"I did. I was supposed to call him back." He checked his watch and grimaced. "I guess it's too late now. He and the band are on the way back here."

"Good. They're twice your size and at least as mean." Her eyes narrowed. "I'll tell them you seduced me. I could be pregnant." She nodded, thinking up lies fast while Quinn's face mirrored his stark astonishment. "That's right, I could."

"You could not," he said shortly. "I never…!"

"But you're going to," she said with a husky laugh. "Just wait until I get out of here and get you alone. I'll wrestle you down and start kissing you, and you'll never get away in time."

"Oh, God," he groaned, because he knew she was right. He couldn't resist her that way, it was part of the problem.

"So you'll have to marry me first," she continued. "Because I'm not that kind of girl. Not to mention that you aren't that kind of guy. Harry likes me and Elliot and I are already friends, and I could even get used to McNaber if he'll move those traps." She pursed her lips, thinking. "The concert tour is going to be a real drag, but once it's over, I'll retire from the stage and just make records and tapes and CDs with the guys. Maybe a video now and again. They'll like that, too. We're all basically shy and we don't like live shows. I'll compose songs. I can do that at the house, in between helping Harry with the cooking and looking after sick calves, and having babies," she added with a shy smile.

He wanted to sit down. He hadn't counted on this. All that had mattered at the time was getting her away from the wreckage and into a hospital where she could be cared for. He hadn't let himself think ahead. But she obviously had. His head spun with her plans.

"Listen, you're an entertainer," he began. His fingers curled around hers and he looked down at them with a hard, grim sigh. "Amanda, I'm a poor man. All I've got is a broken-down ranch in the middle of nowhere. You'd have a lot of hardships, because I won't live on your money. I've got a son, even if he isn't mine, and…"

She brought his hand to her cheek and held it there, nuzzling her cheek against it as she looked up at him with dark, soft, adoring eyes. "I love you," she whispered.

He faltered. His cheeks went ruddy as the words penetrated, touched him, excited him. Except for his mother and Elliot, nobody had ever said that to him before Amanda had. "Do you?" he asked huskily. "Still? Even after the way I walked off and left you there at the lodge that night? After what I said to you on the phone?" he added, because he'd had too much time to agonize over his behavior, even if it had been for what he thought was her own good.

"Even after that," she said gently. "With all my heart. I just want to live with you, Quinn. In the wilds of Wyoming, in a grass shack on some island, in a mansion in Beverly Hills—it would all be the same to me—as long as you loved me back and we could be together for the rest of our lives."

He felt a ripple of pure delight go through him. "Is that what you really want?" he asked, searching her dark eyes with his own.

"More than anything else in the world," she confessed. "That's why I couldn't tell you who and what

I really was. I loved you so much, and I knew you wouldn't want me…" Her voice trailed off.

"I want you, all right," he said curtly. "I never stopped. Damn it, woman, I was trying to do what was best for you!"

"By turning me out in the cold and leaving me to starve to death for love?" she asked icily. "Thanks a bunch!"

He looked away uncomfortably. "It wasn't that way and you know it. I thought maybe it was the novelty. You know, a lonely man in the backwoods," he began.

"You thought I was having the time of my life playing you for a fool," she said. Her head was beginning to hurt, but she had to wrap it all up before she gave in and asked for some more medication. "Well, you listen to me, Quinn Sutton, I'm not the type to go around deliberately trying to hurt people. All I ever wanted was somebody to care about me—just me, not the pretty girl on the stage."

"Yes, I know that now," he replied. He brought her hand to his mouth and softly kissed the palm. The look on his face weakened her. "So you want a ring, do you? It will have to be something sensible. No flashy diamonds, even if I could give you something you'd need sunglasses to look at."

"I'll settle for the paper band on a King Edward cigar if you'll just marry me," she replied.

"I think I can do a little better than that," he murmured dryly. He bent over her, his lips hovering just above hers. "And no long engagement," he whispered.

"It takes three days, doesn't it?" she whispered back. "That *is* a long engagement. Get busy!"

He stifled a laugh as he brushed his hard mouth

gently over her dry one. "Get well," he whispered. "I'll read some books real fast."

She colored when she realized what kind of books he was referring to, and then smiled under his tender kiss. "You do that," she breathed. "Oh, Quinn, get me out of here!"

"At the earliest possible minute," he promised.

The band showed up later in the day while Quinn was out buying an engagement ring for Amanda. He'd already called and laughingly told Elliot and Harry what she'd done to him, and was delighted with Elliot's pleasure in the news and Harry's teasing. He did buy her a diamond, even if it was a moderate one, and a gold band for each of them. It gave him the greatest kind of thrill to know that he was finally marrying for all the right reasons.

When he got back to the hospital, the rest of the survivors had been airlifted out and all but one of them had been treated and released. The news media had tried to get to Amanda, but the band arrived shortly after Quinn left and ran interference. Hank gave out a statement and stopped them. The road manager, as Quinn found out, had gone on to San Francisco to make arrangements for canceling the concert.

The boys were gathered around Amanda, who'd been moved into a nice private room. She was sitting up in bed, looking much better, and her laughing dark eyes met Quinn's the minute he came in the door.

"Hank brought a shotgun," she informed him. "And Deke and Johnson and Jack are going to help you down the aisle. Jerry's found a minister, and Hank's already arranged a blood test for you right down the hall. The license—"

"Is already applied for," Quinn said with a chuckle. "I did that myself. Hello, boys," he greeted them, shaking hands as he was introduced to the rest of the band. "And you can unload the shotgun. I'd planned to hold it on Amanda, if she tried to back out."

"Me, back out? Heaven forbid!" she exclaimed, smiling as Quinn bent to kiss her. "Where's my ring?" she whispered against his hard mouth. "I want it on, so these nurses won't make eyes at you. There's this gorgeous redhead…"

"I can't see past you, pretty thing," he murmured, his eyes soft and quiet in a still-gaunt face. "Here it is." Quinn produced it and slid it on her finger. He'd measured the size with a small piece of paper he'd wrapped around her finger, and he hoped that the method worked. He needn't have worried, because the ring was a perfect fit, and she acted as if it were the three-carat monster he'd wanted to get her. Her face lit up, like her pretty eyes, and she beamed as she showed it to the band.

"Did you sleep at all?" Hank asked him while the others gathered around Amanda.

"About an hour, I think," Quinn murmured dryly. "You?"

"I couldn't even get properly drunk," Hank said, sighing, "so the boys and I played cards until we caught the bus. We slept most of the way in. It was a long ride. From what I hear," he added with a level look, "you and that Hale fellow had an even longer one, bringing Amanda out of the mountains."

"You'll never know." Quinn looked past him to Amanda, his dark eyes full of remembered pain. "I had to decide whether or not to move her. I thought it was riskier to leave her there until the next morning.

If we'd waited, we had no guarantee that the helicopter would have been able to land even then. She could have died. It's a miracle she didn't."

"Miracles come in all shapes and sizes," Hank mused, staring at her. "She's been ours. Without her, we'd never have gotten anywhere. But being on the road has worn her out. The boys and I were talking on the way back about cutting out personal appearances and concentrating on videos and albums. I think Amanda might like that. She'll have enough to do from now on, I imagine, taking care of you and your boy," he added with a grin. "Not to mention all those new brothers and sisters you'll be adding. I grew up on a ranch," he said surprisingly. "I have five brothers."

Quinn's eyebrows lifted. "Are they all runts like you?" he asked with a smile.

"I'm the runt," Hank corrected.

Quinn just shook his head.

AMANDA WAS RELEASED from the hospital two days later. Every conceivable test had been done, and fortunately there were no complications. The doctor had been cautiously optimistic at first, but her recovery was rapid—probably due, the doctor said with a smile, to her incentive. He gave Amanda away at the brief ceremony, held in the hospital's chapel just before she was discharged, and one of the nurses was her matron of honor. There were a record four best men; the band. But for all its brevity and informality, it was a ceremony that Amanda would never forget. The Methodist minister who performed it had a way with words, and Amanda and Quinn felt just as married as if they'd had the service performed in a huge church with a large crowd present.

The only mishap was that the press found out about the wedding, and Amanda and Quinn and the band were mobbed as they made their way out of the hospital afterward. The size of the band members made them keep well back. Hank gave them his best wildman glare while Jack whispered something about the bandleader becoming homicidal if he was pushed too far. They escaped in two separate cars. The driver of the one taking Quinn and Amanda to the lodge managed to get them there over back roads, so that nobody knew where they were.

Terry had given them the bridal suite, on the top floor of the lodge, and the view of the snowcapped mountains was exquisite. Amanda, still a little shaky and very nervous, stared out at them with mixed feelings.

"I don't know if I'll ever think of them as postcards again," she remarked to Quinn, who was trying to find places to put everything from their suitcase. He'd had to go to Ricochet for his suit and a change of clothing.

"What, the mountains?" he asked, smiling at her. "Well, it's not a bad thing to respect them. But airplanes don't crash that often, and when you're well enough, I'm going to teach you to ski."

She turned and looked at him for a long time. Her wedding outfit was an off-white, a very simple shirtwaist dress with a soft collar and no frills. But with her long hair around her shoulders and down to her waist, framed in the light coming through the window, she looked the picture of a bride. Quinn watched her back and sighed, his eyes lingering on the small sprig of lily of the valley she was wearing in her hair—a present from a member of the hospital staff.

"One of the nurses brought me a newspaper," Amanda said. "It told all about how you and Mr. Hale got me out." She hesitated. "They said that only a few men could ski that particular mountain without killing themselves."

"I've been skiing it for years," he said simply. He took off the dark jacket of his suit and loosened his tie with a long sigh. "I knew that the Ski Patrol would get you out, but they usually only work the lodge slopes— you know, the ones with normal ski runs. The peak the plane landed on was off the lodge property and out-of-the-way. It hadn't even been inspected. There are all sorts of dangers on slopes like that—fallen trees, boulders, stumps, debris, not to mention the threat of avalanche. The Ski Patrol marks dangerous runs where they work. They're the first out in the morning and the last off the slopes in the afternoon."

"You seem to know a lot about it," Amanda said.

"I used to be one of them," he replied with a grin. "In my younger days. It's pretty rewarding."

"There was a jacket Harry showed me," she frowned. "A rust-colored one with a big gold cross on the back…"

"My old patrol jacket." He chuckled. "I wouldn't part with it for the world. If I'd thought of it, I'd have worn it that day." His eyes darkened as he looked at her. "Thank God I knew that slope," he said huskily. "Because I'd bet money that you wouldn't have lasted on that mountain overnight."

"I was thinking about you when the plane went down," she confessed. "I wasn't sure that I'd ever see you again."

"Neither was I when I finally got to you." He took off his tie and threw it aside. His hand absently unfastened the top buttons of his white shirt as he moved toward her. "I was trying so hard to do the right thing," he murmured. "I didn't think I could give you what you needed, what you were used to."

"I'm used to you, Mr. Sutton," she murmured with a smile. Amanda slid her arms under his and around him, looking up at him with her whole heart in her dark eyes. "Bad temper, irritable scowl and all. Anything you can't give me, I don't want. Will that do?"

His broad chest rose and fell slowly. "I can't give you much. I've lost damned near everything."

"You have Elliot and Harry and me," she pointed out. "And some fat, healthy calves, and in a few years, Elliot will have a lot of little brothers and sisters to help him on the ranch."

A faint dusky color stained his high cheekbones. "Yes."

"Why, Mr. Sutton, honey, you aren't shy, are you?" she whispered dryly as she moved her hands back around to his shirt and finished unbuttoning it down his tanned, hair-roughened chest.

"Of course I'm shy," he muttered, heating up at the feel of her slender hands on his skin. He caught his breath and shuddered when she kissed him there. His big hands slid into her long, silky hair and brought her even closer. "I like that," he breathed roughly. "Oh, God, I love it!"

She drew back after a minute, her eyes sultry, drowsy. "Wouldn't you like to do that to me?" she whispered. "I like it, too."

He fumbled with buttons until he had the dress out of

the way and she was standing in nothing except a satin teddy. He'd never seen one before, except in movies, and he stared at her with his breath stuck somewhere in his chest. It was such a sexy garment low on her lace-covered breasts, nipped at her slender waist, hugging her full hips. Below it were her elegant silk-clad legs, although he didn't see anything holding up her hose.

"It's a teddy," she whispered. "If you want to slide it down," she added shyly, lowering her eyes to his pulsating chest, "I could step out of it."

He didn't know if he could do that and stay on his feet. The thought of Amanda unclothed made his knees weak. But he slid the straps down her arms and slowly, slowly, peeled it away from her firm, hard-tipped breasts, over her flat stomach, and then over the panty hose she was wearing. He caught them as well and eased the whole silky mass down to the floor.

She stepped out of it, so much in love with him that all her earlier shyness was evaporating. It was as new for him as it was for her, and that made it beautiful. A true act of love.

She let him look at her, fascinated by the awe in his hard face, in the eyes that went over her like an artist's brush, capturing every line, every soft curve before he even touched her.

"Amanda, you're the most beautiful creature I've ever seen," he said finally. "You look like a drawing of a fairy I saw in an old-time storybook...all gold and ivory."

She reached up and leaned close against him, shivering a little when her breasts touched his bare chest. The hair was faintly abrasive and very arousing. She moved involuntarily and gasped at the sensation.

"Do you want to help me?" he whispered as he stripped off his shirt and his hands went to his belt.

"I…" She hesitated, her nerve retreating suddenly at the intimacy of it. She grimaced. "Oh, Quinn, I'm such a coward!" She hid her face against his chest and felt his laughter.

"Well, you're not alone," he murmured. "I'm not exactly an exhibitionist myself. Look, why don't you get under the covers and close your eyes, and we'll pretend it's dark."

She looked up at him and laughed. "This is silly."

"Yes, I know." He sighed. "Well, honey, we're married. I guess it's time to face all the implications of sharing a bed."

He sat down, took off his boots and socks, stood to unbuckle his belt, holding her eyes, and slid the zip down. Everything came off, and seconds later, she saw for herself all the differences between men and women.

"You've gone scarlet, Mrs. Sutton," he observed.

"You aren't much whiter yourself, Mr. Sutton," she replied.

He laughed and reached for her and she felt him press against her. It was incredible, the feel of skin against skin, hair-rough flesh against silky softness. He bent and found her mouth and began to kiss her lazily, while his big, rough hands slid down her back and around to her hips. His mouth opened at the same time that his fingers pulled her thighs against his, and she felt for the first time the stark reality of arousal.

He felt her gasp and lifted his head, searching her flushed face. "That has to happen before anything else can," he whispered. "Don't be afraid. I think I know enough to make it easy for you."

"I love you, Quinn," she whispered back, forcing her taut muscles to relax, to give in to him. She leaned her body into his with a tiny shiver and lifted her mouth. "However it happens between us, it will be all right."

He searched her eyes and nodded. His mouth lowered to hers. He kissed her with exquisite tenderness while his hands found the softness of her breasts. Minutes later, his mouth traced them, covered the hard tips in a warm, moist suction that drew new sounds from her. He liked that, so he lifted her and put her on the big bed, and found other places to kiss her that made the sounds louder and more tormented.

The book had been very thorough and quite explicit, so he knew what to do in theory. Practice was very different. He hadn't known that women could lose control, too. That their bodies were so soft, or so strong. That their eyes grew wild and their faces contorted as the pleasure built in them, that they wept with it. Her pleasure became his only goal in the long, exquisite oblivion that followed.

By the time he moved over her, she was more than ready for him, she was desperate for him. He whispered to her, gently guided her body to his as he fought for control of his own raging need so that he could satisfy hers first.

There was one instant when she stiffened and tried to pull away, but he stopped then and looked down into her frightened eyes.

"It will only hurt for a few seconds," he whispered huskily. "Link your hands in mine and hold on. I'll do it quickly."

"All…all right." She felt the strength in his hands and her eyes met his. She swallowed.

He pushed, hard. She moaned a little, but her body accepted him instantly and without any further difficulty.

Her eyes brightened. Her lips parted and she breathed quickly and began to smile. "It's gone," she whispered. "Quinn, I'm a woman now...."

"My woman," he whispered back. The darkness grew in his eyes. He bent to her mouth and captured it, held it as he began to move, his body dancing above hers, teaching it the rhythm. She followed where he led, gasping as the cadence increased, as the music began to grow in her mind and filtered through her arms and legs. She held on to him with the last of her strength, proud of his stamina, of the power in his body that was taking hers from reality and into a place she'd never dreamed existed.

She felt the first tremors begin, and work into her like fiery pins, holding her body in a painful arch as she felt the tension build. It grew to unbearable levels. Her head thrashed on the pillow and she wanted to push him away, to make him stop, because she didn't think she could live through what was happening to her. But just as she began to push him the tension broke and she fell, crying out, into a hot, wild satisfaction that convulsed her. Above her, Quinn saw it happen and finally gave in to the desperate fever of his own need. He drove for his own satisfaction and felt it take him, his voice breaking on Amanda's name as he went into the fiery depths with her.

Afterward, he started to draw away, but her arms went around him and refused to let go. He felt her tears against his hot throat.

"Are you all right?" he asked huskily.

"I died," she whispered brokenly. Her arms contracted. "Don't go away, please don't. I don't want to let you go," she moaned.

He let his body relax, giving her his full weight. "I'll crush you, honey," he whispered in her ear.

"No, you won't." She sighed, feeling his body pulse with every heartbeat, feeling the dampness of his skin on her own, the glory of his flesh touching hers. "This is nice."

He laughed despite his exhaustion. "There's a new word for it," he murmured. He growled and bit her shoulder gently. "Wildcat," he whispered proudly. "You bit me. Do you remember? You bit me and dug your nails into my hips and screamed."

"So did you," she accused, flushing. "I'll have bruises on my thighs…"

"Little ones," he agreed. He lifted his head and searched her dark, quiet eyes. "I couldn't help that, at the last. I lost it. Really lost it. Are you as sated as I am?" he mused. "I feel like I've been walking around like half a person all my life, and I've just become whole."

"So do I." Her eyes searched his, and she lifted a lazy hand to trace his hard, thin lips. After a few seconds, she lifted her hips where they were still joined to his and watched his eyes kindle. She drew in a shaky breath and did it again, delighting in the sudden helpless response of his body.

"That's impossible," he joked. "The book said so."

Amanda pulled his mouth down to hers. "Damn the book," she said and held on as he answered her hunger with his own.

They slept and finally woke just in time to go down

to dinner. But since neither of them wanted to face having to get dressed, they had room service send up a tray. They drank champagne and ate thick steaks and went back to bed. Eventually they even slept.

The next morning, they set out for Ricochet, holding hands all the way home.

CHAPTER ELEVEN

ELLIOT AND HARRY were waiting at the door when Quinn brought Amanda home. There was a big wedding cake on the table that Harry had made, and a special present that Elliot had made Harry drive him to town in the sleigh to get—a new Desperado album with a picture of Amanda on the cover.

"What a present," Quinn murmured, smiling at Amanda over the beautiful photograph. "I guess I'll have to listen to it now, won't I?"

"I even got Hank Shoeman's autograph," Elliot enthused. "Finally I can tell the guys at school! I've been going nuts ever since I realized who Amanda was...."

"You knew?" Quinn burst out. "And you didn't tell me? So that's why that tape disappeared."

"You were looking for it?" Elliot echoed.

"Sure, just after we got home from the lodge that night I deserted Amanda," Quinn said with a rueful glance at her. "I was feeling pretty low. I just wanted to hear her voice, but the tape was missing."

"Sorry, Dad," Elliot said gently. "I'll never do it again, but I was afraid you'd toss her out if you knew she was a rock singer. She's really terrific, you know, and that song that won a Grammy was one of hers."

"Stop, you'll make me blush," Amanda groaned.

"I can do that," Quinn murmured dryly and the

look he gave Amanda brought scarlet color into her
hot cheeks.

"You were in the paper, Dad," Elliot continued excitedly. "And on the six o'clock news, too! They told
all about your skiing days and the Olympic team. Dad,
why didn't you keep going? They said you were one of
the best giant slalom skiers this country ever produced,
but that you quit with a place on the Olympic team in
your pocket."

"It's a long story, Elliot," he replied.

"It was because of my mother, wasn't it?" the boy
asked gravely.

"Well, you were on the way and I didn't feel right
about deserting her at such a time."

"Even though she'd been so terrible to you?" he
probed.

Quinn put his hands on his son's shoulders. "I'll tell
you for a fact, Elliot, you were mine from the day I
knew about your existence. I waited for you like a kid
waiting for a Christmas present. I bought stuff and read
books about babies and learned all the things I'd need
to know to help your mother raise you. I'd figured, you
see, that she might eventually decide that having you
was pretty special. I'm sorry that she didn't."

"That's okay," Elliot said with a smile. "You did."

"You bet I did. And do."

"Since you like kids so much, you and Amanda
might have a few of your own," Elliot decided. "I can
help. Me and Harry can wash diapers and make for-
mula..."

Amanda laughed delightedly. "Oh, you doll, you!"
She hugged Elliot. "Would you really not mind other
kids around?"

"Heck, no," Elliot said with genuine feeling. "All the other guys have little brothers and sisters. It gets sort of lonely, being the only one." He looked up at her admiringly. "And they'd be awful pretty, if some of them were girls."

She grinned. "Maybe we'll get lucky and have another redhead, too. My mother was redheaded. So was my grandmother. It runs in the family."

Elliot liked that, and said so.

"Hank Shocman has a present for you, by the way," she told Elliot. "No, there's no use looking in the truck, he ordered it."

Elliot's eyes lit up. "What is it? An autographed photo of the group?"

"It's a keyboard," Amanda corrected gently, smiling at his awe. "A real one, a Moog like I play when we do instrumentals."

"Oh, my gosh!" Elliot sat down. "I've died and gone to heaven. First I get a great new mother and now I get a Moog. Maybe I'm real sick and have a high fever," he frowned, feeling his forehead.

"No, you're perfectly well," Quinn told him. "And I guess it's all right if you play some rock songs," he added with a grimace. "I got used to turnips, after all, that time when Harry refused to cook any more greens. I guess I can get used to loud music."

"I refused to cook greens because we had a blizzard and canned turnips was all I had," Harry reminded him, glowering. "Now that Amanda's here, we won't run out of beans and peas and such, because she'll remember to tell me we're out so I can get some more."

"I didn't forget to remind you," Quinn muttered.

"You did so," Elliot began. "I remember—"

"That's it, gang up on me," Quinn glowered at them.

"Don't you worry, sweet man, I'll protect you from ghastly turnips and peas and beans," she said with a quick glance at Harry and Elliot. "I like asparagus, so I'll make sure that's all we keep here. Don't you guys like asparagus?"

"Yes!" they chorused, having been the culprits who told Amanda once that Quinn hated asparagus above all food in the world.

Quinn groaned.

"And I'll make liver and onions every night," Amanda added. "We love that, don't we, gang?"

"We sure do!" they chorused again, because they knew it was the only meat Quinn wouldn't eat.

"I'll go live with McNaber," he threatened.

Amanda laughed and slid her arms around him. "Only if we get to come, too." She looked up at him. "It's all right. We all really hate asparagus and liver and onions."

"That's a fact, we do," Elliot replied. "Amanda, are you going to go on tour with the band?"

"No," she said quietly. "We'd all gotten tired of the pace. We're going to take a well-earned rest and concentrate on videos and albums."

"I've got this great idea for a video," Elliot volunteered.

She grinned. "Okay, tiger, you can share it with us when Hank and the others come for a visit."

His eyes lit up. "They're all coming? The whole group?"

"My aunt is marrying Mr. Durning," she told him, having found out that tidbit from Hank. "They're going to live in Hawaii, and the band has permission to use

One Minute" Survey

You get up to **FOUR** books <u>and</u> Mystery Gifts...

YOU pick your books —
WE pay for everything.
You get up to FOUR new books and TWO Mystery Gifts
absolutely FREE!
Total retail value: Over $20!

Dear Reader,

Your opinions are important to us. So if you'll participate in our fast and free "One Minute" Survey, **YOU** can pick up to four wonderful books that **WE** pay for!

As a leading publisher of women's fiction, we'd love to hear from you. That's why we promise to reward you for completing our survey.

IMPORTANT: Please complete the survey and return it. We'll send your Free Books and Free Mystery Gifts right away. **And we pay for shipping and handling too!** *We pay for EVERYTHING!*

Try **Essential Suspense** featuring spine-tingling suspense and psychological thrillers with many written by today's best-selling authors.

Try **Essential Romance** featuring compelling romance stories with many written by today's best-selling authors.

Or TRY BOTH!

Thank you again for participating in our "One Minute" Survey. It really takes just a minute (or less) to complete the survey… and your free books and gifts will be well worth it!

Sincerely,

Pam Powers

Pam Powers
for Reader Service

"One Minute" Survey

GET YOUR FREE BOOKS AND FREE GIFTS!

✓ Complete this Survey   ✓ Return this survey

1 Do you try to find time to read every day?
☐ YES   ☐ NO

2 Do you prefer stories with happy endings?
☐ YES   ☐ NO

3 Do you enjoy having books delivered to your home?
☐ YES   ☐ NO

4 Do you share your favorite books with friends?
☐ YES   ☐ NO

YES! I have completed the above "One Minute" Survey. Please send me my Free Books and Free Mystery Gifts (worth over $20 retail). I understand that I am under no obligation to buy anything, as explained on the back of this card.

☐ I prefer
Essential Suspense
191/391 MDL GNT4

☐ I prefer
Essential Romance
194/394 MDL GNT4

☐ I prefer BOTH
191/391 & 194/394
MDL GNUG

FIRST NAME   LAST NAME

ADDRESS

APT.#   CITY

STATE/PROV.   ZIP/POSTAL CODE

BUSINESS REPLY MAIL
FIRST-CLASS MAIL   PERMIT NO. 717   BUFFALO, NY

POSTAGE WILL BE PAID BY ADDRESSEE

READER SERVICE
PO BOX 1341
BUFFALO NY 14240-8571

NO POSTAGE
NECESSARY
IF MAILED
IN THE
UNITED STATES

the cabin whenever they like. They've decided that if I like the mountains so much, there must be something special about them. Our next album is going to be built around a mountain theme."

"Wow." Elliot sighed. "Wait'll I tell the guys."

"You and the guys can be in the video," Amanda promised. "We'll find some way to fit you into a scene or two." She studied Harry. "We'll put Harry in, too."

"Oh, no, you won't!" he said. "I'll run away from home first."

"If you do, we'll starve to death." Amanda sighed. "I can't do cakes and roasts. We'll have to live on potatoes and fried eggs."

"Then you just make a movie star out of old Elliot and I'll stick around," he promised.

"Okay," Amanda said, "but what a loss to women everywhere. You'd have been super, Harry."

He grinned and went back to the kitchen to cook. Elliot eventually wandered off, too, and Quinn took Amanda into the study and closed the door.

They sat together in his big leather armchair, listening to the crackling of the fire in the potbellied stove.

"Remember the last time we were in here together?" he asked lazily between kisses.

"Indeed, I do," she murmured with a smile against his throat. "We almost didn't stop in time."

"I'm glad we did." He linked her fingers with his. "We had a very special first time. A real wedding night. That's marriage the way it was meant to be; a feast of first times."

She touched his cheek lightly and searched his dark eyes. "I'm glad we waited, too. I wanted so much to go to my husband untouched. I just want you to know that it was worth the wait. I love you, really love you, you know?" She sighed shakily. "That made it much more than my first intimate experience."

He brought his mouth down gently on hers. "I felt just that way about it," he breathed against her lips. "I never asked if you wanted me to use anything...?"

"So I wouldn't get pregnant?" She smiled gently. "I love kids."

"So do I." He eased back and pulled her cheek onto his chest, smoothing her long, soft hair as he smiled down into her eyes. "I never dreamed I'd find anyone like you. I'd given up on women. On life, too, I guess. I've been bitter and alone for such a long time, Amanda. I feel like I was just feverish and dreaming it all."

"You aren't dreaming." She pulled him closer to her and kissed him with warm, slow passion. "We're married and I'm going to love you for the rest of my life, body and soul. So don't get any ideas about trying to get away. I've caught you fair and square and you're all mine."

He chuckled. "Really? If you've caught me, what are you going to do with me?"

"Have I got an answer for that," she whispered with a sultry smile. "You did lock the door, didn't you?" she murmured, her voice husky as she lifted and turned so that she was facing him, her knees beside him on the chair. His heart began to race violently.

"Yes, I locked the door. What are you... Amanda!"

She smiled against his mouth while her hands worked at fastenings. "That's my name, all right," she whispered. She nipped his lower lip gently and laughed delightedly when she felt him helping her. "Life is short. We'd better start living it right now."

"I couldn't possibly agree more," he whispered back, and his husky laugh mingled with hers in the tense silence of the room.

Beside them, the burning wood crackled and popped in the stove while the snow began to fall again outside the window. Amanda had started it, but almost immediately Quinn took control and she gave in with a warm laugh. She knew already that things were done Sutton's way around Ricochet. And this time, she didn't really mind at all.

* * * * *

Books by Maisey Yates

Gold Valley

Smooth-Talking Cowboy
Untamed Cowboy
Good Time Cowboy
A Tall, Dark Cowboy Christmas
Unbroken Cowboy
Cowboy to the Core
Lone Wolf Cowboy
Cowboy Christmas Redemption

Copper Ridge

Part Time Cowboy
Brokedown Cowboy
Bad News Cowboy
The Cowboy Way
One Night Charmer
Tough Luck Hero
Last Chance Rebel
Slow Burn Cowboy
Down Home Cowboy
Wild Ride Cowboy
Christmastime Cowboy

Visit her Author Profile page on Harlequin.com,
or maiseyyates.com, for more titles!

THE RANCHER'S BABY

Maisey Yates

CHAPTER ONE

MY FAKE EX-HUSBAND died at sea and all I got was this stupid letter.

That was Selena Jacobs's very dark thought as she stood in the oppressive funeral home clutching said letter so tightly she was wearing a thumbprint into the envelope.

She supposed that her initial thought wasn't true—strictly speaking. The letter proclaimed she was the heir to Will's vast estate.

It was just that there were four other women at the funeral who had been promised the exact same thing. And Selena couldn't fathom why Will would have made her the beneficiary of anything, except maybe that hideous bearskin rug he'd gotten from his grandfather that he'd had in his dorm at school. The one she'd hated because the sightless glass eyes had creeped her out.

Yeah, that she would have believed Will had left her.

His entire estate, not so much.

But then, she was still having trouble believing Will was dead. It seemed impossible. He had always been so…so *much.* Of everything. So much energy. So much light. So much of a pain in the ass sometimes. It seemed impossible that a solemn little urn could contain everything Will Sanders had been. And yet there it was.

Though she supposed that Will wasn't entirely contained in the urn. Will, and the general fallout of his life—good and bad—was contained here in this room.

There were…well, there were a lot of women standing around looking bereft, each one of them holding letters identical to hers. Their feelings on the contents of the letters were different than hers. They must be. They didn't all run multimillion-dollar corporations.

Selena's muted reaction to her supposed inheritance was in some part due to the fact that she doubted the authenticity of the letter. But the other part was because she simply didn't need the money. Not at this point in her life.

These other women…

Well, she didn't really know. One of them was holding a chubby toddler, her expression blank. There was another in a sedate dress that flowed gently over what looked to be a burgeoning baby bump. Will had been too charming for his own good, it seemed.

Selena shuddered.

She didn't know the nature of those women's relationships to Will, but she had her suspicions. And the very idea of being left in a similar situation made her skin crawl.

There were reasons she kept men at arm's length. The vulnerability of being left pregnant was one of them. A very compelling one.

As for the other reasons? Well, every woman in this room was a living, breathing affirmation of Selena's life choices.

Heartbroken wives, ex-wives and baby mamas.

Selena might technically be an ex-wife, but she wasn't one in the traditional sense. And she wasn't heartbroken. She was hurt. She was grieving. And she was full of regret. She wished more than anything that she and Will had patched up their friendship.

But, of course, she had imagined that there was plenty of time to revive a friendship they'd left behind in college.

There hadn't been plenty of time. Will didn't have any more time.

Grief clutched at her heart and she swallowed hard, turning away from the urn to face the entry door at the back of the room.

The next visitor to walk in made her already battered heart jolt with shocked recognition.

Knox McCoy.

She really hadn't expected him to come. He had been pretty scarce for the past couple of years, and she honestly couldn't blame him. When he had texted her the other day, he'd said he wouldn't be attending the funeral, and he hadn't needed to say why.

She suspected he hadn't been to one since the one for his daughter, Eleanor.

She tried to quell the nerves fluttering in her stomach as Knox walked deeper into the room, his gray eyes locking with hers. She had known the man for more than a decade. She had made her decisions regarding him, and he…

Well, he had never felt the way about her that she did about him.

He looked as gorgeous as ever. His broad shoulders, chest and trim waist outlined perfectly in the gray custom-made suit with matching charcoal tie. His brown hair was pushed back off his forehead, longer than he used to keep it. He was also sporting a beard, which was not typical of him. He had deep grooves between his dark brows, lines worn into his handsome face by the pain of the past few years.

She wanted to go to him. She wanted to press her thumb right there at those worry lines and smooth them out. Just the thought of touching him made her feel restless. Hot.

And really, really, she needed not to be having a full-blown Knox episode at her ex-husband's funeral.

Regardless of the real nature of her relationship with Will, her reaction to Knox was inappropriate. Beyond inappropriate.

"How are you doing?" he asked, his expression full of concern.

When he made that face his eyebrows locked together and the grooves deepened.

"Oh, I've been better," she said honestly.

A lopsided smile curved the corner of his mouth upward and he reached out, his thumb brushing over her cheek. His skin was rough, his hands those of a rancher. A working man. His wealth came from the chain of upscale grocery stores he owned, but his passion was in working the land at his ranch in Wyoming.

Her gaze met his, and the blank sadness she saw in his eyes made her stomach feel hollow.

She wondered if the ranch still held his passion. She wondered if anything did anymore.

"Me, too," he said, his voice rough.

"Will is such an inconsiderate ass," she said, her voice trembling. "Leave it to him to go and die like this."

"Yeah," Knox agreed. "His timing is pretty terrible. Plus, you know he just wanted the attention."

She laughed, and as the laugh escaped her lips, a tear slid down her cheek.

She'd met Knox at Harvard. From completely different backgrounds—his small-town Texan childhood worlds away from her high-society East Coast life—they had bonded quickly. And then… Then her grandfather had died, which had ripped her heart square out of her chest. He had been the only person in her family who had ever loved her. Who had ever instilled hope in her for the future.

And with his death had come the trust fund. A trust fund she could only access when she was twenty-five. Or married.

The idea of asking Knox to marry her had been… Well, it had been unthinkable. For a whole host of reasons. She hadn't wanted to get married, not for real. And her feelings for Knox had been real. Or at least, she had known perfectly well they were on the verge of being real, and she'd needed desperately for them to stay manageable. For him to stay a friend.

Then their friend Will had seen her crying one afternoon and she'd explained everything. He had offered himself as her solution. She hadn't been in a position to say no.

Control of her money had provided freedom from her father. It had given her the ability to complete her education on her own terms. It had also ended up ruining her friendship with Will. In the meantime, Knox had met someone else. Someone he eventually married.

She blinked, bringing herself firmly back to the present. There was no point thinking about all of that. She didn't. Not often. Her friendship with Knox had survived college, and they had remained close in spite of the fact that they were both busy with their respective careers.

It was Will. Whenever Will was added to the mix she couldn't help but think of those years. Of that one stupid, reckless decision that had ended up doing a lot of damage in the end.

For some reason, she suddenly felt hollow and weak. She wobbled slightly, and Knox reached toward her as if he would touch her again. She wasn't sure that would be as fortifying as he thought it might be.

But then the doors to the funeral home opened again and she looked up at the same time Knox looked over his shoulder.

And the world stopped.

Because the person who walked through the door was the person who was meant to be in that urn.

It was Will Sanders, and he was very much alive.

Then the world really did start to spin, and Selena didn't know how to stand upright in it.

That was how she found herself crashing to the floor, and then everything was dark.

FUCKING WILL. OF course he wasn't actually dead.

That was Knox's prevailing thought as he dropped to his knees, wrapping his arm around Selena and pulling her into his lap.

No one was paying attention to one passed-out woman, because they were a hell of a lot more concerned with the walking corpse who had just appeared at his own funeral.

It was clear Will was just as shocked as everyone else.

Except for maybe Selena.

Had she loved the bastard that much? It had been more than ten years since Will and Selena had been married, and Selena rarely talked about Will, but Knox supposed he should know as well as anyone that sometimes not talking about something indicated you thought about it a whole hell of a lot.

That it mattered much more than the things that rolled off your tongue with routine frequency.

As he watched the entire room erupt in shock, Knox was filled with one dark thought.

At the last funeral he had attended he would have given everything he owned for the little body in the casket to come walking into the room. Would've given anything to wake up and find it all a nightmare.

He would have even traded places with his daughter. Would have buried himself six feet down if it would have meant Eleanor would come back.

But of course that hadn't happened. He was living a fucking soap opera at the wrong damned moment.

He looked down at Selena's gray face and cupped her cheek, patting it slightly, doing his best to revive her. He didn't know what you were supposed to do when a woman fainted. And God knew caregiving was not his strong suit.

His ex-wife would be the first to testify to that.

Selena's skin felt clammy, a light sweat beading on her brow. He wasn't used to seeing his tough-as-nails friend anything but self-assured. Even when things were terrible, she usually did what she had done only a few moments ago. She made a joke. She stood strong.

When Eleanor had died Selena had stood with him until he couldn't stand, and then she had sat with him. She had been there for him through all of that.

Apparently, ex-husbands returning from the beyond were her breaking point.

"Come on, Selena," he murmured, brushing some of her black hair out of her face. "You can wake up now. You've done a damn decent job of stealing his thunder. Anything else is just showing off at this point."

Her sooty eyelashes fluttered, and her eyes opened, her whiskey-colored gaze foggy. "What happened?"

He looked around the room, at the commotion stirring around them. "It seems Will has come back from the dead."

CHAPTER TWO

WILL WASN'T DEAD.

Selena kept playing that thought over and over in her mind as Knox drove them down the highway.

She wasn't entirely clear on what had happened to her car, or why Knox was driving her. Or what she was going to do with her car later. She had been too consumed with putting one foot in front of the other while Knox led her from the funeral home, safely ensconced her in his rental car and began to take them… Well, she didn't know where.

She slid her hand around the back of her neck, beneath her hair, her skin damp and hot against her palm. She felt awful. She felt… Well, like she had passed out on the floor of a funeral home.

"Where are we going?" she asked.

"To your place."

"You don't know where I live," she mumbled, her lips numb.

"I do."

"No, you don't, Knox. I've moved since the last time you came to visit."

"I looked you up."

Knox hadn't come back to Royal since his divorce. She couldn't blame him. There was a lot of bad wrapped up in Royal for him. Seeing as this was where he'd lived with his family most of the year when he'd been married.

"I'm not listed." She attempted to make the words sound crisp.

"You know me better than that, honey," he said, that slow Texas drawl winding itself through her veins and turning her blood into fire. "I don't need a phone book to find someone."

"Obviously, Knox. No one has used a phone book since 2004. But I meant it's not like you can just look up my address on the internet."

"Figure of speech, Selena. Also, I have connections. Resources."

She made a disgusted sound and pressed her forehead against the window. It wasn't cold enough.

"You sent me a Christmas card," he said, his tone maddeningly steady. "I added your address to my contacts."

"Well," she said. "Damn my manners. Apparently they've made me traceable."

"Not very stealthy."

"*And* you're rude," she said, ignoring him. "Because you did not send me a Christmas card back."

"I had my secretary send you something."

"What did she send me?" Selena asked.

"It was either a gold watch or a glass owl figurine," he said.

"What did she do, send you links to two different things, and then you said choose either one?"

"Yes."

"That doesn't count as a present, Knox. And it certainly doesn't equal my very personal Christmas card."

"You didn't have an assistant send the card?" he asked, sounding incredulous.

"I did not. I addressed it myself, painstakingly by hand while I was eating a TV dinner."

"A TV dinner?" he asked, chuckling. "That doesn't jibe with your healthy-lifestyle persona."

"It was a frozen dinner from Green Fair Pantry," she said pointedly, mentioning the organic fair-trade grocery store chain Knox owned. "If those aren't healthy, then you have some explaining to do yourself."

She was starting to feel a little bit more human, but along with that feeling came a dawning realization of the enormity of everything that had just happened.

"Will is alive," she said, just to confirm.

"It looks that way," Knox said, tightening his hold on the steering wheel. She did her best not to watch the way the muscles in his forearms shifted, did her best to ignore just how large his hands looked, how large *he* looked in this car that was clearly too small for him. One that he would never have driven in his real life.

Knox was much more of a pickup truck kind of man, no matter how much money he made. Little luxury vehicles were not his thing.

"I guess I don't get his bearskin rug, then," she said absently.

"What?"

"Don't you remember that appalling thing he used to have in his dorm room?"

Knox shot her a look out of the corner of his eye. "Not really. Hey, are you okay?"

"I am… I don't know. I mean, I guess I'm better than I was when I thought he was ashes in a jar." She cleared her throat. "I'm sorry. Are you okay, Knox? I realize this is probably the first—"

"I don't want to talk about that," he said, cutting her off. "We don't need to. I'm fine."

She didn't think he was. Her throat tightened, feeling scratchy. "Okay. Anyway, I'm fine, too. My relationship with Will… You know."

Except he didn't. Nobody did. Everyone *thought* they did, but everyone was wrong. Unless, of course, Will had ever talked to anyone about the truth of their marriage, but somehow she doubted it.

"How long had it been since you two had spoken?" Knox asked.

"A long damn time. I don't believe all the things Rich said to me before the divorce. Not anymore. He was toxic."

As little as she tried to think about her short, convenient marriage to Will and what had resulted after, she tried to think about Will's friend Rich Lowell even less. Though she had heard through that reliable Royal grapevine that he and Will had remained friends. It made her wonder why Rich wasn't here.

Rich had been part of their group of friends, though he had always been somewhat on the periphery, and he had been…strange, as far as Selena was concerned. He had liked Will, so much that it had been concerning. And when Will had married Selena, Rich's interest had wandered onto her.

He had never done anything terribly inappropriate, but the increased attention from him had made her uneasy.

But then… Well, he had been in their apartment one night when she'd gotten home from class. He'd produced evidence that Will was after her trust fund—the trust fund that had led to their marriage in the first place. And she needed that money. She needed it so she would never be at her father's mercy again. The trust fund had been everything to her, and Will had said he was marrying her just to help her. She'd trusted him.

Rich had been full of some weird, intense energy Selena hadn't been able to place at the time. Now that she had some distance and a more adult understanding, she felt like maybe Rich had been attracted to her. But more than a simple attraction…he'd been obsessed with Will. It almost seemed, in hindsight, as if he'd been attracted to her *because* he thought Will had her.

And what Rich had said that night… Well, it had just been a lot easier to believe than Will's claim that he wanted to help her because they were friends. Trust had never been easy for her. Will was kind, and that was something she'd wanted. Not because she was attracted to him, but because she had genuinely wanted him to be a real friend. After a life of being thoroughly mistreated by her father, hoping for true friendship was scary.

Selena had spent most of her childhood bracing herself for the punch. Whether emotional or physical. It was much easier to believe she was being tricked than to believe Will was everything he appeared to be.

She and Will had fought. And then they had barely limped to the finish line of the marriage. They'd waited until the money was in her account, and then they'd divorced.

And their friendship had never been the same.

She had never apologized to him. Grief and regret stabbed her before she remembered—Will wasn't actually dead.

That means you can apologize to him. It means you can fix your friendship.

She needed to. The woman she was now would never have jumped to a conclusion like that, at least not without trying to get to the bottom of it.

But back then, Selena had been half-feral. Honed into a sharp, mean creature from years of being in survival mode.

The way Knox had stuck by her all these years, the kind of friendship he had demonstrated… It had been a huge part of her learning to trust. Learning to believe men could actually be good.

Her ability to trust hadn't changed her stance on love and marriage. And she fought against any encroaching thoughts that conflicted with that stance.

It didn't really matter that Knox sometimes made her think differently about love and marriage. He had married someone else. And she had married someone else. She had married someone else first, in point of fact. It was just that…

It didn't matter.

"I know this dredges up a lot of ancient history," Knox said, turning the car off the highway and onto the narrow two-lane road that would take them out to her new cabin. Now that she had the freedom to work remotely most of the time—her skin-care company was so successful she'd hired other people to do the parts that consumed too much time—she had decided to get outside city limits.

Had decided it was time for her to actually make herself a home, instead of living in a holding pattern. Existing solely to build her empire, to increase her net worth.

Nothing had ever felt like home until this place. Everything after college had just been temporary. Before that, it had been a war zone.

This cabin was her refuge. And it was *hers*.

Nestled in the woods, surrounded by sweetgrass and trees, and a river running next to her front porch.

Of course, it wasn't quite as grand as Knox's spread in Jackson Hole, but then, very few places were.

Besides, grandness wasn't the point. This cabin wasn't for show. Wasn't to impress anyone else. It was just to make her happy. And few things in her life had existed for that reason up to this point.

Having achieved some happiness made her long for other things, though. Things she was mostly inured against—like wanting someone to share her life with.

She gritted her teeth, looking resolutely away from Knox as that thought invaded her brain.

"Which is now a little bit annoying," she pointed out. "He's not even dead, and I had to go through all that grief, plus, you know…"

"Thinking about your marriage?"

She snapped her mouth shut, debating how to respond. It was true enough. She had been thinking a lot about her marriage. Not that it had been an actual, physical marriage. More like roommates with official paperwork. "Yes," she said finally.

"Divorce is hell," he said, his voice turning to gravel. "Believe me. I know."

Guilt twisted her stomach. He thought they shared this common bond. The loss of a marriage. In reality, their situations weren't even close to being the same.

"Will and I were only married for a year," she commented. "It's not really the same as you and Cassandra. The two of you were together for twelve years and…"

"I told you, I don't want to talk about it."

Blessedly, distraction came in the form of the left turn that took them off the paved road and onto the gravel road that took them to her cabin.

"Why don't you get this paved?" he asked.

"I like it," she said.

"Why?"

That was a complicated question, with a complicated answer. But he was her friend and she was glad to be off the topic of marriages, so she figured she would take a stab at it. "Because it's nothing like the driveway that we had when I was growing up. Which was smooth and paved and circular, and led up to the most ridiculous brick monstrosity."

"So this is like inverse nostalgia?"

"Yes."

He lifted a shoulder. "I understand that better than you might think."

He pulled up to the front of the cabin and she stayed resolutely in her seat until he rounded to her side and opened the door for her. Then she blinked, looking up into the sun, at the way his broad shoulders blotted it out. "What about my car?" she asked.

"I'm going to have someone bring it. Don't worry."

"I could go get it," she said.

"I have a feeling it's best if you lie low for a little bit."

"Why would I do that?"

"Well," he said. "Your ex-husband just came back from the dead, and both of you cause quite a bit of media interest. You were named as beneficiary of his estate along with four other women, and that's a lot of money."

"But Will isn't dead, and I don't care about his money. I have my own."

"Very few people are going to believe that, Selena," Knox said, his tone grave. "Most people don't acknowledge the concept of having enough money. They only understand wanting more."

"What are you saying? That I'm…in danger?"

"I don't know. But we don't know what's going on with Will, and you were brought into this. You're a target, for all we know. Someone is in an urn, and you have a letter that brought you here."

"You're jumping to conclusions, Knox."

"Maybe," he said, "but I swear to God, Selena, I'd rather have you safe than end up in an urn. That, I couldn't deal with."

She looked at the deep intensity in his expression. "I'll be safe."

"You need to lie low for a while."

"What does that mean? What am I supposed to do?"

Knox shrugged, the casual gesture at odds with the steely determination in his gray eyes. "I figured I would keep you company."

CHAPTER THREE

Selena looked less than thrilled by the prospect of sticking close to home while the situation with Will got sorted out.

Knox didn't particularly care whether or not Selena was thrilled. He wanted her safe. As far as he was concerned, this was some shady shit, and until it was resolved, he didn't want any of it getting near her.

All of it was weird. The five women who had been presented with nearly identical letters telling them that they had inherited Will's estate, and then Will not actually being dead. The fact that someone else had been living Will's life.

Maybe none of it would touch Selena. But there was nothing half so pressing in Knox's life as his best friend's safety.

His business did not require him to micromanage it. That was the perk of making billions, as far as he was concerned. You didn't have to be in an office all the damned time if it didn't suit you.

Plus, it was all…pointless.

He shook off the hollow feeling of his chest caving in on itself and turned his focus back to Selena.

"I don't need you to stay here with me," she said, all but scampering across the lawn and to her porch.

"I need to stay here with you," he returned. He was

more than happy to make it about him. Because he knew she wouldn't be able to resist. She was worried about him. She didn't need to be. But she was. And if he played into that, then she would give him whatever he wanted.

"But it's a waste of your time," she pointed out, digging in her purse for her keys, pulling them out and jamming one of them in the lock.

"Maybe," he said. "But I swear to God, Selena, if I have to go to a funeral with a big picture of *you* up at the front of the room..."

"No one has threatened me," she said, turning the key and pushing the door open.

"And I'd rather not wait and see if someone does."

"You're being hypervigilant," she returned.

"Yes," he said. "I am." He gritted his teeth. "Some things you can't control, Selena. Some bad stuff you can't stop. But I'm not going to decide everything is fine here and risk losing you just because I went home earlier than I should have."

She looked up at him, the stubborn light in her eyes fading. "Okay. If you need to do this, that's fine."

Selena walked into the front entrance of the cabin and threw her purse down on an entryway table. Typical Selena. There was a hook right above the table, but she didn't hang the purse up. No. That extra step would be considered a waste of time in her estimation. Never mind that her disorganization often meant she spent extra time looking for things.

He looked around the spacious, bright room. It was clean. Surprisingly so.

"This place is... It's nice. Spotless."

"I have a housekeeper," she said, turning to face him,

crossing her arms beneath her breasts and offering up a lopsided smile.

For a moment, just a moment, his eyes dipped down to examine those breasts. His gut tightened and he resolutely turned his focus back to her eyes. Selena was a woman. He had known that for a long time. But she wasn't a woman whose breasts concerned him. She never had been.

When they had met in college he had thought she was beautiful, sure. A man would have to be blind not to see that. But she had also been brittle. Skittish and damaged. And it had taken work on his part to forge a friendship with her.

Once he had become her friend, he had never wanted to do anything to compromise that bond. And if he had been a little jealous of Will Sanders somehow convincing her that marriage was worth the risk, Knox had never indulged that jealousy.

Then Will had hurt her, devastated her, divorced her. And after that, Selena had made her feelings about relationships pretty clear. Anyway, at that point, he had been serious about Cassandra, and then they had gotten married.

His friendship with Selena outlasted both of their marriages, and had proved that the decision he'd made back in college, to not examine her breasts, had been a solid one.

One he was going to hold to.

"Well, thank God for the housekeeper," he said, his tone dry. "Living all the way out here by yourself, if you didn't have someone taking care of you you'd be liable to die beneath a pile of your own clothes."

She huffed. "You don't know me, Knox."

"Oh, honey," he said, "I do."

A long, slow moment stretched between them and her olive skin was suddenly suffused with color. It probably wasn't nice of him to tease her about her propensity toward messiness. "Well," she said, her tone stiff. "I do have a guest room. And I suppose it would be unkind of me to send you packing back to Wyoming on your first night here in Royal."

"Downright mean," he said, schooling his expression into one of pure innocence. As much as he could manage.

It occurred to him then that the two of them hadn't really spent much time together in the past couple of years. And they hadn't spent time alone together in the past decade. He had been married to another woman, and even though his friendship with Selena had been platonic, and Cassandra had never expressed any jealousy toward her, it would have been stretching things a bit for him to spend the night at her place with no one else around.

"Well," she said, tossing her glossy black hair over her shoulder. "I am a little mean."

"Are you?"

She smiled broadly, the expression somewhere between a grin and a snarl. "It has been said."

"By who?" he asked, feeling instantly protective of her. She had always brought that out in him. Even though now it felt like a joke, that he could feel protective of anyone. He hadn't managed to protect the most important people in his life.

"I wasn't thinking of a particular incident," she responded, wandering toward the kitchen, kicking her shoes off as she went, leaving them right where she stepped out of them, like fuchsia afterthoughts.

"Did Will say you were mean?"

She turned to face him, cocking one dark brow. "Will didn't have strong feelings for me one way or the other, Knox. Certainly not in the time since the divorce." She began to bustle around the kitchen, and he leaned against the island, placing his hand on the high-gloss marble countertop, watching as she worked with efficiency, getting mugs and heating water. She was making tea, and she wasn't even asking him if he wanted any. She would simply present him with some. And he wouldn't drink it, because he didn't like tea.

A pretty familiar routine for the two of them.

"He put you pretty firmly off of marriage," Knox pointed out, "so I would say he's also not completely blameless."

"You're not supposed to speak ill of the dead. Or the undead, in Will's case."

He drummed his fingers on the counter. "You know, that does present an interesting question."

"What question is that?"

"Who died?" he asked.

"What do you mean?"

"There were ashes in that urn. Obviously they weren't Will's. But if he's not dead, then who is?"

Selena frowned. "Maybe no one's dead. Maybe it's ashes from a campfire."

"Why would someone go to all that trouble? Why would somebody go to that much trouble to fake Will's death? Or to fake anyone's death? Again, I think this has something to do with those letters. With all of the women in his life being made beneficiaries of his estate. And this is why I'm not leaving you here by yourself."

"Because you're a high-handed, difficult, surly, obnoxious…"

"Are you finished?"

"Just a second," she said, taking her kettle off the stove and pouring hot water into two of the mugs on the counter. "Irritating, overbearing…"

"Wealthy, handsome, incredibly generous."

"Yes, it's true," she said. "But I prefer beautiful to handsome. I mean, I assume you were offering up descriptions of me."

She shoved a mug in his direction, smiling brilliantly. He did not tell her he didn't want any. He did not remind her that he had told her at least fifteen times over the years that he did not drink tea. Instead, he curled his fingers around the mug and pulled it close, knowing she wouldn't realize he wasn't having any.

It was just one of her charming quirks. The fact that she could be totally oblivious to what was happening around her. Cast-off shoes in the middle of her floor were symptoms of it. It wasn't that Selena was an airhead; she was incredibly insightful, actually. It was just that her head seemed to continually be full of thoughts about what was next. Sometimes, all that thinking made it hard to keep her rooted in the present.

She rested her elbows on the counter, then placed her chin in her palms, looking suddenly much younger than she had only a moment ago. Reminding him of the girl he had known in college.

And along with that memory came an old urge. To reach out, to brush her hair out of her face, to trace the line of her lower lip with the edge of his thumb. To take a chance with all of her spiky indignation and press his mouth against hers.

Instead, he lifted his mug to his lips and took a long drink, the hot water and bitterly acidic tea burning his throat as he swallowed.

He really, really didn't like tea.

"You know," she said, tapping the side of her mug, straightening. "I do have a few projects you could work on around here. If you're going to stay with me."

"You're putting me to work?"

"Yes. If you're going to stay with me, you need to earn your keep."

"I'm earning my keep by guarding you."

"From a threat you don't even know exists."

"I know a few things," he said, holding up his hand and counting off each thing with his fingers. "I know someone is dead. I know you are mysteriously named as a beneficiary of a lot of money, as are a bunch of other women."

"And one assumes that we are no longer going to inherit any money since Will isn't dead."

"But someone wanted us all to think that he was. Hell, maybe somebody wanted him to be dead."

"Are you a private detective now? The high-end health-food grocery-chain business not working out for you?"

"It's working out for me very well, actually. Which you know. And don't change the subject."

A smile tugged at the corner of her mouth.

He was genuinely concerned about her well-being; he wasn't making that up. But there was something else, too. Something holding him here. Or maybe it was just something keeping him from going back to

Wyoming. He had avoided Royal, and Texas altogether, since his divorce. Had avoided going anywhere that reminded him of his former life. He'd owned the ranch in Jackson Hole for over a decade, but he, Cassandra and Eleanor hadn't spent as much time there as they had here.

Still, for some reason, now that he was back, the idea of returning to that gigantic ranch house in Wyoming to rattle around all by himself didn't seem appealing.

There was a reason he had gotten married. A reason he and Cassandra had started a family. It was what he had wanted. An answer to his lifetime of loneliness. To the deficit he had grown up with. He had wanted everything. A wife, children, money. All of those things that would keep him from feeling like he had back then.

But he had learned the hard way that children could be taken from you. That marriages crumbled. And that money didn't mean a damn thing in the end.

If he'd had a choice, if the universe would have asked him, he would have given up the money first.

Of course, he hadn't realized that until it was too late.

Not that there was any fixing it. Not that there had been a choice. Cancer didn't care if you were a billionaire.

It didn't care if a little girl was your entire world.

Now all he had was a big empty house. One that currently had an invitation to a charity event on the fridge. An invitation he just couldn't deal with right now.

He looked back up at Selena. Yeah, staying here for a few days was definitely more appealing than heading straight back to Jackson Hole.

"Okay," he said. "What projects did you have in mind?"

HE NEVER SAID he didn't like tea.

That was Selena's first thought when she got up the next morning and set about making coffee for Knox and herself. Selena found it singularly odd that he never refused the tea. She served it to him sometimes just to see if he would. But he never did. He just sat there holding it. Which was funny, because Knox was not a passive man. Far from it.

In fact, in college, he had been her role model for that reason. He was authoritative. He asked for what he wanted. He went for what he wanted. And Selena had wanted to remake herself in his mold. She'd found him endlessly fascinating.

Though she had to admit, as she bustled around the kitchen, he was just as fascinating now. But now she had a much firmer grasp on what she wanted. On what was possible.

She had felt a little weird about him staying with her at first, which was old baggage creeping in. Old feelings. That crush she'd had on him in college that had never had a hope in hell of going anywhere. Not because she thought it was impossible for him to desire her, but because she knew there was no future in it. And she needed Knox as a friend much more than she needed him as a…well…the alternative.

But then last night, as they had been standing in the kitchen, she had looked at him. Really looked at him. Those lines between his brows were so deep, and his eyes were so incredibly…changed. Physically, she supposed he kind of looked the same, and yet he didn't. He was reduced. And it was a terrible thing to see a man like him reduced. But she couldn't blame him.

What happened with Eleanor had been such a shock. Such a horrible, hideous shock.

One day, she had been a normal, healthy toddler, and then she had been lethargic. Right after that came the cancer diagnosis, and in only a couple of months she was gone.

The entire situation had been surreal and heartbreaking. For her. And Eleanor wasn't even her child. But her friend's pain had been so real, so raw... She had no idea how he had coped with it, and now she could see that he hadn't really. That he still was trying to cope.

He hadn't come back to Texas since Eleanor's death, and she had seen him only a couple of times. At the funeral. And then when she had come to Jackson Hole in the summer for a visit. Otherwise...it had all been texts and emails and quick phone conversations.

But now that he was back in Texas, he seemed to need to stay for a little while, and she was happy for him to think it was for her. Happy to be the scapegoat so he could work through whatever emotional thing he needed to work through. Knox, in the past, would have been enraged at the assessment that he needed to work through anything emotionally. He was such a stoic guy, always had been.

But she knew he wouldn't even pretend there wasn't lingering damage from the loss of his little girl. Selena had watched him break apart completely at Eleanor's funeral. They had never talked about it again. She didn't think they ever would. But then, she supposed they didn't need to. They had shared the experience. That moment when he couldn't be strong anymore. When there was no child to be strong for, and when his wife had been off with her family, and there had simply been no reason for him to remain standing upright. Selena had been there for that moment.

If all the years of friendship hadn't bonded them, that moment would have done it all on its own.

Just thinking of it made her chest ache, and she shook off the feeling, going over to the coffee maker to pour herself a cup.

She wondered if Knox was still sleeping. He was going to be mad if he missed prime caffeination time.

She wandered out of the kitchen and into the living room just as the door to the guest bedroom opened and Knox walked out, pulling his T-shirt over his head—but not quickly enough. She caught a flash of muscled, tanned skin and…chest hair. Oh, the chest hair. Why was that compelling enough to stop her in her tracks? She didn't even have a moment to question it. She was too caught up. Too beset by the sight.

Genuinely. She was completely immobilized by the sight of her best friend's muscles.

It wasn't like she had never seen Knox shirtless before. But it had been a long time. And the last time, he had most definitely been married.

Not that she had forgotten he was hot when he was married to Cassandra. It was just that…he had been a married man. And that meant something to Selena. Because it meant something to him.

It had been a barrier, an insurmountable one, even bigger than that whole long-term friendship thing. And now it wasn't there. It just wasn't. He was walking out of the guest bedroom looking sleep rumpled and entirely too lickable. And there was just…nothing stopping them from doing what men and women did.

She'd had a million excuses for *not* doing that. For a

long time. She didn't want to risk entanglements, didn't want to compromise her focus. Didn't want to risk pregnancy. Didn't have time for a relationship.

But she was in a place where those things were less of a concern. This house was symbolic of that change in her life. She was making a home. And making a home made her want to fill it. With art, with warmth, with knickknacks that spoke to her. With people.

She wondered, then. What it would be like to actually live with a man? To have one in her life? In her home? In her bed?

And just like that she was fantasizing about Knox in her bed. That body she had caught a glimpse of relaxing beneath her emerald green bedspread, his hands clasped behind his head, a satisfied smile on his face...

She sucked in a sharp breath and tried to get a hold of herself. "Coffee is ready," she said, grinning broadly, not feeling the grin at all.

"Good," he said, his voice rough from sleep.

It struck her then, just what an intimate thing that was. To hear someone's voice after they had been sleeping.

"Right this...way," she said, awkwardly beating a path into the kitchen, turning away from him quickly enough that she sloshed coffee over the edge of her cup.

"You have food for breakfast?" he asked, that voice persistently gravelly and interesting, and much less like her familiar friend's than she would like it to be. She needed some kind of familiarity to latch on to, something to blot out the vision of his muscles. But he wasn't giving her anything.

Jerk.

"No," she said, keeping her voice cheery. "I have coffee and spite for breakfast."

"Well, that's not going to work for me."

"I'm not sure what to tell you," she said, flinging open one of her cabinets and revealing her collection of cereal and biscotti. "Of course I have food for breakfast."

"Bacon? Eggs?"

"Do I look like a diner to you?" she asked.

"Not you personally. But I was hoping that your house might have more diner-like qualities."

"No," she said, opening up the fridge and rummaging around. "Well, what do you know? I *do* have eggs. And bacon. I get a delivery of groceries every week. From a certain grocery store."

He smiled, a lopsided grin that did something to her stomach. Something she was going to ignore and call hunger, because they were talking about bacon, and being hungry for bacon was much more palatable than being hungry for your best friend.

"I'll cook," he said.

"Oh no," she said, getting the package of bacon out of the fridge and handing it to Knox before bending back down and grabbing the carton of eggs and placing that in his other hand. "You don't have to cook."

"Why do I get the feeling that I really do have to cook?"

She shrugged. "It depends on whether you want bacon and eggs."

"Do you not know how to cook?"

"I know how to cook," she said. "But the odds of me actually cooking when I only have half of a cup of coffee in my system are basically none. Usually, I prefer to have sweets for breakfast. Hence, biscotti and breakfast cereals. However, I will sometimes eat bacon and eggs for dinner. Or I will eat bacon and eggs for breakfast if a handsome man fixes them for me."

He lifted a brow. "Oh, I see. So you have this in your fridge for when a man spends the night."

"Obviously. Since a man did just spend the night." Her face flushed. She knew exactly what he was imagining. And really, he had no idea.

That was not why she had the bacon and eggs. She had the bacon and eggs because sometimes she liked an easy dinner. But she didn't really mind if Knox thought she had more of a love life than she actually did.

Of course, now they were thinking about that kind of thing at the same time. Which was…weird. And possibly responsible for the strange electric current arcing between them.

"I'll cook," he said, breaking that arc and moving to the stove, getting out pans and bowls, cracking eggs with an efficiency she admired.

"Do you have an assignment list for me?" he asked, picking up the bowl and whisking the eggs inside.

Why was that sexy? What was happening? His broad shoulders and chest, those intensely muscled forearms, somehow seeming all the more masculine when he was scrambling eggs, of all things.

There was something about the very domestic action, and she couldn't figure out what it was. Maybe it was the contrast between masculinity and domesticity. Or maybe it was just because there had never been a man in her kitchen making breakfast.

She tried to look blasé, as though men made her breakfast every other weekend. After debauchery. Lots and lots of debauchery. She had a feeling she wasn't quite managing blasé, so she just took a sip of her coffee and stared at the white star that hung on her back wall, her homage to the Lone Star State. And currently, her salvation.

"Assignment list," she said, slamming her hands down on the countertop, breaking her reverie. She owed that star a thank-you for restoring her sanity. She'd just needed a moment of not looking at Knox. "Well, I want new hardware on those cabinets. The people who lived here before me had a few things that weren't really to my taste. That is one of them. Also, there are some things in an outbuilding the previous inhabitants left, and I want them moved out. Oh, and I want to get rid of the ceiling fan in the living room."

"I hope you're planning on paying me for this," he said, dumping the eggs into the pan, a sizzling sound filling the room.

"Nope," she said, lifting her coffee mug to her lips.

Knox finished cooking, and somehow Selena managed not to swoon. So, that was good.

They didn't bother to go into her dining room. Instead they sat at the tall chairs around the island, and Selena looked down at her breakfast resolutely.

"Are you okay?"

"What?" She looked up, her eyes clashing with Knox's. "You keep asking me that."

"Because you keep acting like you might not be."

"Are you okay?"

"I'm alive," he responded. "As to being okay…that's not really part of my five-year plan."

"What's your five-year plan?"

"Not drink myself into a stupor. Keep my business

running, because at some point I probably will be glad I still have it. That's about it."

"Well," she said softly, "you can add replacing my kitchen hardware to your five-year plan. But I would prefer it be on this side of it, rather than the back end."

He laughed, and she found that incredibly gratifying. Without thinking, she reached out and brushed her fingertips against his cheek, against his beard. She drew back quickly, wishing the impression of that touch would fade away. It didn't.

"Yes?" he asked.

"Are you keeping the beard?"

"It's not really a fashion statement. It's more evidence of personal neglect."

"Well, you haven't neglected your whole body," she said, thinking of that earlier flash of muscle. She immediately regretted her words. She regretted them more than she did touching his beard. And beard-touching was pretty damned inappropriate between friends. At least, she was pretty certain it was.

He lifted a brow and took a bite of bacon. "Elaborate."

"I'm just saying. You're in good shape, Knox. I noticed."

"Okay," he said slowly, setting the bacon down. His gray eyes were cool as they assessed her, but for some reason she felt heat pooling in her stomach.

Settle down.

Her body did not listen. It kept on being hot. And that heat bled into her cheeks. So she knew she was blushing brilliant rose for Knox's amusement.

"I'm just used to complimenting the men who make

me breakfast," she said, doing her best to keep her voice deadpan.

"I see."

"So."

"So," he responded. "There's nothing to do other than work," he said. "Lifting hay bales, fixing fences, basically throwing heavy things around on the ranch. Then going back into the house and working out in the gym. It's all I do."

Well, that explained a few things. "I imagine you could carve out about five minutes to shave."

"Would you prefer that I did?"

"I don't have an opinion on your facial hair."

"You seem to have an opinion on my facial hair."

"I really don't. I had observations about your facial hair, but that's an entirely different thing."

"Somehow, I don't think it is."

"Well, you're entitled to your opinion. About my opinion on your facial hair. Or my lack of one. But that doesn't make it fact."

He shook his head. "You know, if I had you visiting in Jackson Hole I probably wouldn't work out so excessively. Your chatter would keep me busy."

"Hey," she said. "I don't chatter. I'm making conversation." Except, it sounded a whole lot like chatter, even to herself.

"Okay."

She made a coughing sound and stood up, taking her mostly empty plate to the sink and then making her way back toward the living room, stepping over her discarded high heels from yesterday. She heard the sound of Knox's bare feet on the floor behind her. And suddenly, the fact that he had bare feet seemed intimate.

You really have been a virgin for too long.

She grimaced, even as she chastised herself. She hated that word. She hated even thinking it. It implied a kind of innocence she didn't possess. Also, it felt young. She was not particularly young. She had just been busy. Busy, and resolutely opposed to relationships.

Still, the whole virginity thing had the terrible side effect of making rusty morning voices and bare feet seem intimate.

She looked up and out the window and saw her car in the driveway. "Hey," she said. "How did that happen?"

"I told you I was going to take care of it. Ye of little faith."

"Apparently, Knox, you can't even take care of your beard, so why would I think you would take care of my car so efficiently?"

"Correction," he said. "I don't bother to make time to shave my beard. Why? Because I don't *have* to. Because I'm not beholden to anyone anymore."

Those words were hollow, even though he spoke them in a light tone. And no matter how he would try and spin it, he didn't feel it was a positive thing. It seemed desperately sad that nobody in his life cared whether or not he had a beard.

"I like it," she said finally.

She did. He was hot without one, too. He had one of those square Hollywood jaws and a perfectly proportioned chin. And if asked prior to seeing him with the beard, she would have said facial hair would have been like hiding his light under a bushel.

But in reality, the beard just made him look…more masculine. Untamed. Rugged. Sexy.

Yes. Sexy.

She cleared her throat. "Anyway," she said. "I won't talk about it anymore."

Suddenly, she realized Knox was standing much closer to her than she'd been aware of until a moment ago. She could smell some kind of masculine body wash and clean, male skin. And she could feel the heat radiating from his body. If she reached out, she wouldn't even have to stretch her arm out to press her palm against his chest. Or to touch his beard again, which she had already established was completely inappropriate, but she was thinking about it anyway.

"You like it?" he asked, his voice getting rougher, even more than it had been this morning when he had first woken up.

"I... Yes?"

"You're not sure?"

"No," she said, taking a step toward him, her feet acting entirely on their own and without permission from her brain. "No, I'm sure. I like it."

She felt weightless, breathless. She felt a little bit like leaning toward him and seeing what might happen if she closed that space between them. Seeing how that beard might feel if it was pressed against her cheek, what it might feel like if his mouth was pressed against hers...

She was insane. She was officially insane. She was checking out her friend. Her grieving friend who needed her to be supportive and not lecherous.

She shook her head and took a step back. "Thank you," she said. Instead of kissing him. Instead of doing anything crazy. "For making sure the car got back to me. Really, thank you for catching me when I passed out yesterday. I think I'm still...you know."

"No," he said, crossing his muscular arms over his broad chest. "I'm not sure that I do know."

Freaking Knox. Not helping her out at all. "I think I'm still a little bit spacey," she said.

"Understandable. Hey, direct me to your hardware, and I'll get started on that."

Okay, maybe he was going to help her out. She was going to take that lifeline with both hands. "I can do that," she said, and she rushed to oblige him.

CHAPTER FOUR

KNOX WAS ALMOST completely finished replacing the hardware in Selena's kitchen when the phone in his pocket vibrated. He frowned, the number coming up one he didn't recognize.

He answered it and lifted it to his ear. "Knox McCoy," he said.

"Hi there, Knox" came the sound of an older woman's voice on the other end of the line. She had a thick East Texas drawl and a steel thread winding through the greeting that indicated she wasn't one to waste a word or spare a feeling. "I'm Cora Lee. Will's stepmother. I'm not sure if he's ever mentioned me."

"Will and I haven't been close for the past decade or so," he said honestly. Really, the falling-out between Will and Selena had profoundly affected his friendship with the other man.

In divorces, friends chose sides. And his side had always clearly been Selena's.

"Still," Cora Lee said, "there's nothing like coming back from the dead to patch up old relationships. And, on that subject, I would like to have a small get-together to celebrate Will's return, just for those of us who were at the service. You can imagine that we're all thrilled."

If she was thrilled, Knox wouldn't have been able to tell by her tone of voice. She was more resolute. De-

termined. And he had a feeling that refusing her would
be a lot like saying no to a drill sergeant.

"It will be kind of like a funeral, only celebrating
that he's not dead. And you'll be invited. He said he
wanted you to come."

"He did?"

"Not in so many words, but I feel like it is what he
wants." And Knox had a feeling it wouldn't matter if
Will did want it or not. Cora Lee was going to do exactly what she thought was best. "And he wants that
ex-wife of his to come, too. He says you two are close."

"Which ex-wife?" He had gotten the distinct impression that there was more than one former Mrs. Sanders
floating around.

"The one you're close to," Cora Lee responded, her
voice deadpan.

Reluctantly, Knox decided he liked Will's stepmother. "Well, I'll let her know. She went to the funeral,
so I imagine she'll want to go to this." He wasn't sure
he particularly wanted to, but if Selena was going, then
he would accompany her. He was honestly concerned
that the other women who had been named beneficiaries, or whoever was responsible for sending the letter,
might take advantage of a situation like this.

"Good. I'll put you both down on the guest list, and
I'll send details along shortly. You have to come, because I wrote your names down and there will be too
much brisket if you don't."

And with that, she hung up the phone. He looked
down at the screen for a moment, and then Selena came
in, her footsteps soft on the hardwood floor.

He looked up and his stomach tightened. Her long
black hair was wet, as though she'd gotten out of the

shower, and he suddenly became very aware of the fact that her gray T-shirt was clinging to her curves a little bit more than it might if her skin wasn't damp. Which put him in mind to think about the fact that her skin was damp, which meant it had been uncovered only a few moments before.

What the hell was wrong with him? He was thinking like a horny teenager. Yeah, it had been a few years since he'd had sex, but frankly, he hadn't wanted to. His libido had been hibernating, along with his desire to do basic things like shave his beard.

But somehow it seemed to be stirring to life again, and it was happening at a very inappropriate time, with an inappropriate person.

The good thing was that it must be happening around Selena because she was the only woman in proximity, and it was about time he started to feel again. The bad thing was… Selena was the only woman in proximity.

"Who was that on the phone?" she asked, running her fingers through her hair.

"Will's stepmother. She wants us to go to a non-funeral for him in a few days."

"Oh."

She was frowning, a small crinkle appearing on her otherwise smooth forehead.

"Something wrong?"

"No. It's a good thing. I'm glad to be asked. I mean, I was thinking, when I assumed he was dead, that it was so sad he and I had never…that we had never found a way to fix our friendship."

"You want to do that?" He was surprised.

"It seems silly to stay mad at somebody over something that happened so long ago. Something I know neither of us would change."

"The marriage?"

She laughed. "The divorce. I don't regret the divorce, so there's really no point in being upset about it. Or avoiding him forever because of it. I mean, obviously there was conflict surrounding it." She looked away, a strange, tight expression on her face. "But if neither of us would go back and change the outcome, I don't see why we can't let it go. I would like to let it go. It was terrible, thinking he was dead and knowing we had never reconciled."

Knox pressed his hand to his chest and rubbed the spot over his heart. It twinged a little. But that was nothing new. It did that sometimes. At first, he had thought he was having a heart attack. But then, in the beginning, it had been much worse. Suffocating, deep, sharp pain.

Something that took his breath away.

No one had ever told him that grief hurt. That it was a physical pain. That the depression that lingered on after would hurt all the way down to your bones. That sometimes you would wake up in the middle of the night and not be able to breathe.

Those were the kinds of things people didn't tell you. But then, there was no guidebook for loss like he had experienced. Actually, there was. There were tons of books about it. But there had been no reason in hell for him to go out and buy one. Not before it had happened, and then when Eleanor had gotten sick, he hadn't wanted to do doomsday preparation for the loss he still didn't want to believe was inevitable.

Afterward…

He was in the shit whether he wanted to be o

So he didn't see the point of trying to figure out a way to navigate more elegantly through it. Shit was shit. There was no dressing it up.

There was just doing your best to put one foot in front of the other and walk on through.

But he had walked through it alone, and in the end that had been too much for him and Cassandra. But he hadn't known how to do it with another person. Hadn't really wanted to.

Hadn't known how he was supposed to look at the mother of his dead child and offer her comfort, tell her that everything was going to be okay, that *anything* was going to be okay.

But now they had disentangled themselves from each other, and still this thing Selena was talking about, this desire for reconciliation, just didn't resonate with him. He didn't want to talk to Cassandra. It was why they were divorced.

"It's not the same thing," she said, her voice suddenly taking on that soft, careful quality that appeared in people's tones when they were dancing around the subject of his loss. "Mine and Will's relationship. It's not the same as yours and Cassandra's. It's not the same as your divorce. Will and I were married for a year. We were young, we were selfish and we were stupid. The two of you... You built a life together. And then you lost it. You went through hell. It's just not the same thing. So don't think I'm lecturing you subtly on how you should call her or something."

"I didn't think that."

"You did a little. Or you were making yourself feel guilty about it, and that isn't fair. You don't deserve that."

She was looking at him with a sweet, freshly scrubbed openness that made his stomach go tight. Made him want to lift up his coffee mug and throw it down onto the tile, just to make the feeling stop. Made him want to grab hold of her face, hold her steady and kiss her mouth. So she would shut up. So she would stop being so understanding. So she would stop looking at him and seeing him. Seeing inside of him.

That thought, hot and destructive, made his veins feel full of fire rather than blood. And he wasn't sure anymore what his motivation actually was. To get her to stop, or to just exorcise the strange demon that seemed to have possessed him at some point between the moment he had held her in his arms on the floor of the funeral home and when they had come back here.

He had his life torn apart once, and he wasn't in a hurry to tear up the good that was left. At least, that was what he would have said, but this destructive urge had overtaken him. And his primary thought was to either break something or grab hold of her.

He needed to do more manual labor. Obviously.

"I'm not sure you're in a great position to speak about what I do and don't deserve," he said, the words coming out harder than he'd intended.

"Except you're here at my house because you want to protect me, and you just replaced all my cabinet hardware, and it looks amazing. So I guess I would say you deserve pretty good things, since you're obviously a pretty good guy."

"Cabinet hardware isn't exactly a ringing endorsement on character," he said.

He needed to get some distance between them, because he was being a dick. It was uncalled-for. Selena wasn't responsible for his baggage. Not for making him feel better about it, not for carrying any of the weight.

"What about the work you need done outside?" he asked.

"Sorting through the shed. But we're going to need a truck for that."

"Do you have one?"

"I actually do. But I don't drive it very much."

"Why do you have a truck?"

"Extravagance?"

He didn't believe her, since Selena didn't do much for the sake of extravagance. If she had wanted to do something extravagant, he knew she could've gotten herself a big McMansion in town. Some eyesore at the end of a cul-de-sac. God knew she made enough money with that skin-care line of hers. But instead she had buried herself out here in the boonies, gotten herself this little cabin that wouldn't be extravagant by anyone's standard.

"To try and make friends," she said. "It's really helpful when you have something for people to use when they move. You'd be surprised how popular it makes you."

"Honey, this is Texas. I don't think there are enough people around without a pickup for that to be true."

"You'd be surprised," she said. "And my best friend hasn't been back to Texas in so long that I had to resort to making new friends any way I could."

Now she was making him feel guilty. As if he didn't already feel guilty about the illicit thoughts he'd just had about her.

"Well, you're probably better off," he said, keeping

his tone light, brushing past her and heading out the front door.

To his chagrin, she followed him, scampering like a woodland creature out onto the porch behind him. "I don't know about that."

"Do you have the keys to the truck?"

"I can grab them," she said.

For some reason, he had a feeling she was stalling, and he couldn't figure out why. "Can I have them?"

"How about I go with you?"

"Don't you have other things to do? As you reminded me yesterday, you have your own money, and therefore don't need Will's estate, because you're a multimillionaire. Not from nothing, though. You actually run a giant business."

"We both do. And yet here we are. I can afford to take some time off to visit with you, Knox."

That made him feel like an ass. Because he was trying to put some distance between them.

All you do is put distance between yourself and people these days.

Well, he could do without that cutting observation from his own damn self.

"Fine." He didn't mean to grunt the word, but he did, and Selena pretended to ignore it as she went back in the house, reappearing a minute later with keys dangling from her fingertips.

She was grinning, to compensate for his scowl, he had a feeling.

"I will direct you to the truck," she said, keeping that grin sparkly and very much in place.

"You made it sound like you had an old pickup truck

lying around," he said when they approached the shiny red and very new vehicle parked out back.

"I told you I bought it partly for extravagance. I couldn't resist."

Unlike himself, Selena had actually grown up with money, but he had always gotten the feeling her father had kept a tight leash on her. So whatever cash had been at her disposal hadn't really been hers; her life hadn't really been hers.

In contrast, he had grown up with nothing.

No support. No parent who had even bothered to try and be controlling, because they hadn't cared enough.

All in all, it was tough to say which of them had had it worse.

"Just because?"

"Because I do what I want," she said, confirming his earlier thought.

"Yes, you certainly do," he said.

She always had. From going to school, starting her own business, marrying Will when it had seemed like such a crazy thing to do. They had still been at Harvard at the time, and he hadn't seen the damned point in rushing anything.

But she had been determined. And when Selena Jacobs was determined, there was no stopping her.

"I'll drive," she said.

He reached out and snatched the keys from her hand. "I'll drive."

"It's my truck," she protested.

He paused, leaning down toward her, ignoring the tightening feeling in his stomach. And lower. "And I'm the man, baby."

She laughed in his face. He deserved it, he had to admit. But he was still fucking driving.

"That does not mean you get to drive."

"In this case it does," he said, jerking open the passenger-side door and holding it for her.

She gave him the evil eye, but got into the truck, sitting primly and waiting for him to close the door.

He rounded to the driver's side and got in, looking down at the cup holders, both of which contained two partly finished smoothies of indeterminate age. "Really?" he asked, looking down at the cups.

"I have a housekeeper," she said. "Not a truck keeper."

He grunted. "Now, where am I going?"

"You should have let me drive," she said, leaning toward him. And suddenly, it felt like high school. Being in the cab of the truck with a girl who made it difficult to breathe, knowing what he wanted to do next and knowing that he probably couldn't.

Except back then, he would have done the ill-advised thing. The dick-motivated thing. Because back then he didn't think too far ahead.

Well, except for two things. Getting the grades he needed for a scholarship to Harvard and getting laid.

Those things were a lot more compatible than people might realize. And the bad-boy facade made it easy to hide the fact that he was on a specific academic track. Which had been good, in his estimation. Because if he had failed and ended up pumping gas, no one would have been the wiser. No one would have known that he'd had a different dream. That he'd wanted anything at all beyond the small Texas town he had grown up in.

Fortunately, Harvard had worked out.

He had become a success, as far as everyone was concerned.

He wondered how they talked about him in Royal now. Probably a cautionary tale. Evidence of the fact that at the end of the day not even money could protect you from the harsh realities of life.

That you bled and hurt and died like everyone else.

All in all, it wasn't exactly the legend he had hoped to create for himself.

After Eleanor's funeral, someone had told him that you couldn't have everything. He had punched that person in the face.

"Just head that way," she said, waving her hand, clearly not too bothered with being specific in her directions.

He drove across the flat, bumpy property until he saw a shed in the distance, a small building that clearly predated the house by the river. He wondered if it had been the original home.

"Is this it?" he asked.

"If I were driving, you wouldn't have to ask."

"You are a prickly little cuss," he said, pulling up to the outbuilding and putting the truck in Park.

"It's good for the pores," she said, sniffing.

"So it's not all your magic Clarity skin care?"

"That works, too, but you know, a healthy lifestyle complements all skin-care regimens," she said, sounding arch. Then she smiled broadly, all white teeth and golden skin, looking every inch the savvy spokeswoman that she was.

"Question," he said as they got out of the truck.

"Possible answer," she quipped as the two of them walked to the shed.

"Why skin-care products? Is that your passion?"

"Why organic food?" she shot back.

"That's an easy answer," he returned. "That mom-and-pop place I used to go to for deli food when I had a late-night study session was doing crazy business. And it didn't make any sense to me why. When they wanted to retire, I ended up talking to the owner about the business. And how good food, health food, was an expanding market. I mean, I didn't care that it was healthy—I was in my early twenties. I just liked the macaroni and cheese. I didn't care that it was from a locally sourced dairy So when the opportunity came to buy the shop, I took it. It was a risky business, and I knew it. It could have gone either way. But it ended up growing. And growing. And before I knew it, I owned a chain of grocery stores. And it became a billion-dollar industry. All because I liked the macaroni and cheese."

They got out of the truck, slamming the doors in tandem. He looked around at the scenery. He could see why Selena had bought the place. It was quiet. Remote, like his ranch in Wyoming. There was something to be said for that. For being able to go off grid. For being able to get some quiet.

"Now you," he said, prompting her.

She wrinkled her nose, twisting her lips to one side. "I guess it's similar for me. I knew I wanted a business that was mine. I knew I wanted to do something that was under my control. And I did a lot of research about profit margins and low overhead start-up. You know I got a business degree, and I also took all of that chemistry. Just as a minor. The two things are compatible. Skin care and chemistry. And like you said, natural organic products were on the upswing."

"So you're not particularly passionate about skin care."

She lifted a shoulder. "I find that you can easily become passionate about a great many different things. I love having my own money. I love controlling my life. I really like the fact that what I do empowers women in some regard. Skin care is not a necessity, but it's nice. When you feel good about yourself, I think you can do more with your life. Mostly, my passion is in the success." She smiled. "I feel like you can relate to that."

He wasn't sure. Things had changed for him so dramatically over the past few years. "Once you make a certain amount of money, though," he said, flinging the doors to the shed open, "it really is just more money."

"More security," she said. "All of this has to go." She waved a hand around as if it was a magic wand that might make the items disappear.

He looked down at her and smiled. She was such an imperious little thing. Sometimes he could definitely tell she had come from a wealthy family, a privileged background. She gave an order, and she expected to be followed. Or maybe that was just Selena.

"Not necessarily," he said, the words coming out a lot more heavily than he'd intended as he picked up what he thought might be part of an old rocking chair.

"I'm sorry" came Selena's muted reply. "I wasn't thinking when I said that."

"I wasn't thinking of the past either," he said. "It's just that money doesn't let you control the whole world, Selena. That's a fact."

"Well, my father sure thinks it does. And he thought he could use it to control me." She cleared her throat. "That was why... It was why I had to marry Will."

Those words hit him square in the chest, almost like one of the large stacks had fallen square on him. "What do you mean you had to marry him?"

"I just… My grandfather died my freshman year. Do you remember that?"

"Of course I remember that. You were distraught."

She sucked in a deep breath. "He was the only person who ever believed in me, Knox. He was the only person who acted like I could do something. Be something. I loved him. So much. He was also definitely an antique. And there was a trust fund. A trust fund that was set aside for me, but I couldn't access it until I was twenty-five, which was when he figured I would be an adult. Really."

"Twenty-five? That seems…"

"Or I could have gotten married." She looked up at him then, her eyes full of meaning. "Which is what I did."

Her meaning hit him with the force of a slap. He was in shock. And the way he responded to that feeling was by getting mad. He growled and walked out of the shed, heading toward the pickup and flinging the piece of chair into the truck bed. Then he stalked back inside and picked up something else, didn't matter particularly to him what it was. "So you had to marry him because you needed the money?" he asked finally, his heart pounding so hard he was sure it would gallop out of his chest.

All this time he'd thought she'd fallen in love with Will. And that had truly put her off-limits, even after the marriage ended. She had chosen another man when Knox was right there. There wasn't a stronger way to telegraph disinterest.

Their friendship had been too important, way too important, to act on any attraction on his end. Particularly when she'd made it clear how she felt when she'd married Will.

Except she hadn't loved Will. Hadn't wanted him.

"Yes," she said. "I remember that you thought it was crazy when we got married. When we didn't just live together. Well, that was why."

"You didn't tell me," he said, his tone fierce and a hell of a lot angrier than he'd intended it to be. "I'm supposed to be your best friend, Selena, and you didn't tell me what was happening?"

"You had your own stuff, Knox. You were dealing with school. And you were on a scholarship to be there. I didn't want to do anything that would interfere with your grades. And that included bringing you into my drama."

"I was your best friend," he reiterated. "I've always taken your drama. That's how it works. How the hell could you underestimate me like that?" He shook his head. "No wonder the two of you got divorced. You married because of a trust fund."

"I don't want to rehash the past with you," she snarled, picking up a bicycle tire and stomping out of the shed. "It doesn't matter. It doesn't matter what happened between me and Will. Not now. The marriage ended, end of story. It was definitely a bad idea. Don't you think I know that? We divorced. It completely ruined our friendship."

"Why?"

"Are you and Cassandra friends?" she asked.

"No," he said. "But as you have pointed out several times, my marriage to Cassandra was not the same as your marriage to Will. So let's not pretend now. Why did it ruin your friendship with Will?"

She bristled visibly. "Because of Rich Lowell."

"That guy who used to follow Will around? The tool with the massive crush on you?"

"That tool only got interested in me when he thought Will was. And after we married he said some things to me... They didn't seem completely far-fetched. He asked me why Will would suddenly want me when... when he didn't before. He implied Will only wanted my money. Of course, Rich didn't know the details of the trust fund, he only knew I came from a wealthy family, but he made me question... Why would Will agree to marry me only to help me get my trust fund? It was so hard for me to believe he was doing it because he was my friend. That he was doing it because he cared about me. I couldn't imagine anyone doing that.

"When you grow up the way I did... When you have to walk on eggshells around your father, you kind of fold in on yourself. And you focus on surviving. That was what I did. I became this creature who only knew how to scrabble forward. I was selfish, and I couldn't imagine anyone *not* being selfish. So when Rich asked me those questions...it just seemed more likely that Will wanted something from me than that he actually wanted to help me. I got mad at Will. I told him I didn't want anything to do with him. That if he thought he was getting any of my money he was completely insane." She laughed, the sound watery. "You know, that's why it was extra hilarious that he left me that inheritance. I mean, I guess he didn't. Because he wasn't dead. Because he didn't even really write the letter."

Knox had some sympathy for her. He truly did. Because he could remember Selena as she had been. It had been so hard for her to trust. So difficult for her to believe anyone wanted anything for her that wasn't a benefit to themselves.

For a kid from the wrong side of the tracks, knowing Selena had been somewhat eye-opening. He'd discovered that people who lived on the other side of the poverty line still had problems. They could be half-feral. They could be insecure. They could have real, serious life-and-death problems. He had always imagined that if he had money he could buy off all of life's bullshit. Meeting Selena had been his first realization that wasn't the case.

But even with the sympathy he felt, there was anger. So much damned anger. Because he hadn't deserved to be lied to for the better part of the last decade. She had never told him any of the truth, and he couldn't quite stomach that.

The nature of her relationship with Will had always been a secret from him.

He whirled around to face her and she squeaked, taking three steps backward, her shoulder blades butting against the side of the shed.

"You lied to me," he said.

"Well," she shot back, her acerbic tone reminding him of the past. "I didn't realize all of my baggage affected your daily life to this degree, Knox."

"You know it doesn't," he said.

"So why are you acting like it does? Why are you acting like it matters at all? It doesn't. It's ancient history. If I'm not upset about it anymore, then why are you?"

"Obviously, you and Will are upset about it, or the two of you would still speak to each other."

"The rift in our friendship has nothing to do with our divorce. It has everything to do with the fact that I accused him of being a gold digger." She sighed heavily. "You can imagine he was not thrilled with that. He pointed out that he didn't need money, of course. And I said being from rich parents didn't mean you didn't need money. I was exhibit A."

"I understand why that would bother him, but he couldn't forgive you for that? Will was not the kind of guy who took himself that seriously back then, and I can't imagine he's changed all that much in the years since."

She grimaced. "I never asked him to."

"You never asked him to forgive you?" he asked, incredulous. "Even though you accused him of something when he was trying to help you?"

She made a sound that was halfway between a growl and a squeak. "It doesn't matter."

"Then why are you so defensive about it?"

"Why are you acting like this? You're pissed because I didn't talk to you?"

"Because you didn't trust me," he said, moving nearer to her.

She shrank back slightly, turning her head. And her reaction just about sent him over the edge. He knew she'd had a rough past, but that was a long time ago. And he was not her father. He didn't use physical threats to intimidate women, and he had damn sure never done it to her.

He had been nothing but careful with her. And she had lied to him all these years about her feelings for

Will. She hadn't trusted Knox back then. And she was acting like he might do something to hurt her now, when he was here because he wanted to make sure that she was safe and protected.

He reached out, gripping her chin with his thumb and forefinger, forcing her to look up at him. "Don't act like that," he said, his voice hard. "Don't look at me like I'm a damn stranger."

She tilted her chin up, her expression defiant. And then the wind picked up and he caught that sweet smell that spoke *Selena* to him. Lavender and the Texas breeze, and why the hell that should affect him, he didn't know. But it did.

"Then don't act like a stranger," she said.

His blood reached the boiling point then, and before he knew what he was doing, he had leaned in closer, his nose scant inches from hers. "I'm not acting like one," he said, his voice rough. "But I'm about to."

She had never really wanted Will. She had never chosen Will over Knox.

That changed things.

And then he closed the distance between them and pressed his lips to hers.

CHAPTER FIVE

KNOX WAS KISSING HER.

She was sure she was dreaming. Except it was nothing like one of her typical dreams. In those fantasies—which she had always been quite ashamed of—they were always having some nice moment, and then he would capture her lips gently with his before pulling her into his warm, comforting embrace.

In those fantasies, he always looked at her with his lovely gray eyes, and they would soften with warmth and affection before he would lean in.

In this reality, his gray eyes had been hard. He had not been smiling at her. And his lips were... This was not a sweet foray over the line of friendship. No. This was some kind of barbarous conquering of her mouth by his.

This was an invasion. And there were no questions being asked. He was still holding her chin, the impression of his thumb digging into her skin as he tugged down and opened her mouth wide, angling his head and dipping his tongue deep. Sliding it against hers. And she wanted to pull away. She wanted to be angry. Wanted to be indignant.

Because he was angry at her, and he'd been yelling at her. And she was angry at him. He had no right to question her when he had no real idea of what she had lived through. No real idea of what she'd been trying to escape.

Not when he had no idea that the reason she hadn't told him the truth wasn't because she didn't trust him, but because she didn't trust herself. Because what she had really wanted to do, even back then, was ask *Knox* to marry her. But she had known, deep down inside, that with him, a marriage could never be fake. That with him, she would always want everything. And his friendship was so special, she had never wanted to risk it.

Her feelings for him had always been big. Somehow, she had known instinctively that if she made him her husband it would be easy for him to become everything. As painful as it had been, as suspicious and horrible as she'd behaved with Will over their friendship...

Giving in to wanting Knox, to having him...that would have destroyed the girl she'd been.

So she'd kept a distance between them. She'd done what she'd had to do to guard her heart and their friendship. And now he was demolishing all of that good work. That restraint she had shown, that diligence she had practiced all these years.

She was furious. Something more than furious. Something deeper. Something that compelled her to do what she decided to do next.

She shifted, grabbing fistfuls of his shirt, and angled her head, tasting him.

Because it wasn't fair that he was the one who had done this. When she was the one who had spent so long behaving. When she was the one who had worked so hard to protect what they had—to protect herself.

He had no regard for her. No regard for her work.

And he had to be punished for that.

She nipped his lower lip and he growled, pressing his hard chest against her breasts as he pinned her to the side of the shed. He gathered her hands, easily wrapping one of his hands around both her wrists, holding them together and drawing her arms up over her head against the wall.

Bastard.

He was trying to take control of this. Trying to take control of her.

No. He was the one who was ruining things. He was the one ruining *them*. She hadn't gotten the chance to do it. She had been good. She had done her best. And now he wanted all the control?

No. Absolutely not.

She bit him again. This time her teeth scraped hard across his lower lip, and he growled louder, pressing her harder against the wall.

His teeth ran across the bottom of her lip. He nipped her. And somehow, the anger drained out of her.

There was something primal about having her best friend's tongue in her mouth. She had to simply surrender. That was all. Beginning and end.

A wave of emotion washed over her, a wave of need. The entire ocean she had been holding back for more than a decade.

Knox. It had always been Knox that she wanted. Always.

She had messed up everything when she married Will. *Everything.* And when they had divorced it had been too late. Knox had been with Cassandra. And their relationship had been real and serious.

That still bothered her. He had found something real with someone else. She never had.

It would never be the same. Because she had never… She had never loved anyone but him.

And he had loved someone else.

That internal admission hurt. More than that, it made her heart feel like it could shatter into a million pieces with each beat.

But then it just beat harder, faster as Knox shifted, curving his arm around her waist and drawing her against him. She could feel his hardness. Could feel the insistent press of him against her hip that told her this kiss wasn't about teaching her a lesson. Wasn't about anger.

Yes, it had started with anger. But now it was just need. Deep, carnal need between two people who knew each other. Two people who knew exactly what each had been through. There were no explanations required between her and Knox.

That isn't true. There are no explanations required on his end. But I haven't been honest with him. And he knows it. It's why he's angry.

She squeezed her eyes shut and ignored that internal admonishment, parting her lips and kissing Knox deeper, harder.

She was ready for this. Ready to let him undo her jeans, push them down her thighs and take her virginity right there against the side of the shed.

And there was a phrase she had never imagined herself thinking.

Her virginity. Oh, *damn it*. That would be a whole other conversation.

But then suddenly, the conversation became irrelevant, because Knox wrenched his mouth away from hers and wheeled back, his lips set in a grim line, those gray eyes harder than she could ever remember seeing them.

"What?" she asked, breathing heavily, trying to act as though her world hadn't just been tilted on its axis.

"What the hell?"

"You kissed me, Knox. You got mad at me and you kissed me. I'm sure there's some kind of Freudian horror that explains that kind of behavior, but I don't know it."

"You bit me," he pointed out.

"And you pinned my wrists against the wall." She gritted her teeth and turned away from him, hoping to hide the mounting color in her cheeks. Hoping he wouldn't know just how affected she had been by the whole thing. She was dying. Her heart was about to claw its way out of her mouth, her stomach was turning itself over, and she was so wet between her thighs she didn't think she would ever live down the embarrassment if he found out.

"I didn't realize," he said.

"That you pinned my hands?"

"That *that* was there."

"What? Attraction?" She tried to laugh. "You're a hot guy, Knox. And I'm not immune to that. I mean, maybe I'm not up to your usual standards…"

"What usual standards?" he asked. "I was married for ten years, Selena. I had one standard. The person I made vows to. I haven't been with anyone since."

"Oh," she said. "So I guess that explains it." Her stomach twisted in disappointment, then did a free fall down to her toes. "You are super hard up."

"I was angry," he said.

"Awesome," she said, planting her hands on her hips.

"Angry and hard up apparently translates into kissing women you didn't know you were attracted to!"

"I knew I was attracted to you," he said. "But I don't dwell on it."

She paused for a moment, tilting her head to the side. "You...knew you were attracted to me."

"Yes. I have been. Since college. But there's never been any point in exploring that attraction, Selena. You were not in a space to take that on when we first met."

She knew what he was saying was true. She had been attracted to him from the moment they'd met, too, but she'd also built a big wall around herself for a reason.

"I wanted to focus on school," she said, the words sounding lame.

"Until Will and a trust fund came into play?"

"Whatever. You didn't make a move on me. And then our friendship became the thing. And...our friendship is still the thing." No point spilling her guts about what a sad, insecure person she was.

"Yes," he said.

"That's good. I can have sex with any guy," she said, waving her hand as if she had simply hundreds of men to choose from to satisfy her appetites. "You're my only best friend. You've known me for so long and let's just not... Let's not make it weird."

"I just think..."

"You haven't had sex in a while—I get it," she said. Which was pretty damned laughable since she hadn't had sex ever and he was the one who had jumped on her.

"I'd like to think there was more to it than that," he said. "Because there's more to us than that."

She lifted a shoulder. "Fine. Whatever. I'm not that bothered by it. It was just a kiss. Nothing I can't handle."

She was dying inside. Her head was spinning and

she was sure she was close to passing out. She would be damned if she would betray all those feelings to him.

She felt like her top layer had been scraped back, like she was dangerously close to being exposed. All of her secrets. All of herself.

She cared about Knox, she really did, but she kept certain things to herself. And he was poking at them.

"So that's it?" he asked. "We kiss after all these years of friendship and you're fine."

"Would you rather I light myself on fire and jump into the river screaming?"

"No," he said closely, "and that's an awfully specific response."

"Knox," she said, "you don't want me to be anything but fine. Believe me. It's better for the two of us if we just move on like nothing happened. I don't think either of us needs this right now."

Or ever.

She wanted to hide. But she knew that if she did hide, it would only let him know how closely he'd delved into things she didn't want him anywhere near. Things she didn't want anyone near.

"Yeah," he said. "I guess so."

"You don't want to talk about our feelings, do you?" she asked, knowing she sounded testy.

"Absolutely not. I've had enough feelings for a lifetime."

"I'm right there with you. I don't have any interest in messing up a good friendship over a little bit of sex."

Knox walked past her, moving back into the shed. Then he paused, kicking his head back out of the doorway. "I agree with you, Selena, except for one little thing. With me, there wouldn't be anything little about the sex."

KNOX WASN'T SURE what had driven him to make that parting comment to Selena after they had kissed against the shed wall. But she had been acting strange and skittish around him ever since.

Not that he could blame her. He had no idea what in hell he'd been thinking.

Except that even though he was angry at her, she also looked soft, and tempting, and delicious. Finding out she had violated his trust, that there were things about her he didn't know, made him feel like their friendship was not quite what he had imagined it was. And in light of that realization, it had been difficult for him to figure out why he shouldn't just kiss her.

Asshole reasoning, maybe, but it had all made perfect sense in the moment. In the moment when he had brought his lips down on hers.

Yeah, it had all made perfect sense then.

The next few days had been incredibly tense, in a way that things never usually were between them. But he could at least appreciate the tension as a distraction from his real life. It was strange, staying with Selena like this in close quarters—that kiss notwithstanding. Because it reminded him a lot of their Harvard days. It wasn't like he'd been blind to how gorgeous she was then. But he'd made a decision about how to treat their friendship, due in large part to Will.

In many ways that decision had made things simple. Though the kiss was complicated, it was nothing compared to loss or divorce or any of the other things he had been through since.

But now they had that party for Will, and they had to actually go be in public together. And she had to try and act like she was at ease with him rather than looking at him like he might bite her again.

Though *she* had started the biting.

Knox buttoned up his dark blue shirt and tried not to think overly hard about all the biting. And the fact that it had surprised him in a not-unpleasant way.

Damn. He really *did* need to find a woman.

But every time he thought about doing that he just felt tired. He didn't want to cruise bars. He didn't want to find strangers to hook up with.

If he was that desperate for an orgasm he could use his right hand

He had been in love with Cassandra, once upon a time. Though it was hard to remember the good times. Not because they had faded into memory, but because they hurt.

They also ruined the idea of anonymous sex for him.

He was over that. Done with it. He knew what sex could be like when you *knew* someone. When you had a connection with them. He didn't have any interest in going back to the alternative.

He knew a lot of guys who would kill to be in his position. Away from the commitments of marriage. Knox just didn't see the appeal.

He had never found it monotonous to be with the same person. He had thought it offered far more than it took. To know somebody well enough that you could be confident they were asking for what they wanted. To just know what they wanted at a certain point.

He'd been with his wife for over a decade. The only woman for all that time. It had never seemed a chore to him.

The idea of hooking up—that seemed like a chore.

But damn, he needed to get laid. He was fantasizing about getting bitten by his best friend, so obviously something had to change.

That was the funny thing. Because while he remembered and appreciated the married sex he'd had with Cassandra, he didn't specifically fantasize about *her*. Possibly because she was bound up in something too painful for him to fully relive.

He and Cassandra were over. Done. Everything in him was done with what they'd had.

But he still found himself in the midst of a sex paradox.

He gritted his teeth, walked out of the bedroom he was occupying at Selena's and stopped still.

She was standing in the middle of the living room wearing a bright red dress that conformed to her glorious figure. Her long black hair was styled in loose waves around her shoulders, and she had a flower pinned on the side, part of her hair swept back off her face. She looked beautiful, and effortless, which he knew wasn't the case.

She had spent a good while affecting that look, but she did a damned good impression of someone who hadn't tried at all.

He wanted to kiss the crimson lip color right off her mouth. Wanted to pull her into his arms and relive the other day.

And he knew he couldn't. Knew he couldn't touch her again, and he couldn't look like he was standing there thinking about it, because they had to get to that party. And he had to manage to get there in one piece, without Selena chewing him up and spitting him out because he was acting like an ass.

MAISEY YATES 257

He reached over and grabbed his black cowboy hat off the shelf by the door. "I'm ready," he said, positioning it on his head. "Are you?"

"You're wearing jeans," she said.

He lifted a brow. "I'm a cowboy, honey. We wear jeans to parties. Plus, it's Texas."

"I'm wearing *heels*," she said, sticking out one dainty foot and showing off the red stilettos and matching toenail polish on her feet. As if he hadn't already taken stock of that already, with great interest. "The least you could have done was throw on a pair of dress pants."

"I have cowboy boots on," he returned. Then he stuck his arm out, offering it to her. "You go with me as is or you go by yourself, babe. Up to you."

She sighed, an exasperated sound, and reached out, taking hold of his arm before moving to the front door with him. This was the first time she had touched him since the kiss. And damn it all if he didn't feel a hard shock of pleasure at the delicate contact of her hand against his arm, even though it was through fabric.

Selena, for her part, seemed unaffected. Or at least, she was doing a good impersonation of someone who was.

"I'll drive," she said, producing her keys and moving to her little red car before he could protest. He had a feeling he would hate butting up against Selena's temper right about now even more than he hated letting someone else drive, so he didn't fight her on it.

"You can drive in those shoes?" he asked when Selena turned the car out onto the highway.

She waved a hand. "You know, Ginger Rogers did everything Fred Astaire did backward and in heels. I can drive a car in stilettos, Knox," she said, her tone crisp and dry like a good Chardonnay.

He would like very much to take a sip of her.

"Good to know," he said.

"You're not impressed with my logic," she said, sounding petulant.

"The fox-trot isn't driving, so no."

"Don't worry, Knox." Her tone was the verbal equivalent of a pat on the head. "I'll get us there safely. You can be my navigator."

He grumbled. "Great."

"The Chekov to my Kirk."

"Come on," he said. "I'm Shatner. Everyone knows that."

She laughed. "No one knows that. Because it isn't true."

"Clearly I'm the captain of the starship *Enterprise*, Selena."

"O Captain! my Captain! I'm the one driving."

"Technically, as you are the one in red, I would be very concerned by the metaphor."

"This is going into serious nerd territory, Knox." She chuckled. "Do you remember we used to stay up all night with the old *Star Trek*, eating ice cream until we were sick when we were supposed to be having study group?"

"We studied," he said. "We all took it pretty seriously."

"Yeah," she said. "But at a certain point there was just no more retaining information, and we ended up vegging."

"Our college stories are pretty tame compared to some."

"Yeah," she said. "But I don't think you and I ever wanted to compromise our good standing at the university by smoking a lot of weed. We had to get out there and make our own futures. Away from our families."

"True," he returned.

"Which is why we are the successful ones. That's why we're the ones who have done so well."

He felt like he was falling into that great divide again. He wasn't sure what those words meant anymore. Hadn't been for some time. "I guess so."

Tough to think that he had spent all that time working like he had. Through school, and in business, only to reach existential crisis point by thirty-two. It was surprising. And a damn shame.

"Well," she said. "I think anyone who ever doubted us has been proved wrong. How about that?"

He shook his head, watching the familiar scenery fly by. It was so strange to be back here in Royal. He'd met Cassandra in Royal when visiting Will, and he'd decided he'd move there after college to be closer to her. They'd started their life here, their family.

He took it all in. The great green rolling hills and the strange twisty trees. So different from the mountainous terrain in Wyoming. So different from the jagged peaks that surrounded his ranch, which he'd always kept even during the time he'd lived in Royal. The ranch made him feel like he was closed in. Protected. In another place. In another world. Rather than back here where time seemed too harsh and real.

"True enough."

At least he had found a way to talk to Selena again. At least, they'd had a moment of connecting. A moment where the weirdness of the kiss hadn't been the only thing between them. They had a history. She'd known him as a college kid, out of step with the privileged people he was surrounded by, determined to use that opportunity to make something of himself. She'd known him as a newlywed, a new father, a grieving man. A newly single man.

Selena was one of the most important people in his life.

"I know you think you're the captain," she said softly. "Just like I know you don't like tea."

A jolt went down his spine. "What?"

"You don't like tea."

"I…know. I didn't think you knew. You serve it to me all the time."

"And you never say anything."

"My mama would have slapped me upside the head," he said.

He didn't talk about her much, and for good reason, really. WillaMae McCoy was a hard, brittle woman who had definite ideas about right and wrong, until it came to the men she shacked up with and the bottle of liquor she liked best to dull the heartache of losing them.

"Really?" Selena asked.

"Yes. She was big on 'Yes, ma'am,' 'No, ma'am.' Good posture and holding the door open for a lady. And I certainly wouldn't have been allowed to turn down a cup of tea."

"Even if you didn't like it?"

He lifted a shoulder. "Manners."

"Well. Don't do that with me. You can always tell me."

Finally, they arrived at Will's family ranch, the place decked out for a big party. The lights were all on inside the house and he could make out a faint glow coming from behind the place.

And just as he had told Selena, most of the men were in jeans and button-up shirts, wearing white or black cowboy hats. It was Texas. There was no call to put on a tie. Though some of the men wore bolos.

"You okay?" he asked. Because lost in all the strangeness of the past few days, lost in the revelation that Will and Selena had married for reasons other than love, had been the fact that Will was her ex-husband. And it was possible that—even though they had actually gotten married for the trust fund—she was still hurt by the entire thing.

She hadn't said she wasn't, and she had spent all these years avoiding Will. Seeing as she'd gone to his funeral, she'd imagined she'd missed the chance to ever connect with him again.

But look how that had turned out.

"I'm fine," she said, forcing a smile. "It's a good thing," she said. "Getting to see Will. I'm glad that I got this chance."

"All right," he said.

Without thinking, he rounded to her side of the car and opened the door for her, taking her hand and helping her out of the vehicle.

Then they walked into the party together. He placed his hand low on her back as he guided her through the front door of the massive ranch house. She whipped around to look at him, her eyes wide.

He removed his hand from her back. He hadn't even thought about it, how possessive a move it was. He had just done it. Because it had felt reasonable and right at the time.

He could tell by the expression on her face that it had actually been neither.

He stuffed his hand in his pocket.

The housekeeper greeted them and then ushered them out into the yard, where Cora Lee was waiting, greeting them with open arms and kisses on both cheeks.

When she pulled away, Knox had that sense again that she was the kind of woman you didn't want to cross. Sweet as pie, but there might be a razor blade buried in the filling.

Or at least, if there needed to be one, there would be.

"So good of you to come," she drawled.

"Of course," Selena said. "I'm just thrilled that Will is okay."

"So are we all, sugar," she said.

They moved back through the party and Selena shivered. He fought the urge to put his arm around her again. Obviously, she wasn't having that. Clearly, she was not open to him touching her. In spite of the fact that they had been friends for years.

It was that kiss.

And as he stood there, conscious of the newfound boundaries drawn in their relationship, he asked himself if he regretted that kiss.

No, sir. He sure as hell did not.

Because it had woken up some things inside of him he hadn't thought would ever wake up again.

And those thoughts put his mind back at the place it had been while he was getting ready for the party. He wasn't sure how he was going to move forward.

But maybe the desire for anonymous sex would come next.

He damn sure hoped so. Because relationships…
Marriage. None of that was ever happening again.

And that, he realized, standing there in this crowded,
loud Texas party with country music blaring over the
speakers, was the real tragedy.

He had reached the point that so many people ide-
alized. He had crawled out of the gutter, bloodied his
knuckles getting there. He'd found love. He'd gotten
married. He'd had a child.

And it had all come crashing down around him

He knew what it looked like to achieve those things,
and he knew what it looked like standing on the other
side of losing them.

They were nothing but heartbreak and rubble.

He didn't want them again. He just couldn't do it.

He took a step away from Selena. He was not going
to touch her again. That much was certain.

CHAPTER SIX

SELENA FELT KNOX'S WITHDRAWAL.

Although he had taken only a slight step to the side, she could sense that something had changed.

His eyes were distant. And he looked a lot more like the sad, wounded man she had first seen after his daughter's funeral than he looked like the friend she'd reminisced with in the car about their nerdy college life.

She started to say something, but he spotted someone they both knew from college and gave her a cursory hand gesture before walking away.

She felt deflated.

She knew she was acting a bit twitchy. But damn, Knox looked handsome in that outfit. In those jeans that hugged his muscular thighs and ass. And that hard place between those muscular thighs that she had felt pressed up against her body just the other day.

The cowboy hat. Oh, the cowboy hat always made her swoon. Cowboys weren't her type. If they were, she would have her pick. She lived in Texas.

No, sadly *Knox* was her type. And that had always been her tragedy.

She was brooding, and pretty darned openly, too, when her friend Scarlett McKittrick spotted her from across the lawn and headed her way. Scarlett being Scarlett, she *bounded* across the lawn, her eyes sparkling with determination in the dim light. She was like a caffeinated pixie, which was generally what Selena liked about her, but also part of why she'd been avoiding Scarlett since Knox had come to town. She didn't want her friend to grill her on why he was hanging around, or to start asking questions about what was happening between them. She'd end up telling Scarlett everything and confessing she wanted Knox. She just didn't want to have that conversation.

It made her feel a little guilty since Scarlett's adoption of her son had just been finalized and she knew Scarlett might feel like the baby was why Selena wasn't hanging around as much. But that wasn't the reason. She and Scarlett had been friends for years, even though the bond wasn't as intense as the one Selena shared with Knox, which was unsurprising, since Selena didn't secretly harbor fantasies about making out with Scarlett.

"Hi," Selena said, trying to sound bright.

"Hi, yourself," Scarlett said, her eyes assessing Selena in her overly perceptive manner. "I have escaped by myself for the evening, so I'm feeling good." She ran her hand through her short hair and grinned. "Thanks for asking."

"Sorry," Selena said. "I'm a terrible friend."

Scarlett waved a hand. "Yeah. A bit. But I'll live. What's happening with you and Knox?" The subject change nearly gave Selena whiplash.

"Nothing," Selena said, lying through her teeth.

"He seems… I mean, I haven't seen him *since*."

"I know," Selena said. "He's made himself scarce."

Scarlett bumped her with an elbow. "So have you recently."

"I'm sorry. I've been dealing with all the stuff with

Will. And Knox came to stay at my house after the funeral that wasn't and he hasn't exactly left."

Scarlett's eyebrows shot up. "Really?"

"Yes," she said. "Don't go thinking weird ideas about it. There's nothing weird."

"If you say so. But he looked... He doesn't look good, Selena."

She took a deep breath of the warm night air, catching hints of whiskey and wildflowers, mingling with smoke from a campfire. "I know. He's not the same. But how could he be?"

"Yeah. I guess if he was, you'd be forced to think he was pretty callous. Or in denial."

Selena shook her head. "Well, I can say he's not in denial. He's pretty firmly rooted in reality."

Except for that kiss. That kiss had been a moment outside of reality. And it had been glorious.

"Anyway," Selena said, "he's feeling paranoid because of everything with Will. I mean, *someone* faked Will's death. And *someone* wanted me and everyone else at that memorial service. It's weird. And it is nice to have Knox here just in case anything goes down."

"Yeah. I questioned the wisdom of having a party tonight, even though the only people Cora Lee invited were those of us at the service when Will walked in. But also, it's Texas, and at least eight percent of the people here have a sidearm, so anyone who tried to cause trouble would end up on the wrong side of a shoot-out."

"No kidding."

"Hey," Scarlett said, obviously ready for a new topic. "When are you guys coming out to Paradise Farms? Or if you'd rather do something different, the ranch next door to mine is doing a thing where you can go glamping."

Selena blinked. "I'm sorry—what?"

"You know—" Scarlett waved her hand around "—*glamorous camping.*"

"I don't know anything about that. Mostly because I don't know anything about camping, Scarlett. As you well know."

"It's not like regular camping. Yes, you ride horses, and go on one of the long trails that takes two full days to complete, and there's an overnight checkpoint. But the food that's included is amazing and the tent that's set up is a really, really nice tent, luxurious even."

"I… I don't know." The idea of being alone with Knox on an abandoned trail, riding horses, sleeping under the stars—or under the canvas top of a very nice tent—all seemed a little bit…fraught. And by fraught, she meant it turned her on, which was probably a very bad thing considering their situation.

"Well, think about it. It'd be a great way to take a break from all the drama here in town. The invitation is open. Because it's new, the schedule is really vacant. And I know they'd be happy to have testimonials from both of you. You can come out to Paradise Farms and use my horses. Right now, people are bringing their own to ride the trail."

Selena tried to smile and not look like she was pondering Knox and close quarters too hard. "I'll think about it."

"Do that." Scarlett grinned. "And text me. I'm dying at home buried under diapers and things. Babies are a lot of work."

"Okay. I promise."

Scarlett shifted. "Okay. Well, do text me. And…if anything…comes up. If you need to talk about *anything*. Please remember that you can call me."

"I will. Promise."

That left Selena standing alone as Scarlett went off to talk to someone else. She tapped her fingers together, and a passing waiter thrust a jar of what she assumed was moonshine into her empty hands.

She leaned forward, sniffing gingerly, then drew her head back, wrinkling her nose.

"I'm surprised you came."

She turned to see Will Sanders, her ex-husband—sort of. They hadn't spoken in so long it was weird to have him here next to her, talking to her. And it also made the years feel like they had melted away. Like there had been no fight. No stupid marriage. No accusations. Like greed and money—her greed—had never come between them.

"Yeah," she said, "fancy meeting you here. Especially since I thought you were dead."

"I would've thought you were pretty psyched about my demise, gingersnap."

"I've never understood that nickname. I'm not a red-head."

He winked, but it was different somehow than it had been. "No, but you're spicy with a bit of bite."

"Right. I guess I bit you a time or two." But not the way she'd bitten Knox. Not the way Knox thought she might have bitten Will. Her mind was terminally in a gutter right now.

"Yeah. But that's water under the bridge. A lot is thrown into perspective when you've been through what I have." She examined him for the first time. The hard

line of his jaw, the slightly sharper glint to his eyes. He
was not the same man he'd been. That much was certain. She could make out faint scarring on his face and
wondered how much surgery he'd had to have to get
himself put back together. She'd heard someone mention that Will had been in a boating accident in Mexico
and left for dead. He'd been recovering and trying to
make his way home all this time.

She wondered if there was anything that could put
his soul back together.

"I'm sorry," she said. "And that was so easy to say it
makes me seriously question why I didn't do it earlier."

"I know why you didn't do it earlier. Because you
were angry. Because you were scared. It's fine, Selena.
I'm not the kind of guy you need in your life anyway."

"Oh, I know," she said. "But it would be nice to be
on speaking terms with you."

"I'm sorry if I hurt you," he said.

"You did not hurt me," she said, making a scoff-
ing sound.

"I thought that was why you got so angry at me. Because you were in love with me."

In spite of herself, in spite of the absurdity of the situation, Selena let out a crack of laughter. "Will Sanders,
you thought I was in love with you?"

"Yes."

"You are so full of it!" she all but exploded. And
for some reason, she felt lighter than she had in days.
Weeks. *Years.* "I was not in love with you."

"You asked me to marry you to help you get your
trust fund. And then you got mad at me…"

"Because I thought our friendship was too good to
be true, Will. I didn't have it the easiest growing up. I

didn't have people in my life I could trust. I trusted you. And when Rich planted that seed of doubt…"

Everything in Will's body went hard like granite. Right down to his expression and the line of his mouth. "Right. Well. Rich has a lot to answer for."

"I just…" She tapped the side of the jar. "I wanted so badly to believe that what we had was real friendship. I guess maybe that wasn't super common for you with women, but it meant something to me."

"So—" he frowned "—you weren't in love with me?"

She laughed. "No."

"Then why did you ask me to marry you? You could have just as easily asked Knox. Did I win a coin toss?"

Unbidden, her gaze drifted across the expanse of lawn, and her eyes found Knox. Effortlessly. Easily. Her eyes always went right to him.

"I see," he said, far too perceptive. Old Will would never have been so perceptive. "Well, this does make a few things clearer."

"I'm sorry I was such a terrible friend," she said. "I'm sorry I let my issues drive us apart. And I'm sorry I listened to Rich when you had never given me a reason to mistrust you. You would make a horrible gold digger, Will, and I see that now."

"Yeah, well, nothing like dying and coming back to life to make people think better of you," he commented. "Of course…the thing with my life at the moment is I can't have it back."

"What?"

"Someone has been living it for me, Selena. I didn't write you that letter. I didn't write letters to anyone."

"Will…" She stared at him, at the changes in his face. "What happened, Will?"

"Not talking about that yet," he said, his voice tight. "I don't know what's actually going on and until then... until then I'm just keeping watch on everything."

Silence settled between them, and Selena swallowed hard and nodded. "Well...well, I'm glad you're okay. And I'm really glad you're not dead."

Suddenly he smiled, and she thought she saw a glimpse of the Will she'd once known. "You know, when this is over I think I'm going to start a line of greeting cards. The Awkwardly Interrupted Funeral line. *So glad you're not dead. Hey, you rose from the grave and it's not even Easter.*"

"That sounds great," she responded, laughing.

Well, at least one relationship in her life wasn't a total mess.

"I have to make the rounds. As a reanimated corpse, I'm extremely popular." He stuffed his hands in his pockets and winked again. It seemed a little try hard at that point, but she could understand.

Will's life couldn't be totally normal at the moment, all things considered.

"Great," she said, a smile tugging at her lips.

She wrapped her arms around herself and looked at who was attending the party. She caught sight of Will's stepbrother Jesse Navarro, who was always a dark and sullen presence. Selena didn't know him personally, but she knew of him. She had moved to Royal after college, lured by Will's tales of it as some sort of promised land.

And it always had been for her. She'd found a sense of home here. Part of that was because at first she'd had Knox, since she and Will hadn't been on speaking terms. But even after Knox had left...

The town was special to her. Even if she was a late-comer.

She had seen Jesse at events before. Even without being a member of the Texas Cattleman's Club, it was impossible to move in the moneyed circles in Royal and not have some clue about who the people were in your age bracket.

She also saw the woman who'd had the child at Will's funeral. And she wondered if that was Will's baby. Wondered if she knew the truth about anyone.

Because the fact remained that if Will was the one responsible for all that heartbreak she'd been standing in the middle of at the funeral, as much as she might like him, he had a lot to answer for. A lot to atone for, now that he was back.

Suddenly, Jesse's gaze landed on that woman, and his eyes sizzled with heat.

Selena felt like she had to look away, like she was witnessing an intimate moment.

When she looked back, whatever connection she thought she'd spotted seemed to be gone. And the woman hadn't seemed to notice at all.

She looked around again, trying to get a visual on Knox, and saw that he was gone. Then she saw a figure standing just outside the lights on the lawn, holding a bottle of beer. She knew that was him. She knew him by silhouette. That wasn't problematic at all.

She ditched the moonshine in the jar and reached for a bottle of her own beer, walking gingerly across the grass in her heels, making her way to where he was standing.

"Hi," she said.

He didn't jump. Didn't turn. As if he had already

sensed her. That thought made the back of her neck prickle. Was he as aware of her as she was of him?

"Hi," he returned, lifting his bottle of beer to his lips. He took a long, slow pull. And she was grateful for the shroud of darkness. Because had it not been so dark, she would've watched the way his lips curved around the bottle, would have watched the way his Adam's apple moved as he swallowed the liquid.

And her whole body would have burned up. A lot like it was doing now, just imagining such things.

"I talked to Will," she said.

"Did you?" he asked, the words laden with a bite.

"I think we made amends, for what that's worth. It was something that needed to happen. There's a lot of stuff in my past, and I'm all bound up in it. No matter how successful I get, no matter how far I move forward, it's just there."

He lifted a shoulder. "I can relate to that."

Except she knew he was talking about something a lot more grave, and she felt instantly guilty.

"Why aren't you at the party? Don't you want to talk to Will?"

"I decided I wasn't really in a party mood once everything got going."

"All right." She wrapped her arms around herself to keep from wrapping her arms around him. "Do you want to leave?"

"That's fine. If you're having fun."

"I'm not sure I would call laying a ghost to rest fun. Just potentially necessary."

"Right."

Then she did reach out and touch him. Her fingertips

brushed his shoulder, and she felt the contact down to her stomach, making it clench tight. "Knox."

His name was a whisper, a plea. But she didn't know what for. For normalcy? For an explosion?

His muscles tensed beneath her touch, and she felt like her stomach had been scooped out. Felt like she had been left hollow and wanting, aching for something that only he could give her.

She remembered what it felt like when his mouth pressed against hers. Finally, after all that time. She had kissed other men. Half-hearted attempts at finding a way she could be attracted to somebody who wasn't her best friend. It had never worked. It had never excited her.

This kiss haunted her dreams. It haunted her now.

She wanted to kiss him. She wanted to give him comfort. In any way she could. And they were out here in the darkness on the edge of this party. Where Will Sanders had come back from the dead and everything was just freaking crazy.

So she decided to be crazy, too. She slid her hand upward to his neck, curving her fingers around his nape. And then she brought herself around to the front of him, placing her palm on his chest, directly over his heart, where it was raging hard and fast.

"Selena," he said, a word of warning. A warning she wasn't going to heed.

She stretched up on her tiptoes—because she was still too short to just kiss him, even in these heels—and a rush of pleasure flooded her, a rush of relief, the moment their mouths met.

She was lost in it. In the torrent of desire that overtook her completely as his scent, his flavor, flooded her senses.

It was *everything*. It was everything she remembered and more. Kissing him was like nothing else. It was like every fantasy colliding into one brilliant blinding firework.

Oh, how she wanted him. How she wanted this. She wrapped her arms around his neck, still clutching the bottle of beer tightly, and then he dropped his bottle, grabbing hold of her hips with both hands and tugging her heat against his muscular body. She could feel his arousal pressing against her stomach, and she wanted… she wanted to ride it.

She wanted to ride *him*.

"Please," she whispered.

She didn't know what she was begging for, only that if she didn't get it she would die.

He moved one hand down to her side, then down her lower hip around to the back of her knee. Then he lifted her leg and drew it up over his hip, opening her to that blunt masculine part of him.

She gasped and tilted her hips forward, groaning when a shot of pleasure worked its way through her body. She tilted forward, riding the wave of pleasure. Allowing herself to get caught up in this. In the rapturous glory of his mouth on hers, of his hard, incredible masculinity.

She would let him take her here, she realized. Let him strip her naked on the edges of this party and lay her down in the damp grass. Sweep her panties to the side and thrust inside of her, even though she'd never let another man do it before. She wasn't afraid. Not even remotely.

This was Knox McCoy and she trusted him with all that she was. Trusted him with her body.

I don't trust him. There's so much I haven't told him.

But if she told him everything, then he wouldn't look at her the same. What if he saw the same abused girl she always saw when she looked in the mirror, rather than the confident businesswoman she had become?

She couldn't stand for that to happen. She truly couldn't.

So maybe if there was this first. Maybe they could both find something in it. Something they needed.

He drew away from her, suddenly, sharply, his chest heaving with effort. She wished she could see his face. Wished she could read his expression. Then he slowly released his hold on her thigh, and she slid an inch or so down his body. Not the most elegant dismount, that was for sure. She was grateful for the darkness, because he couldn't see the fierce blush in her cheeks, couldn't get an accurate read on the full horror moving through her at the moment.

"I'm not sorry," she said, pulling her dress back into place.

"Did I ask you to be?" he bit out, his words hard.

"No," she said, "but you stopped."

"I stopped because I was close to fucking you right here at a party. Is that what you want?"

"I…" She was dizzy. She couldn't believe she was standing here listening to her friend say those words, directed at her. "That's a complicated question, Knox."

"No." He shook his head. "It's really not. Either you want to get fucked on the ground at a party by your best friend or you don't."

She looked away, feeling self-conscious even though

she knew he couldn't see her expression. "Maybe not...
on the ground...at a *party*."

"Selena," he said, gripping her chin, leaning forward and gazing at her with his dark, blazing eyes.
"I can't give you anything. I can't give you anything
other than sex."

"I didn't ask you for anything," she said, her voice
small.

"We're friends. And that means I care about you. But
I'm never, ever getting married again."

"It's kind of a long leap from fucking in the grass to a
marriage proposal, don't you think, Knox?" she asked,
self-protection making her snarky, because she needed
something to put distance between them.

"I just meant this doesn't end anywhere but sex, baby.
And I need our friendship. I haven't had a lot of bright
spots in my life lately, and I hate to lose the one I have."

"But you want me," she said, not feeling at all awkward about laying that out there. Because he did. And
she knew it.

"That doesn't mean having."

And then he just walked away. Walked away like
they were in the middle of having a conversation. Like
her heart wasn't still pounding so hard it was likely to
go straight through her chest. Like she wasn't wet and
aching for satisfaction that he had denied her, yet again.

And that was when she made a decision. She was
going to have Knox McCoy. Because there was no going
back now. They wanted each other. And she had been
holding on to all those feelings for him for so long that
she knew a couple of things for certain. They weren't
going away, and no man could take his place as it was.

She had known a lot of girls in college who had

thought they needed to get certain guys out of their systems, which had always seemed to her a fancy way to excuse having sex when you wanted it, even though you knew it was a really bad idea and the guy was never going to call. It had always ended in sadness, as far as she had seen.

But Knox had been in her system for so long, and there was no other way he was getting out of it. She knew that. This wasn't a guy she had met in class a few weeks ago, a guy she had exchanged numbers with at a party.

She had known Knox for the better part of her adult life and she wasn't just going to wake up one morning and not want him.

So maybe this was the way forward.

She pulled her phone out, still not ready to go back to the party, to go back into the lights where people might see her emotional state. Where they might be able to read what had just happened. And she texted Scarlett.

So, about that glamping.

CHAPTER SEVEN

KNOX HAD STUCK it out at the party just to be a stubborn cuss. By the time he and Selena got back in the car and started to drive to the ranch, he expected her to unleash hell on him.

Instead, she didn't. Instead, she was silent the entire way, and he didn't like that. He didn't like it at all. He'd enough of hard, sad silences. He preferred to be screamed at, frankly. But Selena didn't seem to be in the mood to give him what he wanted.

And he said nothing.

Then when they pulled in the driveway and finally got out, heading into the house, she spoke. "We're going glamping tomorrow," she said, her expression neutral, but vaguely mischievous.

"What?"

"Scarlett suggested it. We're going on a trail ride. And we are staying overnight in a luxury tent."

"I was going to head back to Jackson Hole," he said, lying, because he had no plans to do that at all. And for the first time, he questioned why.

He didn't like that all these interactions with Selena forced him to do things like ponder his motivations.

"I don't care. Change your ticket. You're rich as God, Knox. It's not like it's a problem."

"No," he said slowly.

"You're coming glamping with me, because you're still not okay, I'm clearly not okay, and we need to do something to get back on track. We are not leaving our friendship here. You are not going off to Wyoming for however the hell long and not seeing me. Because it's going to turn into not seeing me for months, for years, as we avoid all the weirdness that has sprung up between us."

Oh, he was personally all right with avoiding the weirdness. But obviously, she wasn't.

"Okay," he found himself agreeing, and he couldn't quite fathom why.

"It'll be fun," she said, grinning at him, all teeth. And it made him damn suspicious.

"I'm not overly familiar with fun," he said, purposefully making his tone grave.

"Well," she said, "this will be."

He had his doubts, but he also knew Selena Jacobs on a mission was not a creature to be trifled with. And not one easily derailed.

So they would go on a trail ride. They would go camping.

Once upon a time he'd liked to ride, he'd liked to camp. Why the hell not?

Maybe she was right. Maybe it would remind him of some of the things he used to like.

Although, privately, he feared that it would go much the same way as the party had gone. That all it would do was reinforce the fact that he couldn't enjoy things the way he used to. That he had nothing left to look forward to in his life.

Because he couldn't think of a single dream he hadn't

achieved. Then two of them he lost. And one of them just didn't mean a thing without the others.

And he had no idea where the hell you went from there.

Camping, it seemed.

He shook his head and followed Selena into the house.

BY THE TIME they were saddled up and ready to ride, Selena was starting to have some doubts. But not enough to turn back.

They were given a map and detailed instructions on how the trail ride would work, and then she and Knox were sent off into the Texas wilderness together. Alone, except for each other.

And the condoms Selena had stuck in her bag.

Because this was a seduction mission more than it was anything else, and she was completely ready to go there.

Well, except for the nerves. And the doubts. There were those. But that was all virgin stuff.

Oh, and the fact that she was going to see her best friend's penis.

The thought made her simultaneously want to giggle and squeeze her thighs together to quell the ache there.

Her cheeks heated as she realized the rhythm of the horse's gait did a little something for it. Her face flamed, her whole body getting warm.

Knox McCoy had turned her into a sex-crazed pervert. And they hadn't even had sex yet.

He might not want to have sex with me.

Yes, that was the risk. She might get Knox alone in a tent, around a romantic campfire, and she might strip herself completely naked and get denied. It was possible. It was not a possibility she was hoping for. But it might happen. The idea did not thrill her.

But there was no great achievement without great risk. And anyway, if there was one thing she had kind of learned from this whole experience with Will's death-that-was-not-actually-a-death, it was that time was finite.

She had stood at Will's funeral and had regretted leaving things bad between them. She didn't want to regret Knox.

Somewhere in the back of her mind she knew that if this ruined her friendship with Knox she was going to regret that. She was going to regret it a whole hell of a lot. But at least she wouldn't wonder. Right now, it seemed worth the risk.

Maybe on the other side it wouldn't. But she wasn't on the other side yet.

She squared her shoulders and they continued to ride down the trail.

It was beautiful. The land was sparse, filled with scrub brush and twisty, gnarled trees that were green in defiance to their surroundings. She had been told that the trail would wind toward some water, and that it would get shadier and greener there, which was why it was good to do this leg early in the morning, before the sun rose high in the sky and the heat and humidity started to get oppressive.

But the view around her wasn't her primary reason for being here, anyway. It was him. It was Knox.

"So," she said, "it's nice out."

"Yeah," he responded, taciturn like he had been last night.

It was funny, how she had gone from the one being all angry about the kiss to him being all angry. What a delight.

She hoped that banging him was slightly more delightful.

The thought made her nerves twitch.

"So, how many hours is it to camp?" he asked.

"About six," she said.

"That seems a little bit crazy," he responded.

"I know," she said, and then she frowned. Because she hadn't really considered that. The fact that she was going to launch a full-out seduction after having been on the back of a horse all day. Honestly, there was a sweat situation that might be problematic. Not that she minded if he was sweaty. She was all okay with that. It was pheromones or something. She had always liked the way Knox smelled when he'd been sweating. After he had gone for a run in college and he would come back to hang at her dorm for a while, steal some food off her and her roommate. He had walked by her, and her stomach would go into a free fall.

It was so funny, how she had buried that reaction down deep, and how it was all coming up now. Bringing itself into the light, really.

She had been in full denial of her feelings for him for so long. While she had definitely known they were there, she didn't focus on them. But now she was admitting everything to herself. That she was a sucker for the way he smelled. That his voice skimmed over her skin like a touch. That in so many ways she had been waiting for him. Waiting for this. And that excuses about how busy she was, how important the company was, were not really the reasons why she didn't date.

It was because no man was Knox, and never would be.

As she made idle chatter for the rest of the ride, she fought against cloying terror. She was headed toward what was her undeniable destiny and almost certain heartbreak.

But she'd come too far to turn back now. She simply couldn't.

Eventually, they did come to that river, and they found themselves beneath the canopy of trees as the sun rose high in the sky. They arrived at camp before the sun began to set, a glorious, serene tent out in the middle of nowhere right next to the river.

There were Texas bluebells in the grass that surrounded it. A little oasis just for them. There was a firepit, places to sit. It really was the most civilized camping she had ever seen.

"I am going to jump in the river," Knox said. He got off the horse and stripped his shirt off over his head.

And she froze. Just absolutely froze as the shirt's fabric slowly rolled up over his torso and revealed his body.

Lord, what a body.

"What?" he asked.

Well, great. She'd been caught staring openly. At her friend's half-naked body. Talk about telegraphing her seduction plans.

"Nothing." She blinked. "I'll go… We can get the horses settled and then I'll get my swimsuit."

But her gaze was fully fixed on his broad, bare chest. On all those fantastic, perfect muscles. Which she had felt through his shirt a time or two in the past few days. But now… Seeing it like that, dusted with just the right amount of pale hair, glistening with sweat… She wanted to lick him.

She imagined the rules of friendship generally prevented that. But she was fully violating those anyway, so she was just going to embrace the feeling.

"Come on," he said, nodding once. "Let's get the horses into the corral."

She went through the motions of leading the horses into the gated area and making sure there was fresh water in the trough, but really, she was just watching Knox.

The way the sun glinted on his golden hair and highlighted the scruff on his face—she wanted so badly to run her fingers over it. The way the muscles in his forearms went taut as he removed the horses' bridles and saddles…

He bent down low, setting about cleaning their hooves, his body putting on a glorious play of strength and sculpted masculinity that took her breath away.

He was such a familiar sight. But in context with desire, with what she wanted to have happen later, he was like a stranger. And that both thrilled and excited her.

When they finished taking care of the animals, he straightened, and she was momentarily struck dumb again by his beauty. It was a wonder she'd ever managed to get to know the guy. His looks were a serious barrier to her ability to form cogent thoughts and words that were more than noises.

"Why don't you go on in and get your suit?" he asked, handing her her pack.

His fingers brushed against hers and she felt the touch like a bolt of lightning. All the way through her body.

Selena scurried into the tent, barely able to take in the glory of it. There was an actual bed inside, seating, a woodstove, all surrounded by beautifully draped canvas. The bed was covered in furs and other soft, sumptuous things. It was the perfect place to make love to a man you had been fantasizing about all of your life.

And when darkness fell, she was going to do just that.

The corners of her lips turned upward when she realized there was only one bed in the place. And she wondered if Scarlett was matchmaking. If Selena had been that damned transparent. She changed quickly into a black bikini, ignoring the moment of wishing it covered more of her body, and headed outside.

She was gratified when Knox's expression took on that similar "hit with a shovel" quality she had been pretty sure her own had possessed a few moments ago when he had stripped off his shirt.

"Nice suit," he said.

He was wearing a pair of swim shorts that she wondered if he'd been wearing beneath everything else the whole time. Or if he had just quickly gotten naked outside.

And then she thought way too long and hard about that.

"Thank you," she said.

The shorts rode low, revealing every sculpted line just above that part of him that was still a mystery to her. She was doing her best not to look like a guppy spit out onto the shore. Gaping and gasping. She had a feeling she was only semi-successful.

"There's only one bed," she commented. "I didn't realize that."

As if that mattered. She was planning to seduce him anyway.

"Oh," he said. "Well, I can sleep on the floor."

"Let's worry about that later," she said, because she hoped that both of them would be completely all right with the fact that there was only one bed just a little bit later.

They went down toward the river, and in spite of the heat, when she stuck her toe in the slow-moving water, she shuddered slightly.

"Oh, come on," he said. "It's not that cold."

As if to demonstrate all of his masculine bravado, he went straight into the water, wading in up to his hips and then lying flat on his stomach and paddling out toward the center of the wide body of water.

She took a deep breath and followed suit, screeching as the water made contact with the tender skin on her stomach. "It is cold," she shouted at him.

"You're a baby," he responded, turning over onto his back and paddling away from her.

"I am not a baby," she said. She swam toward him and then splashed at him. He laughed, reaching out and grabbing her wrist, drawing her against him. She didn't know what the intent had been. Maybe to stop her from splashing him, but suddenly, her legs were all tangled up with his and her breasts were pressed against his bare chest. The wet swimsuit fabric did absolutely nothing to provide a barrier between them. Her nipples were hard, sensitive, partly from the chill of the water and partly just from him. From her desire for him.

"Knox," she said. "If you don't like it, tell me. I don't want to be tea."

"You're not tea," he said.

"Good. I'd hate for you to sleep with me because of good manners. A girl wants to be wanted."

And something in his eyes changed. His jaw was

tight, the lines by his mouth drawn, deep. And she could see the struggle there. The fight.

"I don't need forever," she said. Her seduction plan had just gone out the window. This electricity between them was sparking right now. And she was going to make the most of it. She was going to take it. "I just need you. For a little while. I've wanted you... Always. I have. This isn't new for me. And it's not going away." She raised her hands, trusting him, trusting his strong, steady hold to keep her afloat. She traced those deep lines on either side of his lips with her thumbs, stroking him. Touching him the way she had always dreamed about touching him. Freely, without holding back.

That was the sad thing. She felt a whole hell of a lot for him, and yet she'd always, always held it back, held back a part of herself.

She was tired of that. And she was surrounded by reminders of why it was wrong. Time wasn't infinite. She'd thought she'd missed a chance to apologize to Will.

She wasn't going to miss this chance.

"You want this?" he asked, his voice rough. "You want me right now? Let me tell you, Selena, all I can give you is selfish. I haven't had sex in two years. A little bit more, maybe. Because it's not like there was a whole lot going on during the divorce. During the grief. And I... I don't have any control left in me. I wanted to do the right thing. I wanted to be honest with you about what I could and couldn't give you, but if you keep offering it to me..."

"If I keep offering it to you then you need to trust me." She met his gaze and held it. Tried to ignore her breathlessness, her nerves. "I'm your friend. I've been your friend for a long time. Haven't I always taken what you've given to me? Haven't we always been there for each other? That's what this is. I want to be there for you. And I want this, too. This isn't pity sex, Knox. I want it. I want you. I think you want me. So let's… Let's just trust that we'll find our way. Because we are friends. We've been through hell together. It wasn't my hell, Knox, but I walked alongside you. Trust me. Trust me to keep walking with you."

She was on the verge of tears, emotion clogging her throat, and crying wasn't what she wanted. It wasn't what this was supposed to be. It was supposed to be physical, and it was becoming emotional. But too late she realized, as she clung to him while he treaded water for them both, with Knox it was never going to be anything but emotional. Because they cared for each other.

And emotion was never going to stay outside of the sex. It was never going to be sex in one column and friendship in the other. They were bringing sex into a friendship. And that was big and scary, and not something she could turn away from.

"Trust me," she said, a final plea before he closed the distance between them.

CHAPTER EIGHT

KNOX HAD KNOWN he was lost the moment she had come out of the tent wearing that bikini. He hadn't even given himself a chance. When he had grabbed hold of her in the water... It hadn't been to stop her from splashing him. It had simply been because he couldn't stand to not touch her anymore. He had to do it. He'd had to bring her against his body. Because he couldn't stand to not have his hands on her.

And as he held her he had the fleeting concern that this was going to be the most selfish sex on the face of the planet, and he was going to treat his best friend to it. She didn't deserve that. She deserved more. She deserved better. But he didn't have control. Not anymore.

He was a man stripped of everything. Life had simply stolen every fucking thing from him in the last two years. He couldn't fight this. Not with what he had left.

He just wanted. And he was so tired of wanting. There were so many things he couldn't have. He could not have Eleanor back, no matter how much he wanted her.

He couldn't fight death. No matter how he wanted to. How he wished that there was a sword he could have picked up so he could do battle with death. Instead, he'd had to stand by helplessly, not able to do a damn thing. For a man who had never accepted the limits of life, losing to death with such resounding finality had been incomprehensible.

But he could have this. He could have Selena.

He didn't have to fight it, and he damn sure wasn't going to. Not anymore.

So he kissed her. He kissed her like he was drowning in this river and she was the air. He kissed her like there wasn't going to be anything after it. Because for all he knew, there wouldn't be. Life was a bitch. A cruel, evil bitch who took as much as she gave, so he was going to take something of his own.

Maybe anger at the world wasn't the way to approach a seduction. Maybe it wasn't the way to engage with his best friend, but he couldn't help himself. Couldn't do anything but lean into it. Lean into her. When she parted her lips and slid her tongue against his, he forgot to keep kicking, and they sank slightly beneath the water, the surface slipping past their shoulders. "We need to get out of here," he said, paddling them both toward the shore.

"There's that bed," she said softly, stroking her hand over his face, over his shoulders, the slide of skin against skin slick from the water.

He looked into her dark eyes to get a read on what she was thinking. "Did you plan this?"

"No," she said, looking very much like the picture of pristine innocence. In a black bikini that looked like sin.

"You didn't." Her eyes sparked with a little bit of heat, and a lot of the stubbornness he thought was cute about Selena at the best of times. It was cuter now, considering he was holding her nearly naked curves.

"Well." Her smile turned impish. "I didn't know there would be one bed. But I did know that I wanted you. And I figured this was as good a way as any to go about having you."

"Minx," he said, kissing her again. Kissing her until they were both breathless, out there in the bleached Texas sun.

Then he swept her up and carried her back toward that tent.

He didn't bother to dry either of them off when he deposited her on the plush bed at the far side of the canvas wall. He stood there, looking at every delicious inch of her. Those full breasts, barely contained by the swimsuit top, her small waist and firm stomach. Those hips. Wide and delicious, and her thighs, which were full and lovely. Shaped like a delicious pear he definitely wanted to take a bite out of.

He pushed his wet shorts down his thighs, careful with his straining arousal. And it was gratifying to watch her mouth drop open, to watch her eyes go wide.

She squeezed her thighs together, drawing one leg up slightly, biting her lip.

"See something you like?" he asked.

She nodded. "Yeah," she said. And it was rare for Selena to not have a snarky comment follow.

"Do you want this?" he asked.

"Yes," she said, the word breathless. "I want it so much." She rolled to her side, her wet hair falling over her shoulder, her eyes wide. "Don't change your mind."

He glanced down at his extremely prominent erection. "Oh, I'm not in a position to change my mind. Or to do much of anything with my mind at the moment, especially thinking."

She settled back into the blankets, looking satisfied with that statement. "I'm okay with that."

He got onto the bed, moving over her, kissing her again, reaching behind her neck and undoing the tie on her bikini top in one fluid motion. Then he did the other one, taking the wet cups away from her breasts.

His breath caught in his throat as he looked at her. At that glorious, golden skin, her tight, honey-colored nipples.

He leaned forward, flicking the tip of one sensitive bud with his tongue, gratified when she gasped and arched against him. He sucked her deep into his mouth, lost completely in his own desire. His need to feast on her, to gorge himself on her beauty.

He wasn't thinking about anything in the past. Wasn't thinking about anything but this. But her. There was no room for anything but desire inside of him. There was nothing else at all.

He smoothed his hands down her narrow waist to those full hips, gripped her bikini bottoms and tugged them down her legs. And he groaned when he saw that dark thatch of curls at the apex of her thighs. He kissed her stomach, all the way down low to that tender skin beneath her belly button. Then he forced her legs apart, his cock pulsing, his stomach muscles getting impossibly tight as he looked at his friend like this for the first time. He felt her try to close her legs, try to move away from him.

He wasn't going to let her get away with that.

She might have orchestrated this little camping trip. Might have thought she could conduct a seduction. And he was seduced; there was no doubt about that. But she wasn't in charge. Not now. Hell no.

He leaned forward, breathing in the scent of her. Musk and female and everything he craved. His mouth watered, and he leaned forward, sliding his tongue over her slick flesh, flicking that sweet little clit with the tip of his tongue. She gasped, her hips bucking off the bed, simultaneously moving toward him and away from him. He held her fast, grabbing hold of both hips, drawing her roughly against his mouth where he could have his fill and maintain control of the movements.

She tried to twist and ride beneath him, but he held her fast, pleasuring her with his lips and his tongue, pressing his fingers deep inside of her until she cried out, until her internal muscles pulsed around him.

"Knox," she said, his name thin and shaky on her lips, her entire body boneless. And that satisfied him. Because it had been a long damn time since he'd had a woman, and there was a deep satisfaction to making her come that he couldn't even describe.

He could do that to her body. This need, this skill existed inside of him, and the desire to practice it was there. He'd left that need boxed up inside of him for years. In a stack in the corner of his soul. Anything that wasn't work, anything that wasn't breathing.

Right now, this felt like breathing. And he didn't simply feel alive. He felt like Knox.

He wanted to do it again. Again and again. He wanted to make her scream his name. But she was reaching for him, urging him up her body, urging him to kiss her again. Who was he to deny her?

He was going to give her everything.

Everything he had.

He settled between her thighs, kissing her deeply. He wanted this to last longer. Wanted to go on. But he just didn't possess the control. He needed to be inside of her. And he needed it now. He could only take so much satisfaction from her orgasm without desperately needing his own.

He pressed the head of his cock to the entrance of her body, found her wet and ready for him. Then he slid himself upward, drawing his length over those slick folds, teasing her a little before moving back to her entrance and thrusting in hard.

Then he froze as she tensed beneath him. As she let out a cry that had nothing at all to do with pleasure.

Somehow, Selena was a virgin.

SELENA TRIED *SO* hard not to be a baby when the sharp, tearing pain moved through her. He had just made her feel so good. And really, she wanted this. She wanted him. But the invasion of his body into hers hurt and she hadn't been able to keep back the cry of shock when he had entered her.

Screaming in pain was probably not the best move on her part. A pretty surefire way to kill the mood. Knox froze, looking down at her with anger written all over his handsome face.

She felt him start to move away from her, felt his muscles tense as he prepared to pull back. So he could stop touching her. So he could run out into the desert in the late afternoon and take his chances with the sun and snakes rather than with her. But she didn't want him to go.

So she clung to him, desperation probably leaving marks behind on his skin, digging her nails into his shoulders and kissing him fiercely, rocking her hips against his, ignoring the pain. She didn't want him to stop. It was too late anyway. Her virginity was gone. The hard part, the scary part, was over.

She didn't want to stop. Not now.

He tried to pull away again but she moved her hands down, clapping them over his muscular ass and holding him to her. She shook her head, her lips still fused to his.

He said nothing. Then he just continued on, slowly withdrawing from her body before thrusting back inside. He shuddered, lowering his head, his forehead pressed to hers. And she recognized the moment where whatever reservations he'd had were washed away by his own tide of need.

She'd had an orgasm already; he had not.

"Yes," she whispered as he began to move inside of her. As he began to establish a steady, luxurious rhythm that erased the pain she had felt only a moment before.

She wrapped her legs around his narrow hips, urging him on, chasing the pleasure she had felt before. And it began to build, low and deep inside of her, a band of tension that increased in intensity, drawing her closer to a second release. But this one seemed to come from somewhere deeper.

This time, when she shattered, it was just as he did, as his muscles tensed and his body shuddered, as his own orgasm washed through her, his thick, heavy cock pulsing as he spilled himself into her.

And when it was over, they lay there gasping, and she knew she was never going to be the same again. That there was no getting anyone out of her system. That her need for him would never change.

But along with that realization came a deep sense of peace. One that she was sure would vanish. But for now, she clung to it. For now, she clung to it and him, because reality would hit soon enough.

And she was in no hurry.

Because she had a feeling as soon as the afterglow receded there would be questions. She had a feeling there were in fact going to be quite a few follow-up questions. And what she really hadn't thought through in this moment was that there were going to be a lot of questions about Will.

She closed her eyes. Of course, she had already alluded to the fact that their marriage wasn't everything it seemed. So maybe Knox wouldn't be completely shocked. Maybe.

Well, even if he was—maybe that wasn't the end of the world. Maybe it was time to share the truth with him. She had closed him off. And now... Now he had been inside her body. So maybe that time was over. Maybe she just needed to go for it.

There was only one way to find out.

"Yes," she said, finding courage from deep inside that she hadn't realized existed. "I was a virgin."

He swore and moved away from her. She looked over at him just in time to see him scrubbing his hands over his face in what one might be forgiven for assuming was despair.

She folded her hands and rested them on her bare stomach, staring up at the canvas ceiling. "I assume you have queries."

"Yes," he responded. "I have several."

"Well," she said. "My marriage to Will wasn't real. I mean, we were never in a relationship."

"Never?" He treated her to a long hard look.

"No," she said. "We were never in a relationship at all. It was purely to help me get the trust-fund money."

"Why didn't you come to me? You could have picked

either of your friends to help you out with this and you asked him?"

Panic fluttered in her breast and she took a deep breath, trying to tap it down. She wasn't going to tell him that she hadn't asked because she couldn't face the possibility that living with him wouldn't have felt fake to her. She wasn't going to bring up her feelings at all. "I just… Look what happened with my friendship with Will afterward. Don't tell me I was wrong in trying to protect our friendship from problems like that. Choosing Will seemed necessary. Marrying him seemed like the only thing I could do to make sure that you and I were going to be okay. You were always more important to me, Knox. I just didn't…"

"That's bullshit, Selena," he said. "I know it is. Give me a straight answer."

"Why?" she asked. "I don't want to give you a straight answer. Because there is no good answer."

"I want the truth."

"Fine," she said. "I was afraid we would end up like this." She swept her arm up and down, indicating their nudity. "I didn't worry about that with Will. Not at all. It was just never like that between us. I never had those feelings for him."

"You had them for me."

"Yes," she said. "That's kind of obvious, considering we are lying here naked."

"But even back then?" he asked.

He'd already confessed to being attracted to her, but she hadn't handed out a similar confession. For her it felt so raw. So deep.

"I wanted you. But I knew I wasn't in a position to have you. I thought maybe someday… And then…marrying Will was a bad choice, Knox. And it's one I've never been particularly interested in interrogating. It ruined a lot of things."

"About the time you got divorced I was with Cassandra."

"Yes," she said. "In a lot of ways, I was grateful for that. Because it helped us preserve our friendship. I don't regret that neither of us made a move. I feel like it was actually better. I feel like if it had happened when we were young, we wouldn't have been able to…process this. We wouldn't have been able to separate the attraction from the friendship."

"And you think we can now?"

"I think we're both tired," she said, obviously. "I think we're both fatigued after spending a long time denying what we wanted. It's a pattern. In both of our lives. I'm not going to pretend to compare my struggle to yours. I'm really not. But…why fight this? We both wanted it. And for the first time, we're in a place where we can both take it. It was always wrong, and maybe in the future it will be wrong again. Maybe it will just naturally fade away."

"Is that what you really believe?"

"Yes," she said. "I do. I believe this is something we can work out. This is something we can have."

"But… Hell, Selena," he said. "You've really never been with another guy?"

"No. I was really busy. I was really busy growing the company and…"

"Yeah, usually that's the kind of thing people say when they miss a lot of coffee dates. Not when they just kind of forgot to have sex ever."

Now this, she could not be honest about. She was

not going to have a discussion with him about how no man had ever seemed to measure up to him in her mind.

Because that was beyond sad.

"It really wasn't something that mattered to me. And then… Over the past few weeks with you…" She cleared her throat. "I'm attracted to you. I always have been. But it's not something I dwell on. I mean, you were married to somebody else. You had another life. And I always respected that. I did. What you had with Cassandra… I would never have dreamed of encroaching on it. I care about you like a friend, and I kind of want to tear your clothes off and bite you like a crazed lioness, and those two things are separate. But there was never any crazed lioness fantasies while you were married." That was a little lie. There was the occasional fantasy, but she had known she could never act on it.

He paused for a moment, then placed his hand on her. "So your attraction went dormant?"

"Yes," she said. "Your marriage was the winter of our attraction. It hibernated."

"Your libido hibernated," he said, his tone bland.

"Yeah," she said. "And my burrow was work. Work and friends and establishing my life in Royal." She let out a heavy sigh. "I never wanted to get married and have a family," she admitted. "My father was… You know he was difficult. And it's…" She knew it was time to share everything. They were naked, after all. They were naked and he had just taken her virginity, and there really were very few secrets left between them. But the last one was hers. She was holding it. She had to give it up.

"My father used to beat us. He was violent. His temper was unpredictable. We walked like there was broken glass under our feet all the time. Doing the very best we could not to bring that temper up. It was terrible. Terrifying. I will never, ever submit myself to that kind of thing again."

"So is that why you avoided relationships?"

"I would say that's why they weren't a priority. I'm not sure that I avoided them. I just didn't pursue them."

"You're being difficult."

"Yeah, well," she said. "I reserve the right to be difficult. I *can* be difficult now. That's the beauty of life on your own terms."

"And you think that's the key to happiness?" he asked, brushing his knuckles idly over her hip. It was a question void of judgment, but it made her chest feel weird all the same. Mostly because she'd never thought of it in those terms.

"It's a luxury. One that I appreciate. That's why I was so desperate to marry Will," she said. "Because I needed that money. Because I needed to be able to control my life. Because if I couldn't, then I was always going to be under my father's thumb."

"He *hit* you?" he asked.

"Yes," she said. "All the time. For anything. For attitude, disrespect. For not complying with his wishes when he wanted us to. We didn't have any control. We had to be the perfect family. His perfect wife. His perfect daughter. He didn't want me to go to college. He didn't want me to have any kind of autonomy at all. My grandfather is the one who helped me enroll in Harvard. But then he died. And I knew I wasn't going to find any more support. I wasn't going to have the resources for college. I was going to have to go back home, Knox, and I couldn't face that. I didn't want to need my father again. Ever. And I needed to get my hands on that trust fund in order to make that happen. In order to protect myself. To protect my mother. After I got it, I moved her out of the house. I installed her somewhere he couldn't get to her. I did everything I could do with my money to make sure we were never beholden to him again."

He shifted, tightening his hold on her. "I didn't know it was that bad." His words were like ground glass, sharp and gritty, and it gratified her to know that Knox was holding her tight with murder on his mind, because he couldn't stand the thought of her being hurt.

She was right to trust him.

"We all have our own struggles," she said, working to keep her tone casual. "I never wanted anyone to look at me like I was broken. Like I needed to be treated gently. I've always felt strong. Growing up that way, I had to be. But I protect what I have. I protect what's mine.

"You can see how our relationship, love, all of that never figured into my plans. I could never see myself submitting to a man controlling my life. To anyone controlling my life. To love controlling my life. Because that was my experience. It took so much for my mother to leave because she loved him, not just because she was afraid of him. Because part of her wanted to make it work. Wanted to find the man she had once known. The one who had made her fall for him in the first place. No matter how much I tried to tell her that man never existed, it was difficult for her to accept."

Selena took a deep breath before continuing, "She refused to press charges in the end. She used to cry. And say that I ruined her life by breaking up the marriage. By sending her to live in Manhattan, far away from him, and safely ensconced in an apartment there.

She would think about going back to him, and it was only her fear that kept her away. She skips therapy all the time, no matter how many appointments I set up. I just... I never wanted to be that creature. Ever."

Knox grabbed hold of her chin, met her gaze. "You never could be."

She reached up, curled her fingers over his wrist and held his arm steady. "Any of us can be. At least, that's what I think. One step in the wrong direction and you're on that path, and at some point you're too many steps in, and you can't imagine going back. I've never thought I was above anything. I've never thought I was too good, too smart... Because that's not it. That's not what does it. We can all get bound up in it."

He looked genuinely stricken by that. "I never thought of it like that," he admitted.

"I know. It's human nature to want to believe people are at fault for their own bad situations. And oftentimes they are complicit. But I don't think it was a fundamental personality flaw that made my mother stay with my father. It was fear of change. A fear of losing what she had. Because what if she ended up with less?"

"But she stayed in a house with a man who hit her daughter. You might be able to excuse that, Selena, but I don't think I can."

She looked away from him. "Sometimes I have a hard time with that. I won't lie to you. I can't have a relationship with my father. He's not a good man. He hurt me. He hurt my mother. He was made of rage that had nothing to do with us. I'm convinced it had everything to do with some kind of anger at himself. But whatever it was, it's nothing I want touching my life. So yes. I feel like I could be angry at her. Maybe I would even be justified. Because you're right. She did stay. Her fear was bigger than her desire to take action to get us out. In the end, my fear of living in that hell forever is what made me take action. And I just... We are out. And I don't have the energy for anger anymore. I want to have at least one relationship with one family member that isn't toxic. I want to heal what I can."

"That's pretty damned big of you," he said.

She laughed, lifting her shoulder. "Sure, but then, I also don't want to have a romantic relationship, so I'm emotionally scarred in other ways."

"I can appreciate that."

Silence fell over them and she allowed herself to fully take in the moment. The fact that she was lying there, skin to skin with her best friend. With the man she had fantasized about all of her life. She had told him everything. She had finally laid bare all the secrets she had been so scared to roll out. But on the heels of sharing everything came the revelation she had been working on avoiding. The real reason she had been afraid of confiding in him all this time.

It wasn't just that she cared for him. It wasn't just that she was attracted to him. She was in love with Knox McCoy, and she always had been. In love with a man she could never allow herself to have, because she had sworn that she would never get involved in those kinds of relationships.

And she was such a fool. Because she had been in love with him from the moment he had first walked into her life. She had thought she could keep him as a friend, and ignore the bigger feelings, the deeper feelings, but that was a lie. There was no avoiding it. There never had been.

But she didn't tell him that. She had let out all her other secrets and replaced them with another. One that she hoped he would never discover.

Because as horrifying as it was to admit to herself that she was in love with him, it would be even worse to have him know and have him reject her.

So she laid her head on his chest and focused on the rhythm of his heartbeat, on the way his skin felt beneath hers.

It wasn't love. But for now, maybe it was enough.

CHAPTER NINE

THEY FINISHED OUT the trail ride the next day in relative silence. Knox was saddle sore, because it had been a while since he had ridden a horse. And it had been a while since he had ridden a woman. But he and Selena had definitely indulged themselves the entire night. He still wasn't sure what to make of any of it. Of the fact that he'd made love to his best friend, of the fact that she had been a virgin.

Yeah, he didn't even the hell know. But things weren't terribly awkward, which was a miracle in and of itself.

When they arrived back at Paradise Farms he noticed that Selena was pretty cagey with Scarlett as they deposited the horses and thanked her for the generous loan.

"She knew, didn't she?" Selena asked when they got back into the car and headed down the highway.

"Do you think so?"

"Well, I wonder, because she obviously knew the tent only had one bed."

He chuckled. "So you think she was trying to set you up?"

"I think she was trying to set *you* up," she said. "She thought you seemed sad."

"I am," he responded, his tone dry. The answer more

revealing than he'd intended it to be. He had meant to make the comment kind of light, but it was difficult for him to keep it light these days.

"I'm sorry," she said.

"Don't apologize," he said. "There's no damned reason to. You didn't do anything. Nobody did."

"I'm not apologizing, not really. I'm just sorry that life is so messed up."

He huffed out a laugh. "You and me both. I'm not sure what you're supposed to do with a bunch of broken pieces," he said, the words torn from him. "When they're all you have left. When you had this full, complete life and then suddenly it's just gone. I don't know what the hell you're supposed to do with that."

"I don't either," she commented. "I really don't. I guess you try to make a new life, new things. Out of the broken bits."

"I don't think I have the desire or the energy," he said.

"What's the alternative?" she asked, her voice hushed. "I'm not trying to be flippant. I'm asking a serious question. If you don't rebuild, what do you do? Just sit there in the rubble? Because I think you deserve a hell of a lot more than that."

"What's the point? Everything you do, everything you are, can be taken from you." He didn't know what had gotten him into such a dire place. He'd just had sex for the first time in years and now suddenly they were talking about the fragility of life. "All these things you make your identity out of. Husband. Father. Billionaire. They're just things. They get taken from you, and then what? It's like you said about your mother last night. You lose sight of who you are, and then you're just

afraid of what will be left. Once you lose those titles
that defined you then…then there's just nothing. That's
how it feels. Like I'm standing on a hell of a lot of nothing. Somehow I'm not in a free fall…but I don't trust
this will last. I don't trust that the whole world won't
just fall apart again."

They turned up the dirt road onto her property and
didn't speak until they were inside the house again.
Then finally she turned to him, her dark eyes full of
compassion. He didn't like that. The compassion. Because it was so damned close to pity.

"I don't know what to say," she said, when they got
into the house. She looked at him with luminous eyes,
and he could read her sincerity. Her sadness.

He didn't want either.

He reached out, grabbing hold of her wrist and wrapping his arm around her waist, crushing her to his body,
because he couldn't think of anything else to do. He
needed something to hold on to, and she was there,
like she had always been. In the middle of that horrible breakdown that he'd had at Eleanor's funeral, she'd
been there. And she was here now. There was a yawning, horrific ache inside of him, and she was the only
thing he could think of that would fill it.

"I used to be a husband," he said, his voice rough.
"I used to be a father. And now I'm just a man with a
hole inside, and I don't know what the hell I'm going to
do to fix it. I don't even know if I want to fix it. I don't
know who I am."

"I do," she said softly. She lifted the hand that was
currently free and brushed her fingertips against the
side of his face, tracing the line of his jaw. "You're a

man, Knox. A man that I want. For now…can that be enough? Can you just be that for me?"

Everything inside of him roared an enthusiastic hell yes. He could be that. He could do that. It was actually the one damn thing he knew in that moment. That he could be Selena's lover. That he could satisfy them both. He didn't know what the hell was going on in the rest of the world, but he knew what could happen here, in her bedroom.

And so he picked her up, holding her close to his chest as he carried her to the back of the house and deposited her on her bed. He stripped them both of their clothes, leaving the lights on so he could drink his fill of her beautiful body. He was about to do to her what he had done last night, to force her legs open and taste her as deeply as he wanted to. But she sat up on the bed, moving to the edge and pressing her hands to the center of his bare chest.

"Let me," she whispered. She pressed a kiss to his pectoral muscle, right next to his nipple. "Let me show you. Let me show you how much I want you."

He tensed, his entire body drawn tight like a bow. She continued an exploration down his torso, down his stomach, and lower still until she reached his cock. She curved her fingers around him, leaning forward and flicking her tongue over the head. His breath caught sharply, his entire body freezing.

"I've never done this either," she said. He looked down at her and saw that she was making eye contact with him, her expression impish. "If you were wondering."

Of course he had wondered, because he was a man, and damned possessive even if he shouldn't be. And the fact that she was doing this for him, only for him, and had never done it for anyone else was far too pleasing a revelation by half.

She braced herself on his thighs and took him deeper into her mouth, arching her back and sticking her ass in the air. He pressed his palm down between her shoulder blades and tried to keep himself from falling over as she continued to pleasure him with her lips and her tongue. It was a hell of a thing, accepting pleasure like this. He hadn't fully realized what he'd been doing to himself all this time. Punishing himself. Taking everything away that he possibly could.

Sex. Leisure time. All of it.

He hadn't allowed himself to enjoy a damned meal since his daughter's funeral. It was all hurry up and then get back to work. Leave work and then exercise. Work the ranch. It was only during this past week while he'd been here with Selena that he had begun to get in touch with some of the things he had left behind. Things like the company of people he cared about. Like going to an event and seeing people you knew. Like how much he enjoyed the touch of a woman. And he didn't know what he felt about all these revelations—the knowledge that he'd been punishing himself and the fact that he had started letting go of that punishment this week.

Piece by piece.

He felt a sharp pang of guilt join with the overriding sense of pleasure she was pouring onto him with all that sweet, lavish attention from her mouth.

Need was roaring through him now, and it was almost impossible for him to keep himself in check. He knew he needed to, but part of him didn't want to. Part of him just wanted to surrender to this completely, surrender to her completely.

But no, she deserved better than this.

In the end, she deserved better than him, but he was too weak to turn her away.

He didn't have the power. And that was what it always damn well came down to.

That when it came to the important things, he didn't have the strength to make an impact.

But he could make it good for her. And he would take that.

"Not like this," he said, his voice rough.

He grabbed hold of her arms and pulled her up his body, claiming her mouth in a searing kiss, his heart pounding hard, his breath coming in fierce gasps. Then he laid her down on the bed, hooked her leg up over his hip and thrust into her deep and hard, taking her until they were both breathless, until they were both completely caught up and consumed in their release.

When it was over they lay together. Just a man and a woman. Who had wanted each other. Who had needed each other, and who had taken steps to act on that need.

It was simple. Peaceful. He let his mind go blank and just rested. Listened to her breathe in and out. Focused on the feel of her silken skin beneath his touch. The way her hair spread over his chest in a glossy wave.

It didn't last long.

Didn't take long before he remembered who he was. Who they were. Before he had to face the fact that even though he felt like he might have been washed clean by what happened between them, he was still the same. Deep down, he was still the same.

Selena curled more tightly against him and he

wrapped his arm around her, relishing the feel of her warmth, of her feminine softness, of her weight against him. Those words, those thoughts, triggered terror inside him. So he pushed it away.

"Are you going to stay away forever again?" she asked, her tone sleepy.

"What do you mean?"

"I mean, this is the first time you've been back to Royal since…well, you know since what. You've been in Wyoming. I had to chase you down over there to even see you."

"I know," he said.

"Is that what we are going to do? Are you going to leave and put distance between yourself and Texas again?"

And between himself and her. That part was unspoken, but he sensed it was there. And that it was a very real concern.

"It's hard to be here," he said. Finally. "The life Cassandra and I made together was here. It was a good life. It's one that I could have lived till the end. This beautiful house… Our beautiful family. It was good. It really was. I made it. I had all the things you think you want when you picture reaching that perfect position in your life. Then it crashed into a wall." He shook his head. "Nobody likes to go back to the scene of an accident. And that's what it feels like to me."

"I can't even imagine," she said, her voice muffled. She buried her face against his bare shoulder and he curled his hand around the back of her head, holding her. It was strange, to touch her like this, so casually. As if it all hadn't changed between them just last night. Because touching her like this felt natural. It felt right.

"Grief is a hell of a thing, though," he said. "It doesn't really matter where you are. It doesn't really care. It's in a smell, a strange moment that for some reason takes you backward in time. It's seeing a little girl that's the same age as Ellie would've been now. Or a little girl the same age she was when she died. Just seeing people walking together. Couples walking through life. It's freezing in the grocery store because you've picked up a box of crackers."

He tried to laugh, but it was hard. "We carry these crackers in the store. You know, graham crackers. Organic, obviously. And they were her favorite." He cleared his throat but it did nothing to ease the pressure in his chest. "I can't walk by that damn shelf, Selena." The words were broken, tearing through him, leaving him bloody and ragged inside. "Because I remember the way she used to wipe her mouth on my shirt and leave a trail behind. She would just…ruin all these really nice shirts. It was frustrating, and I think it annoyed me, even though I never got mad at her. Because she was just a baby. Just a little girl." It was surreal. Lying there, talking about this. Like he was watching someone else do it. But if it was another man's life, it wouldn't have hurt so much. "I'd give anything—my damned life—to wash graham cracker out of a shirt again."

He felt wetness on his shoulder and he realized she was crying, and then he realized there was an answering wetness on his own cheeks. "I didn't need to stay away from Texas to protect myself. There's no shielding yourself from something like this. I can lose my shit over a fucking cracker."

She buried her face in his chest. "I wish I could fix it," she said. "And those are the most frustrating words

I've ever said. Because they don't give you anything. And they don't fix anything."

"Between the two of us I think we have a lot of broken pieces," he said, clearing his throat.

"I guess so."

"I won't stay away this time," he said, moving his hand up and down her bare curves, down her waist, over her hip. "I don't think I could." He was quiet for a long time. "I haven't told anyone that story." She didn't have to ask which one. "I just kept all this stuff to myself."

And he knew it was why his marriage had ended, or at least it was part of the reason why. Because he'd gone inside of himself, and Cassandra had retreated into herself. And neither one of them had known how to find their way back to each other, and they hadn't had the energy—or the desire, really—to even begin to try.

"Thank you for telling me," she said. "Thank you."

"You said you felt like you hadn't done anything. But you have. You did. You gave me this. This memory. This moment. The first thing I've really enjoyed in years. That's not nothing."

"What are friends for?" She smiled, and then she kissed his lips.

And after that, they didn't speak anymore.

CHAPTER TEN

KNOX SPENT THE next week at Selena's house, and he didn't really question what he was doing. Yes, he had an inkling that he was avoiding his real life. That he was avoiding dealing with the charity event that his ex had organized, that he was avoiding the reality of life in general, but he didn't much want to focus on any of that.

The mystery surrounding Will's return hadn't been solved, but there had been no more fake letters and no attempts by anyone to contact Selena. Knox was leaving all of that to the investigators and Will's family.

Instead, he wanted to focus on this newfound layer of his relationship with Selena. Wanted to focus on enjoying the way things felt again. Sex. Food. He and Selena were enjoying a lot of both.

And he was still helping her sort out her property. Slowly, though, because he really wasn't in a hurry to finish. He was working out in the shed, while Selena took care of some business things in the house, when his phone rang.

It was from a number he didn't recognize, so he picked it up just in case it was a business call. "Hello?"

"Knox," the voice on the other end said.

Cassandra. The impact hit him like a punch to the stomach. And his initial response was rage. Absolute rage that she was intruding on this peaceful moment in his life. On this new thing that was happening with him.

He didn't want to hear her voice. Not while he was standing here in Selena's shed, mounting a new shelf so she had adequate storage.

"I don't know this number," he said.

"I got a new phone," she responded, her voice tenuous.

"Why did you call?"

And he felt like an ass for being impatient with her. For being such a jerk, because it wasn't like she had ever done anything to him. They had never really done anything to each other, and that had been the problem in the end.

"You never responded to the invitation for the Ellie's House fundraiser," she said.

"Did I need to? I wrote a check."

"I want you there," she said. "Ellie's House is really important to me. It's the only thing that makes me feel like what I went through—what we went through—wasn't completely pointless and cruel. I want this to be important to you. I want you to be there. To lend your connections. Your appearance matters."

"Don't say it like that," he said. "Don't say it like the charity isn't important to me. Like *she's* not important to me."

There was a long pause on the other end. "I didn't mean it like that. I really didn't. I did not call to have a fight with you, I swear."

He shifted, looking out the door of the shed at the field and trees off in the distance. The leaves blowing in the breeze, the sun shining down on it all. Like the world wasn't really a dark and terrible place. Like he wasn't being torn to shreds every time he took a breath. "We didn't fight while we were married. What's the point in fighting now?"

That produced another long silence. "There isn't one." Cassandra took a breath. "It would mean a lot to me if you could come. And I need to tell you something. Something that… I don't know how to say. I don't know…where to begin."

His chest tightened. "What?"

"Knox… I… I'm getting married."

He had not expected that. Neither had he expected the accompanying feeling of being slapped across the face with a two-by-four. "What?"

"I met someone." Something in her voice changed. Softened. Warmed. Happiness, he realized. He hadn't heard it in her voice in a long time. Certainly not when talking to him. "I didn't expect it. I wasn't looking for it. I didn't even want it. But he's… He makes me happy. And I didn't think I could be happy again. I have purpose with Ellie's House, and… I really want you to come. And I want you to see him. To meet him."

"I'm sorry—why the hell would I want to meet your fiancé, Cassandra?" he asked. He could feel his old life slipping away. Moving into the distance.

Or maybe she was moving on and life was going past him.

"You don't love me," she said. "You're not *in* love with me, anyway."

That wasn't even close to being part of the visceral, negative reaction to her announcement. That much he knew. He didn't want Cassandra. He'd had her, they'd had each other, and they hadn't tried to fix things.

There was something else. Something he couldn't pinpoint. But it wasn't about wanting her back.

"No," he said.

"But we still care about each other, don't we? We were together for ten years. It's such a long time. Our whole twenties. It was you and me. We went through something... You're the only other person on earth who will ever know how I feel. You're the only person who experienced the same losses as me. You'll always matter to me for that reason. I just need you there. I need this closure. Please come."

Those words hit him hard. And somehow, he found that he didn't have the strength to turn her down. "Okay."

"Bring somebody," she said. "I mean it. Find a date. Find...something. We deserve to be happy."

After that, they got off the phone, and he struggled with his feelings about what she'd said. Because at the end of the day, he wasn't entirely sure he deserved to be happy.

He stumbled out of the shed and went into the house. Selena was sitting in there, her dark hair piled up on top of her head in a messy bun. She was holding a pen in her mouth and staring down at her laptop.

She was so damned beautiful he could barely breathe. "Hey," he said.

She looked up and she smiled at him, and it felt like the sun coming out from behind the clouds. Which, for a man who had spent the past two years in darkness, was a pretty big thing.

"Do you want to come to a charity thing with me?"

"Sure," she said, giving him a strange look.

"It's Cassandra's thing," he said.

"Oh," Selena said, her expression cautious. "For El-lie's House?"

He frowned. "You know about that?"

She bit her lip. "About the foundation, yes. I wasn't invited to any charity event. But I sent some money in a while back."

He cleared his throat and shoved his hands into his pockets. "Well, she told me to bring a date."

The corners of her lips turned upward, just slightly. "Then I'm happy to fulfill that role."

"Great," he said, trying to force a smile.

It was only later that he questioned the decision. He realized he was committing to bringing Selena to a public function, as his date. Which had less to do with how it might look—he didn't care, and anyway, it was well established that they were friends—but that he was bringing her along as a plus-one to his grief. That he was basically submitting himself to showing it all to the public.

But it was too late now. He'd already agreed. He'd already asked her to come with him. He was just going to have to get a handle on himself. To get some of his control back.

Because everything was moving in a direction he wasn't sure he liked. All that was left to do was try and keep a handle on himself.

KNOX ACTED STRANGE for the next week. Which was not helped at all by the fact that Selena was starting to feel a little bit strange herself.

She was trying not to dwell on it. Was trying not to dwell on anything other than the good feelings Knox created in her. Who knew how long all this would last?

She didn't want to waste any time being upset or worried. Didn't want to waste time being hypersensitive to his moods or to her own.

There was way too much good happening. And she knew it was temporary. So she planned to just pull herself together and enjoy.

She tried to shake off her lethargy as she looked in the mirror and finished putting her makeup on. She was just so tired. She didn't know if it was because of the lack of sleep since Knox had moved in, or what. Stress, maybe, from the upcoming event for Ellie's House.

Because as much as she knew that he wasn't making a statement by bringing her, it still felt momentous that he'd asked her to come with him. He would probably be annoyed with her for thinking that. But she was coming to an event with his ex-wife and his ex-wife's fiancé. An event for a charity his ex-wife had created for the daughter they had lost.

He could have easily gone by himself. And Selena had a feeling that a few months ago that was exactly what he would have opted to do. Since he had been doing things on his own for the past couple of years.

The fact that he'd reached out to her was probably why he was acting weird. The intensity of the whole situation. She really couldn't blame him.

She checked her reflection in the mirror and had a momentary feeling of uncertainty. And then a flash of jealousy followed closely by a bite of guilt.

She had to wonder if he might compare her to his tall, blonde ex, who was more willowy than she was curvy. And Selena wouldn't really be able to blame him if he did. She and Cassandra were so different. The idea of standing next to Cassandra and playing a game of compare and contrast had been making her feel ill.

Of course, that wasn't what was going to happen. And Cassandra had always been very nice to her.

It'd been strange when she and Knox had gotten divorced, because Selena had genuinely liked her. As much as you could like the woman who had ended up with the man of your dreams, *obviously*.

But as Selena had recused herself from having those kinds of dreams, she'd never really been angry with Cassandra. Knox being married had always been both a relief and a heartache. There was really no other way to describe it. A relief because that feeling of *what if* had abated slightly since there had been no more *what if* left. But also it had just burned sometimes. Knowing he was with someone else. That he'd loved someone else.

But she'd never let herself dwell on it. She hadn't been able to be with him romantically, not when a relationship like that would have required risk and a trust she hadn't been willing to give. But she'd also needed him in her life, and she wasn't about to let something like a marriage come between them.

Now, had Cassandra been a bad wife, Selena wouldn't have been able to stand for it. But Cassandra had always been great. Exactly the kind of woman Selena thought Knox should have been with. So getting all bent out of shape about Cassandra and comparisons now was just pointless.

She twisted her body slightly, frowning as she smoothed her hand over the front of her fitted gold dress. A strange sense of disquiet raced through her as she adjusted herself in the halter top. Her breasts hurt. Like they were bruised.

That was very, very strange.

She knew of only one thing that caused such intense breast tenderness and…no. That was ridiculous. Except her breasts had never been tender before. Her eyes dropped down to her stomach. She looked the same. She couldn't believe…couldn't believe there could be a baby in there.

And the first time…she and Knox had forgotten condoms. That had been in the back of her mind, niggling at her consciousness, ever since. At the time, it had been lost in confessions of her virginity and the deep pain he'd expressed when talking about his daughter.

But the fact remained…the condoms had been forgotten.

The stomach she was currently scrutinizing felt as though it dropped down to her toes.

She could not be pregnant. Well, she could be pregnant—that was the trouble. She really could be. She and Knox had unprotected sex and she was… Well, she was late.

"No," she said to her reflection, bracing her arms on the dresser. "No," she said.

"What's going on?"

She turned around to see Knox standing there wearing a suit and a black tie, and if her stomach hadn't already been down in her toes, it would have done a full free fall.

"Nothing," she said, turning around quickly, still holding on to the dresser. "I just was afraid that I couldn't find my earrings. But I did."

"The ones you're wearing?"

"No," she said, grabbing for another pair on top of the cluttered dresser. "These."

And he kept staring at her, so she had to change into the earrings that she had already decided against. She took out the pair that looked absolutely perfect with her gold dress and sadly discarded them on the top of the dresser. Then she put the others in, smiling. "See?"

"Right," he said, clearly not seeing a distinction between the two. Because he was a man. Which was the only reason that her excuse actually worked. Because otherwise he would know that the other pair was clearly better.

"Are you ready to go?"

"Yes," she said.

"I got us a room at the hotel where the charity event is being held. You know, so that neither of us has to be the designated driver."

He was keeping his tone light, but she definitely sensed the hint of strain beneath it.

"Sounds good," she said.

At the mention of alcohol, she realized that she actually couldn't bring herself to drink a glass of champagne before she knew for sure.

Before she knew for sure if she was pregnant.

Oh, she was going to pass out. She really was. She wasn't sure how she was supposed to get through tonight. She needed to sneak away from him and get a test.

This wasn't happening.

It wasn't fair.

It definitely couldn't crash into the event tonight, because the event was way too important. For the memory of his daughter.

Suddenly, Selena was sure she was going to throw up.

"Are you okay?"

"I guess," she said. "I'm nervous." She opted to be honest about part of her problem so she could leave out the big, scary part. "I haven't seen Cassandra since your divorce. And the two of us are... You know."

"She's engaged," he said.

"It's not her that I'm worried about."

He frowned. "Are you afraid I'm going to see her and want her? Instead of you?"

"I don't know," she said, lifting a shoulder. "Yes."

"I'm not harboring secret feelings for Cassandra," he said. "We'll always be... We're linked. She and I created a life together. And then we both had to go through the experience of losing it. Losing Ellie. So it's not the same as if we were sharing custody or something. But..."

"I'm all right with that. I mean, I get it. I really do. And I am not upset about that at all. I just... She's prettier than me," Selena said finally.

He frowned. "You are the prettiest damned woman, Selena Jacobs," he said. He reached out and brushed his fingertips across her cheek. "I... I haven't felt this good in a long time. And the fact that I still feel pretty good even with all of this Ellie's House stuff looming on the horizon... It's a testament to you. I don't long for my marriage. The man who was married to Cassandra doesn't exist anymore. That's the only real way I can think to explain it. We changed too much and we didn't change together. Nobody's fault. It just is. But the woman she is now has found a different man. The man I am now wants you. Nobody else. I can't even compare the two of you. I don't want to. You're you. You always have been. You occupy a special place in my life no one else ever has."

Her heart felt swollen, like it might burst through

her chest. It wasn't quite a declaration of love, but it almost was. He put his arm around her and started to guide her out of the bedroom, and then they headed to the driveway, where he got into the driver's side of her car and started down the road that would take them to downtown Royal for the event.

This felt right, being with him for this event to celebrate his daughter's memory. She had to wonder what that meant. She had been so convinced that there was no future between herself and him. Had been utterly and completely certain that the two of them could have nothing but sex and friendship.

But they were in some different space where all those pieces had woven together, and her feelings for him were so big. So deep and real. She just didn't know where they were anymore. And she wondered why she was resisting at all. Because when she had decided she wasn't going to have a husband and children, when she had decided that love wasn't for her, that idea had been attached to an abstract man. Some version of her father who might someday betray her.

But this relationship she'd started wasn't with an abstract man. It certainly wasn't with anyone who resembled her father.

It was with *Knox*.

Knox, who had been one of her best friends for all of her adult life. She trusted him, more than she trusted just about anybody. She wasn't afraid of him. She wasn't afraid of loving him. He was a safe place for all those feelings to land.

And if she was having his baby…

She had no idea what to make of that. Had no idea what it would mean to him. She knew he'd said he didn't want to have a relationship again, but what if they were having a child? What would that do to him?

Suddenly, the whole situation seemed a lot more fraught than it had a moment ago. Just one moment of peace, and then it had evaporated.

Surely he would want another child, though—if she was really pregnant. He had been a wonderful father, and it wasn't as if a new baby would replace the little girl he had lost.

Her brain was still tying itself in knots when they arrived at the hotel. Cars and limousines were circling the area in front, valets taking the vehicles away to be parked, doormen ushering people inside. Knox stuck his black cowboy hat on his head and smiled at her, and then the two of them got out of the car and headed into the hotel. She clung to him, mostly because she thought if she let go of him she might collapse completely.

And not just because of those strange feelings of jealousy she'd had earlier. No, not at all. It had very little to do with that. It was just…everything else. Suddenly, what she and Knox were doing, what they were sharing, felt too big.

They made their way into the lobby of the hotel. It was art deco with inlaid geometric designs on the floor reflected in gold on the ceiling panels. There was a banner hung over the main ballroom, welcoming the distinguished attendees to the first annual fundraiser for Ellie's House.

But it was the picture on the stand, right in the entry of the ballroom, that stopped her short and made her breath freeze in her chest. It was a photograph of a little girl. Beautiful. Blonde.

With the same gray eyes as her daddy.

She was lying in a field with her hands propped beneath her chin, yellow-and-purple wildflowers blooming all around her.

Selena's heart squeezed tight and she fought to take a breath. She clung even more tightly to Knox, whose posture was rigid. She sneaked a glance at him and saw that he was holding his jaw almost impossibly tense. It hurt her to see that picture. In memoriam of a child who would be here if life was fair. She couldn't imagine how it was for him.

He paused for just a moment, and she looked away as he brushed his fingertips lightly over the portrait. It felt wrong to watch that. Like she was intruding on a private moment. On a greeting or a goodbye. She wasn't sure.

He straightened, then began moving forward. She rested her head on his shoulder as they walked, and she had a feeling they were holding each other up now.

The ornate room was filling up, but it didn't take long for her to spot Cassandra, her blond hair pulled back into a bun. She was all pointed shoulders and collarbones, much thinner than she had been the last time Selena had seen her. But as beautiful as ever. Cassandra had always been a stunning woman, and tonight was no exception. She was wearing an understated black dress, with a ribbon pinned to the top.

She rushed over to greet them, her expression harried, her face a bit pale. "I'm so glad you made it," she said. She took a step forward, like she was ready to hug Knox, and then thought better of it. Instead, she reached into her clutch and produced two ribbons, pressing them into Knox's palm. "If you want to wear these."

"Thank you," he said.

"Hi," Cassandra said to Selena.

Selena broke the awkwardness and leaned in, embracing Cassandra in a hug. "Hi," she said. "It's good to see you."

Cassandra looked between them, her expression full of speculation, but she said nothing. Instead, she just twisted the large yellow diamond ring on her left hand.

"Is your fiancé here?" Knox asked.

"He was," Cassandra said. "I sent him out to get me some new nylons because I put a run in mine. He's good like that."

"He sounds it," he said, a slight smile curving his lips.

"Well," Cassandra said. "You know me. If there is a nylon in the vicinity I will cause a run in it."

"I'm glad you have someone to get you a new pair," he said.

"Me, too." After a beat of silence, she said, "I'm sorry—I have to go back to getting everything in order, but I'll find you again later tonight."

"You're gonna make tons of money," he said.

"I hope so," she said. "I hope we do. I hope I am part of making sure that in the future this doesn't happen. Not to anyone." Cassandra's blue eyes filled with tears and she looked away. When she looked back at Knox, her smile was in place. "Sorry. I have to go."

She turned abruptly, brushing her hands over her face, her slim shoulders rising and falling on a long breath. Then she strode forward resolutely, mingling with the other people who were starting to fill up the ballroom.

Selena could only be impressed with the way that Knox handled himself the whole evening. He had pinned the ribbon that Cassandra had given him proudly on his lapel, and Selena had done the same, to the top of her dress. And she did her very best to keep her focus on what was happening around them. Ellie's House— Ellie's memory—was simply too important for Selena to get caught up in her own worries.

There was a buffet, which Selena noticed Knox never went near. And she made a point of acting like she hadn't noticed. But when the band started to play, she asked him to dance.

He surprised her by complying.

He swept her into his arms, and for the first time in hours, she felt like things might be okay between them. "This is a wonderful tribute," she said, softly.

"Yes," he responded, the word clipped.

"I'm sorry." She lowered her head. "I said the wrong thing."

"No. It's just…still hard to accept that my daughter needs tributes. I guess I should be more used to it by now."

"No. Don't do that, Knox. You were caught off guard earlier."

"It was a nice picture," he said, his voice rough. "I remember the day it was taken. Out at the Jackson Hole ranch where we used to take picnics. I don't… I don't even like to remember. Even the good times hurt."

Selena didn't say anything. She just rested her head against his chest and swayed with him on the dance floor. They didn't speak much for the rest of the evening. Knox focused on talking to potential donors, rather than to her. But Selena was used to these types of events and it was easy for her to go off and do the same, to make sure she did her part to bring in money for the charity.

Cassandra gave an amazing speech about the impor-
tance of medical research, and the progress that was
being made in the effort to treat childhood cancers and
other childhood diseases. She talked about the function
of the charity, how they donated money to innovative
research teams and to housing for the various hospi-
tals, so families could stay near their children while
they received treatment and not be buried under the
financial burden.

Selena found that she could only be impressed with
Knox's ex-wife. She couldn't be jealous. She was just
proud. And it seemed…okay then, that Knox would always have a connection with Cassandra. It seemed important even. Selena certainly wanted to be involved
in supporting this effort with Ellie's House, and she
thought it was amazing what Cassandra had done with
her grief.

As the clock drew closer to midnight, Selena hit a
wall, so tired that she was barely able to stand. Knox,
on the other hand, was still moving dynamically around
the room, stumping to have more checks written. It was
amazing to watch the way the fire had been lit inside of
him since they had arrived. Clearly he had a desire to
make all of his family's suffering count for something.
To make the loss count for something.

Suddenly she felt so nauseous, she thought she might
collapse. Fuzzy-headed. Sleepy. It could just be stress
and fatigue. It had been a crazy few weeks and a hard
evening. She was just so overly…done.

She walked over to Knox and touched his arm. "I
need to go to bed," she said.

He gave her a cursory glance, obviously still focused
on the event. Which was fine with her. She imagined

he would want to stay till the end. She *wanted* to stay; she was just going to fall over if she tried.

"I'll see you up in the room," he responded.

If he was disappointed about the fact that she would be asleep when he got there, rather than ready for sex, he didn't show it. But then, he was busy. And she could appreciate that. She could more than appreciate that. It was good to see him passionate about something, especially something involving his daughter's memory. Good to see him involved.

Selena slipped out the back of the ballroom and wrapped her arms around her midsection as she walked through the lobby. She felt so awful. So tired she thought she might fall asleep where she stood.

And though it *could* be stress and fatigue.

Or something a lot scarier.

There was only one way to find out whether or not she was carrying Knox's baby.

Maybe the timing sucked, and she should just go to bed. But now that she started thinking about the possibility again, she couldn't wait. Not another minute, and certainly not until tomorrow morning.

She stopped walking, pausing for a moment in front of the concierge desk. Then she took a tentative step forward.

"Is there a pharmacy close by?"

CHAPTER ELEVEN

KNOX FELT GUILTY about letting Selena leave the party without him. But he was engaged in a pretty intense conversation with a local business mogul about donations and ways to raise awareness, and he felt…like he was able to do something. Like he could be something other than helpless.

Tonight, Cassandra made much more sense to him. She had thrown herself into this. At first, her drive had been difficult for him. Because every reminder of Eleanor was a painful one. But now, after participating in the fundraiser, he understood.

Looking around at all of this, he couldn't help but understand. She was doing the only thing she could. Her mother's heart compelled her to let their daughter live on somehow, while Knox had been consumed in the grief.

He hadn't had it in him to take that kind of generous approach. To make sure what had happened to his daughter didn't happen to anyone else. But he had found it tonight. He had found something that he had thought long gone—hope. Like there was a future in this world that was worth being part of.

And that made him feel…like a little piece of himself had been recovered. A piece he had thought he might never access again. A piece that allowed him to be a part of the world, that allowed him to enjoy being alive. To enjoy the taste of food. The touch of a woman. The desire to accomplish something. Anything.

And, yes, the fundraiser had made a difference, but the catalyst for this change was all Selena.

As the night wore on, the crowds began to thin out, and finally, he was left with Cassandra, who sat up on the stage. She looked exhausted, and she looked sad.

"You did a good thing," he said, walking over and taking a spot next to her.

"Thank you," she said, treating him to a tired smile. "But I know."

"Isn't this exhausting?" he asked.

"What?" she asked. "Charity events?"

"Reliving this all the time," he said.

"I do anyway," she said. "So why not make something of it? This charity helps me feel like I'm moving on. Even though it all…stems from her, losing her. I don't know how to explain it, really. Like I'm taking the tragedy and making something positive with it."

He looked across the room and saw Cassandra's fiancé, who was helping with cleanup. He seemed like a good man. A great man. One who had jumped into all of this without having known Ellie at all, but who supported the charity just because it meant so much to Cassandra.

It occurred to Knox then that the truth of the matter was that Cassandra *was* a hell of a lot more moved on than he was.

And he didn't know what to feel about that. He didn't know how to reconcile it. He didn't know if he *wanted* to move on.

And yet moving on was what he had just been thinking about. That experience of beginning to enjoy life again.

Was that what she had now? Could she be thankful to be alive? Was she able to love this man? And not be afraid of loss?

Part of him still wanted to hold on to the past. Wanted to fight against blurry images, fading pain and the normalcy he was starting to feel on some days. Wanted to fight against the past slipping away. He wanted to go back out front and stare at that portrait of his daughter lying in a field of flowers. To memorize her face.

He just didn't want to forget.

He didn't *want* to come out the other side of this grief.

Suddenly, he felt like he was sliding down into a dark pit, and he had no idea what in hell to do about it. If he wanted to do anything about it at all. He had no idea what to do with any of these feelings. Had no idea what had happened to the good feelings from a few moments before, and even less of an idea about why he resented having those good feelings now.

Grief didn't make sense. All of the guides talked about stages and moving on. For him, it wasn't stages. It was waves, coming and going, drowning him. The memory of his child acting like a life raft in his mind.

How the hell could he move on from his own life raft?

Cassandra had said earlier that he was the only person who had been through what she had been through. And that was true. But now he was sitting here alone with these feelings. She had moved on. And there was no one. No one at all.

It scared him.

What would happen if they both went on with their lives like Ellie hadn't existed? If she became only this monument to a greater cause, instead of the child they loved so much.

And suddenly, he needed to get out of there. Suddenly, he needed to find Selena.

He knew she was asleep, but he needed her.

"I'm going up to bed," he said, and if his departure seemed sudden, he didn't much care. He walked out of the ballroom and headed through the lobby, getting into the elevator and checking the key in his wallet to see which room he and Selena were in. Then he pushed the appropriate button and headed up to their floor.

He got to the room and pushed the key card into the door, opening it slowly. When he got inside, Selena was not asleep as he'd expected.

She was sitting on the edge of the bed, her head bent down. She looked up, her face streaked with makeup and tears and a horrific sense of regret.

"What's going on?" he asked. "I thought you were going to sleep."

Then he looked down at her hands. At the white stick she was clutching between her fingers.

THE LOOK ON Knox's face mirrored what she was feeling.

Terror. Sheer, unmitigated terror.

But even through the terror, she knew they could do this. They would get through it as they had every other thing life had thrown at them over the years. They would make it work together.

She trusted him, and that was the mantra she kept repeating to herself, over and over again.

She had given Knox her heart slowly over the past decade. And now he had all of it, along with her trust.

She loved him.

She always had. But sitting there looking at the test results, she knew she was in love with him. The kind of love built to withstand. The kind that could endure.

She loved him.

They could weather this. She was confident they could.

"I'm sorry," she said. "I didn't want you to find out like this."

She had fully intended to talk to him tomorrow, but then she had ended up sitting on the edge of the bed, unable to move. Completely and utterly shell-shocked by what was in front of her in pink and white.

The incontrovertible truth that she was pregnant with Knox McCoy's baby.

She had cried, but she wasn't sad. Not really. It was just so much to take in, especially after spending the evening at the charity event. Especially after seeing the portrait of his daughter by the door and witnessing all the small ways grief affected him. The small ways that loss took chunks out of him over the course of an evening like this.

Now he was finding out about this. It just seemed a bit much.

"You're pregnant," he said.

"Yes. We didn't… We forgot a couple of times," she said, her voice muted.

That first time, down at the camp.

That second night, in her room when they had talked about Eleanor and graham crackers and her heart had broken for him in ways she hadn't thought she could recover from.

"I can't do this," he said, his voice rough.

"I mean…" She tried to swallow but it was like her throat was lined with the inside of a pincushion. "A baby isn't tea. I can't…not serve it to you. I can't… Maybe this is our sign we have to try something real, Knox."

The words came out weak and she despised herself for them.

"I can't," he said again.

Her heart thundered so hard it hurt. Felt sharp. Like it was cutting its way out of her chest.

"We *can*," she said. "We can do this together, Knox. I know that it's not…ideal."

"Not ideal?" he asked, his words fraying around the edges. "*Not ideal* is a damned parking ticket, Selena. This is not *acceptable*."

Anger washed through her, quick and sharp. At him. At herself. At how unfair the whole world was. They should just be able to have this. To be happy. But they couldn't because life was hard, and it had stolen so much from him. She hurt for him; she did.

But oh, right now she hurt so much for herself.

"I'm sorry that the pregnancy is unacceptable to you, but it's too late. I'm pregnant."

"Selena…"

"I love you," she said. "I didn't want to say that right now either. I didn't want to do it like this, but… Knox, I love you. And I know that I've always said I didn't want a husband and children, but I could do it with you. If we are going to have a baby then I can do it. I *want* to do it."

She straightened her shoulders as she said the words,

realizing just then that she was committing to her baby. "I... I want this baby."

He looked at her for a moment, his eyes unreadable.

"Then you're going to have it on your own."

She felt like she had been blasted through with a cannonball, that it had left her completely hollowed out. Nothing at all remaining.

Pain radiated from her chest, outward. Climbing up her throat and making it feel so tight she couldn't breathe.

"You don't want this?"

"I can't."

She felt for him. For his loss. She truly did. But it wasn't just her being wounded. It was their child. A child who was losing a chance at having him for a father.

She had thought...

She had no idea how she could have misjudged this—misjudged him—so completely.

She'd thought...if she knew one person on earth well enough to trust them it should have been him.

This was her nightmare.

But it wasn't just heartbreak over losing the man she loved, over losing the future she'd so briefly imagined for them before he walked into their suite.

No, she was losing her friend.

And bringing a child into the heartache.

"So that's it. You don't want to be a father again." Dread, loss, sadness...it all poured through her in a wave. She felt like she was back in the river with him but this time, he was pushing her under instead of holding her up. "You don't want me."

"Selena, I already told you. I've had this. I've had it

and I lost it, and I cannot do this again. There is no mystery left in the damned world for me. I know what it's like to bury my child, Selena. I will not... I can never love another child like that. Ever."

She had trusted him.

That was all she could think as she stood there, getting ripped to shreds by his words.

As a young woman, she had been convinced that the hardest thing, the most difficult thing in the world, was enduring being beaten by a man with his fists. Her father had kicked her, punched her while she was down.

But this hurt so much worse. This was a loss so deep she could scarcely fathom it. This was pain, real and unending.

She couldn't process it.

She pressed her hand against her stomach. "Then go," she said, her mouth numb, her tongue thick. "Go. Because I'm not going to expose my child to your indifference. I'm not going to be my mother, Knox. I'm not going to have a man in my child's life who doesn't care about them."

"Selena."

"No. You're the one who said it. Why couldn't my mother love me enough to make sure I was in the best situation possible? Why didn't she protect me? Well, now I'm the mother, the one making choices. I'm going to love this baby enough for both of us. I'm going to give it everything I never had and everything you refuse to give it. Now get the hell away from me."

He was operating from a place of grief, and she knew it, but he was an adult. She knew full well that her duty was to protect her child, not Knox's emotional state.

She was sick, and she was angry. And she didn't think she would ever recover.

"I just can't," he reiterated, moving toward the door of the hotel room.

"Then don't," she said. "But I don't believe the man who pulled himself up out of poverty, got himself into Harvard, stood by me as a good friend for all those years and came to Will's funeral, even though it was hard—I don't believe that man can't do this. What I believe is that you're very good at shutting people out. You go into yourself when it gets hard, rather than reaching out. Reach out to me, Knox. Let's do this together. I don't need it to be perfect or easy. We have a bunch of broken pieces between us, but let's try to make something new with them."

"I can't." He looked at her one more time with horribly flat, dark eyes, and then he turned and walked out of the hotel room, leaving her standing in a shimmering gold ball gown, ready to dissolve into a puddle of misery on the floor.

There was pain, and then there was this.

Knowing she was having her best friend's baby. And that she would be raising that baby alone.

CHAPTER TWELVE

HE DRANK ALL the way back to Jackson Hole. He drank more in the back of the car as his driver took him back to the ranch. And he kept on drinking all the way until he got back to his house and passed out in bed. When he woke up, he had no idea what time it was, but the sun was shining through the window and his head was pounding like a son of a bitch. He was also still a little bit drunk.

Best of both worlds.

He could hardly believe what had happened earlier. It all seemed like a dream. Like maybe he had never gone to Royal and had never gone to a funeral for Will that hadn't actually happened. Like maybe he had never slept with Selena. He had never gone to that charity event in honor of his daughter. And then Selena certainly hadn't told him she was pregnant with his baby.

Because why the hell would she be pregnant with his baby since certainly they had never really slept together?

And they certainly hadn't been living together like a couple. Playing house, reenacting the life that he had lost. A life he could never have again.

He got up and saw half a tumbler full of scotch sitting on the nightstand. He drained it quickly, relishing the burn as he fumbled for his phone. He checked to see if he had any missed calls and saw that he didn't. But he did see that it was about three in the afternoon.

He frowned down at his phone for a long moment, then scrolled through his contacts. "Hello?"

"Cassandra," he said, the words slurred.

"Knox?"

"Yes," he said. "I am drunk."

"I can tell." She paused, because clearly she wasn't going to help him with this conversation. She wasn't going to tell him why he had called. He wished she would. He sure as hell didn't have a clue. Didn't know why he was reaching out to her now when he hadn't done it during their marriage.

When he hadn't been able to do it when it might have fixed something.

"Are you all right?" she pressed.

"Fuck no," he said. "I am not all right."

"Okay." Again, she gave him nothing.

"How come you're happy?" he asked. "I'm not happy. I don't want to be happy. What happens if both of us are happy and we forget about her? We forget how much it hurt? And how much she mattered?"

He heard her stifle a sob on the other end of the line. "We won't. We won't."

"What if we do?" His heart felt like it was cracking in two. "I don't want to replace her. I can't."

"You won't," she said. "You won't replace her ever. Why would you think that?"

"Selena is pregnant," he said, "and I don't know what to do. Because it's like I traded our life in for a new version. That's not fair to anyone. It's just not."

His words didn't make any sense, but all he knew

was that everything hurt, and he couldn't make sense of any of it.

There were no words for this particular deep well of pain inside of him.

"You're not," she said, her voice cracking. "You're *not*."

"I'm sorry," he said. "I think I called to be mad at you. For being okay. For moving on. But now I'm just sorry. I should've been there for you. Maybe we should have been there better for each other."

"Maybe," she said. "But I didn't want to be."

Silence fell between them. "I didn't either."

"I loved our life," she said. "And it took me a long time to realize that I think I loved our life more than we loved each other. And when we lost Ellie... It wasn't that life anymore. And what we'd had wasn't enough to hold us together."

"Yeah," he agreed, her words making a strange kind of sense in his alcohol-soaked brain. "Yeah, I think so."

"You need to find somebody you love no matter the circumstances. Not just someone you love because she fits a piece in your life. Because she fulfills a role. Not a wife—a partner."

"I'm afraid," he said, the words ripped from somewhere down deep.

Cassandra laughed, soft and sympathetic. "Join the club. Believe me. Nobody is more afraid than me. I mean, maybe you. But it's hard. It's hard to open yourself up again. I think so... I think you already did. I think you're already in love. So don't keep yourself from it. That's not protecting yourself. That's just punishing yourself. And if that's what you're really doing... you need to stop."

"How?" he asked. "How am I supposed to stop punishing myself when I'm here and she's gone? When I couldn't protect her? How am I supposed to move on from that?"

When Cassandra spoke again, her voice was small. "You have to move on from it, Knox, because she isn't here anymore. And as little as either of us could do for her when she was ill, there's nothing we can do for her now. There's nothing you can do by holding on to your grief. She doesn't need you anymore. She doesn't need this from you."

He couldn't speak. His throat was too tight, his chest was too tight and everything hurt.

"Selena *needs* you," Cassandra continued. "The child you're going to have with her needs you. And you're going to have to figure out a way to be there for her, for this child, or you really aren't the man I met all those years ago."

He couldn't speak after that. And Cassandra let him off the hook, saying goodbye and hanging up the phone.

Because he wasn't that man. He wasn't. He didn't know how to be. He didn't want to be. He was changed. Hollowed out and scarred. Like a forest that had been ravaged by wildfire, leaving behind nothing but dead, charred wood.

Selena needed him.

Cassandra's words continued to echo through him. Selena needed him. Not Eleanor. Eleanor was gone, and it was unfair. But there was nothing he could do about it but grieve. And he knew he would do that for all of his life. There was no way to let go of something like that. Not truly. But maybe there was a way to learn to live. To live with the grief inside of you, to allow good memories to come back in and take residence along-side the pain.

To let love be there next to it, too.

Maybe moving on wasn't about being the man he used to be. Maybe it was about doing what Selena had said. Maybe it was about making something new out of the broken pieces.

Selena needed him. Their baby needed him.

He was beginning to suspect he needed Selena, too. That without her he was going to sink into the darkness forever.

The question was whether or not he wanted to let in the light.

SELENA HAD GONE to the doctor to confirm her pregnancy after securing someone else's canceled appointment, and then had gone to Paradise Farms to visit Scarlett and see how baby Carl was doing. While she watched her bright-eyed friend play with her new baby, Selena felt a strange mix of pain and hope.

She had made choices to protect her baby. To protect this little life growing inside of her that she already loved so much.

Watching Scarlett brought it all into full Technicolor. Made impending motherhood feel real.

"Do you like it?"

"What?" Scarlett asked, looking up from Carl's play.

"Being a mother."

"That's a funny question."

Selena lifted a shoulder. "I'm in a funny mood. Indulge me."

"Yes. Although there are periods where I'm so tired I just want to lie on the floor and sleep." She shifted her hold on the baby and looked down at him, smiling. "And I have done that. Believe me. Sometimes I ask myself why I made this choice. Why I decided to have a baby before I had a life. But… I do like it. Adopting Carl has been the most rewarding thing I've ever done. Even though sometimes it's really hard. But I love him. And adding love to your life is never a bad thing."

Selena tapped the side of her mug of tea, looking out the window. "I like that. It's adding love."

"And a lot of work," Scarlett said. "Are you thinking about adopting?"

Her friend was likely joking, judging by the lightness in her tone. Because Selena had never given any indication she had an interest in adopting a baby. In fact, she was probably the least maternal person Scarlett knew. There was no way to ease her friend into this. No way to broach the subject gently.

So Selena figured it was time to drop the bombshell. "No, I'm not thinking of adopting. I'm pregnant."

Scarlett stared at Selena in shocked silence, opening and closing her mouth like a fish that had been chucked onto dry land. When she finally recovered her ability to speak, it came out as a shocked squeak. *"What?"*

Selena looked down into her teacup. Tea leaves were supposed to tell the future. Her Yorkshire Gold only contained the reflection of her own downtrodden expression. "It happened on the camping trip."

"Damn," Scarlett said. "I guess those tents really are romantic."

"Romance wasn't required," Selena said, grimacing. "It was more than a decade of pent-up lust."

She sighed and leaned back on the couch. "But he's not ready for this. He doesn't want anything to do with me."

Scarlett frowned. "He doesn't? That's just… I don't know him that well, but everything I do know about him suggests that he's a better man than that."

"He is," Selena said. "He's a good man. But he's also a scared man. He's not doing a very good job of handling his fear. It just got all messed up. I found out I was pregnant the night we were at the gala fundraiser for the charity his ex-wife created in honor of their daughter. He freaked out. And I kind of don't blame him. The night was an emotional marathon."

Her eyes filled with tears, and her throat felt strange, like she had swallowed a sword, making it painful to breathe. "I only just found out I was pregnant and I got it confirmed today. And while I was sitting there waiting for the lab results to come in I just… It already hurt to think that I might lose the baby. That maybe I wasn't really pregnant or something had gone wrong with the first test. I don't even have a little person to hold in my arms yet and my love is so big. Knox lost a child… I'm angry at him for hurting me. But I can't fathom what he's gone through, the grief he feels. And as much as he deserves it, I can't even hate him for walking away."

"You don't need to hate him," Scarlett said. "You might need to punch him in the junk."

"I don't want to do that either. Okay. I want to do it a little bit. But I just… I'll do this parenthood thing by myself. You're doing it, right? I'll raise the baby. I can take care of us. I have plenty of money. My child is never going to want for anything."

Scarlett looked down at Carl and stroked a finger over his downy cheek. "You're going to be a good mother."

"You say that with a lot of confidence."

"Because I know you. You'll probably be tired, and you'll probably make mistakes. I know I'm making mistakes all the time. But it all comes back to the love. Love covers a whole lot of things, Selena. I truly believe that."

"I just wish love could cover this." Tears she hadn't even been aware of began to slide down her cheeks. "I love Knox so much. I want him. For me. For the baby. But I also just wish he could have had a different life. Even if it meant losing him, I would give him a different life. But there's nothing I can do to ease his grief."

"Sure there is," Scarlett said, looking surprised.

"What?"

"Go after him."

Like it was the most obvious thing. And maybe to her fearless, confident friend, it was. But Selena was different. She didn't think she could survive getting turned down again.

"He doesn't want me to go after him," she said. "He walked away. He said he couldn't be a father to this baby. He said he didn't love me."

Scarlett shook her head. "Because fear makes you stupid. And that's exactly what *he's* letting happen. But you're letting him hide. You're letting him give in to it. Don't let him. Or at least make him tell you no again. Come on, Selena. He can be a coward all he wants, but you're not a coward. Make him look you in the eye in the light of day and say he doesn't want you or the baby. Make him tell you he doesn't love you. And then make him tell you he's not just saying no because he's afraid."

Selena's heart thundered faster. It hadn't even occurred to her that it might not be over. That there might be something she could do to fix this. "But if he rejects me…"

"Then he rejects you." Scarlett shrugged, looking pragmatic about it.

Selena closed her eyes. "I never wanted to be that woman. That woman who was such a fool over a man. My mother… She stayed with my father even though he was awful. Even after she left him, she missed him. The man who abused her, Scarlett—she said she missed him. I just don't… I don't want to be that person."

Scarlett frowned. "I can understand that. Really. But you know, hopefully, if you go make a fool of yourself for him, he'll make a fool of himself for you at some point, too. If you're going to be together for your whole lives, then there should be a lot of chances for both of you to chase each other down. For both of you to be idiots over love. I guess that's the big difference, right? Your mother was the one doing all of the giving, and your father did all of the taking."

Selena bit her lip. "It would never be like that with Knox."

"Well, there you go," Scarlett said, extending her arm out wide. "It's not the same."

Selena shook her head and sighed deeply. "No. I guess it's not." She put her hand on her stomach. "I don't feel in any way emotionally prepared for this."

"Well, good," Scarlett said, laughing. "Because if you did, I would have to break it to you that you're actually not. It would be up to me to tell you that you are in no way prepared. No matter what you might think."

"It's that different?"

Scarlett nodded. "Harder. Better, too."

Like love in general, Selena supposed.

She stood up, wobbling slightly, her balance off. She blamed the last few days.

"I have to go," Selena said.

"Where to?"

"I have to fly to Wyoming."

CHAPTER THIRTEEN

Knox had spent the rest of the day hungover and then had spent the next day working out on the ranch. Doing what he could to exhaust himself mentally and emotionally while he got all his thoughts together.

He had been pretty determined about what he wanted to do regarding Selena, but he had to be sure he was going to say the right thing. Because when you told a woman you didn't want her you had to prepare a pretty epic grovel.

He wasn't going to do anything to cause Selena more pain than he already had. And he had a lot of digging to do to find the right words. Through the dark and dusty places inside of himself.

He'd been restless and edgy in the house, and he'd decided to go out for a ride on the property. He urged his horse onward through the field, and he continued on to the edge of his favorite mountain. One with jagged rocks capped in snow that reached up toward the sky, like it was trying to touch heaven. Something he wished he could do often enough.

He wasn't a man who liked graveyards. But then, he supposed no one did. He just didn't find any peace in them. No, he found peace out here. With nature. That was when he felt closest with Ellie.

He looked around at the wildflowers that were

blooming, little pops of purple and yellow against the green. Life. There was life all around him. A life to be lived. A life to enjoy. Maybe even a life to love, in spite of all the pain.

It was like that picture of Ellie. Sitting right here in this field surrounded by flowers.

He knew he wouldn't find her here, and yet he'd needed to come to this place. He'd avoided riding out here for the past two years.

Today had seemed like the day to go again. The last time he'd ridden out to this field, the last time he'd seen this view, he was a different man with a different future.

A man who'd known who he was and where he was going.

Now he was a man alone. Struggling to figure out what came next. If he could heal. If he wanted to heal.

An image of Selena flashed into his mind, of her hurt and heartbreak that night in the hotel room. She needed him. She needed him now.

Selena wasn't gone. Selena was here. And they could be together.

"I've got to figure out how to find some happiness, baby," he said, whispering the words into the silence. Whispering the words like a prayer. "I'm never going to forget you. I'm never going to stop loving you. But I'm going to learn how to love some other people, too. I'm going to take some steps forward. That doesn't mean leaving you behind. I promise."

He closed his eyes and waited, letting the silence close in around him. Letting himself just be still. Not working. Not struggling or fighting. Just existing. In the moment and with all the pain that moment carried.

The breeze swirled around him and he kept his eyes

closed, smelling the flowers and the snow, crisp on the air as it blew down from the mountaintop.

That was assurance. Blessed assurance.

Letting go didn't mean forgetting. Moving forward wasn't leaving behind.

And in that moment, as he took a breath of the air that contained both the promise of spring and the bite of winter, he realized it was the same inside of him, too. That he could contain all of it. That he could hold on to that chill. That he could welcome the promise of new life.

There was room for all the love. For the bitter. For the sweet. For everything in between. There was no limit, as long as he didn't set it.

He knew what love could take away. He also knew what it could give. He had despaired of that for so long. That there were no mysteries left available to him. That he knew all about the heights of love and the lows of loss.

But he realized now that he had the most powerful love yet ahead.

The love he chose to give, in spite of the knowledge of the cost.

He just had to be brave enough to take hold of it.

He got down off his horse and bent to pick the brightest, boldest yellow wildflower. He held it between his thumb and forefinger. Ellie's flower. Just like in that picture. He stroked his thumb over one petal and a smile touched his lips.

He put the flower in his shirt pocket, just over his heart, and looked at the view all around him. A view he hadn't allowed himself to enjoy since he'd lost his daughter. A place that was full of good memories. Good memories he'd shut away so they couldn't hurt him.

But they were part of him. Part of his life. Part of her life. And he wanted them. Wanted to be able to think of her and smile sometimes. Wanted to be able to remember the joy loving her had given him, not just the sorrow.

That was what he'd forgotten. How much joy came with love. Of course, you couldn't choose what you got. Couldn't take the good without risking the bad.

But you could choose love. And he was ready to do that.

It was time to walk forward. Into the known and the unknown.

And as long as Selena would have him, he had a feeling it was going to be okay.

He closed his eyes and faced the breeze again, let it kiss his face. Then he mounted the horse and took off at a gallop across the field, heading back toward the homestead.

He got his horse put away and strode out toward the front of the house. He needed to get his private plane fired up, because he had to get back to Texas, and he had to get back fast.

After what he had said to her, a phone call wasn't enough. He needed to go and find her. And he needed to tell her. To tell her he was sorry. To tell her they could do this. They could be together.

To tell her that he was done running.

There was something big, something fierce expanding in his chest. Something he hadn't felt in a long time.

Joy.

Selena.

And almost as if those feelings had brought her out

of thin air, he looked up when he reached the front of his house and there she was. Standing in the center of the driveway, looking small and pale and a little bit lost. Selena Jacobs didn't do lost, and he had a feeling he was the cause of that desolate look on her face.

His heart clenched tight, guilt and love pouring through him.

"What are you doing here?" he asked.

She lifted her chin. "I came to get you."

"You can't be here to get me. I was about to get on a plane to go get *you*."

Her bottom lip wobbled. "What?"

"I don't know what you're here for, Selena. But you have to hear me out first. Because I have to tell you. I have to tell you about everything I've realized. It's been a hell of a time."

"Yeah," she said, her tone dry. "You're telling me."

"I'm sorry," he said. "I'm sorry that I hurt both of us, but most especially you. I'm sorry that I did so much damage. I was afraid to move on. Because...because of the guilt. I just... The guilt and the fear. It isn't that I don't want the baby. It isn't that I don't love you. I do. I want you, and our baby, so much I ache with it. I want so much that it scares me, Selena, because I haven't wanted a damn thing in years. I haven't let myself want anything. Not even food. Because wanting, needing, *loving*, in my experience has meant devastation. I can't come up with another excuse. It's just that. I am so afraid that I might lose you someday. That if I love you too much, want to hold you too close, that something will happen, and I'll have to face that dark tunnel again. I couldn't survive it, baby. I couldn't. You've meant everything to me for a long time. And now, wanting you as a lover, loving you as a woman, I know that the loss of you would destroy me. The loss of our life. The loss of our child…

"But I can't live that way. I can't live in fear. I can't live holding on to only bad feelings to try and protect myself."

He walked toward her, took her hands. "I called Cassandra. Drunk off my ass. She said something to me… She was right. She said you have to love the person you find more than you love your life together. What Cassandra and I had felt perfect. But only as long as it *was* perfect. Once that fractured, we couldn't put it back together. We didn't want to. We loved what we had more than we loved each other. But when I fell in love with you, Selena, we had nothing. Nothing but those broken pieces. And what you said… I think it's the way forward. That we put these broken pieces together and we make something new. I can't go back. I can never be who I was. But I can try to be something new. To be something different. I can try to be the man you deserve."

She said nothing. Instead she sobbed as she threw her arms around his neck and clung to him, her tears soaking into his shirt. "Seriously?" she asked, the word watery.

"What seriously?"

"You really want to do this?"

"I need to," he said. "I need you. I realized something today, walking around the property. Winter and spring exist side by side here. It's been winter inside of me for a long time. And there's a part of me that's afraid of what letting go of that means. That it means I don't love Ellie enough. Or that I didn't."

"Of course you loved her enough," Selena said. "Of course you do. I know that in our lives together I want to honor that. This baby, this child, is never going to replace what you lost."

"I know," he said. "That was what I realized. I can make room in my heart for both of them." He reached into his pocket and removed the yellow flower, holding it out for her. "This is us. This spring. New life. A new season. I want to make room inside of me for that. I want less cold. Less fear. More of this."

"Please," she said, smiling and taking the flower from his hand. "Yes, please. More spring. A lot more."

"I love you," he said. "I love you knowing that love is the most powerful thing on earth. That having it makes everything brighter, that losing it can destroy your whole world. I love you knowing what it might cost. And maybe that's a strange declaration, but it's the most powerful one I've got."

He cupped her chin, lifted her face to meet his. "When you're young, you get to dive into things headlong. You get to embrace those big, scary feelings not knowing what might wait for you on the other side. I know. But I want to choose a life with you. More than anything, I want to love you. If you want to love me." He let out a long, slow breath. "You know, if you still can love me."

"I do love you," she said. She held on to his face, met his eyes. "I love you so much, Knox. And the thing is, I could never tumble headlong into it when I was younger because I was scared. But I've grown up. I trust you. And trust has always been the key. I know what kind of man you are. I was afraid of love for a long time, but I was never afraid of you."

"But I hurt you."

"Yes," she said. "You did. But you were hurting, too. You didn't hurt me because you were a bully or because you enjoyed causing me pain. You did it because you were running scared. I get that. But that doesn't mean I'm not going to make you pay for it later."

"Oh, are you?"

"I am." She smiled. "I'm going to make you give my skin-care line preferential shelving in your supermarkets."

"Corporate blackmail."

"Yes," she said, "corporate blackmail. But it could be worse. It could be sexual blackmail."

He wrapped his arm around her waist and drew her up against his body. "Honey," he said, "you couldn't stick to sexual blackmail."

"I sure as hell could," she said, wiggling her hips against him. "And you would suffer."

He leaned forward and nipped her lower lip. "You would suffer."

"Okay," she said, her cheeks turning pink. "Maybe I would."

"Will you marry me, Selena? Marry me and make a new life with me? I'll never be the man that I was. But I hope the man I am now is the one for you."

Her smile turned soft. "He is. Believe me," she said, "he is."

"So that's a yes?"

"Yes," she said. "I never thought I would walk down the aisle for real. But, Knox, if ever I was going to, it had to be with you."

He looked down at Selena, at the woman he had

known for so many years, the woman he'd gone on such a long journey to be with.

"Right now," he said, "this moment… It can only ever be you. You're the one worth being brave for. You're the one who made me want to start a new life. And I'm so damned glad that you did."

"Me, too," she said and then squeaked when he picked her up off the ground and held her to his chest.

"I'm also glad that you saved me a flight," he said, heading back toward the house with her in his arms.

"Well, I'm glad to be so convenient."

"You're more than convenient," he said. "You're inconvenient. You made me change. Nobody likes that."

"Oh dear," she said, "however will you punish me?"

He smiled. "I'll think of something."

"You've always been my best friend," she said, hours later when they were lying in bed together, thoroughly sated by the previous hour's activities. "And now you're more. Now you're everything."

"I'm happy to be your everything, Selena Jacobs. I'm damned happy that you're mine."

He kissed her, a kiss full of promise. A kiss full of hope for the future.

And he smiled, so happy that for the first time in an awfully long time he had both of those things.

And more important, he had love.

EPILOGUE

A CHILD'S LAUGHTER floated on the wind, and Selena ran to keep up with the little figure running ahead of her. She had long, dark hair like her mother, and it was currently bouncing with each stride.

She had her father's eyes.

Selena's husband was lingering behind her, his speed slowed by the fact he was holding their new son.

Selena turned to look at them both. Knox was clutching the five-month-old baby to his chest, his large hand cradling the downy head. Knox was such a good father.

He was caring, and he was concerned, and he had a tendency to want to rush to the doctor at the very first sniffle, but she couldn't blame him. And watching the ways in which their children had opened him up…it made her heart expand until she couldn't breathe.

"Carmela!" Selena shouted. "Slow down."

Their daughter stopped and turned to look at them, an impish grin on her three-year-old face. She stopped, in the field of yellow-and-purple flowers, with the snow-covered mountains high and imposing behind her.

Selena turned back and saw that Knox had stopped walking. That he was just standing there, staring at Carmela.

Selena took two steps back toward him and put her

hand on his forearm. "Are you okay? Do you need me to take Alejandro?"

"No," he said, his voice rough.

Carmela was turning in a circle, spinning, careless and free out in the open.

Knox couldn't take his eyes off her. He was frozen, his expression full of awe.

"What is it?" Selena asked.

"I just can't believe it," he responded. "That I have this again. This chance to love again. To love her. To love him." He brushed his hand over baby Alejandro's head. And then he turned those gray eyes to her. His desire for her was hot, open. It made her shiver. "To love you."

He leaned in and kissed her, and she shivered down to her toes.

"I remember feeling like I had nothing," he said. "Nothing to hope for. Nothing to hold. And now… I have hope. I have a future. And my arms are full."

Selena wrapped her arms around him and rested her head on his chest. "My best friend knocked me up on accident," she said. "And all I got was…this whole wonderful life."

He kissed her one more time, and when they parted she was breathless. Then the two of them walked on toward their daughter, toward the future. Together.

* * * * *

We hope you enjoyed reading

Sutton's Way

by *New York Times* bestselling author

DIANA PALMER

and

The Rancher's Baby

by *New York Times* bestselling author

MAISEY YATES

Both were originally Harlequin® series stories!

From passionate, suspenseful and dramatic
love stories to inspirational or historical,
Harlequin offers different lines to
satisfy every romance reader.

New books in each line are available every month.

"Come here," he said, his voice suddenly hard. "I want to show
you something."

There was a big white tent that was still closed, reserved for
an evening hors d'oeuvre session for people who had bought
premium tickets, and he compelled her inside. It was already set
up with tables and tablecloths, everything elegant and dainty,
and exceedingly Maxfield. Though there were bottles of Cowboy
Wines on each table, along with bottles of Maxfield select.

But they were not apparently here to look at the wine, or indeed
anything else that was set up. Which she discovered when he
cupped her chin with firm fingers and looked directly into her eyes.

"I've done nothing but think about you for two weeks. I want
you. Not just something hot and quick against a wall. I need you
in a bed, Wren. We need some time to explore this. To explore
each other."

She blinked. She had not expected that.

He'd been avoiding her and she'd been so sure it was because
he didn't want this.

But he was here in a suit.

And he had a look of intent gleaming in those green eyes.

She realized then she'd gotten it all wrong.

"I…I agree."

She also hadn't expected to agree.

"I want you now," she whispered, and before she could stop herself, she was up on her tiptoes and kissing that infuriating mouth.

She wanted to sigh with relief. She had been so angry at him. So angry at the way he had ignored this. Because how dare he? He had never ignored the anger between them. No. He had taken every opportunity to goad and prod her in anger. So why, why had he ignored this?

But he hadn't.

They were devouring each other, and neither of them cared that there were people outside. His large hands palmed her ass, pulling her up against his body so she could feel just how hard he was for her. She arched against him, gasping when the center of her need came into contact with his rampant masculinity.

She didn't understand the feelings she had for this man. Where everything about him that she found so disturbing was also the very thing that drove her into his arms.

Too big. Too rough. Crass. Untamable. He was everything she detested, everything she desired.

All that, and he was distracting her from an event that she had planned. Which was a cardinal sin in her book. And she didn't even care.

He set her away from him suddenly, breaking their kiss. "Not now," he said, his voice rough. "Tonight. All night. You. In my bed."

Don't miss what happens next in…
Claiming the Rancher's Heir
by New York Times *bestselling author Maisey Yates!*

Available November 2020 wherever
Harlequin Desire books and ebooks are sold.

Harlequin.com

⊞ HARLEQUIN
DESIRE

Luxury, scandal, desire—welcome to the lives of the American elite.

Save **$1.00**

on the purchase of ANY Harlequin Desire book.

Available wherever books are sold, including most bookstores, supermarkets, drugstores and discount stores.

Save $1.00

on the purchase of ANY Harlequin Desire book.

Coupon valid until November 30, 2020.
Redeemable at participating outlets in the US and Canada only.
Not redeemable at Barnes & Noble stores. Limit one coupon per customer.

52616769

5 65373 00076 2   (8100)0 12461

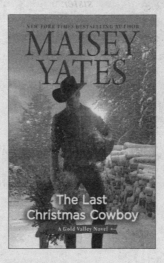

SPECIAL EXCERPT FROM

HQN

This Christmas, cowgirl Rose Daniels is determined to play matchmaker for her sister. She enlists the reluctant help of family friend Logan Heath, but his insistence that she doesn't understand chemistry is exasperating. Until they share one electrifying moment that shows her exactly what chemistry is all about...

Read on for a sneak preview of
The Last Christmas Cowboy
by New York Times and USA TODAY bestselling author Maisey Yates.

There was a breath where Logan stopped. Just one. Rose's eyes went wide. Her chest hitched upward, and her lips parted.

And then he closed the distance between them.

The taste of her exploded through him, shrapnel from the impact embedding in his chest. He didn't know what he had imagined. That it might be gentle or easy because she was young. That he would have control over it because she was inexperienced and he knew it.

It wasn't gentle. It wasn't easy.

And he did not have control.

Her mouth was so damn soft, and it was the softness that he thought might bring him down to his knees.

He would brawl with any man at a bar, even if he was twice Logan's size. He would be confident in his ability to win. Strength didn't scare him.

He would test himself against a sheer rock face, and he wouldn't be intimidated. He was a man who had survived so much there wasn't a whole lot that scared him. Wasn't a whole lot he thought might be able to bring him to his knees.

But this softness could.

This softness very nearly did.

PHMYEXP0920

It wasn't an avalanche. Wasn't an explosion. It was like the sun. Warming him through, melting ice in his veins he hadn't even realized was there. And it hurt. Like when your hands froze solid out working without gloves and you came inside and pressed them up against a heater.

It always hurt. When feeling returned to parts of your body that had lost it.

That was this kiss.

It wasn't what he intended. The bet had been to teach her a lesson, and hell…he'd had to follow it through. And part of him wanted to punish her for torturing him, for refusing to listen. He thought to crush her mouth beneath his and make her take the desire that rioted through his chest, whether he wanted it to or not.

Instead, he found himself just holding her there, her mouth against his, immersed in that softness, damn near devastated by it.

Then she moved.

A whimper beginning in the back of her throat, her hands coming up and taking handfuls of his T-shirt. He didn't know if she was planning on pushing him away or pulling him more firmly against her. He didn't give her a chance to make the choice.

He wrapped his arm around her waist and pulled her more firmly against his body, fitting her petite curves to his chest.

He could feel her fingers tightening on his shirt, could feel the way that she tugged him to her, even just slightly.

She wasn't pushing him away.

No, she wasn't pushing him away at all.

He angled his head, slipping his tongue between her lips, and she gasped, reeling backward and stumbling away from him. Her eyes were wide, her lips flushed pink and swollen looking.

It was the most intoxicating aphrodisiac he'd ever come into contact with.

Rose. Rose Daniels, looking like a woman aroused, flushed and turned on because of him.

Don't miss The Last Christmas Cowboy
by New York Times *and* USA TODAY *bestselling
author Maisey Yates, available October 2020,
wherever HQN Books and ebooks are sold.*

HQNBooks.com

PHMYEXP092